The Leaven of The Pharisees

Beware of the leaven of the Pharisees, which is hypocrisy.

But there is nothing concealed that will not be disclosed, and nothing hidden that will not be made known.

For what you have said in darkness will be said in the light; and what you have whispered in the inner chambers will be preached on the housetops.

Luke 12:1-3

On behalf of the State and of all citizens of the State, the Government wishes to make a sincere and long overdue apology to the victims of childhood abuse for our collective failure to intervene, to detect their pain, to come to their rescue.

Bertie Ahern, An Taoiseach
May, 1999

1

Clothes were strewn all over the bedroom, with shoes scattered across the floor, while Molly stood in the airless calm of the hurricane's eye, packing a suitcase. "You're not going," Stan screamed at her, his tone getting louder in an attempt to coerce her into recognizing his authority.

The sweater that Stan had torn from the suitcase and flung across the room was retrieved, folded and returned to the open case. Reticent like her late father, unruffled by storm or tempest, Molly rolled up a pair of stockings and tucked them into a corner of the bag, ignoring her husband so completely that his face began to redden in frustrated anger.

"I've got a business to run, damn it, and you're not going when I'm up to my ass in work," Stan continued with his one-sided harangue.

It was absolutely futile to argue with her, and he should have learned that after all these years. Any minute now, he was sure to accuse her of being just like her father, close-mouthed and cold as stone, but she took it as a compliment when he meant to insult her. Not at all part of the stereotypical Irishman, but Molly was proud of her Hibernian roots and she did not put any stock in college mascots or cartoon characters that hyped sugary cereal. She was as Irish as her father had made her, as Irish as any other daughter of an immigrant from Dublin. Exactly like the recently departed Frank Devoy, his daughter made a lie of the image of the jolly, happy Irishman, dancing across the gridiron or cavorting through a shower of marshmallow lucky charms. They could be morose and taciturn, masking sadness under a cheery grin that hid their true emotions. They kept secrets.

Molly could feel Stan's eyes burning into her skull, watching her get ready to leave for Ireland while he acted as though she would not dare to go against his direct order. He was trying to see what was going on in her head, but every thought was invisible, hidden behind a face that was as unchanging as a marble carving. He could holler all he wanted but Molly was stubborn and she would not bend for him. She would bow like a sapling in the wind for her beloved father, and she was doing all this for a man who had made Stan Bellush an underling.

Waving a shoe at her, Stan lashed out again, changing direction. "He'll be just as dead next January as he is today. Wait until work slows down."

His request might be reasonable, but Molly had been moving towards the door since the day she walked in it and this had become the best time to go. The kids were spending two weeks with her brother's family. There would be no drama, no scenes to bring the neighbors to their windows, no holy show. Not one person on the block would see that Molly and Stan did not have a marriage, they had a business and she was the employee who had no hope of being fired. She was quitting without giving notice.

How could she stall, when her father had left such specific instructions? After the will was read and the attorney handed her the box of documents, she took it as a sign that her father might, after all, have loved her. He wanted her to dispel the fog that obscured her vision; he wanted to open up to her in a way that he never had when he was living. By going to Ireland, she would discover what he was talking about on that New Year's Eve all those years ago, when he told her flat out that he had made a mistake, that he had failed to tell her the truth. "It's in you, and you'll pass it on to the little ones," Frank assured her. "It won't die with me unless we take it out, once and for all." He promised to correct the omission one day, to remove the cloud that blotted out the sun, but he could wax poetic and hopelessly obscure after a couple of drinks. Molly believed that he was finally making good on his vow.

"You leave now, damn it, and don't bother coming back," Stan issued his most powerful threat.

The weighty cask, an elaborate box of varnished oak carved with a Celtic cross, contained approximately half of Frank Devoy's ashes, the part of him that he wanted to rest in Irish soil. With love, Molly placed the box in her carry-on bag, to keep him with her for every minute that remained before she had to give

5

up her father for good. Next to his coffin she tucked the official documents that allowed Frank's earthly remains to fly back across the ocean he had traveled as a young man, when he decided to fight the Nazis alongside the Yanks instead of the Brits. Twice, Molly checked the paperwork to be sure that it was all there and in order.

She shut the large suitcase before Stan took out anything else. When riled, as he was now, he could be incredibly childish, and Molly was so tired of his tantrums that she decided to put an end to it. Whatever he had taken out, whatever was missing, she could buy in Dublin. He was delaying her departure, something that she would not let him do.

"You got it, huh, do you hear me?" he repeated his vow. "Don't bother coming back."

Taciturn and tight-lipped, Molly went back to stuff a few essentials into the carry-on. Verifying that her passport was in the inside pocket, she wedged a paperback guidebook next to a bundle of documents. Last week, when she booked a room and bought the plane ticket, she had no idea where anything was. Blindly, she rented a car and made an appointment to see her father's attorney in Dublin, jotting down directions that were nothing but strange names. The long plane ride would have to serve, to give her the time she needed to research the streets, get her bearings, figure out how to get from Dublin Airport to Derry House, and from Derry House to wherever her father was sending her with his itinerary.

Never had the man spoken of his childhood or his life in

Ireland with the same carefree abandon that his wife used to describe her giddy youth in Chicago. Mom could regale her children for hours on end with an outpouring of words that flowed easily, sharing memories without seeming to think about them or hold anything back. She could laugh over her sister's escapades with the sailors at the USO dances, but Dad was hardly as easy with his words when he told them about his sister. "She grew up," he would say with a shrug, "and they thought that she wasn't quite right in the head."

Any details about how his widowed mother was able to raise two small children on her own was talked around until the circle grew big enough to touch on another topic. To his face, Molly laughed and called her father the Man of Mystery, but that was exactly what he was. Mom liked to think that her husband was a man of few words, disinterested in anything domestic, and that suited Dad just fine. He was reticent, close-mouthed, and he kept his past close to the vest until he died, a lifetime of silence.

The key to Frank Devoy's life was crammed into the large bag, a stack of neatly organized documents that Molly had inherited along with orders to finish up some business. For years, he had maintained these same records, a rough draft or an outline of his memoirs that recorded his existence. Along with sufficient funds to cover the trip and expenses, Molly had received her father's bequest, with surprisingly specific instructions on when to read each individual packet. This was as much guidebook as he felt she needed, with a compilation of addresses, names and information that would help her trace her father's footsteps through Dublin during the Great Depression. Frank Devoy was dead, but he still wanted his daughter to discover the child who grew up to be her father, a reticent man whose eyes were clouded by a sadness that was impossible to fully disguise.

A list of strange names and symbols started the memoir. Dermot Downey, late, HMS *Hood* was tagged with a cross. Sisters of Mercy, Booterstown, and Carriglea School in Dun Laoghaire, all were listed but the meaning was as obscure as her father's past. After a final inspection, Molly clicked the lock shut and hoisted the cumbersome bag onto her shoulder. Ignoring Stan as if he was not even there, she walked down to the foyer.

Without saying goodbye, Molly closed the door on Stan's final demands and threats. She slid into the driver's seat of her car, a flashy Mercedes that she bought to appease her husband's sense of mobile display, his financial acumen on wheels. In Dublin, she would drive something small and cheap, and she looked forward to getting behind the wheel of some nondescript vehicle and blending into the crowd. At the end of the driveway, she took a last look at the perfectly manicured front lawn and then watched it slowly disappear in the rear view mirror. This could all be a mistake. Inside, she was empty, a hollow core of loneliness. How could her father remove something when there was nothing there?

Walking through the concourse at O'Hare's International Terminal, Molly presented a picture of a businesswoman, embarking on yet another trip for the home office with her mind focused completely on the goal. Her grip loosened on her suitcase, her sweating hand slipping on the handle. "Well, this is it," Molly said under her breath. She presented her ticket at the check-in counter and slid into a seat, waiting to board.

Frank had never been very affectionate, not as much as Barbara at least, and not comfortable with all the bussing that went on in Barbara's family. He never was close to anyone, always keeping a certain emotional distance. Molly had never paid much attention to it before, but her travels were meant to take her to uncharted territory and there was a great deal of the unknown to be explored.

An old woman, apparently lost, started up a conversation that put an end to further pondering. Helping her to check the flight number on the ticket, offering to sit next to her and hold her hand, Molly felt that she was celebrating her father's memory. While he was not inclined to hug and kiss at random, he had practiced Christian charity with a vengeance, and she followed his example at every opportunity.

Settled into her seat, with her newfound friend clutching the armrests next to her, Molly continued to contemplate her father and the way he was. If Aunt Nuala was not completely sane, then her brother was not mentally whole either. There had been something different about the way that Frank hugged his children, as well as a peculiar stridency when he taught them wrong from right. Opening the guidebook, briefly glancing at the contents, Molly hoped that the cause of her father's behavior was contained in the notebooks and sheets of paper that were covered with names and addresses, dates and recollections, the legacy that was given to Molly Nuala Devoy. Brother and sister, touched by the same disease, and her father had seen that she was infected as well. She very much wanted to be cured.

Standing on tiptoes to see over the rail, Frank stood in the dock, fighting to hold in the tears, struggling to be a credit to his dear daddy in heaven. Nuala had been standing there only a few minutes ago, until M'lud sent her back to Mammy. More than anything, Frank wanted to go back to Mammy, to press his head against her breast and fill his nose with her warm, soothing soap and lavender smell. Behind the forlorn boy in his Sunday best, his sister was wailing, while he bit down on a quivering lip. His wool stockings were growing more unbearably itchy by the minute, but he did not dare to fidget, too afraid of a stern rebuke from the mean man in the black robe or the scowling nun in the black habit. If he stood very still, and if he did not cry, he was sure that M'lud would let him return to Mammy and find shelter.

The halls and the courtroom were full of strange people, swarming with nuns and priests, mothers who had sobered up for the occasion and fathers who hung their heads, broken and defeated. Frank wanted to tuck his head against Mammy's shoulder, to blot out the faces of the women keening over their losses and the poor widows who moaned with the melancholy of the powerless. He did not want to see their raggle-taggle clothes or their children's pale cheeks streaked with tears.

When M'lud spoke again, Frank looked at him, pleading with his eyes, asking without words to be told what it was that he had done, begging to learn why he was in the dock in a room full of horrible sounds, rank odors and crushing fear. Last night, he had overheard them talking. They said it was not his fault, but then why was he standing in the dock, on trial? He would never mess about in the road again, not ever, if only he could have Mammy's arms around him. He would be as good as Saint Patrick himself, if only he could get out of the stuffy courtroom.

2

Dead tired and queasy from one drink too many, Molly lurched off the plane and walked into another world, her father's world. Abruptly, she fell into a sea of brogues that mingled with the strange signs that were printed in Irish, as if she had arrived overseas but gone a little past her intended destination. Her first thought was that it was not too late to turn back, but the tug on her arm was her father asking her to carry on for his sake. The weight of his ashes suddenly pulled at her elbow and she adjusted the carry-on bag to ease the sting in her joints.

"Welcome home, Miss Devoy," the customs official said. Perusing her documents, the gentleman's smile slid into a concerned frown. "Sorry for your troubles. It must have been difficult for you."

"Yes, thank you," Molly said. Her Irish passport, her dual citizenship, had been meant as a pleasant surprise for her father, but then they never did make the trip. He wanted to come home, to show her what he never talked about, but it was too late now for anything but regrets.

Things were going relatively smoothly until Molly stood next to the rented car and discovered that the Irish drove on the left side of the road. For some irrational reason, she had never expected to find any vestige of British culture or habits in her father's homeland, but now she had to deal with a strange place while driving on the wrong side of the road. Cold sweat beaded on her forehead and upper lip as Molly gave some serious thought to giving up right then and there. Putting the carry-on bag in the passenger seat, she told herself that her father was with her, sitting next to her for the start of the trip.

"Okay, let's go, Daddy," she murmured. Walking around to the driver's side, she took her seat and tried to stir up the same feeling of suffocating protection that had been given by her father when she was a little girl. "This is it. We're going. Remember how you used to say you were keeping an eye on me when I went out? Can you do it now?"

The driving directions that she had pulled off the Internet were specific, down to fractions of kilometers, but the unfamiliar streets and scenery were unnerving. At the roundabout, she followed the information and the signs, taking the second exit to join the M1 motorway, then searching for the sign to South Quays. Molly steered the car with her heart pumping madly, even painfully, in her chest. When St. Anne's Road popped up, she veered sharply through the turn, frantically searching for house numbers and hoping for a façade that spoke of Protestant Ascendancy elegance. When she pulled up in front of a non-descript little cottage, Molly was in full-blown panic, a strange woman in a strange place with her father's stern warnings ringing in her ears.

Without a doubt, she was on the correct street, and Molly got out of the car to verify that it was the Grand Canal on the other side of the road. It was all as Mrs. Devlin had described it, including the pots of geraniums in the tiny front garden. When Molly noticed the flowers, she also noticed that the lace curtain hanging in the front window had just moved. A shadow flashed away from sight, and within seconds, a rather old and very fair-skinned woman was standing in the doorway, her gray eyes sparkling with a warm welcome.

"Is that you, Miss Devoy?" the white-haired figure inquired in a slight lilt, the pattern beyond the Pale. Molly could hear her father's musical brogue in Mrs. Devlin's voice.

"Your directions were perfect," Molly said, awash in a profound sense of relief to have arrived in one piece.

"In you go, then, and have a cup of tea," Mrs. Devlin insisted. "You've come a long way."

The wheels of the overstuffed suitcase squeaked happily as Molly strode up the short walk, her carry-on perched on top for the ride. "Your house is lovely," she told her hostess.

Like so many older people, Mrs. Devlin was alone and lonely, so she rented rooms to people traveling on a budget. For Molly, it would be the best room, upstairs in the front of the house. She was given a key with a plastic tag labeled 'back door' which allowed her to come in late at night without disturbing the other guests, although the place was so quiet there didn't seem to be another living soul in the place.

On and on Mary chattered as they climbed the stairs, offering the warm hospitality of her parlor, the daily newspapers, television or conversation. Her desire to babble was in such direct contrast to Frank's reticence that Molly was not so sure that her father was a typical Irishman after all.

"There's three rooms altogether that I let, but only one other is in use, that's the honeymoon suite. There's a couple here from Sligo, newlyweds, a lovely couple, but I don't see much of them."

"They say that Americans always ask a lot of questions," Molly said. "I hope you won't be offended by me, but I'm really going to need some help and there are so many things I need to know."

"No trouble at all, Miss Devoy." Mary pushed open the door to Molly's room. "It's a sacred duty, to bury your father in the old sod. You come to me any time, day or night. You're a good girl, to come so far for such a sorrowful thing."

It took no time to scan the whole space, which was nothing more than a bedroom in a small and very simple home. The double bed was covered with a pretty quilt, and the lampshades on the side tables picked up the pink tones of the homemade curtains. There was a time when the two Devlin daughters shared the room, but they were grown up and Mary rented the place to lodgers who caught her fancy.

"It's charming," Molly said. Not bothering to unpack, she shoved her big case into a corner and plopped the carry-on onto the bed. Frank's ashes were lovingly removed and placed with respect on the dresser top.

"You'll wake him in my house and that's an end of it," Mary asserted. "I'd be honored, and insulted if you turn me down."

Molly thought that she saw someone in the hallway, just over Mary's shoulder, but she was so jet-lagged and tired that she was not sure what she was seeing anymore. "You're so kind, Mrs. Devlin. I hadn't thought about a wake. Anyway, I have to get started." Molly looked at her watch, then began to take out her documents. "No time to lose."

With subtle grace, Mary backed out of the door, to let Molly get on with settling in. The minute that Molly was back down the stairs, the old woman's voice rang out from the sitting room, offering more tea.

"Thank you, but just a quick cup," Molly said. "I have to get a move on if I'm going to organize a funeral before next Thursday."

"Tell me where you want to go, and I'll see if I can get you there."

"Well, I have to contact a priest from St. Michael's in Inchicore, to arrange the Mass and the burial." Molly began to reflect on her father's instructions. "From there, if there's time, I'd like to drive past his old house."

"St. Michael's," Mary mumbled with rapture. "When I was a girl, I went there every year for their May procession. They don't do that any more, parade the Consecration through the

16

streets, with people carrying statues all decked out with beautiful flowers. It's a shame, really. All the girls would dress up in their First Communion dresses, with the white veils, and we were all so pretty. We'd walk in the procession with our hands folded, praying and singing with the priest."

Mary's hands eased readily into an age-old reflection of prayerful contemplation as she sank into a sweet reverie. With her eyes half shut, she replayed the scene of her special day, when she walked along the streets of Inchicore, participating in one of the Church's most elaborate rituals. Ladies' sodalities and gentlemen's societies paraded out of her memories, everyone dressed in their finest clothes for the special occasion.

"I'm from the Coombe here, just south of the Liberties. I wonder if I ever knew your dad."

As Molly suspected, Mrs. Devlin had never met Frank Devoy or his older sister Nuala. The old woman could not recall anyone named Fran, born Francis, Devoy, or his wife Maire who had been a member of *Cumann na mBan* during the Easter Rising. Unable to help in one area, Mary turned to the map, to offer some assistance that was within her range of experience.

"You'll have an easy time of it," Mary said. "Stay on the South Circular Road, see here, it crosses Kilmainham, and here you find Inchicore Road, and then right around the corner to Thomas Street."

A jumble of streets lined the area under Mary's forefinger, a hodgepodge that was not even remotely similar to Chicago's neatly organized grid work. Molly could not decide if she was afraid of getting lost or afraid of being disappointed. Several years back, Frank had asked her to join him on a visit to his native city, with a faint hint of longing in his voice. Without her father to paint pretty pictures, Molly was worried that she would see only old facades or empty lots that held no charm without Frank's memories to resurrect a lost era.

"Even though you're from a big city," Mary said quietly, "don't go forgetting that Dublin is not all charming pubs and friendly faces."

"I know, Mrs. Devlin." Molly patted her guardian's hand. "My father always told me that a lady should stay out of pubs and keep off the streets."

Mary's smile never left her face, but a shadow darkened her eyes. "The neighborhoods nearby aren't good, to be blunt about it. Knackers and hooligans all about; keep an eye open and keep with the crowds."

"I understand," Molly assured her. "I'll watch my back."

What Mary warned of, Molly saw to be a fact. The streets were dirty, very much like the most rundown areas of Chicago that she avoided. Buildings were old, constructed without heart or soul; windows were dressed in rags and tatters. Groups of young toughs were hanging around street corners, the girls in skintight fashions and the boys in voluminous, baggy clothes. They did not appear threatening, only hopeless, like social misfits who had no future to look forward to, children lacking dreams. In posture, dress, and manner, they were no different from their American counterparts.

The need to maintain a state of full alert was wearing, and it did not help that Molly was worn out from traveling. When she saw the signs for the car park for Kilmainham Museum, she pulled in to rest and regain her bearings. Somewhere in the back of her mind, she could hear her father prattling on about executions, Kilmainham Jail, and martyrs. Molly had been eleven years old when her father had too many beers at the family picnic, and now she was sorry that she could not recall even half of what he had said. His homeland's history had always held a special place in his heart, but with regret, Molly realized that she had not shared that love as fully as she could have.

Ireland's young people were losing touch with their history, and Eoin MacNeill did not want his son to forget how difficult it had been to achieve freedom. Ever since Dermot was weaned, he had taken his son on afternoon outings in an informal custody arrangement, usually going to the zoo or the Phoenix Park if the weather was cooperative. Now that Dermot was sixteen, and increasingly surly, Eoin switched tactics and dragged the boy all over Dublin, indoctrinating him in Irish history and coming clean about the hypocrisy of the Irish Free State. His own life was an outstanding example.

"What's next, the dinosaurs at the museum?" Dermot griped.

"American schoolchildren travel miles to see their country's birthplace," Eoin contended, sounding like a fool and knowing it.

"Excuse me, is it true?" Dermot asked the lady with the enormous street map and the dazed expression.

An American accent stood out in the small crowd that was assembling at the cashier's station, and Dermot was just brash enough to approach a complete stranger and behave boorishly.

"Sorry?" She jumped in surprise.

"In America, do the kids trip over their feet in a mad dash to see the ancient battlefields?" Dermot asked with childish sarcasm.

"The kids love going to Washington when they finish their last year of primary school," she said.

"No prison tours?" The caustic tone remained.

"Not prison, exactly, just the local jail. And that's only part of the anti-drug curriculum. Jails are pretty scary when they're full of inmates."

Crumbling in embarrassment, Eoin cleared his throat loudly to get his son's attention. "I'm sorry, but he's sixteen, you see," he mumbled.

"Really? I have a daughter the same age. Good thing she's not with me, or I'd have my hands full," she said, winking at Dermot.

"You seem to be lost," Eoin ventured.

"Yes, a bit. I'm looking for St. Michael's Church."

"It's just across the road," Eoin said. "Can I give you a lift?"

"Across the street?" she asked.

"No, I meant, an escort. It's a rough area." He felt Dermot's elbow nudging his arm, but Eoin missed the meaning.

"Is it safe to visit Goldenbridge Cemetery?" she asked, a hint of a tear beading on her eyelashes. "My grandparents, and then my father's funeral next week."

"Let us go with you," Eoin offered at once.

"No, I couldn't." The lady touched a fingertip to the corner of her eye. "You've already paid for the tour."

Dermot made himself useful by folding up the map, a task that fairly screamed out his relief that he would not have to be subjected to the sob-inducing story of Joseph Mary Plunkett and his beloved Grace, married in the chapel of Old Kilmainham Gaol the night before Joseph's execution. In school, he had learned all about the Easter Rising and he had no interest in the re-enactment at three o'clock.

"Kilmainham will still be here tomorrow," Eoin said. "Were you born in Ireland?"

The affable father and his relieved son guided the American woman across Kilmainham Bridge, one glad to put the museum behind him and the other shocked by his bold behavior. Eoin had no business inquiring into this person's affairs, but he was doing just that as they promenaded along Emmet Road.

"It's not exactly across the way, is it?" Dermot complained at the long walk.

21

"My God, my father lived here," she gasped, her head turning in circles. Inchicore was a long, long way from American suburbia, and Eoin could hardly suppress a wince as the woman made a most unflattering comparison.

"Didn't you ever come to visit him?" Dermot barged in.

"He didn't die here." She was almost whispering, lost in amazement at the depressed area, shocked at the scruffy industrial aura of the neighborhood. "He went to Chicago after the war, World War Two. I was born in Chicago. I've never been here before."

"He never would have recognized the streets," Eoin expounded. "The old tenements were torn down years ago, not long after the Civil War ended. They were some incredibly blighted slums, and now we have these lovely Eastern Bloc concrete slabs in their place. More spacious, but still hideous."

"We have them too." The woman quickened her pace, nervously catching the inquisitive stares of the women who passed the trio on the street.

"Dermot, run back and bring the car around," Eoin said quietly. This was not an area for a casual walk, and he was beginning to realize that their destination was not as close as he had thought at first.

"No, please," she blurted out in panic. "I can drive, I think I can figure out how to get there."

She turned around and they all headed back to the car park, walking briskly. They were crossing Kilmainham Bridge for the second time when Eoin figured out the reason for her hasty departure. Beware of strangers was dogma, but beware of strange men was a woman's creed, the gospel to be observed. Based on the way her eyes flitted about, he guessed that she was just as concerned that someone might think she was a streetwalker picking up a couple of tricks in the middle of the afternoon. Her fast pace indicated that the latter reason was far more important, as if she would take her chances with a crazed murderer but never brook aspersions cast on her character.

"Oh, my God, I am sorry," he babbled. "I'm a professor at university, I swear to you, I am only trying to be helpful. Tell her, Dermot, we aren't up to anything."

"What are you talking about?" the young man asked.

"You've both been too kind, thank you," she said. Her muscles tensed, as if she was on the verge of running.

Trying to tell his side of the story, Eoin put a hand on the lady's arm to stop her from sprinting off through a dangerous neighborhood. "I'll drive, and you can follow us. Please, miss, you can't wander around here by yourself."

The danger was obvious, marked by the seedy characters that lingered in doorways. "He told me, my father, he told me it was too dangerous for me to go without him," she said. In a small voice, she added, "*Mo mhuirnin*, I can't go alone and it isn't safe for you. But then he made me come here."

"I'm Dermot, Dermot MacNeill, and this is my father Eoin," the boy made introductions. "He is a university professor, at University College Dublin, like he said. Looks like a pervert though, doesn't he?"

The good-natured jibe was full of adolescent wit, enough sass and sharp tongue to calm her nerves slightly. Eoin did indeed look like a professor, with salt and pepper curls that were a little too long to be fashionable, and dark eyes that gave an impression of brooding in a deep, philosophical way. His half-smile was given tentatively, to complete a picture of the slightly distracted intellectual who doubled as Good Samaritan. When she extended her hand in greeting, his grin spread across his long, equine face.

"Molly Devoy," she shook Dermot's hand and then Eoin's. "Please excuse me, I'm making a fool of myself."

"I'm the fool, Miss Devoy," Eoin apologized. "When I descend from my ivory tower, I forget how the real world spins."

After issuing some explicit directions, Eoin drove off, slowly navigating the streets of Inchicore and watching out for Molly in his rear view mirror. His son took a long glance through the back window of the car. "She's good craic, Dad," Dermot mentioned. "Too bad for me that the daughter's at home."

"Dermot, American women are not preternaturally horny," Eoin corrected a myth. "They are no more sexually active than any other female."

"Speaking from experience?"

"Don't be cheeky."

"I'm not saying that they're abnormal, I'm saying that they are perfectly normal. Pop a pill every day, and they're free. Everywhere in the world except Ireland."

"Things change." Eoin glanced back to check on his follower. "We were under England's thumb for eight hundred years and the Catholic Church was the only rallying point. Look at Poland, and how they have made progress."

"Look at Poland sixteen years ago," Dermot said.

"You'd rather have been aborted than born, is that it?"

"Christ, Dad, I never said anything about chucking me down the pan. But you would have gotten married again, wouldn't you? And my mother would have met someone else and I'd have brothers and sisters."

The car wheels crunched on the gravel drive in Goldenbridge Cemetery, and Eoin pulled to a stop in front of the office. He was sorry that his son was denied a large family, but no one could go back in time to change it. Of course, if he and Sheila had entered into the marriage with a genuine intention of making a full commitment, but young people never thought of the consequences of their brainstorms.

He hated these discussions because it was impossible to explain an affair that was based entirely on a nonsense. They were friends before they were lovers, and they became lovers because Sheila admired the combination of intelligence and athleticism that he brought to the mix. No man could tell those things to his son, that two people came together to create a brilliant, talented child, even though it was a child that was very much wanted. At the altar of St. Mary's Church they made vows that they had no intention of keeping, and when they walked out the door, they went their separate ways. Only once had Eoin

25

begun to explain their reasoning, but somehow, with all his keen intellect, he could not find the right words. Dermot called him a hypocrite, and Eoin could not refute the boy. The rebellion had been crushed before it began.

"Father Cahill, I'm so sorry that I'm late, but I got lost." Molly marched in to the office with Eoin and Dermot on her heels, the American woman on a mission. "They told me you were here when I called at St. Michael's."

If the priest were a day younger than eighty-five, Eoin would never have believed it. He could see the old brain processing Molly's greeting, which had been delivered in a rapid patter that rocked the octogenarian back on his heels. "Not at all, not at all," Cahill rebounded. "I thought I'd made the mistake and was to meet you here, but it's all to the good. I see that your husband came along after all."

Now it was Eoin's turn to be off balance, but he recovered quickly enough. "If only I were, Father," he said with mock sorrow. "As it is, I'm only the tour guide. Eoin MacNeill, and my son Dermot. If you don't mind, we'll wait and see that your guest is returned safely home."

"Cup of tea, Miss Devoy?" Cahill asked, indicating that the party was to enter the cluttered back room where he met with the bereaved. "Now then, about opening your grandfather's grave."

Molly reached into her large handbag and extracted a letter-sized envelope. "In accordance with my father's will, I am making a bequest of twenty thousand dollars to St. Michael's

Church," she stated with icy bluntness. The priest looked through her, behind her, his rheumy eyes seeing something that only he could see.

Never in his forty-eight years had Eoin observed anyone, let alone a female, take complete control with stunning confidence and ruthless insolence. In very plain terms, Molly was bribing the ancient cleric, and she made no bones about it. Without a doubt, Dermot was all ears, fascinated by a method of behavior that he had heard of but never witnessed. Father and son fixed their attention on the bargaining couple, amazed and amused by Molly Devoy.

Until Dermot gave him a nudge and a wink, Eoin did not realize that he was thoroughly examining the unusual ring on Molly's left hand. The sapphire and diamonds were set in white gold and delicate filigree, a very lovely antique ring that could never be mistaken for a wedding band. Returning his son's sly nod, Eoin offered up a little prayer that it was not an engagement ring either, although engagements could be easily broken.

"How large is the coffin?" Cahill acquiesced with panache.

"Only half his ashes, Father, and the wooden box is about six inches by three by three." Molly leaned over to pay up. "I could dig the hole myself with a garden trowel."

"Go on with you," the priest said. Pocketing the check, he changed the subject. "I'm semi-retired, you know. Well, with time on my hands, I took the liberty of putting a notice in the *Times*. What you told me when we spoke on the phone last week, it was inspirational. A man comes out of the Liberties and falls to the Strand, dirt poor, and strikes out on his own, going to America and making a success of himself. Four boys educated by the Christian Brothers like himself, I had to include the mention, and with all four in professions, it made for a grand story."

"You have four brothers, Miss Devoy?" Dermot sounded jealous.

"Yes, two in the medical field and two in banking," she said, speaking as if it were commonplace.

"And herself, a surgical nurse," Cahill continued.

"Taught by the Sisters of Scant Mercy," she snickered, but as the words came out of her mouth her silly grin twisted into an embarrassed grimace.

Dermot snorted and began to laugh. "We call them Show No Mercy," he said.

To dare to disparage the religious in front of a priest was unheard of in Eoin's generation. The kowtowing had begun early and lasted for seventy years, starting with the departure of the British in 1922. He knew enough Irish history to admit that the Irish Free State of that time was not at all free, because it was a shadow state run by the Catholic bishops of Ireland. No one stood up to them when the Church of Rome demanded special status in the newly minted constitution, and Eoin had a theory about why it had come to pass.

Men like Frank Devoy might have voiced a protest, and the Protestants of Ulster definitely would have balked if they had seen fit to join in a united Ireland. The sort of men who descended from the Famine immigrants might have shouted out, but those who were dissatisfied had pulled up stakes and gone away. The best and the brightest, the energetic and the scrappers, had all gone to America or England. Those who would question were quizzing their priests, but they were not in Ireland any more, they were in New York and Boston and Baltimore, while the devout of Ireland closed their eyes and prayed. Only now, with the new millennium and a new economy, was Ireland opening up as well, to join the western world in a candid examination of the hierarchy.

"Let us pray," Cahill said. Molly rolled her eyes with tired impatience and Dermot covered a snicker. The litany began and seemed to go on for hours, with chants of "Pray for us" punctuating every petition to nearly every saint in the pantheon. The trio almost sprinted out of the office after a final "Amen".

"You look like you could use a drink," Eoin said.

"I didn't mean to be spiteful," she said, looking around to be sure that Father Cahill was well out of earshot. "It was the brogue, the way he talked; it reminded me of my father and things just slipped out."

"Then it was your father who thought so highly of the good Sisters," Eoin quipped.

"Yeah, well, to tell you the truth, he gave money to Brother Rice High School every year, and when I was at Mother McAuley, he wouldn't give them a penny," she said. "Looking back, I think that he actually encouraged me to be a hellion. He was forever telling me not to listen to a word that they said. The only reason I was sent to that school was because my mother was an alum, and she put her foot down."

"Sisters of Scant Mercy," Eoin repeated the line, shaking his head and chuckling. "You're a bold one, to say it out loud."

"Jet lag made me do it," she replied. "My father was so Victorian when it came to women. Can you believe it, but when I started dating, I had to take one of my brothers along as a chaperone. Guard your reputation; Christ, that was drilled into my head, and the whole time my brothers got away with murder."

"Isn't that the way of the world? Girls get the leftovers after the boys have feasted. I'm afraid that you have the impression that Ireland and America weren't very different when you were growing up."

"I think I'm making it out to be worse than it was. My dad always supported me, took my side every time I was called in to the Mother Superior's office. I always wanted to ask him why, but I don't think he would have told me." She paused, lost in a reverie, but her face quickly brightened. "I called him the Man of Mystery."

"I'm afraid Father Cahill was a bit of a Man of Mystery himself in there," Eoin said, indicating the cemetery office.

"That pompous ass knew my father and claims he can't remember a thing about him," Molly said. "Oh, yes, the messenger boy, he says, and as soon as I told him I never knew that my father was a messenger, his memory fails him."

"Perhaps they had a run-in, you know, rivals for the same lovely colleen," Eoin said.

"No, I'm sure it involved my aunt."

"There you go, he probably broke the girl's heart," Dermot suggested. "Did she pine away as a spinster?"

"Dermot, I don't know what happened to my aunt," Molly said. "It's best not to know, some things are best left unspoken, that's all I ever heard. Don't speak of it and it never happened, or keep quiet and it will go away."

"Consider the times," Eoin said. "There's a vein of hypocrisy running through this country, and it's only in Dermot's generation that people are looking back with open eyes and open mouths. Don't think less of us for something that's in our blood."

Rubbing her eyes wearily, Molly sighed. "I could use a drink, thank you."

"It's in you as well," Eoin said as he shut her car door. "Back at Kilmainham, you weren't afraid of me at all, were you? You were worried about those other people, what they were thinking of you and your reputation. That's how it was, even when I was a lad in Killrossanty."

"My Irish genes," Molly agreed.

"You know, I've brought you this far. Let me be your guide through Ireland's soul. Dinner to go with the drink?"

"Eoin, thank you. Really, I can't express how grateful I am."

"Before you think too highly of me, I'll admit that I'm not entirely charitable. It's for Dermot as well. I want him to learn about the world before he's out there in the middle of it."

History had never been Dermot's favorite subject, but his father was remarkably interesting over pints of Guinness. This was not the dry as dust sort of lesson, for the trio bandied about social mores and the role of the Catholic Church in Ireland over the centuries. Molly's American viewpoint was a glimpse of Chicago-style sensibility, seasoned with an equally refreshing notion that people were entitled to some things and they had a right to take them.

Listening to Molly, Dermot discovered that taking no for an answer was not part of her cultural heritage, because she believed that she had a right to the truth. Those were the same concepts that Eoin wanted him to absorb, because he wanted his country to reclaim the best of the immigrants' lives and bring back to Ireland what had flown away in famine and hardship.

The motorcade wound back to the Coombe and St. Anne Road at eight o'clock, when Molly's jet lag blossomed into full-blown exhaustion. Like a proper gentleman, Eoin walked Molly to the back door and turned the lock for her.

"Are they spying on you?" he said, catching a fleeting glance of an old woman at the upstairs window.

"I think this place is haunted," Molly whispered. "I've seen things, or at least I thought I did, but then no one was there."

"By the way, Molly, I'm on holiday now, for the summer. I thought, if you need help, I'm willing to drive you all over town. Looking up your father's old friends is going to be a lot of work, and I know Dublin quite well."

"No, I can't drag you into this," she said. "But I am grateful, truly grateful."

She was shaking his hand goodbye, but then she reached up to give him a peck on the cheek, to better express her sincerity. Quick as a flash, Eoin turned his head and kissed her lips.

3

Not one to sleep past eight o'clock, despite the greatest fatigue, Molly was wide-awake. Unfortunately, it was two a.m. in Dublin when it was eight o'clock back home, and she stared up at the shadows on the ceiling, tired as could be. Frank's voice had woken her as he spoke in her nightmares, a scene that took place in Mother McAuley High School, a rerun of an old discussion in the office of the Mother Superior.

"You took enough blood and sweat out of the Devoys," Frank hissed with restrained fury. "Stealers of souls, never ask me for charity again."

He had been a deeply religious man, pious and severely conservative in his doctrine. When she was a teen, Molly had chafed under the restraints that she saw as discriminatory, largely because her brothers seemed to have free rein to roam as they pleased. Lying in Mrs. Devlin's house, Molly measured the crack in the plaster and explored her father as she had never done before. Why he wanted her to take this tour with him before, and why he ordered her to undertake the journey after he had died, were two questions that she puzzled over until she dozed off, to dream of Mrs. Devlin and the votive candle that the kind lady had placed in front of Frank Devoy's miniature coffin.

"Look, Rose, he was a student at Carriglea," Mrs. Devlin said in Molly's dream. "She'll help you. She'll understand."

By half past five, Molly had given up and she dragged herself out of bed. Pulling open the drapes, she looked out at the street-lit scene below, a landscape that was utterly foreign and dismally ordinary, yet strikingly beautiful. The Grand Canal reflected the lights, twinkling like submerged stars in a world turned upside down. Off in the distance, rows of townhouses presented their bare, flat facades to the world, as modest and unadorned as holy nuns. Molly tried to put herself in her father's shoes, looking out on a city that he had wandered as a young man. There were so few anecdotes to draw on that she could not quite paint a picture of little Frank Devoy, hand in hand with his sister Nuala, walking along the street on their way to the May Procession in Inchicore.

Commandeering the communal bathroom because no one was likely to be up so early, Molly soaked in a tub of warm water. Before long, she heard Mrs. Devlin on the ground floor, probably fussing in the kitchen over the freshly baked soda bread. Relaxing in the scent of lavender bubbles, Molly started to think about Eoin, the unintentional charmer who kissed quite well. He was unassuming in his manner, like a small town lad with no pretensions of grandeur once he made his mark in the big city. In a way, he reminded Molly of her father, but her mind was only trying to create similarities by projecting Frank onto a gentleman like Eoin.

Frank had set out a detailed itinerary, and Molly dutifully followed it. On Tuesday, she was scheduled to look up a couple of colleagues from the General Post Office, which Molly had recently learned was more than a place to buy stamps. Eoin had explained it to her at the pub, to help her understand how her father could be an employee of the postal service and not deliver a scrap of mail. He wanted her to fully comprehend because he wanted her to absorb Irish culture and custom, and instill an appreciation for the Irish way of life.

Thumbing through the folder to find the street address of Mr. Brendan Rea, Molly stopped short on the steps as she was descending. Someone had been at her notes because the pages were not in the same order as they had been left the night before. Tucked in the back of the accordion-fold portfolio were a few newspaper clippings that she did not recall seeing. A sort of disorientation took hold, an unnerving sensation of uncertainty with a sure thing.

After tossing her maps and notes on the bottom step near the telephone table, she popped out to drop an extra sweater in her car. Invigorated by the different smells and sounds of Dublin, she strolled up the driveway to the street, to watch St. Anne Road come alive in the early morning mist. Eoin was sitting in his car, a tiny Fiat, parked at the curb.

"*Dia duit*," he greeted her.

"Good morning," Molly said. "You sound like my father."

"I sound old? I don't know that to be such a compliment," he said.

"No, it is. I was thinking about him and I was sad, and now you've made me happy."

"Back to Inchicore today?"

"No, off to Tallaght, a place on Barcroft Close."

"Buy you breakfast? Full Irish fry."

"I hope Mrs. Devlin isn't offended if I duck out."

Her sense of timing was not coincidental. Mrs. Devlin must have been watching the scene through her parlor window. She stepped out onto the stoop with a great deal of noise, obviously attracting Eoin's attention. Molly made the introduction that Mrs. Devlin was longing for, and the old woman's curiosity pushed her to invite the gentleman to join them. "My other guests are late risers," she told Eoin when he balked. "It's no trouble to set an extra place."

The innkeeper enjoyed company, and she chatted freely with Eoin, asking after his family as if she had known the college professor for years. Plates piled with rashers, eggs and puddings were passed back and forth across the dining room table as the party discussed modern Ireland.

"The Americans are so wasteful," Mary clucked when Molly declined the black pudding. "And now our young people are getting into the same habits. In my time, we knew how to save and make do."

"Irish thrift," Eoin said. "My grandparents made use of every part of the pig when they butchered one."

"Even the squeal?" Molly replied. "That was the motto for one of the slaughterhouses in Chicago. They liked to boast that they used everything but the squeal."

"The butcher must have been an Irishman," Eoin said. "Bread fried in drippings, I haven't had it since I was a boy. You're a wonderful cook, Mrs. Devlin."

The tastes brought Molly back to the St. Paddy's Days of her childhood, when her mother would back real soda bread for the occasion and her father would fry the slices, soaking up all the bacon fat. She was sure that the recipe came from the poor man's cookbook, the Devoys surviving hard times with extreme thrift.

Back in Mary's youth, Dublin was the poorest city in Europe, a place where she was fortunate to have one doll, and that home-made from rags and scraps. With a woeful shake of her head, Mary remarked on her own grandchildren, with crates stuffed full of plush toys and dolls. Not one of their numerous possessions was precious to them, not like Mary's love for her rag doll, which she still had, tucked away in the box room.

"Did you ever know hunger?" Molly asked.

"Children don't remember being hungry." Mary waved off the hardship. "What I do recall is my father, and his grief that his babes were in need."

Molly noticed that her hostess was agitated, although it was not a dramatic display of anguish. As a trained nurse, Molly picked up on nuance, such as the grimace that a patient could not restrain when they did not want to admit to deep pain. Mary's body language was vaguely reminiscent of Frank's stress many years ago, when he asked his daughter to make the journey that she had finally undertaken.

"It's not the hunger, nor the patchwork clothes and bare feet," Mary went on. Her hands came together, as if she was about to pray, but then she twisted them, rubbing her fingers and clutching the palms. She worried her napkin until Molly feared that the linen fibers would snap at the crease that was pressed in, over and over, by Mary's work-worn fingers. "The children. Some of them. Taken away. That's what I remember."

Startled by an odd noise, Molly jumped and swung her head towards the kitchen door. A whimpering or muffled sob had come from there, but when she looked back at Eoin and Mary, they evidently had not heard a thing.

"Is this house haunted?" Molly asked.

Much to her surprise, Molly noticed that Mary was smiling at her. "There's many ghosts in Ireland, and only those with a special gift can see or hear them," the old woman said.

"As well as those who have not had much sleep," Eoin said. "What children were taken away, Mrs. Devlin?"

"The orphans, mostly. Back then, the bishops and the priests didn't want women to work after they married, and that's how it should be," Mary said. "It was the law back then. A married woman raised her children and didn't go off to a job every morning, dropping off the babies at a creche."

"Religion is what kept the rebellion going," Eoin said. There could be no doubt that he was a college professor, accustomed to giving lectures. He proceeded to wax prolific on the clergy maintaining their elevated status in the face of horrific poverty, the infrastructure of the newly born nation in disrepair, and the survivors of the Easter Rising trying to make a silk purse out of a sow's ear. He concluded by noting that orphanages were dreadful places, but the current foster care system wasn't a marked improvement in his mind.

"There was a family I knew well, seven children and the father passed on," Mary said. "The parish priest lodged a complaint and the children were taken. He saw Mrs. Noonan smoking on the street, a sign of loose morals in those days, and now the Dail's gone and banned smoking. And the priest from my church will sit in my kitchen with a cigarette when he pays us a visit."

The teacup was perched halfway to Molly's lips and it stayed there while she stared wide-eyed at Mary. "That's why," she mumbled.

"Why what?" Eoin asked.

"When I was eighteen, my father saw me smoking in front of the hospital where I was volunteering for the summer," Molly said. "He slapped me, right there, in public, but not out of concern for my health. He didn't really care that I smoked, but I was never to be seen with a cigarette, he said."

"Considering the temper of the times, I'm not surprised that he would be so angry at you," Eoin said. "All around him, and this during his formative years, he got the message that women were expected to behave in a certain way."

"Sounds like a police state to me," Molly said.

Before Mary could put together a response, Eoin jumped in with his opinion, suggesting that the global economic depression that gave rise to fascism had its origins in the common experience of poverty and hardship. After all, America had its fans of communism and fascism as an answer to the economic crisis, and Ireland was no different. The government slipped into fundamentalism to hold things together, and the Irish Free State was marked by oppression and a fear of socialism. Mary could only marvel at the drastic changes she had witnessed, with the explosion of prosperity that marked the end of the Twentieth Century in Dublin.

Molly pictured Spain under Franco and Germany under Hitler as Eoin maneuvered his car through the narrow streets. "Do you have any reason to believe that your father was put in an orphanage?" he casually inquired.

"His father had been an insurance man, which is why my father became an underwriter out of college," Molly said. "I know that my grandfather left some money to my grandmother, and part of that was used to pay for school. Dad never mentioned anything else. He never mentioned much of anything."

"It must have been difficult for his family," Eoin said. "Limited capital that had to be stretched until your father was old enough to work and support his mother, and with the world economy in the tank, it would have been extremely stressful."

Never once had Frank told her to be grateful for what she had, like so many of her friends' parents. He put a positive spin in things, always saying that the Devoy family was blessed, no matter what was happening. Only now did Molly have a sense of her father's ability to clutch at straws. The small inheritance probably spelled the difference between abject poverty and the everyday variety that was normal existence. There but for the grace of God went the Devoys.

The discussion turned to the beer-infused conversation of the night before. Molly had some unanswered questions, a few things she was too fatigued at the time to put into words.

"Why did you feel that you had to get married?" Molly asked. "I mean, it was the eighties."

"Maybe so, but I was born in the fifties," he said. "Unwed mothers were brought to special homes to hide the shame back then, or they left the country. If a girl was lucky, her mother could pretend to be pregnant while her daughter went off to visit some newly discovered aunt in the farthest corner of Ireland. There are a few people my age who have called their mother 'Sis' all along and never known the truth. Taking a position in England was another excuse, and then the girl would come home after a year, like the job didn't work out."

"That's horrible."

"But that's how it was. Don't be fooled by Dublin, by the trendy cafes in Temple Bar. Ireland is still a rural nation, all small farm towns and isolation. To this day, you can find little villages that are run by the parish priest, where things haven't changed in a hundred years."

"My dad had a baby sister who died in infancy. Do you think that's his secret? That my aunt Nuala was pregnant and not married?"

"There would be a strong wall of silence erected around that event," Eoin assured her with a chuckle.

"I'm not ashamed of it, if that's the case."

"Nor should you be. Just remember, though, that these old turkeys would be, and they may hurt your feelings with their old notions."

The warning was issued while Eoin eased the car into a spot across the road from the home of Mr. Rea. Molly sized up the little row house, so different from her father's four bedroom, two and one-half bath in Illinois. In celebration of the mild climate, the window boxes were filled with flowers that matched the pot near the front door, a blaze of colorful geraniums and petunias that brightened a gray day. The house was not as large, but it was just as warm and inviting as the Devoy homestead.

Mrs. Rea's parlor was spotless, neat and stunningly cramped. Molly sat on the love seat with Eoin, with Mr. Rea so close by in his matching armchair that their knees bumped if anyone moved. The retired postal supervisor stared at his guest, leaving the conversation to his wife. Having just met the couple, it was hard to tell if Mrs. Rea was a natural chatterbox, with her husband forced to wait for an opening to get a word in. After a few minutes, though, Molly found it odd that Brendan seemed to

43

choose his every word with great care, as if he was afraid to say the wrong thing, or say too much.

"How could you hire such low bred, such jailbirds?" Mrs. Rea fumed.

Brendan and Frank's boss at the GPO, Mr. Tully, hemmed and hawed as the two boys stood at his side. Brendan's mother was beside herself with rage, making the Inspector of Messengers fidget. Arguing with a woman was a sensitive issue, especially when her son was watching the proceedings.

"The lad took top honors in the National Exam, Mrs. Rea," Tully said, a plea for understanding. "Highest score on the application test, and that is why he has top seniority among the new boys. I can assure you that the boys that are sent to us from Carriglea are the finest, every one recommended by the Christian Brothers. How can you accuse the good Brothers of sending an unsuitable boy to me?"

"A leopard cannot change its spots, Mr. Tully, and a delinquent is a delinquent," she ranted. "You are exposing my son to the worst sort here, mingling in their Institute upstairs. I'll not have my boy in company with the likes of him."

Frank stood there mutely, his crisp messenger's uniform hanging heavily on his slight shoulders. There had been humiliation without end at school, but this morning's tongue-lashing was physically painful. To his face, he was denigrated and shamed, unable to run away and escape the abuse. With eyes downcast, he looked over at Brendan, who was blushing beet red with embarrassment at his mother and her ingrained prejudice. Brendan knew that his new friend was a fine, decent fellow who had been unlucky in his youth, but no boy would dare to defy his mother. As much as he might have wanted to, as much as he had promised he would, he did not speak up to defend Frank.

*"You see to it that my son is kept away from that boy,"
Mrs. Rea concluded. "That lad should be kept apart from any decent person."*

"I watch out for all my boys," Mr. Tully said. "Now go on home and tend to the house, Mrs. Rea, while I see to my job."

"Did he speak of me?" Brendan asked, his eyes alight with expectation.

She wanted to be diplomatic and kind, but the truth was perhaps not as grand as Mr. Rea was hoping. "Good old Brendan at the GPO, now there was a lad." Molly repeated a phrase that she had heard once or twice. "That's how he referred to you."

"We were sorry to hear of his passing," Adele Rea said. "They got together when your grandmother left us, before you were born I expect, and what a hooley we threw that night. Do you remember, Brendan, when Frank Devoy came to call?"

"I always knew he'd go far." Brendan went off on a tangent, running away from some hidden thoughts. "Did he ever tell you how he came to be employed?"

"No, please tell me," Molly said.

"We came to see Mr. Tully, all twelve lads who scored well on the test, and he gave us a final examination. There was one more requirement besides our book learning to be made a messenger boy. Can you ride a bicycle, son, old Mr. Tully says to each of us, and to a man we declare that we could ride from Dun Laoghaire to Punchestown and back again." Brendan was a natural storyteller, emoting dramatically and raising a laugh from his audience. "Now, to me, your father confesses the truth. I've never been on a bicycle in my life, what do I do? Sit on it and pedal, says I, like Dick Burke over there."

Studying the faces of his audience, satisfied that he held them spellbound, he continued after a dramatic pause. "It comes to Frank, and he gets himself seated and says a little prayer. I give him a push to start, and off he goes, a bit unsteady but by God he was determined. And wouldn't you know it, Mr. Tully is busy talking to Mr. O'Malley the whole time. Frank pedals right past him because he doesn't know how to stop, and I grabbed the handlebars before your dad rode straight into the wall."

"So I take it he passed the test?" Eoin said.

"God surely answered his prayers that day," Brendan said. "It was the least the Almighty could do for him."

They cut the visit short when Molly noticed that Brendan was growing fatigued. A mention by Adele of her husband's heart condition confirmed what Molly had suspected, and she politely took her leave before Brendan's strength was sapped any further. She was growing weary as well, but it was reminders of her father that taxed her emotions. The Man of Mystery had told Brendan all about his children through years of correspondence, detailing their lives and their triumphs. On the other hand, Molly knew absolutely nothing about Brendan Rea, an old friend who was kept in the shadows, held close to the vest.

"Did you feel it?" she asked Eoin while he motored along the Tallaght Bypass. "I can't tell if it's jealousy or admiration, but I'd swear that Mr. Rea thinks life cheated him."

"What your father did with his life, Molly, is more out of the ordinary than I can explain. A job at the Post Office was special; it implied a little status, a position in society. Especially at the end of the Depression, when unemployment was rampant." Eoin slipped into another lecture. "It was expected, and maybe it still is, that a man would start at the bottom and work up, which is what Mr. Rea did. When he retired, he was a supervisor, and that's not a job to be brushed off. Your father didn't settle for that route, you see, he reached for the top."

"Do you think he could have done as much if he had stayed in Dublin?"

"Probably not, come to think of it. The opportunities weren't there during the post-war years." He steered in the direction of Upper Camden Street. "How about lunch?"

"Thanks, yes, I need a rest," she said.

"Your Irish is showing," he teased. "You're growing melancholy."

"My father used to lapse into the doldrums every now and then," she replied. "Maybe it's something genetic that I inherited."

The only other GPO chum that Frank asked Molly to see was living in a nursing home, and it was obvious that Con McCreevy was too senile to carry on a conversation. He babbled about telegrams, recalling the war years, but he did not remember anyone named Devoy. Taking a chance, Molly asked if he had ever met Nuala, but he only stared at a wall and tried to explain that his sisters were working at a creamery. His illness was another reminder to Molly that she could have learned a great deal about her father, if only she had come four years ago when he first asked.

"Are you tired yet, or can I take you to dinner?" Eoin asked after the mind-numbing session with Mr. McCreevy.

"I'm sorry, Eoin, but I'm just all in," Molly said. "It's been an up and down day, but it's ending on a down note."

"We're not far from my place," he said. "Have a lie down, and I'll be sure to wake you in an hour or so. You'll feel better after a rest."

"I can't, you've done too much for me already."

"Come on, it's quiet and you're ready to collapse. Your hostess is very nice, but she'll wear you out if you go back to your room."

"I know, she loves to talk and I just can't face up to it now. Only an hour, that's it, all right?"

"Absolutely. You need to rest your mind, and I won't trouble you at all. A little quiet music, low lights, very peaceful and serene."

She checked an urge to make a remark about his offer, which did not sing of rest but of romance. One look at his rather homely face, the very image of a weary plow horse, told Molly that he was honestly offering shelter, and seduction was a foreign language. "You are the sweetest man I have ever met," she said with a grateful smile.

4

"Exposed to moral danger," announced the severe old man in the black robe. Frank would never forget those words.

"Please, M'lud, please, don't take my children," Maire Devoy begged, her desperate tone twisting the knots in Frank's stomach.

"Put away in separate institutions until the age of sixteen," the judge's bored droning continued, the same phrase that Frank had heard all morning, over and over again.

Sitting on the tram, nearly suffocated by Mammy's embrace, he heard her mumble, "Sister Keogh's doing. Half-truths and false words. And a blessed nun at that. What's the good of my words against hers?"

Frank's father had been dead for four years, and in all that time it seemed that his mother was forever fretting about money, about paying bills and stretching a shilling to reach a half-crown. At her wits end, she sometimes told her friends when the family went shopping on Thomas Street. From overheard conversations, Frank had learned that Mammy's suitor, the man they called Uncle Joe, had something to do with their latest problems, but a little boy could not understand the law and the clergy's idea of suitable conduct *for a young widow who wanted more children and a father for her young son.*

Never once had Joe O'Brien stayed overnight, a fact that Frank was quite sure of because he was a light sleeper and always woke up when Uncle Joe left. The last time that Sister Keogh came to the house, and he was hiding under Mammy's bed with Nuala, they heard the nun accusing Mammy of something that made her weep. Nuala told him that Uncle Joe wanted to get married, but Mammy was not sure about him, and maybe that was the problem. Marriage was something that lasted for life, as Nuala informed her little brother, and a woman could not just run over to the church without giving things some serious thought

"Mammy, if you marry Uncle Joe," Frank began to ask, but he stopped when he realized that his mother was silently crying.

"Too late for that," she said. Her lips were forced into a cheerful smile, but the tears that rolled down her cheeks made a lie of her assurances. "It's not to be so bad as that. You are both going on lovely holidays, with lots of other children to play with."

On the day that Mammy left the house with Nuala, to bring her to the nuns at Booterstown, she stopped long enough to talk to Mrs. Connelly, the woman who lived next door and who loved to mind other people's business. Frank heard a few words, bits and pieces about the wounds of the Civil War, the Shinners being made to suffer by the holier-than-thou Free Staters, and former members of Cummann na mBan being persecuted. Never before had Frank heard his mother speak with such venom, with bile poisoning her every word.

The ceili band played until after midnight, and Molly stayed until the last note had died out. In some way, she felt as though she had connected with her father, making up for the distance that they both kept. As if she was paying homage to her father, she danced gaily as she had danced as a girl, feet flying in a pounding rhythm that had once made Frank Devoy proud of his baby.

"Mom, why did you marry Dad?" Molly said into the phone at two in the morning. After Eoin dropped her back at the bed and breakfast, she had an urge to call her mother. There were questions that had to be answered at once, things to be sorted out that could not wait until later.

"Well, he had some very fine qualities," Barbara said, taken aback by the odd interrogation. "Why, did you hear of something bad?"

"No, I just need to know what attracted you to him."

"He was so shy," Barbara said. "A little unsure of himself, maybe a touch of insecurity, I don't know exactly, but he was so vulnerable. Your father was really a very sensitive person under his rough exterior."

"Come on, Dad was not shy. I saw him at parties, and he was the one with the lampshade on his head," Molly said. "Even at the office, I watched him once and he was sure not shy about telling off people who screwed up."

"He taught himself to be more outgoing. Like his sister, he once said. Supposedly, your aunt was very bubbly as a child, but then something happened to change her. I think she went crazy and your father was too embarrassed to tell anyone."

"Maybe she had a nervous breakdown," Molly said, but her theory was created out of mist and vapor.

"Who knows? Anyway, honey, I married your father because I fell in love. What more does a girl need?"

"Just that, I guess."

"What's wrong, Molly?"

"I wish that Dad was with me."

"He is, honey, he's always with you. Do you want to come home early?"

"No, I'm not ready to leave. If I could, I think I'd stay here longer. Oh, did you know that Dad's first job was delivering telegrams?"

The vigil candle was still burning, maintained lovingly by Mrs. Devlin. She had added a holy card of St. Patrick to the shrine of Frank Devoy, and Molly somehow felt better because of Mary's concern. Soothed into tranquility, she fell asleep almost before she climbed into bed, her reveries filled with images of Mary Devlin, her father and Eoin and the old boys from the GPO.

With Eoin tied up in meetings the following day, Molly planned on going it alone. Over a breakfast of oatmeal and hot tea, Mrs. Devlin acted the part of guide for the day's itinerary. She knew Fitzroy Street, a rather grand area in its time, which meant that the Devoys were somewhat well off when Frank's father was alive. In modern Dublin, however, the street was no longer grand and its residents far from well-off. Mary warned her to be careful.

"My father did claim that his parents were comfortable, but certainly not rich by American standards," Molly said.

"In my childhood days, anyone who could afford a two story cottage was rich," Mary said with a generous dollop of humor. "And if there was a flat to let in the building, you were riding high on the pig's back."

"It's sad, but I can't get a handle on how poor most people were."

"How could you, dear? The best you'll find is a taste of it from the memories of the old ones, like me. We had simple pleasures back then, not like today's children with their computers and games. Not everyone had electricity, now that should give you an idea of poverty. Some had battery-operated radios, but not everyone. We had gas lighting, and my mother made her penny's worth stretch to the limit. Still, it's a shame to give that up, the thrift and the scrimping. I can't waste, to this day."

The day's drive was a pilgrimage into Frank's past, an almost religious undertaking that would bring Molly to the

54

source of her father's hidden sorrows. She turned back to the list, to get Mary's take on the place where Frank lived after his father had died.

"Don't go there, Molly, I won't allow it," Mary said. "I know for a fact that the house your father lived in after he finished school was torn down long ago. You're a headstrong girl, so I'll tell you the honest truth to keep you away from there. I know the area from my younger days, and your people were living in a single room in a tenement, that's what this street offered. There's no doubt of it, I promise you."

"So my grandfather's money must have run out."

"Even one living on Fitzroy Street in Drumcondra would be hard-pressed to put enough aside to keep a family in spuds forever."

"What did a family do?" Molly asked, not expecting an answer.

"The worst slums in the world were right here in Dublin, and the poor lived in hovels, in squalor, and glad to find a roof even if it was leaking. You'd find one toilet in the yard, next to the only tap, and you'd share the facilities with all the neighbors."

"No help from the government?"

"It wasn't done, not in those days. We were just as afraid of communism as America was, back then, and some things that should have been done weren't done out of fear."

"Are these areas safe?" Molly asked, pointing to the second and fourth locations on Frank's roster. "He lived here before he went to school, and this is where my grandmother was living when she died."

"Northbrook Terrace used to be a nice place," Mary said. "Around 1970 or so, I would say, the wrong sort began to move in. Parts of the block were pulled down and corporation housing went up. Your grandmother's home is still there, in a lovely area that's getting popular with young couples."

"Good old urban renewal," Molly said. "There isn't much in Dublin that's old, I mean, things like ancient monuments and such."

"There never were any, my girl," Mary said. "There are some grand country houses that were built by the English landlords, and we have a few castles, but you have to remember that the Irish people had nothing. It's a wealthy man who builds a monument, and we had few wealthy men."

"Dr. MacNeill drove me around Merrion Square last night and explained the Protestant Ascendancy and the destruction in the city's center after the Rising. Whatever grandeur did exist was gone by the time my father came along."

"When some of the old buildings along the Liffey were pulled down, there were those who complained. I never cared for the modern style myself," Mary said. "The beauty of Ireland is not in her cities. They're ordinary, as ordinary as every other city in any other country. The beauty is in the countryside, in the heart of Ireland."

The drive along Fitzroy Street and Northbrook Terrace was made with the doors locked and the windows rolled up. Like any other town, the once-fashionable neighborhoods gave way to decreasing fortunes, and the lovely cottage that sheltered little Frank Devoy was now decrepit. Without her father there to fashion a different model of a time long past, Molly did not have a pleasant image in her mind as she left the place behind. If Eoin had come, she was sure that he could have blurred the sharp edges and helped her erase the garbage in the streets, the boarded up windows, and the strung-out addicts lounging at the corner.

The garda pulled her over when she was about four blocks from the place that her father had called home when he got his first job. Despite the fact that Molly resembled the Devoy side of the family, she dressed like a Yank and she drove like a scared tourist, making her easy to pick out.

"I'm looking for James Street," she said, with the bold insufferance of an American.

"Now why would you be wanting to go there?" the constable asked with a raised brow.

"My father lived there for a time," Molly said. "Before the war. I mean the Emergency."

"For your own good, miss, I can't let you proceed. If you want to see something, drive back the way you came and stroll across Ha'penny Bridge."

"But," Molly protested.

"Unless you've come to buy drugs, which is what most visitors are after around here."

"I should say not," Molly said. "Then can you tell me how to get to Drimnagh?"

"And did your dad live there as well?"

"Yes, after he finished school and got a job. My grandmother lived there until the day she died."

"Then he did well for himself." The officer nodded with gallant panache before delivering a set of driving directions that made Molly's head swim.

What were called corporation houses in Ireland would prove to be their version of public housing, a Caucasian Cabrini-Green, the projects for the light of complexion. Each and every unit in the estate was the same, although everything was now sixty years older and showing its age. For Molly, the stark contrast between what her father had, where he fell to, and then what he climbed for, provided a perfect understanding of Frank's pursuit of the American dream. He had known grinding poverty, but through hard work he had bettered himself. As much as his life had improved, it was not enough, because Frank had gone away to find even greater success, a grander house, and a completely different life.

Flushed with elation over her joyous discovery, Molly did not realize that she had forgotten all about lunch. Instead, she carried on with her mission, following the road signs back to City Centre and a meeting with a Dublin attorney. At once, she disliked his tone, his questions about why she was pursuing a Freedom of Information request, forcing the government to turn over some documents. She turned the tables on Mr. O'Rahilly and asked him why Frank had started the process in the first place.

"Mr. Devoy did not tell me precisely why, nor did I take the liberty of asking. About four years ago, we began corresponding, and when I heard of his passing I was afraid that his heirs would be denied some important information. You see, Ms. Devoy, these documents were of great interest to your late father. The fact that he sent you here confirms my suspicions."

"Mr. O'Rahilly, could you file a request to dig up information on my aunt? If she married, or if she emigrated, would there be something in the government files?"

"What do you know of your father's past?" O'Rahilly asked. "Do you know where he was schooled, or where he worked, any of that?"

Molly pulled a bundle of papers out of her satchel. "What I know is in here, names and addresses, with a set roster that I'm to follow. Yesterday, I found out that my dad was a telegram messenger at the GPO, when I spoke to a couple of men he used to work with. Now tomorrow, I plan to meet several of his old schoolmates from Carriglea, which is a high school or secondary school, as I understand it. I just noticed, I'm working backwards. I suppose my last stop will be the maternity ward where he was born."

"Did he speak of his experiences at school when you were growing up?" O'Rahilly continued.

"Never. Although he was a firm supporter of the Christian Brothers' school in Chicago, and he spoke very well of

59

the order," Molly said. "It seems to me that his experiences must have been positive, even though he never expressed it verbally."

"Before that, though, in primary school?" O'Rahilly pressed.

"What is this all about?"

"Shortly before your father died, he asked me to pursue a request for his sister's records. The paperwork was filed, and now I will exert a bit of pressure on the right places to move the wheels of bureaucracy a little faster. Excuse me for running out, but I have a meeting in twenty minutes. I am representing a class in a lawsuit against the Sisters of Mercy. I'll tell you about it another time; you'll find it very interesting."

The clerk handed Molly a sealed court order, the magic key that would open up Frank Devoy's past. With surprise, she learned that she was being sent to Kilkenny, over seventy miles from Dublin. At a facility named St. Patrick's, Molly would at last uncover the origins of the Man of Mystery, and with her hands trembling with excitement, she turned to the next section of her father's saga.

"At St. Patrick's in Kilkenny, you will be crushed," he warned from the grave. "Forgive me, *mo mhuirnin*, but I call on you to speak for me when I am silenced in death."

The Man of Mystery never failed to intrigue, and Molly went to her afternoon meeting with such overwhelming curiosity that she feared she could not concentrate on the task at hand. Her host would be Mr. Patrick Grady, who was proud to consider himself Frank's closest chum. His was the only name that Molly knew well, someone she had wished Merry Christmas to over the phone every year. Michael O'Keefe was joining the party, and Dan Garrity had promised to drop by. If not for Pat, it would be nothing more than a collection of strange names, a gathering of Frank's past that was kept hidden.

Sounding just like he did on the phone, Pat was gregarious, making fun of O'Keefe and Garrity for running late because O'Keefe was doing the driving and if the two of them arrived by Saturday it would a miracle. He mentioned some of the other lads, although Molly had no idea who they might be, promising her that they would be at the wake without fail.

Meeting Mrs. Grady was a bit disconcerting because the woman stared and scowled, saying very little as she set up the tea service in the neat little parlor. Every inch a sweet Irish grandmother in her flowered dress and sensible shoes, she looked at Molly suspiciously, as if the young lady were here to seduce Mr. Grady.

"Why don't you run over to Cissie's, mother," Pat said.

"What of serving our guest?" she asked.

"We can see to ourselves," he said.

"Look, Mrs. Grady, if you'd rather stay, I'm fine with it," Molly said, attempting to relieve the tension.

"I told you, Niamh, she's not a doctor come to put you away," Pat said with impatience.

"No, not at all," Molly vowed. "I'm only a nurse, and you look just fine to me."

That was enough to appease the old woman, who put on a sweater and lifted the strap of her handbag onto her forearm with a smile. "Is it your father who passed away?" Niamh asked, even though Pat had explained things to her five times already.

"Bit of old age, a little forgetful." Pat tossed his head towards the door as Niamh closed it behind her. "Any stranger comes in and she thinks I've sent for the asylum to get her."

"I'm sorry, the poor thing," Molly said. "You don't mind that I've come?"

"Mind? I'd be a poor friend if I didn't welcome Frank Devoy's little girl. It's as if I've watched you grow up, through the pictures he sent, and now here you are in the flesh."

"He wanted me to see you, to talk about Carriglea."

"We had some good times, and some of the finest teachers in the country. There must have been three hundred boys enrolled in those days, and Brother Conrad knew every one of us. I saw him once, on Grafton Street, about fifteen years ago, and he still remembered my name."

"That's remarkable. Every boy must have been important to him, to make such an effort."

"The building is still there, but back in our day Dun Laoghaire was out in the country. Dublin's built up and around it now."

Their chat was interrupted by the arrival of Mike and Dan, as they insisted on being called. Three old men, short of stature, white-haired and wizened, looked Molly over carefully, assessing the quality of Frank's upbringing until they were satisfied that his daughter was a credit to her father.

"Do you remember the play that we staged, the one that Brother George wrote in Irish?" Dan took a turn at an anecdote.

"Can you believe it? The government wanted Irish to become the official language and replace English." Mike shook his head in wonder. "Brother George tore into the subject with his own ideas, teaching us Irish the way we had learned English as children, by speaking it. Ho, the inspector gave him what for when he came in to check the curriculum."

"And how do my grandchildren learn the language today?" Pat asked. "The same way as Brother George wanted to teach us, without the dry grammar lessons. We learned plenty of Irish until the government decreed that we had to memorize rules and regulations."

"Do you remember the bread from Kennedy's Bakery?" Mike switched topics. "Frank hated it, so I always let him have a long dip in the drippings to mask the sour taste."

"What was that for, a midday snack or something?" Molly asked.

"Snack? That was breakfast, my girl, one quarter of a loaf of bread and one quarter of the bowl of drippings. Add a cup of tea and that was our meal, except on Friday, of course, and then it was margarine on the bread," Mike said.

"We did have elevens," Pat said. "That was more bread, at recreation time out in the yard. They'd wheel out a cart, filled with slices of bread, and we'd eat right there, standing up, winter or summer, we ate outdoors."

"With nothing to wash it down," Mike added, lighthearted. "Brother Comerford said it made us masticate thoroughly."

All three men began to chortle with glee over the Brother's quaint phrase. Molly, on the other hand, was horrified. Bread and bacon grease was not a meal, not a wise choice for a daily repast. Catching herself, she mentally berated her American ideas of suitable food. Of course the Irish would use drippings, because it was wasteful to discard perfectly edible food that provided a big dose of calories to active boys. It may not have been particularly healthy, but it beat starving by a long way.

"So if you boys had the drippings, who ate the bacon?" she asked.

"The Brothers, of course," Pat said, as if that were only natural. Carrying on with his summary, he returned to the menu. Boiled, chopped beef at three, with boiled spuds, and who could forget the cabbage which, he said after a pause, they did indeed manage to forget to eat if they could avoid it.

From inedible cabbage came a recollection of beef soup, another thing best forgotten in Dan's mind. The recipe was simple, consisting of the water left behind after boiling the beef, dumped into a cup with the congealed grease floating on the top. Not one of the old men could recall seeing a single boy put that cup to his lips.

"The hogs feasted on potato jackets, cabbage and beef soup," Mike said. "Some of the lads at Carriglea came from farms, and they studied farming. We had a lovely farm at the school, and they grew all our potatoes and cabbage. Sometimes they'd butcher one of the hogs and we'd have sausage instead of beef at dinner. Wasn't it grand, boys, when we had sausage?"

"Of course, come Friday, you never knew what they'd find in the kitchen to feed us." Pat sat back in his chair, at ease with his school days. "No meat so no drippings, as we said, but we'd be given cheese in place of the beef. Sometimes they'd make up a lovely custard, and I prayed to be chosen to clean the pans that night. That was a treat, to scrape out the custard scraps, you'd feel like a king."

"We could buy extras, mind you," Mike said. "My mother sent me six penny stamps every week, and the Brothers cashed them in for me. There was a little commissary, and your Dad worked there for a time, selling sweets and the like. In fact, he was allowed to go into town to replenish the store when the goods ran low."

As if a cloud had descended, the air in the room grew heavy and dark. Pat fingered the crease in his trousers as he recalled Frank, a kind-hearted lad who earned a bit of money with his work in the commissary, a bounty that he never failed to share with his division. The gloom grew deeper as Dan spoke of Dermot Downey, probably one of Frank's closest companions at the school.

"Dermot was a clever chap," Dan said. "Loved ships of any kind."

"His most proud possession was his full set of British warships from the Players' cigarette packages," Mike added. "We'd trade them back and forth, but Dermot wouldn't part with one of his ships. Couldn't wait to get out of Carriglea and join the navy. Poor lad."

The time flew by as the schoolmates regaled Molly with wild stories of the school play that became a fiasco. For the first time, she learned that her father played a clarinet in the school band, which performed at concerts for the public and was always featured in the most important religious processions in the area. Dan stumbled over a mention of some concert in Marino, when Frank's mother could come to see him because it was within walking distance of her home. He cleared his throat and changed the subject so quickly that Molly never had a chance to encourage him to elaborate on his tale.

A neighbor brought Niamh Grady home at five o'clock, and the men clammed up completely when she walked in. The atmosphere in the lounge changed so radically that Molly decided it was best to leave. Knowing that she would see them again at the funeral, she shook hands all around and gathered up her impressions. On the surface, her father's days in the Christian Brothers school seemed quite pleasant, though stark, and that explained Frank's respect and devotion to the order. Nothing had been said to explain his loathing of the Sisters of Mercy, however, and the point of confusion lingered as she

66

turned the key in the ignition of the car. She had a few more pieces of a large puzzle, pieces that were not fitting together easily.

Pat walked his friends to the curb, where they could speak privately on the quiet suburban street. "I'll go to my grave the same as old Frank. I'll never tell my family that I was in Carriglea, and if they find out after I'm gone, I won't be here to see their shame," he said quietly.

"We played it well, lads," Mike said. "So it was a boarding school, she says. Frank would have wanted it this way, to send her home with only our happy times."

"It was like paradise after Kilkenny," Pat said. "When we told her of Downey, I almost wanted to let her know that we all were forced into the mold of military men."

"They trained us like soldiers, didn't they, with that damned bugle every morning. Marching to Mass in regiments, messing together like sailors. Is it any wonder that Downey talked of nothing but the Royal Navy?" Mike sniffled, pretending to a spot of congestion. "He wanted to sail away from the disgrace, the same as the rest of us."

"Frank did well for himself," Pat said, rapping the door of Mike's car in a farewell salute.

"Died peacefully," Mike agreed. "I'll come by on Thursday morning and give you a lift."

"He wants it told, my boys," Pat warned. "That's why she's come. He's sending her to St. Patrick's."

"Maybe it should be told," Dan said. "Frank was always sharp as a tack. I'd trust him, trust his judgment."

Pat waved goodbye and went back into the comfort of his secure home. He could smell pork chops frying, a delicacy he did not taste until he was seventeen years old. Stretching ahead of him, he faced a long night of tossing and turning, with the nightmares returning. Already he knew that he would try very hard not to close his eyes. Reflexively, he clutched his hand into a fist, feeling again the sting of Brother Damien's leather strap and the pain of trying to play a clarinet with fingers that were aching and swollen after yet another biffing.

Driving back as the sun went down, Molly had a vague notion that things were not quite as they had been presented. The old men bantered in spurts that were spaced apart by furtive glances and very brief silences, as each word was weighed before delivery. She had a terrific ability to judge when the whole truth was being cut up and served in tiny bits. Stan did that so often that she had become an expert at reading the downcast eyes, the sigh and the false smile.

As soon as she walked into the front door of Derry House, Mary called her into the parlor to help with a memory scrapbook that would be given to her grandchildren. "My fingers are a little tired of cutting," Mary said. "Can you trim these pages for me?"

The sheet that Mary gave her was yellowing with age, and Molly noted the date of the article, which was four years past. "Last Days of a Laundry," the banner trumpeted, but Molly only read those few words, concentrating her efforts on neatly clipping the excess paper. As she worked across the long edge, she glanced at a sentence that mentioned the proliferation of automatic washing machines, and how that could account for the laundry's demise. Molly smiled, picturing Ireland being dragged into the Twentieth Century, kicking and screaming at all the electronic gadgets, while the rest of the universe prepared to step into the Twenty-first.

"That nice professor called for you," Mary said in her romantic lilt.

"I was afraid he had forgotten me by now," Molly said.

"He left his number, but I told him in no uncertain terms that it was his duty to call you, and not the other way around."

"Women do phone men these days, Mrs. Devlin."

"Here now, what did I tell you about that?"

"Okay, okay, women phone men, Mary."

"I'm sure they do. But a gentleman rings up a lady." Mary raised an eyebrow. Looking up at the clock on the fireplace mantle, Mary made a quick calculation. "Let's see now, he called at four and again at half past five. Six-fifteen he's due."

The article from the *Irish Times* was carefully placed on the heavy pasteboard and covered with plastic to preserve the morsel of Dublin history. "Is this your picture?" Molly caught sight of a page covered with snapshots.

"The lovely bride, that's me. I was a fair colleen in those days, I must admit. Mr. Devlin in his Sunday suit, what a handsome man." Mary's fingertip barely touched the page of her memory book, her delicacy a result of reverence. "This one is his mother, and these other lads are his brothers. His sister Lily was already married and living in England when we were married. Her husband had been a mechanic in the RAF, and he had a fine job after the war. Can you see, back behind the lads, that's their other sister."

"She's a shy one," Molly said. The young lady in the picture definitely seemed to be hiding behind her brothers, disappearing into the background.

"Oh, my yes, very shy. But pretty as a picture, the prettiest girl in the Coombe my John liked to boast."

Just then, the phone rang and Mary insisted that Molly answer. It was not quite six-fifteen, but Mary had been fairly accurate in her prediction.

"I should have called yesterday," Eoin apologized. "Last night, I tumbled in the door and fell asleep at once, I'm sorry to say, like the old man that I am."

"Don't worry about it, Eoin," Molly said.

"But I don't want you to think it was a one-night thing," he said. "On holiday, it's one thing, but, well, I don't know what I'm trying to say."

"Women do go out to find men, Eoin; women sleep with guys because they want sex. It's normal desire, we all have it, and it's nothing to be apologizing for."

"So if I never saw you again, you'd think I used you and it wouldn't bother you?"

"Not used, just not making a big deal out of nothing important."

Her statement was more bold than he expected, and he teased her about the legacy of America's days of free love and sexual liberty. He praised her as his icon, a testament to all that he had missed because he had to grow up in Ireland, all buttoned up and confined in a corset while the rest of the world was dropping its collective knickers in rebellion against the old ways. Molly heard the longing in his voice, a tone that bemoaned the loss of youth and missed opportunities.

"Do you have any plans for tomorrow?" he asked.

"Nothing set in concrete. I was thinking of running down to Kilkenny to get my Dad's school records, but I can wait until Monday. Do you have a better offer?"

"Come to Waterford with me. My father is a relic of your dad's era, and I thought you might benefit from an interview with him. You need a solid background in Irish life in the Twenties and Thirties if you're going to understand your father, and really appreciate what he wanted you to learn when he sent you here."

"But will he hold back like everyone else? All my life, anything sensitive or unpleasant was best not to know of. I visited with a few of my father's old school friends, and I could tell that they were hiding things from me. I'll go with you, Eoin, and I'd love to see the countryside. I just need to know if I'll be disappointed before I get there."

71

"Opening up to strangers is not in our nature," he said. "Take what comes out of the old man. A drop or a waterfall, it's better than being dry."

Pat Grady sat in front of his television, his granddaughters noisily arguing over a doll's dress. He drummed his fingers on the armrest, thinking of calling, to tell Frank's daughter the whole story about the farm at Carriglea. Not even Frank knew, because Pat had never been able to tell his closest confidant. To throw water on Frank's adoration of the Christian Brothers seemed too cruel, and Frank had done nothing to deserve being totally disillusioned. It was to the best that Frank had gone to his grave thinking that the Brothers were selfless and devoted to teaching, but Pat could not decide if it was all to the best that Molly be kept in the dark.

The more scholarly lads, like Pat and Frank, took up tailoring because they had to choose a course of study that would lead to an occupation, even though they hoped for something better when they left school at sixteen. They did not mingle very much with the country boys, the ones who were taken off the farm and allowed to choose agriculture as their area of specialization, working on the school's acreage to hone their skills. Frank knew all about Seamus O'Rourke, who excelled at his coursework and went straight to Saville Row in 1938, eventually owning a respectable gentlemen's haberdashery. It was the other side of the picture that Frank never saw, the dark side that was hidden behind murky shadows and scattered on distant farms all across Ireland.

Needing advice, Pat rang up Mike O'Keefe, to mull over the issue of Bob Emmett, the wizard of animal husbandry at Carriglea. His knowledge had been of great benefit to the hog farmer who hired him, but it had been of no use to Bob's destitute mother and sisters. His wages were paid directly to the Christian Brothers, with Bob never seeing a farthing. Beaten regularly if he did not work fast enough, slaving away day after day for twelve or fourteen hours a day, he ran away and joined a British regiment at the start of the war. Pat finally heard the story forty years later, the sad tale passed along from mouth to mouth among the former students.

"Liam Wynne made out better than he would have without the Brothers," Mike pointed out. "He was sent to a good family who welcomed him as a son, and when he married the daughter they couldn't have been happier. It's not the clergy alone, Pat; it's us, the Irish people. Leave it be."

5

From the passenger's seat of Eoin's car, Molly finally discovered the Ireland that poets and bards had immortalized, a land of impossibly green hills, rolling fields and dots of white sheep that painted a dream world of beauty. Off in the distance, the low-slung mountains framed a picture that a mere photograph could never capture, not when the reality was far more picturesque than the travel brochures could reveal. There was a majesty to the sweep of the pastures, hung with long strands of fieldstone in a jewel box of emerald. This was the country that her father had loved, the land that claimed his heart. Molly grew morose as they left County Wexford behind and plunged ahead to County Waterford.

"I let my father down," she said. "He wanted to show all this to me, and I deprived him of a great joy. He never scolded me, never told me to my face that I was making a mistake. I felt it, though, every time I disappointed him. I wish he would have yelled at me, just once, so I would have opened my eyes."

"Would you have opened them, Molly? Or would you have closed them a little tighter? Maybe he knew you well enough to get you headed in the right direction. He couldn't live your life for you."

"My marriage was a mistake."

"So was mine. You followed your heart and I followed my head. Did either one of us come out better than the other?"

"I didn't insult you when I called you a martyr the other night, did I?"

"Martyr is a much overused word in this country. Every other word in our history books is 'martyr'. It's so ingrained in our psyches that I suspect the biology department at UCD is going to announce the discovery of a martyrdom gene in Irish DNA."

They left the main road and veered northwest, driving through the rich farmland of Waterford. The little town of Kilrossanty appeared in the distance, its presence defined by the small stucco buildings erected at the very edge of the narrow lane, rising straight up out of the ground like proud soldiers on parade. Eoin slowed the car to point out the sights, which consisted of a few shops, the pub, and the omnipresent church at the center of town and the center of life.

"How are you keeping yourself, Eoin?" the butcher greeted them as they entered the white tiled shop.

"Molly, I'd like to introduce my brother Declan," Eoin said. "He's taken over the shop."

"Fourth generation," Declan boasted. "A pleasure, Molly. I've heard great things about you already."

Her eyes flicked sideways at Eoin, a little ripple of annoyance at his audacity. To find out that she was being talked about behind her back raised her hackles, and the pungent odor of disgrace teased at her nose. To make matters worse, a young girl of twelve dashed from the back of the shop and stood behind the counter, gawking.

"Can't you say hello to your uncle, Jess?" Declan gave the girl a little nudge. "His friend will think we've no manners in our town. Does Kilrossanty put you in mind of Chicago, Molly?"

"You know where I'm from?" Molly said through clenched teeth.

Despite Eoin's desperate hand gestures, his brother would not zip his lip. "A girl from town went to Chicago six months ago, to work as a nanny for a rich family. She's living in a suburb; what's it called, Jess?"

"Kenilworth, Daddy, like the book," Jess said, but she never stopped staring.

"They sure are rich," Molly agreed.

"Are you rich, Miss Molly?" the little girl asked with delightful innocence.

"I have two girls and a boy, so I'm as wealthy as can be," she said.

"Jess, take Miss Molly up the street to show her the town," Declan said. "Mammy's waiting lunch for us, go on now."

Jess could not move fast enough, to claim the honor of escorting a visitor through Kilrossanty. With the innocence of the small town, she pulled Molly out of the door, boasting of her newfound status as an acquaintance of a genuine American. She would be the talk of the town for months, she gushed to her newfound friend, immediately commencing on a quiz session to acquire some fragments of information that could be exchanged for the awe of her classmates.

The little bell over the door tinkled its high pitch, and then the door clicked shut. "She's got a lovely ass, Eoin," Declan said. "What does she see in you, I'd like to know? Is she a good ride?"

"It's none of your business, you filthy pervert," Eoin said, chucking his brother on the arm.

"That's a strong yes. Come on, I'll tell Peter to watch the shop for a minute. Your friend will need a drop before she faces himself," Declan said. He hung his butcher's coat on a peg behind the counter and walked towards the shop door. "Sweet Jesus, she's been waylaid by Mrs. Rafferty."

The woman who owned the general store across the road was making small talk, examining Eoin MacNeill's unexpected lady friend while Jessie puffed up with pride of ownership. Americans were mythical beings in this tiny farming hamlet, sometimes seen at The Farmhouse bed and breakfast outside of town, but otherwise existing only as television images. Eoin took in the view, a scene that had not changed in over forty years, and marveled at how out of place Molly appeared.

In neatly pressed khakis and a tailored wool blazer, Molly was the picture of elegance, standing in sharp contrast to the old women in housedresses and tatty cardigans, and their younger equivalent in jeans and shapeless flannel shirts. There was much more than her clothing that betrayed her national origin. She looked quite well to do in her outfit, with her ginger-colored hair cropped short in a fashionable bob, not unlike the professional women of Dublin. What completely gave her away was her walk, a stride that reflected a confidence that only American women carried, with head high and shoulders back, taking on the world that they believed they owned. Her presence in little Killrossanty reflected on him, the local boy who had done well and now appeared to be doing even better.

With the meal concluded and the children sent outside, the adults sat around the dining room table, discussing Irish life for Molly's edification. Unfortunately, the old parish priest had died three years earlier, and his trove of experience was gone with him. Offering up what he could, Declan tried to explain how the priest clung to the old ways, struggling to maintain a tight grip on the parishioners until well into the 1980's. That was the turning point, in Declan's mind, when people started to ask questions and Father Duggan ceased being the law in Killrossanty.

"What do you mean by 'law' exactly?" Molly asked. "Judge and jury, that sort of thing?"

"There was a young couple, both from farms, and they were messing about, as young people will do. They weren't in any hurry to get married, but if it came down to it, the boy was ready to take that step." Declan said. "The Father gets wind of their hanky-panky, and wouldn't you know it, he marches off to Quinn's house and orders the girl to get married. Be at the church at four o'clock tomorrow, he says, or I'll put you away on Gloucester Street."

"Wasn't this after the place was shut down?" Eoin asked.

"Not a month after, but poor old Duggan was getting senile and he slipped back to the Fifties. The Quinns all went on holiday to Liverpool, but Susan changed her mind and they came back on the same ferry," Declan prattled, telling a story that required more knowledge of the listener than Molly possessed.

"Don't you remember, Eoin, the Sheehan lad?" Declan's wife Kathleen added. "It was a lovely wedding, Father Kelly's first marriage ceremony. Thank goodness they sent him, so they could put old Duggan out to pasture."

"Heaven help us, Kathleen is going to start in on hypocrisy," Declan said. "Beware of the leaven of the Pharisees, which is hypocrisy."

"Well, that's just what it is," she argued.

"There came a time when we took to laughing at Father Duggan's sermons," Declan continued. "He was at the far end, and falling off the edge, with his talks about the girls in this town. A person would think we were raising a pack of tramps and whores to hear him going on, as if half the young men were being seduced every night. What was needed was the middle ground, to keep the boys and girls in line without sounding silly. No one would listen to him after a while."

"Are you sure it wasn't our father up there in the pulpit?" Eoin asked.

"Our father and half his cronies," Declan said. "And your father as well, Kathleen. But that's what they were taught as boys in school by the nuns, and then by the priests when they were older."

"People who shunned sex teaching sex," Molly said. "They couldn't let go of the old notions. I saw it in my father, the way he treated me compared to my brothers."

"To this day, the Church will condemn a film if the bishops think it's not suitable," Kathleen said. "Of course, that guarantees a box office smash."

"It's a very Catholic country, isn't it?" Molly uttered an enormous understatement.

"Ah, but His Holiness in Rome loves us." Declan raised his glass in a toast.

Seeing a country through native eyes gave Molly a picture of Frank's Ireland that was as close as she could hope to find. Through Eoin's father, she got a glance at her father's soul, and uncovered the old world that he moved through. Con MacNeill was older than Frank Devoy, but he clearly recalled the days of his childhood, which he related with blunt honesty and affection. Kilrossanty was as isolated as the Arctic Circle back then, in the days before cars were a common sight. The clergy and religious provided a link to the outside world, but they gave only as much as they wished to let in, and their word was law. The Catholic Church and the Dail Eireann worked as one, to create a dream world of secular life in a country that had endured centuries of occupation and religious oppression. As an American, Molly saw Con's world as a hellish place that was as repressive as fascist Italy or socialist Russia. She could not shake the impression she formed of Con MacNeill's life, any more than she could bring herself to like him.

He certainly didn't endear himself to her when he called Eoin's ex-wife an adulteress for taking another husband, divorce or not divorce. And Eoin had to lie in the bed he had made as well, not to remarry until Sheila was dead and he was free in God's eyes.

Giving up on a masquerade, Eoin fumed openly at his father's ranting. Molly threw him a tender smile, feeling sorry for a man with such a strict father. Frank had been firm, not strict, and if anything, he was downright indulgent. His upbringing in Dublin had shaped him, just as Con had been molded by hard times in the back of beyond. She did find a similarity in Con's reserve, a reticence that most likely developed as an outgrowth of poverty. Molly could imagine that those who had made a habit of scrimping and scraping to get by had a tendency to use their words and their emotions with the same economy.

"That went well," Eoin said sarcastically when the evening ended at last.

"He's very bitter," Molly said.

"Maybe that's it. In part, I think he's mad at the world. He missed out on things growing up because his father died when he was fourteen. My grandmother wouldn't bring a man in to work in the shop because she was afraid of a scandal, with the family living here above the store. My dad had to leave school early, and when I went off to university, he pulled on his black boots and stomped all over us."

"Not sleeping on the sofa?" Molly asked as Eoin crawled into her bed, seeking the warmth of her skin on a chilly summer evening. "Don't you feel weird, having sex in your old bed?"

"Not weird, Molly, just incredibly horny."

He nuzzled her neck and tickled her, inducing a silly giggle that she tried hard to suppress. His lovemaking that night was slow, intense and so pleasurable that she could not contain the low moans that escaped from deep within her. Sighs mingled with the squeak of the bedsprings to create an erotic symphony, the pace building to a crescendo of groans that nearly became a shout. When he woke her in the middle of the night to make love again, she readily agreed, aroused by his insistence and his strong desire. In the morning, she changed the sheets and tidied the room, and then watched him toss the condom wrappers on the dresser top, where they were reflected in the mirror, impossible not to see. He told her to leave them exactly where he left them.

82

Back at Mrs. Devlin's cottage in the Coombe, Molly called her brother's place in Michigan to check on her children before checking in on Stan. Eoin was content to wait in the lounge, sitting with Mrs. Devlin and her storehouse of old anecdotes that began with "Did you know the Tierney family on St. Thomas Road? Maybe they were gone when you came to Dublin," and away she sailed through the war years.

Not wishing to be seen crying, Molly bounded up the stairs and flew into her room, to grab a handful of tissues from the box next to the bed. A few words from her brother and she saw with brilliant clarity that it was over between her and Stan. In her heart, she didn't want to go back to their house, to pick up where they'd left off. Accepting reality brought the tears to her eyes, made her weep over the result of keeping the peace with her mother after Stan proposed. Molly liked being alone, not having to depend on others because they were unreliable. She had learned that from her father, the same man who didn't like Stan but never told her outright. Make-up repaired, she went back to the parlor as if nothing at all had gone wrong.

"We'll be back late, Mrs. Devlin, don't wait up," Molly said with a casual air, adept at hiding what she felt inside. "Mr. MacNeill tells me that a night on the town can run until the wee hours."

"Why didn't you tell her you'd be gone all night?" he grumbled, pouting as he drove away from the curb. "I wanted you to spend the night with me."

"I just couldn't, Eoin, I couldn't tell her," Molly said.

"You're not who you seem, or who you claim to be, Molly Devoy," he said. "The time will come when you'll wish you had been honest with yourself."

"I know my mind," she answered. "It isn't necessary to lay everything out for public consumption."

"Keep your secrets, then," he said.

The honeymoon couple was gone back home to Sligo, and Mrs. Devlin was attending Sunday Mass by the time that Molly crawled down the stairs for breakfast. Her head was throbbing, a piercing hangover that served as a reminder that she was too old to drink and party all night. Hearing a noise in the kitchen, Molly rushed in, ready to confront a burglar. The petite old lady at the stove looked so shocked at the intrusion that Molly feared she had caused a stroke.

"I'm sorry, I didn't know that anyone was here," Molly said.

The white-haired woman's eyes flitted nervously all around, reminding Molly of a caged parakeet facing the house cat. Without a doubt, the poor lady's hands were visibly trembling.

"You'd better sit down," Molly suggested, and the Irish bird did as she was told. "My name is Molly. I'm staying here. Do you work for Mrs. Devlin?"

Molly had taken the woman's hand and gently checked her pulse, her nurse's training always coming into play. With tremendous effort, the elderly lady pulled herself together and extended her right hand in a movement that was oddly starchy. "How do you do? I am Rose Devlin."

At once, Molly pictured an addle-headed maiden aunt, kept by her brother out of a sense of duty. There was an air about Rose, a manner that called to mind Frank Devoy's phrase "not quite right in the head."

"Do you come in on Sundays?" Molly asked, taking note of Rose's flushed cheeks and nervous perspiration.

"I live here," Rose whispered.

"How could I never have seen you?"

Molly felt as if her voice was booming, but she was not shouting. She had an odd sensation that she was an enormous hulk, taking up the entire kitchen. It was only due to Rose's diminished sense of self, as she shrank into her space in an attempt to disappear.

"I'd like to go to St. Stephen's Green, please?" Rose asked, not looking Molly in the eye while her hands twisted with agitation.

"I'd like to see that myself," Molly said. She had no plans for Sunday, and Rose appeared quite harmless, though not altogether there.

At once, Rose got up and went to the pantry, returning with a hat on her head, a handbag on her arm, and a heavy cardigan sweater swathed around her body, buttoned up to her neck.

"Shall I leave a note for Mrs. Devlin, then?" Molly asked.

85

A few gulps of tea had to serve as breakfast, since Rose was determined to charge out the door. "I forgot my name once," Rose confessed as Molly hastily scribbled her memo.

"It happens, Rose, don't let it concern you."

"I like it when people call me Rose."

"It's a very pretty name. I wish I had named my girls something pretty, but my husband thought that French names sounded classy."

"A wife has to keep the peace."

Molly stopped in her tracks, caught off guard by an echo of her own thoughts. When she began to laugh at her insight, Rose's face crinkled up in confusion, a puzzlement that relaxed once the old woman was seated in the car.

"Do you know how to get there?" Molly asked. She opened up her map and spread it across the steering wheel.

"I've never been."

Recalling that Rose was described as the shy girl, Molly was not particularly surprised at her inexperience. Social anxiety could easily cripple a woman, becoming a habit if not treated properly. Equally possible was an untreated case of agoraphobia, in which Rose did not know what she had and the family had settled on some other excuse for her inability to leave the house. That Rose had a sudden urge to make an excursion was completely illogical, but Molly had seen the confusion of elderly patients in the surgical unit. Old age was not pretty.

"Okay, I've got a route," Molly announced.

"I need flowers. A wreath," Rose said, speaking always in a tiny voice.

The unlikely couple arrived at the park with two of Mary's bright red geraniums. Rose knew that she wanted to go to the general vicinity of James Clarence Mangan's bust, and the garda was very kind as he escorted the ladies to a bench.

"Rose, what is a Magdalene laundry?" Molly asked. She read the memorial plaque that was set into the park bench. When she turned to look at Rose, Molly was shocked at the woman's face, gone dead white.

"It's best not to know," Rose gasped, choking on some internal terror.

"I shouldn't have brought you here," Molly said. "Come on, Rose, let me get you home."

The two geraniums were deposited on the bench and Rose crossed herself, pausing to offer a silent prayer. "I haven't set foot in the church since then," she stated strongly, a hint of anger in her inflection.

"I try not to miss," Molly said, using her strength to push Rose into a sitting position. "Can you make it back to the car? Take it easy for a minute, catch your breath. I don't know if I can move the car any closer to pick you up; you might have to walk."

Perched gently on the seat, Rose tenderly touched the brass plaque. "How could God let them do what they did?" she mumbled. Her thin finger, gnarled by a lifetime of hard work, stroked the individual letters of the inscription. Since she was growing calm, and her color was returning, Molly sat next to her, waiting patiently for Rose to do whatever she needed to do. "They are silent now. Silent. Unknown."

After a while, Rose simply got up and started to walk back along the path, her business concluded and her outing finished. She took Molly's arm, though it was not for support but for protection that she held her body close, recoiling from the few people who were out for a stroll on an overcast Sunday morning. A glance from a passerby was enough to make Rose cringe, clinging a little tighter to Molly's upper arm. By the time they reached the car, Molly felt as if Rose had almost retreated into her, attempting to hide from the world.

"Have you ever seen this part of Dublin before, Rose?" Molly asked, taking note of the little glances that swept underneath downcast eyes.

"No. Never."

"We can stay if you like. I can drive you around if you like. Would you like to go for a ride in the car?"

"You don't mind? With me here?"

Knowing but few streets, Molly watched the road signs carefully, making a loop that crossed the Liffey at O'Connell Street before heading along the quays towards Inchicore, where she retraced her route from her first day in Dublin. Back on St. Anne's Road, Rose began to weep, making a beeline for her room and shutting the door behind her.

"Please forgive me, I am so sorry." Molly expressed her deepest regrets. "It was too much for her, and it's my fault that she's so agitated now."

Cocking her head, Mary listened to her husband's sister, sobbing in her little room at the back of the house. "It had to be done, Molly," Mary said. "She had to do it before she passed on, and now she has finally done it. Thank you, thank you a hundred times over for helping us."

"I'm really glad to help, Mary, but I'm not qualified for this sort of treatment. It can be dangerous to intervene without a competent psychiatrist making the proper diagnosis. She can be helped, but it would be better to seek the right kind of medical practitioner. How long has Rose been mentally ill?"

"We don't speak of it, Molly."

6

Eoin begged her to postpone the trip to Kilkenny for one more day, for purely selfish reasons. He had already made plans to give his full attention to Dermot on Sunday, and he went home that night with a longing to hear Molly's funny Chicago accent. Talking Molly into a delay was not all that difficult. As far either one of them could determine, she would be given some school records that would be as dull as it sounded, and Tuesday was as good a day as Monday to shuffle a bundle of papers.

Molly ran down her itinerary for Mary's benefit at breakfast, mentioning a few tourist sights and seeking her landlady's opinion as to interest or attractive features. When Rose burst into the dining room, even Mary was shocked.

"Please, I must see Glasnevin Cemetery," Rose said, in the voice of a woman who did not think she was deserving of the favor.

"Will you take her, Molly, please," Mary begged. "She's never asked before, not once. It's a resurrection, that's what it is, she's coming back to us."

"We'll have to go first thing this morning," Molly said. "Mr. MacNeill and I have plans. Wait, there's one other thing. I'm happy to go, but I would like your promise, Mary, that you will make an appointment for Rose to see a therapist."

"We can't thank you enough." Mary dabbed at her eyes. "It's been so hard, these fifty years. She'll get treatment now, Molly, she's ready."

"Fifty years?" Molly said. "Mary, there are fantastic medications available that would help Rose. You aren't doing her any favors by keeping her locked up like this."

"Dear Molly," the old woman said, patting Molly's hand. "She is locked up in her mind, not by the door. Ever since my late husband brought her to us, fifty years ago, she's kept to herself, being a great help to me, bless her, but she will not go out on the street without one of my boys with her."

"Do you mean to say that she's closeted herself in this house and never leaves?"

"If the boys call on us, she'll take a walk, but they live out in the suburbs and only come by but two or three times a month. She's had some notions for the past few years, but she never asked the lads to take her as far as Glasnevin. She asked you."

"No one is ever too old for therapy. The best help that I could give Rose would be to drive her to a psychiatrist's office."

"There are some who have done that," Mary said. "But Rose wants to start out in her own way, to meet her demons head on or sneak up on them from behind, as she sees best."

"I'm really not qualified for psychiatric nursing," Molly protested.

"There's other kinds of qualifications," Mary said. "And look, here's Rose, all ready to go. You look lovely in that hat, Rose. Doesn't it set off her eyes, Molly?"

The compliment did not elicit a smile, but a frown of embarrassment. Rose shrank into herself again, but Molly realized that the woman did not physically change, it was Rose's soul that was fleeing, responding to some ancient, and irrational, alarm.

Glasnevin Cemetery was one of the places that Eoin had mentioned as a sight that was well worth seeing. The most illustrious people from Ireland's rich history were laid to rest there, sleeping beneath the sod with the brightest lights of Irish literature and art. Poets and statesmen, revolutionaries and soldiers could all be found. The greeting center provided maps and anecdotes, along with clear directions for the many tourists who descended on the hallowed ground.

"My friend would like to see the memorial to the Drumcondra women," Molly explained to a very sweet old matron who sat behind the reception desk.

The lady peered at Rose for a moment, as if a reason to visit the memorial was written on the woman's face. "Let me show you on this map," she said, her expression a warm embrace that enveloped Rose.

Bundled back into the car, Molly took her time driving to their destination, taking advantage of an opportunity to study the monuments and contemplate the names. Unlike a typical Chicago graveyard, with an ambience that hinted at parkland and discrete death, the row upon row of tombstones, shrines and memorials declared quite plainly that this was a place for the dead. Rose nervously clutched a bouquet of flowers, creating an annoying racket with the crinkling of the cellophane.

"Who is buried here, Rose?" Molly asked while they stood at the monument.

"The ones who had no names," Rose said softly. "I could have been one of them."

A cursory glance brought to Molly's mind a similar situation in the United States, another tragedy that befell a group of poor women. "There was a fire in New York, maybe one hundred years ago, at a sweatshop. The girls were locked in and hundreds died in the fire."

"Locked in, yes, they were," she mumbled. "Abandoned and cast off and locked in."

"Rose, come on, you're getting upset. Let me take you home."

"I was a pretty girl back then. The Father had to put me away."

"Yes, you were very pretty. Mary showed me a picture of you."

"Was your grandmother pretty?"

"Now how can I honestly answer a question like that?" Molly made light of it. "I think she was drop-dead gorgeous. In the photos, her eyes look really bright, and her smile, well, I like to think I have her smile."

"My friend ran away, over the wall. Sister beat her when her father brought her back. The big keys, she used those, on the head."

The care and treatment of the mentally ill was nothing less than barbaric fifty years ago, and Molly chided her modern self for criticizing practices that were done in ignorance. Even so, beating a girl was not any sort of proper care, it was the rage of a frustrated caregiver who should have recognized her anger and stepped aside. Those sorts of things went on, and Molly was aware that inmate abuse still went on, because no one was looking over a shoulder, to relieve those whose duty was to look after the infirm with kindness. It was a phenomenally stressful occupation, and only the most patient were suited to look after those whose care required patience in abundance.

"That sounds awful," Molly said.

"They shaved my head," Rose said, her voice growing stronger though her tone remained flat.

"Did you have lice?"

"Beautiful hair. Black and wavy, my beautiful hair that my mother used to brush and put up in a big bow on Sunday. They had to punish me. The other girls envied my hair."

"Jesus Christ," Molly mumbled through her teeth. "What kind of asylum did they run over here?"

"When I get home, I am going to call Tommy," Rose declared. "He can take me to talk to the attorney. I'm going to join them."

"Will you get therapy, Rose?" Molly asked, tentative and gentle in her approach. "It's a good idea, to call Tommy. Let's get home so you can make that call, and I'll speak to Mary about mental health counseling."

"I can talk to you, Molly. It helps me if I talk to you."

"It will help you more to talk to someone who knows how to ask the right questions and can prescribe the right medicines."

"First, I have to see that lawyer," Rose insisted.

"Rose, you sound like an American," Molly teased. "Sue the bastards, right?"

"This never happened in America, though," Rose said.

Nuala screamed her lungs out while the nuns fought with her to get her into the drab, gray, shapeless dress. She took pride in her appearance, and the rag she was supposed to wear was not even suitable for a rag picker's daughter. "Your name is Lilith," Sister Augusta shouted, slapping the girl into a form of submission. "From this moment on, you are Lilith. Your mother is a tramp, and I pray that you never turn out like her."

Later that day, when she was put into bed, Nuala burrowed under the bedclothes and hid. A child with a fertile imagination, she pretended that she was not in an orphanage, and made believe that her mother would be waiting for her in the Mother Superior's sitting room until morning, when Nuala could go home. She was not Lilith, nor would she ever be Lilith.

"My name is Nuala Devoy," she said to herself, over and over, repeating the phrase in her mind until she fell asleep.

Even though he knew that his mother would be coming home alone, it was still a shock to see her, unashamedly weeping on the street, holding a box and clutching Jenny. Frank started to cry when he saw that, because Nuala never went anywhere without her precious Jenny, the doll that their father had given her when she was born. He felt as if his sister had died, and been taken to St. Anne's Orphanage to be buried. His mother's first words when she came through the door where heartbreaking, because she said she would never see her little girl again, not allowed to visit, and he asked if Nuala was dead. Mammy mumbled something that sounded like nine years dead, but he was afraid of asking her what she meant when he was trying so hard to be the man of the family and not upset her any more.

"She'll come back to us," Mammy said at last, gathering her son into her arms. After a while, he wanted to run outside and play, but his mother was not letting go.

Early the next morning, they boarded the train to Kilkenny. Frank had never been so far from home, growing

96

tired of the long ride and begging to go back home. Weary, he began to cry, fidgeting in his seat while he insisted that he did not want to ride the train anymore.

"It's a grand adventure," Maire claimed, but her weeping did not help to convince Frank that he was going to be happy.

The convent attached to St. Patrick's was as gloomy and forbidding as the rest of the place. The remnants of the Devoy family sat in St. Anthony's Parlor, where the nuns conversed with Mrs. Devoy while Frank sat as close to his mother as he possibly could. All at once, two Sisters grabbed him, tore him from his mother, and forcibly dragged him to the dormitory, with Frank fighting with all his five-year-old might. They stripped him of his clothes and tossed him into a disinfectant bath, a humiliating treatment for a boy who was regularly bathed at home. Two nuns, menacing in their black habits and face-pinching wimples, scrubbed and toweled with a violence that was unknown to Frank. It would soon become customary, almost expected, and a part of his existence.

The journey through terror did not end after the women forced some rough woolen trousers and stockings onto his kicking legs. Mr. Clancy appeared, and he went at Frank's hair with a cruel delight, shaving the boy's head and nicking ears in retribution for the squirming and wailing.

For the next four days, Frank was kept in the infirmary. Petrified with intense fear, he screamed and wept for his mother without stopping, becoming physically ill. Over the course of his confinement to St. Patrick's, Frank would spend a great deal of time in the sick room, contracting every childhood illness and succumbing to a constant assault of sties and boils as his misery erupted on his skin.

Before long, he forgot what life had been like, becoming accustomed to the regime of an orphanage. Mr. Clancy's whistle ruled his life, with a toot first thing in the morning that signaled the march to morning Mass. The whistle called the boys to class, it announced break times, it signaled bathroom time and lights out and bedtime and every single activity of every day. Somehow he understood that his new life was cold and sterile, but that was simply how things were at St. Patrick's Orphanage. Mr. Clancy was king and the little boys were at his mercy.

Every spring, the inmates spent a day in re-stuffing their horsehair mattresses, a business that a few other convents in Dublin offered as a moneymaking sideline. "Please, Mr. Clancy, I need to go out to the yard," Frank said, even though the boys were supposed to concentrate on the task.

"You just went ten minutes ago," the despot growled. Visits to the toilet were at set times, whether a little boy's body was on the same schedule or not. "Come on then, but I'll be watching to make sure you aren't trying to sneak off."

The child had grown accustomed to using a toilet in a crowd, because the boys went as a group, not unlike a bunch of soldiers marching off to the latrine. For some other reason, the full bladder shriveled away under Mr. Clancy's stern glare, and Frank could not force a trickle to save his life.

Abruptly, Mr. Clancy grabbed Frank by the wrist and brought his ever-present leather strap across the child's fingers. Howling in pain, Frank could not escape, and Clancy continued with the punishment by beating the other hand. In agony, Frank urinated, unable to control his bladder.

"Here's a baby that pees his pants," Clancy announced loudly, and he paraded Frank and his wet trousers through a line of boys in the schoolyard. If Satan had appeared just then, Frank would have gladly sprinted off to Hell. The eternal flames, the fiery torment, could not be any worse than this.

The urge to go came frequently, and Frank lived in fear of a repeat performance. When he got up for the third time during the night, Judy stopped him. The girl who was in charge of the under-tens, an orphan who had lived all of her thirty years with the Sisters of Charity, was not one to tolerate any alteration in routine. Employed as a caretaker to a large group of small boys, Judy was not the least bit qualified for her job, either by training or by temperament. Raised on violent discipline, she meted out punishment with a maddening unpredictability.

Under Judy's fierce scowl, Frank could manage the slightest passing of water. "It's an odd color," the monitor noted. "Go see Matron in the morning."

For good measure, Judy caned Frank's bare bottom after he had marched back to bed. Under Judy's rule, the children went to bed at half past six and they were to stay there until Mr. Clancy blew his whistle in the morning. Any talking was punished by a caning, but that often included imaginary talking, and Frank had been woken from a sound sleep many times to receive several blows of Judy's bamboo stick. Despite Frank's emergency, Judy had her rules, and she let him have a few swats to make him think more carefully about getting up during the night.

The boy was grateful for his time in the infirmary, where he was treated for a kidney infection. Despite the intense heat of the room, wafting from a stove that Matron kept blazing day and night, Frank was content to exchange one torment for another. It was better to lie in bed, mouth parched and skin glowing with sweat, than to face Judy's cane and her merciless, brutal regime.

"Here's a lovely marble for this poor chap," Mrs. Morley cooed. The patroness of St. Patrick's, a wealthy woman of social standing, came at least once a month to visit her 'dear ones', making a special point of spending a few minutes with the sick. The boys loved her because she was the only adult they saw who ever uttered a kind word.

To own a toy of any sort was so spectacularly wonderful that Frank's eyes nearly popped out of his head. At Christmas, his mother sent him a second-hand wind-up train and a set of tracks, but it had been broken by the other boys in no time. Frank's prized possession was a worn cog from an old engine that served as a spinning top, but to acquire a real toy, his very own brand-new, shiny marble, was the greatest joy he had experienced since arriving at the orphanage.

Sister Julia took it from him on the day he was released back to the dormitory. "This was given to the infirmary for the sick children," she explained. "It stays here."

Frank never saw his marble again. Whenever he noticed Sister Julia in the hallway or at chapel, he pictured his marble, rolling around in the deep recesses of the nun's habit. He mourned its loss, and he would never forgive the Sister for taking his toy, which he firmly believed she had claimed for her own selfish reasons.

Recreation time was much anticipated, especially in the summer, because Frank could finally get some water to drink. Mr. Clancy trilled his big whistle, and the boys dashed off for the toilets in the recreation yard. Pat Grady flushed, and Frank thrust his hands into the stream, shoveling water into his parched throat as rapidly as he could. He then did the same for Pat, as all the boys slaked their thirst in the only way that they had.

"Judy's got a bowl of lettuce leaves," Pat said when they returned to the yard. "It must be as hot as hell if we're getting that."

Pat devoured the single green leaf, sucking off the drops of wash water that remained. Frank watched him eat the slug that clung to the leaf, wondering if Pat was somehow singled out to get a little something extra, or if Judy was playing a cruel trick. At least she left the bowl behind, so that little fingers could dip into the puddle on the bottom and moisten dry tongues.

Time was governed by the liturgical calendar, as Lent gave way to Easter and then the Feast of the Ascension. There was Ordinary Time and saints' days that came around with exacting regularity, but other signs served to mark time, like the plum puddings hanging in the rafters of the refectory that spelled Christmas, even before the four Sundays of Advent. The mouth-watering aroma of Barbados rum, plump raisins and sweet currants made little boys dream of the unique tastes of Christmas, flavors that were reserved only for the nuns with nary a crumb given to the children.

"I heard that St. Nicholas is coming this year," Bobby said. "This year for sure."

"Don't be a fool, Bob," Frank scoffed. "He only visits the rich children, not poor boys like us, or orphans like Kevin Mullhall. No one wants anything to do with us, especially not a saint."

They did not need a calendar to know that it was Christmas Day, not when they were given a dollop of rice with a spoonful of jam on top, instead of their usual bread and margarine. When they were not marched off to work at their jobs, they gratefully accepted the gift of a day of leisure, hours of rest and carefree abandon. The boys were restless with anticipation as the day wore on, eager for Reverend Mother's call to the largest classroom, where they would find her seated next to a large glass cabinet filled with a sumptuous array of toys. As would be expected, the children rushed to get a Christmas present. Whether it was a lead soldier, a wooden top or a small mouth organ, just having a genuine toy to play with was marvelous.

Frank came away with a balloon, having obediently queued up instead of behaving like a greedy savage. He took his gift gratefully, knowing that he was lucky to have received a present from his mother and 'Uncle' Joe, his new daddy. The annual gift of toy train and tracks was definitely better than one of Mother Superior's treats, and Frank could look forward to playing with it until it was smashed, after which he could trade the broken bits with other boys for miscellaneous other broken bits that their imaginations turned into playthings.

For his birthday in March, his mother sent him a small tin box that once contained John Players' tobacco, now stuffed with sweets. "I'll give you a peppermint for a cigarette card,"

Frank offered. Like everything else that fell into a boy's hands, the candies could be exchanged for something else that was needed or craved. What Frank really wanted was the box, but that was never given to him. The nuns assured him that the box was returned to his mother so that she could fill it again, but Frank had no proof of it, other than the sweets that the Sisters doled out to him as if they were pieces of gold.

"How about this one?" Joe White said. "West Highland Terrier card. You like dogs."

"Deal," Frank agreed, and the treasures traded hands.

"Your people must be well off," Bob said. "Your mammy and daddy get a tour of the building every year, looking at your bed in the dormitory like it's a holy well and sitting in your seat in the refectory."

"My real daddy was the one who was well off," Frank boasted. "My Aunt Maggie is his sister, and she sends me a shilling every Christmas. It's only because my father left money behind for my schooling, that's what Uncle Joe says, that's why the Sisters are so nice to my people."

"Does your aunt have a house, like Peter and his family in our readers?" Joe asked, his tone expressing his sense of wonder. "And a dog, like Peter's dog Toby?"

"Aunt Maggie's dog is mean and ugly, not a proper pet like Toby. It's white without any spots, and it's always snapping at everyone. My Uncle Mike works for Jacob's, and they eat biscuits every day at tea." Frank embellished his little fairy tale. He had dreams of tea and biscuits, sitting in Aunt Maggie's spotlessly clean parlor, like Peter in the school's reading textbook. Like Peter in the story, Frank imagined that he, too, had a mother and a father, and they lived all together in a house. Those were the things that Frank yearned for, wanted so badly that he could hardly stand living.

All the orphan boys were given jobs when they turned eight. Some were put to work at repairing the hundreds of shoes that were used by the inmates, and others had to mend and repair the clothes. Frank was given a job that he absolutely hated. It fell to him to polish the woodwork of the chapel and the endlessly long corridors of the convent's public areas. He was supervised by Margaret, who was yet another product of the Sisters of Charity orphanage system, thoroughly institutionalized and socially unskilled. Frank dusted the crevices of the altar rail and Margaret cuffed him for missing a spot. He re-did his work, and she cuffed him for being too slow. For a small boy, the task of polishing was backbreaking and hard, but Margaret gave no quarter. She was never satisfied, and Frank was always being punished.

"I'm going to the yard," she growled one afternoon. "See to it that every pew is gleaming when I get back, or you'll feel it."

Visiting Day in August, the one day that Maire could get the bank holiday reduced tram fare, had come and gone only three days ago. Kneeling on the very spot where his mother *had prayed on that wondrous, magical day, Frank gave in to the despair of homesickness that swamped him. He missed his mother and sister, he missed a gentle touch, a loving caress, and a soft word. Once a year, in August, Frank savored his mother's kiss, her hugs and her lovely smiles. For the rest of the year, he dwelled on the recollection, making himself sick.*

Sobbing, he prayed to his mother, to come back and take him away from the horrible place he had been sent to, but the prayers were entirely in vain. He was so engrossed in his pleading that he did not acknowledge Sister Loretta when she came in to change the altar cloth. That afternoon, Frank learned that he was going to be made an altar boy, the one orphan who was so fervently devoted to Our Lord that he would serve at the nuns' early mass. An uncommon child, according to Sister Loretta, but it felt like some sort of punishment. He had to get up even earlier every morning to attend to this added duty. The days became more endless, with night and Judy's cane to be dreaded, on top of Mr. Clancy's sadistic tortures. He implored his Creator for salvation, confident that eventually God would hear his heartfelt pleas.

"How is your flighty friend?" Eoin asked. He waved cheerily to the old woman who was standing in the window, watching his every move. "Is she a new guest?"

"Remember when I thought that this place was haunted? She's my ghost," Molly said. "She took her sister's newspaper clippings and put them with my papers during the night. At least I'm not the one who's nuts."

"The dotty maiden aunt in the garret," Eoin said. "At least you've seen Glasnevin Cemetery. It's rather like Arlington Cemetery in Washington, in a way, with Westminster Abbey sprinkled in."

"I'd rather see the Book of Kells."

"Are you sure that you don't need my help getting to Kilkenny?"

"You really want to go, don't you?"

"I'd like to know if your father was a scholar or some dull-witted sort."

"He went to college, you know." Molly had to laugh at Eoin's silliness.

"On the G.I. Bill, and what would an American university know of an Irish leaving certificate?"

"I never thought of that," Molly said with fresh admiration for her father's brashness. "Secondary schools issue a diploma after four years, and people start college at eighteen. My dad finished school when he was fifteen."

"There it is, he must have been brilliant. Leaving certs were earned at sixteen."

"Clever at least. The other day, his best friend in Ireland told me how my father came to find new housing after he started his job. I don't know why my dad never told me himself, it's a great story."

"Well, I'm waiting," Eoin said.

"The school nurse at Carriglea had been engaged to a man who was executed after the Rising, and she was friendly with my dad because my grandmother had been a member of Cumann na mBan."

"You're from a rebellious strain, I see. My grandmother busied herself in the butcher shop and never cared who was in charge of the government, as long as people kept buying roasts and chops and rashers."

"Here's the best part. He knew that the nurse was a close friend of Mrs. Thomas Ashe, the hunger strike martyr Ashe."

"It's a name that needs no explanation in this country," Eoin assured the storyteller.

"Anyway, Mrs. Ashe was an alderman in Dublin, so my father goes to City Hall and says he has a telegram for Mrs. Thomas Ashe, but he didn't really. Once he got to her office, he told her that he was a friend of Nurse Scanlon, which was true, and then he told her about his living conditions. My grandmother had put her name on the list for better housing a long time before, but my father went right to the top to make things happen. They did move, out to a new development in the suburbs."

"The gift of Blarney," Eoin said. "Your grandmother was probably a sweet lady who followed the rules and obeyed orders, very meek and mild. In short, she was the perfect Irish woman of her time."

"Was it shocking, what my father did?" Molly asked.

"There are always those who step up," Eoin said. "Our history is filled with tales of men who took it upon themselves to take action while those around them wrung their hands, and not just the martyrs of 1916."

"The Christian Brothers told him that he would go far, and he did," Molly said.

"Let me drive you to Kilkenny, please. We can make a day of it, go to see some sights while we're there. What is the point of traveling this far and not seeing the Rock of Cathon?"

Able to sightsee while Eoin drove, Molly watched every farmhouse and stone wall go by, hoping to commit to memory the exquisite beauty of the Irish countryside. She was a bundle of nerves, shouting out an announcement that they were at Kells Road where they had to make a turn. In a way, this stop would be like standing in her father's shoes, looking out at his world, but through her own eyes.

"He never said a word about his primary school, are you certain?" Eoin asked.

"He hated the Sisters of Mercy with a passion," Molly said.

"Then prepare yourself for some bad news."

"No, wait, he did say something. It's funny, how these things pop up in my head that I had forgotten. If you don't have any expectations, you will never be disappointed. That's what he told me he had learned at school."

The facade was not in the least inviting, a Georgian pile of coldness that was broken up by windows that failed to lighten the gloomy and sad appearance. In passing, Eoin noted that it was now a school for the learning disabled, although an orphanage did still occupy part of the space. He stopped talking abruptly, changing the topic, suggesting that they set off after her meeting with the director and get roaring drunk. Or go back to his place and reflect, or whatever she would need to do.

They went up to the door and Eoin held it open, taking a long look at her face as if he was trying to imprint her image in his brain. Then he told her that he was going to wait in the car, jabbering about taking in the view in a disjointed string of words that were close to nervous splutters. He glanced at her again, a peculiar stare, like she was going to look different when she came out and he would have to recognize her by her clothes or the pearl stud earrings that she had bought on Grafton Street. As she slid past his outstretched arm, he turned away, unable to meet her eyes.

"You won't be long," he said.

Alone in the foyer, she was swept by a sense of awe, having walked through the same portal that her father had entered many years ago. The sense of history was coupled with the excitement of discovery, until Molly analyzed the peculiar odor that assailed her nose. There was a scent of disinfectant, cleaners and wood polish that she associated with her former grade school and the attached convent. Her father had loathed the aroma to such an irrational degree that Barbara never once put polish on a stick of furniture, and she had to be careful what brands of cleaners were used on the kitchen floor. He had avoided going to his children's grade school, becoming physically ill unless he covered his nose with one of Barbara's perfumed handkerchiefs.

Sister Attracta was waiting in her office for the visitor from Chicago. Molly was feeling a bit shaky, after sizing up the building's exterior and finding nothing but institutional proportions and the fraying edges of a place that was not beloved by the former pupils. Her father had warned her that she would be crushed, but if it was only a matter of a rundown and cold facility, she could handle that well enough.

"Our mission has changed since your father was enrolled here," the nun said warmly, even proudly, of her order's dedication. "Of course, the interior is wholly different. The dormitories, and even the classrooms, are so radically altered that you would never have a sense of your father's surroundings. However, if you did wish to tour the buildings, I would be happy to show you around."

"Thank you, Sister, but I'd rather not. If it was unchanged, if you could point to a bed and say, this is where your father slept, but it's gone now," Molly said.

"You have the court order?" Sister asked, babbling about former residents coming in so often these days.

They exchanged papers, Molly's sealed envelope for a thick packet of very old documents, the record of one boy's passage through childhood. Molly dropped into a chair, a huge and eager smile on her face.

"Please don't open it here," the nun's words rushed out.

"Why not?" the audacious American asked, untying the string that held the records together.

"Consider the times," Sister said.

The top sheet was the personal record that had been typed on March 31, just one week after Frank's fifth birthday. Molly looked it over, the smile falling from her face as her mouth gaped in shock. She read the words again and again; 'ordered to be detained' and 'what charge' began to dance and pulsate like flashing lights. Tried and convicted, her father had been tried and convicted as a little boy, a baby.

The words that ran through her mind popped out, her shock unable to rein in her emotions. "What the...?" she said, just above a whisper. "What the fuck?"

7

Christmas of 1931 was a time of miracles. Because Frank's father had been a man of some small means, the state extracted a part of his legacy to cover his children's education expenses. It put Frank in a slightly different light, and because of his special status, he was put on the train to Dublin to spend three days at home. Maire met her boy at the station, showering him with hugs and kisses and copious tears.

The baby girl that was born eight months ago was already dead and buried, events that occurred far away from St. Patrick's which did not mean anything to Frank. He had never seen his half-sister, and she might just as well not have existed at all for as much as Frank could judge. The effects of Maude's loss were evident in his mother, awash in an overabundance of sorrow that spilled out, turning the Christmas visit into the most important event of a lifetime.

For three days, Maire walked all over Dublin, dragging Frank around to visit his countless relations. He could not quite remember them, having not seen them for so long, and a once yearly call did little to refresh his memory. "Does Nuala come home after Christmas?" he asked, strolling along on the way to visit Aunt Celie.

"No, dear, she's not allowed to leave the convent," Maire replied easily, not completely masking the pain in her heart.

"She never writes back to me, Mammy," Frank complained. "Are you sure that she has my address?"

"She's not allowed to write to us, Frank. I write to the Mother Superior, and she then writes to me to send word of Nuala. Your sister does beautiful crochet work, isn't that grand?"

They walked home to James Street because the tupenny tram fare was too great a strain on the budget. Frank hated coming back to the dingy tenement, and he had to hold back a sob the first time he saw how wretched his mother had become. His dearest mother was living in conditions so desperate that Frank wanted to cry. All her old furniture, the heavy mahogany pieces that were so stylish in the early Twenties, were crammed chock-a-block into the single room, leaving only narrow passageways to move through. Several gilt mirrors hung on the walls, along with a couple of broken clocks that represented Maire's past comfort with Fran Devoy. One sash window provided all the light that filtered in from the yard, making the space dark and morbidly depressing, in a building without electricity to power a single bulb.

"Where's Uncle Joe?" Frank searched around, hoping that Uncle Joe was in another room that had somehow escaped Frank's notice. Such an extra room did not exist.

114

"Gone to the bookie's," Maire said, with a strong note of embarrassment in her voice.

Unfortunately for Maire, Joe won a few shillings that day, and he spent every penny on beer. He came home drunk, and Frank discovered the true nature of his stepfather at an early age. Joe had bad teeth before, but now, three years later, he had but a few yellowed fangs remaining in his shiny, bald head. He flew into a tirade at dinner, tearing into Maire because the boiled beef was too tough for his gums. That did not stop him from eating his fill, leaving nothing for Maire but a few potatoes. In between bursts of loud insults, he droned on and on about the horses he had played, rambling into an extended discourse that was so incredibly dull that Frank was amazed at the tedium.

Gradually, Frank came to see why his mother had her doubts about Joe. She confessed a little to her son, needing someone to talk to, even if he was too young to appreciate her fate. It was foolish, but Maire had to defy the State and have more children, something that they could not stop her from doing, and therein lay her downfall. Recalling how fond Joe was of her children, calling Nuala his princess, she admitted that all the man really wanted was money. The bequest that Fran Devoy had provided to maintain his little family, along with the many porcelain and silver trinkets that once decorated the cottage on Northbrook Terrace, were gone. Joe had run through the money in no time, and then pawned

115

everything he could get his hands on. The money was gone, the cottage was gone, everything was gone, except Joe O'Brien. Divorce was not an option, and all Maire had left were everlasting days and nights of regret. It was doubtful that she would have more children, not after Maude's birth.

"I've never worked a day in my life," Joe bragged to his captive audience while Maire went out to the yard to wash her dishes under the tap.

"Why don't you get a job?" Frank asked, with a child's innocent delivery.

"War injury, Frank, my boy," Joe said. "Bad back, Mother of God, the pain. I draw my pension every week, thanks to my service to the Crown during the Great War. It ain't much, but what can a man do?"

The conversation returned to racing forms, which occupied Joe's attention as he calculated and scribed with his pencil. His monologue ran towards bizarre terms that Frank did not comprehend, as Joe explained to his stepson how he planned to play the horses after he had picked up his weekly government stipend and a half crown gift from Aunt Maggie. The complexities of gambling were lost on Frank, who longed to flee from Joe's steady stream of babble.

On Christmas Day, after Mass, Maire prepared a pig's cheek and a plum pudding, giddy with joy to share the holiday with at least one of her children. She had saved up all year, cutting corners until she sliced into the center, squirreling away the handouts she received from Fran's many sisters and miscellaneous relations to afford the luxury. St. Nicholas gave Frank a wind-up car and some sweets, and on St. Stephen's Day the round of social calls resumed, to visit still more aunts that he did not remember. Shillings and half crowns were put in his palm, and he accumulated nearly a whole pound before his holiday ended.

"Remember Nuala in your prayers," Maire reminded Frank at the train station when the holiday was over. "Don't cry now, I've tears enough for both of us."

Homesickness and depression engulfed Frank, filling the train car and nearly drowning him before the engine chugged into Kilkenny. He thought longingly of Nuala, and of the fun they could have shared on Thomas Street, visiting with their old neighbors in the Liberties. He thought of writing to her, to tell her that Mammy's plum pudding still acted like a dose of castor oil in solid form, but then he recalled that letters were forbidden by the nuns in Booterstown.

"Sisters of Scant Mercy," his mother mumbled that August, when Frank was sent home for a week's holiday. He understood that his sister was not granted any such reprieve, and even at his young age, he realized that something was wrong. His mother's hatred was subdued, but very much alive.

"He was not begging, that was only a pretext to conform to the laws for incarcerating children," Sister Attracta assured Molly. She was failing in her attempt to disguise the shame she felt at her order's devious tactics. "The new government, what was called the Irish Free State, they were all about cleaning up the slums. Poor children were swept up and confined to places like this, and if the Sisters of Charity, or the Good Shepherds, or whatever order, did a good job or a poor job, no one monitored the schools."

"My God, my God," Molly said, consumed by heartbreak and fury. "This was a prison. A prison for innocent children. Perfectly good families, ripped apart."

"The industrial schools fell under the supervision of the prison system. It was stupid, stupid and insensitive. Orphans were reviled in those days, and not only here in Ireland."

"But my father was not an orphan," Molly said. "His mother was living, and he had a stepfather."

Perusing Frank's medical records through tears, Molly saw the depth of her father's torment. As a nurse, she fully understood the effect of emotional distress on health, and her father had been in the infirmary so often that it was a wonder they saved a cot for him in the dormitory. It was inconceivable to her that anyone with a heart could take a child from its mother because the family happened to be poor. It was appalling to learn that such had been her beloved father's fate. At that instant, she wanted to demolish St. Patrick's Industrial School for Boys brick by brick and bury the Irish people under the rubble.

Searching for something that could sound like a reasonable explanation, Sister Attracta spoke of the trickle of old men who came into her office, every one of them leaving in tears. More than anything, she wanted to give solace, but there were no words. All she could offer was a feeble excuse, that the Sisters of Charity who ran St. Patrick's were not even aware of what was going on when they were not looking, and with few nuns distributed through a large compound, they rarely looked.

So many years after the fact, none of the religious were still alive, to explain why they had not bothered to check on the boys at night, when a sadistic dormitory monitor woke them up and caned them because she thought she heard a sound. Sister Marian, Sister Clare and Sister Devaney could not speak from the grave to tell the world why they did not know that the school's custodian often forced a boy to touch the electric generator, and then laughed gleefully when the child was jolted by a blast of electricity.

"I am so terribly sorry," Sister Attracta said, but her words rang hollow. The lessons had been learned, and she monitored her staff with a zealot's intensity. For those who paid the price of past neglect, it was scant remuneration.

The caustic words of Con MacNeill reverberated in Molly's brain, his assertion that industrial schools were for juvenile delinquents, the hooligans who were removed from the streets by the blessed Sisters. Kept under lock and key where they belonged, the inmates, kept away from decent people.

"My father was not a delinquent,' Molly said, aware of a grievous insult that had been unknowingly thrown at her father, and therefore at her.

"No, Miss Devoy, he was not. The records show that he was a very good boy," Sister assured her.

"He kissed me goodnight. Every night, until the day I married."

"He gave to you what he did not have here. What was done then was wrong, Miss Devoy. It was wrong."

Frank also gave to Molly what had been incorporated into his being at St. Patrick's, and the feeling twisted her stomach into a knot. Her inheritance from the industrial schools was shame, a sense of being inferior or worthless, and Molly was now too embarrassed to face Eoin. Her father was an industrial school inmate, the lowest dregs of Irish society when poverty was the norm. Frank had taught his daughter to value her reputation, and Molly knew exactly what that reputation was to men like Con MacNeill, a low rank that submerged Frank Devoy beneath contempt. Eoin had not defended the industrial school boys that night in Kilrossanty, instead remaining silent, with a silence that spoke more loudly than meaningless words.

Shell-shocked and aching, she went outside, too shaken to wish Sister Attracta a farewell of any kind. She saw Eoin, sitting in his car and listening to music as he sang along, full of cheer and merriment. "Take me to Dun Laoghaire," she said, resenting her dependency on someone she dreaded seeing again. By rights, the shame should fall on his head, not hers, but there was no fair play in this country.

"You need a drink," he said, startled by the abrupt change of attitude.

"Just drive," she ordered, not even looking at him.

Grabbing her arm, he gave it a shake to rattle her back to sanity. "Don't you dare speak to me like that," he said. "What's wrong with you?"

Without answering, Molly rummaged about in her satchel, finally locating the material that the attorney had obtained for her and delivered on Monday. She was supposed to read it first, before going to St. Patrick's, but she had been so busy with Rose and then with Eoin that she had put the packet aside. Perhaps it was too late to read it now, but she pulled the folder open anyway.

"Damn it, Molly, you will answer me, and answer me right now," Eoin insisted. "What is wrong?"

"This is what's wrong," she said. She waved the papers under his nose, so close that he had to pull his head back to avoid being slapped. Tossing the folder into his lap, she pulled the top page out of the folio she had just been given and held it only inches from his eyes, obstructing his view of anything else. "And this. Your father did this to mine. Your family, your precious republic and your goddamned clergy."

Eoin was not surprised when she uttered a string of curses, a clear demonstration of her shock at uncovering a truth that had long been buried. Her act of childish petulance served as a warning to him, that history's dirt had just drifted into his car, foul and filthy. He looked at the papers that were scattered across his lap, trying to read and put them in order at the same time. The corner of the folder had nicked his chin, but he did not feel the sting.

From the first words, the picture became more clear. Frank Devoy had been convicted of receiving alms as a child of five, and that explained the nature of the packet that had thudded onto his lap. The transcript of the court case read like a screenplay, but as he read further, he saw that Francis and Nuala Devoy were charged with a different crime altogether, one that did not exist in written form, one that had nothing to do with alms or neglect.

"Sister Keogh" was printed in block letters in the left margin, followed by her lines. "A gentleman has been seen entering and leaving her home, without a chaperone present."

"Did you speak to Mrs. Devoy about her scandalous conduct?" the Court inquired.

"Oh, dear God," Eoin groaned. "Your father as well, swept up by the cruelty man."

He flipped the hideous words into the back seat, started the engine, and threw the car into reverse. Tires squealing, he floored the accelerator, flying to Dun Laoghaire as fast as he dared to go past the speed limit.

For an hour, they traveled in silence, a hush that was marred by Molly's occasional sniff and murmured apology for throwing things at him. He tried to take her hand but she pulled away, crowding up against the car door as if she longed to get as far away from him as she possibly could. "Ever since the term ended, I've been working on my lecture notes," he said at last. "Some of this, I know about, but I'm an economist, and that's how I've approached the subject. For years, I've taught about the economic impact of the new government's policies, about dealing with poverty and urban renewal from a monetary standpoint."

"It's always the money, isn't it," Molly said.

"As soon as de Valera got in, they cut the taxes, but that left nothing for social services. The upper and middle classes were happy, but the poor got poorer. They were a bunch of idealists, Molly, a crowd of utopian dreamers running a country when they didn't know how to do it. No background or knowledge of finance, just a lot of good intentions, and intentions don't put shoes on a child's feet. Maybe we all wanted to worship some heroes so we covered up their failings. I don't know, I won't suggest I know."

He was so like her father, hiding behind lectures and skating away into historical homilies. Rather than speak honestly, he delivered Economics 101 at a safe distance from the truth. "Keep the peace," she mumbled. "Keep the goddamned peace."

They had spoken of Dun Laoghaire, the ancient heart of Dublin, the area that Molly knew from her father's rare recollection of Sunday cycling excursions. In its heyday, when the British called it Kingstown, it was a popular resort area.

123

Now, under Irish rule and with its beautiful name restored, it was a mecca for tourists who enjoyed its Victorian architecture and atmosphere. Thinking that Molly needed to immerse herself in her father's happy memories, Eoin drove to the pier while babbling on through Molly's silence. He was ashamed of the cruelty that once was ignored in the recent past, and he would have crawled into a hole if one were available. Trying to ease her mind, he parked his car where they could watch the ferries crossing the Irish Sea. It was time to come clean, to lay things out and talk them over.

"There are women's groups that organize charters," he said. "More than one of those boats is filled with Irish girls, going on holiday to England. Abortion cruises, Molly."

She turned her head away, as if she were about to be sick. He did not want to punish her further, or fill her with enough disgust to send her running back to Chicago, but he had to say some things so that she would understand

"Sheila and I didn't want that, she sincerely wanted a baby, we both did. We come from provincial towns, little hamlets, that's all they are. She wanted a child but not a husband; she was focused on her career and she was looking at thirty coming at her. You understand, Molly, it's the sort of thing we read about in the papers, about American women having it all. I was willing to get her pregnant. Christ, was I ever willing."

When Molly got out of the car, Eoin followed, not wanting to pass over a chance to confess to someone who had the power to forgive his hypocrisy. She started to walk away, not going anywhere in particular, and Eoin followed at her elbow.

"Her father told her to get married, or never show her face at home again," he nearly shouted over the noise of people, boats, cars and waves. "My father told me to deny my responsibility because it was her problem. Do you see why we went through the motions, Molly, made things legal?"

"St. Eoin, the martyr of Kilrossanty," Molly said. "Is it any wonder that the Irish people were under England's thumb? Cry over your sorry fate and don't stand up, or someone might slap you down. Don't take a chance that they might run away like bullies always do."

"It's not that easy, miss," Eoin said. "You're full of big words, but you've never had to make a choice like that. Everything's come easy to you, all your life, everything handed to you, that's all you know. Now you're finding out that the rest of the world doesn't live with a hand held out, expecting it to be filled with gold. I tried to stand up to the bullies, but I was a coward and I backed down. Would you be any more brave?"

His words struck home. Molly stopped pacing, stopped clenching her fists as if she were shadow-boxing against the ghosts of the past. Wrapping his arm around her, he surrounded her with the warmth of security and the comfort of empathy. Carefully, he guided her back to the car where he sat for a moment, listening to her breathing while he contemplated his next move.

"My grandmother was courted by a man whose wife had died and left him with three children. She was left with four. They probably weren't in love, but they needed each other. The priest told her that she was no better than a whore to have a man in the house. She thought that her children were adequate for chaperones, but the saintly Father didn't agree." Eoin paused for a moment.

"She was threatened, wasn't she?" Molly said.

"She did what her priest told her to do. People trusted the clergy, Molly, they believed in them because the clerics were educated when most people were happy to be literate. A priest was God's representative here on earth, and they could do no wrong, they couldn't lie and they certainly could not make mistakes."

"Gods with feet of clay," Molly murmured.

"You can control people with guns and force, but you can control them just as readily through poverty. A man will care about finding enough food to feed his children, and social policies can be hanged. Policy and discourse won't fill anyone's belly."

"I know that," Molly agreed, sounding defeated.

"You love your father, that's why this is so hard to take. You might not have understood him before, but now you see what kind of world he came from. It hurts, Molly, I know it's painful. It hurts me, to have to tell you all this."

126

"He knew that I was poisoned by the same sickness that damaged him," she said. "That's why he sent me here, to be healed."

"Maybe he did," Eoin said. "Maybe he thought you were too interested in material possessions and he wanted you to appreciate the basic necessities."

"I know what he saw. I see it now." Molly covered her eyes, leaning forward as if her head were too heavy for her shoulders.

"Let's get this over with, and we'll spend a quiet evening," he suggested, backing his car out of the parking space. "You've had a weight dropped on your shoulders and I think you need time to rest and let the bad news settle in."

"I have to find my aunt," Molly declared. "Whatever else my father wanted for me on this trip, that's the one thing that I think he wanted me to do more than anything else. That's why he asked me to come here in the first place, not just for his life story."

"It's out of the question, Father," Maire stated simply.

The superior of St. Saviour's Orphanage in Dublin looked intently at Frank's mother. For a fee of ten pounds, Frank could be admitted to the seminary, a fate already recommended by Sister Loretta. The status that visited the family with a member in the priesthood was highly elevated, and Father O'Donovan could not believe that such an opportunity was being passed over. Not only that, but the brother of the Mother Superior at St. Patrick's had put in the first word, and becoming a Dominican seemed like a golden future.

"There's no possibility to meet any fee whatsoever," Maire continued. This conversation stung her pride, with its reminders of her powerlessness and poverty. She wanted to end the discussion quickly. "I am sorry that we've wasted your time."

Accompanied by Sister Loretta, the party walked back to the train station, where Frank would be returned to complete his time at St. Patrick's. His mother chatted with the nun, who made sure to place herself between Frank and Maire. "It's one of the best," Sister said. "Their boys regularly take top honors in the National Examination every year. With his father's bequest falling to them, they will reserve a spot for him. He can transfer in September at the start of the new term."

When it was time to turn the corner towards the tram terminal, Maire looked down at her boy, wondering if he felt as much love for her as she had for him. His farewell hug was so full of intense longing that she wanted to shout, to tell the world and Sister Loretta that she was Frank Devoy's mother, now and forever. The little prisoner of the black robed Sisters of Charity was her flesh and blood, and there was nothing that could be done on earth to change what God had decreed.

"You're going to Carriglea Industrial School, Frank," Maire said, smiling through her tears. "You'll be happy there, I promise."

The smile that he returned was filled with relief, as if he understood that she meant a better day was coming, when the tortures of St. Patrick's would be replaced by a center of learning. He promised to devote himself to his studies, in a voice that carried an absolute guarantee of his sincerity. For good measure, he assured her that one day, when he was grown up, they would have a home of their own like they used to, and be a family again. It was with great restraint that Maire suppressed the smirk that she longed to throw at the nun.

"Is Nuala at a different school now?" he said, extending the leave-taking.

"No, Frank, she's still with the good Sisters in Booterstown."

"Will you write to her, to tell her I'll be closer to her?"

"Of course I will. She'll be happy to hear of it."

Maire watched the pair walk away, her heart breaking anew at every separation. Nuala could have been put away on the North Pole for as much contact as the mother had with her daughter. The Mother Superior of St. Anne's claimed that the girl was doing well, but Maire was not so sure that she could take a nun's word. She could never forget Sister Keogh's testimony.

8

Girls arriving at St. Anne's were given new names, as if the children were only just born when they entered into the care of the Sisters of Mercy. All traces of their old life were washed away, like another baptism, and Nuala wondered if she had been as confused about her name the first time around. Something from the Bible was supposed to be better than something from Irish mythology, but she felt very strongly that her dear daddy in heaven had picked her name for perfectly good reasons. Besides, if the priest had approved the name at the baptismal font, there could be nothing wrong with it, and she could not accept the new label that set her teeth on edge every time she heard it.

Everything about her new life at the orphanage was horrifying, particularly the public toilets. She was shocked when she found that all the girls did their business in a large room lined with water closets, where she could hear everything, and it was not in the dormitory but in a separate building in the schoolyard. They lacked toothbrushes and never cleaned their teeth, and for a prissy little girl, it was disgusting. Getting up at seven was not terribly unpleasant, but she quickly grew tired of going to Mass each and every day.

For the first few days, the little girl was so sick with misery that she could not eat her breakfast of bread and margarine, and for the first few days, Sister Ursula caned her for being wasteful. The child's hands ached, with bruised palms and swollen fingers.

"I called you to the front of the room, Lilith," Miss Ahern said, her sharp teeth bared in anger. She was glaring at the idiot girl who ignored a teacher's demand, but the frightened child did not yet recognize her new name.

The teacher strode down the aisle and wrenched Nuala from the desk by her ear, dragging the girl to the front of the room. Yanking Nuala's arms into an outstretched position, she slapped the bamboo cane across the open palms.

"You will speak when spoken to," Miss Ahern said, her words accompanied by a fierce whack of her cane. Holding her face only inches from Nuala's, she lashed out. "You are wicked and disobedient. Repent your sins, Lilith, or you will burn in hell for all eternity."

"I'm sorry," Nuala sobbed, "I'm sorry."

"Do you wish to become a tramp like your mother?"

"No, Miss Ahern," the little girl said.

The Sisters of Mercy who ran the vast complex in Booterstown were committed to their mission. They preached endlessly that women were in such danger of sin and immorality that they took it upon themselves, at the state's urging, to rescue the daughters of the poor and unsavory, the

131

countless dissolute women who populated the Irish Free State. Every female on earth was eligible for inclusion in the ranks, because all women were sinners. It all started with Eve, and it was all in the Bible.

Separate from the orphanage was the convent school, where the outside girls were drilled in reading, writing and morality. For the inmates of the adjoining orphanage, the lessons had to be much more severe and rigorous, because the wards of the state had been exposed to the evils of sex by their mothers. It was implied, or at least that was how Nuala saw it, that she could not have any contact with her mother because the nuns were afraid that all their hard work would be reversed by her mother's lewdness. How a widow could be termed lewd because she was going to get married again made no sense, but Nuala quickly learned that no explanation would be forthcoming.

The closest thing that she saw that resembled a family connection was the occasional sweet, which she knew had been sent by her mother. Once a week, beginning with the Sunday after her birthday and extending for twelve weeks, she was given a bull's-eye caramel or a horehound drop. After that, there were twelve more goodies that followed Christmas, and pennies from Aunt Maggie that she could use at the commissary, where she bought Oxo beef bouillon cubes to make the soup taste better.

Every Friday, a regiment of girls would bath while the rest made do with washing up, every unit divided carefully by age to shield the younger girls from the pubescent bodies of the seniors. Sister Ursula took advantage of the wet skin to administer weekly discipline, which consisted of as many blows on a bare bottom as she felt was necessary to achieve submission. For spilling her tea, a girl re-named Myra was whacked twice, leaving thick red welts where the heavy leather strap had been applied. 'Lilith' received three lashes for failing to learn unquestioning obedience.

After eighteen month, Nuala was well versed in the rules of the game and was rather adept at appeasing the Sisters before they beat her. No one could develop a method to overcome the endless mental abuse, and before she was nine years old, Nuala was buying into the idea that she was not yet fit to join decent society. Sister Ursula warned her that she presented a great threat to men's souls because she was exceptionally pretty and had a beautiful voice, two traits that could lead her straight to the pit of hell if she did not use those gifts for God's work. In a low undertone, the Sister often reminded her that many women succumbed to the temptations of the flesh, just like Nuala's mother, and the orphans at St. Anne's would be trained to resist. Nuala had no idea what Sister Ursula was going on about.

She was supposed to be one of the lucky ones, according to Sister Agnes, but Nuala failed to see it. As a junior girl she had a job, three hours a day for six days a week, but she did not have to scrub clothes or floors or patch stockings. Those chores helped to make the orphanage self-sufficient, but Nuala was involved in a duty that actually made money for the Sisters of Mercy. The exquisite Irish lace doilies and tablecloths that were purchased by pious Irish Catholics in Boston and New York and Baltimore were not actually made by the Sisters in their Booterstown convent. The export market was driven by slave labor, the work of children as young as eight, and Sister Agnes assured Nuala that it was an honor and a privilege to be chosen as a lace maker. It seemed an odd way to show affection, to choose her to manufacture the lace trim that Clery's put on the christening gowns, but then again, the other nuns had their own strange ways of showing how much they liked Nuala.

"Vanity is woman's greatest sin," Sister Ursula declared as the girls were rapidly scrubbing their skin. In three groups of ten, the under-tens bathed in one tub, with the last group getting the dirtiest water.

"A woman who loves God does not admire herself," the nun continued, passing between the tub and the two rows of wet children standing at attention. "Hell's torment awaits the girl who thinks herself more beautiful than another. Only our Holy Mother is beautiful, and her beauty lies in her sacrifices to God. Those who would be saved will follow the example of

Blessed Mary, ever virgin, and worship Our Lord above all earthly things."

Those in need of a flogging were whacked, and then all thirty were allowed to don a nightdress. Typically, they would then kneel at the side of their cot, ready for evening prayers with the other seventy-five children who shared the dormitory. Tonight, Sister Ursula told them to line up at the end of the beds along the center aisle, standing in two neatly ordered columns. 'Lilith' was brought to the head of the line, where Sister took a large shears and hacked off Nuala's long, strawberry blond hair. Tears rolled down little cheeks as she watched the tresses fall gently to the floor, coming to rest like the dead leaves of autumn. When Nuala felt the cold metal of the razor scraping her scalp, she wished that God would be merciful and kill her on the spot.

"Blessed are the meek, blessed are the humble, for they shall see God," Sister Ursula proclaimed. "Pick up the hair, Lilith."

Doing as she was told, a quietly weeping girl clutched her lovely tresses in her tight fists.

"Now, Lilith, you will carry this emblem of your sin to the stove in the infirmary. We will burn your sin, as you will burn in hell if you do not repent of your wickedness. Together, we will pray for your soul."

They marched side by side to the stove that warmed Matron's office. The hair was tossed into the flames, and

Nuala knelt to watch her soft curls turn to ash, as Sister reminded her that women are ashes and dust, to return to ashes and dust in death. "Is that so pretty, Lilith?" The nun pointed at the debris in the hearth.

"No, Sister."

"Are you so pretty that you can elevate yourself above others?"

"No, Sister. I didn't mean to do it. I'm sorry, Sister; I don't know how to be better. I'm going to hell when I die," Nuala said.

"That is why you are here, child. You have gifts, Lilith, given to you by God and meant to be used to serve him. You have a gift that I have seen in my sister, do you recall, when she came to visit with us?"

"Oh, yes, Sister, I remember her very well," Nuala said, wiping away the tears. The Benedictine nun had been fascinating, telling stories of her inspiring activities as a missionary in South Africa.

"My sister noticed you, in a classroom of thirty girls, in an orphanage of two hundred children, she noticed you, Lilith. Follow the examples that are set by the good Sisters who surround you. Give yourself up to God; do not be afraid, as our Blessed Mother was not afraid. Give up all earthly desires, and some day you will serve Our Lord through a woman's highest calling. He chooses few, Lilith. He chose my sister, whom I love and admire. Do not disappoint us."

Sister Ursula shocked Nuala into frenzied weeping by kissing the child's forehead, sighing with pleasure at this example of deep piety. In reality, it was nothing more than a small child breaking under intense pressure. Being the pet of the nuns had isolated her from the other girls, and she felt more alone at that moment than she ever had before.

"Lilith is a boy," was the mockery of the morning ablutions, abuse that was encouraged by Mary Josephine, the caretaker of the under tens. Like every other supervisor in every other industrial school, Mary Josephine was a product of the system, and she held tightly to the traditions of the past. Nuala lifted her chin proudly, cast a suspicious glance at Mary Josephine and mumbled something about lice and whom it came from to begin with. The girls steered clear of Mary Josephine for several days.

On the morning of her ninth birthday, kneeling at morning Mass, Nuala looked up at the gory depiction of the crucified Christ, prominently featured above the altar. She had observed all the paintings that hung in the dormitory and lined the walls of the corridors, and like the depictions in the chapel, they all represented brutal suffering. Everything that she looked at, from the time she woke up until she closed her eyes at night, were alike in that one respect.

Saint Stephen, pierced by hundreds of arrows and bleeding profusely with his face contorted in agony, graced the *wall next to the dormitory nun's cell. St. Roque was the patron saint of invalids, and his portrait featured enormous leg wounds being licked or bitten by vicious dogs. It hung in the infirmary, where it terrorized the sick children into health. St. Agatha looked up to heaven with eyes glowing in rapture, loving God from her perch in the refectory.*

"Two cream cakes, with a cherry on top," Mary Josephine claimed was the saint's offering to God, carried on the tray that Agatha held stiffly. When she was much older, Nuala would come to find that those were St. Agatha's breasts, the symbol of her martyr's torment, suitable to be displayed as an example of chastity and perpetual virginity in girls' schools only.

The story behind every painting and statue in St. Anne's Orphanage was one of torture and of sexuality denied, the same message that was imprinted on young female minds. Nuala determined that being a Catholic meant that one suffered the most brutal agonies, did endless penance and endured persecution. In short, she felt a strong bond between her religion and her life because they matched so seamlessly.

The orphans knelt in the chapel and Nuala thought of what she would buy with her birthday money that was sure to be deposited with Reverend Mother Laurentia. Prayers to St. Mary Magdalene, the most reprehensible of women who had been saved by Jesus himself, were being intoned when Nuala stopped daydreaming and realized that they had a new chaplain. He seemed to be looking at her as he approached the communion rail, or so she thought, and she prayed that God and the priest would forgive her for letting her mind wander through the Consecration and the Agnus Dei.

Called out of the crochet room that afternoon, Nuala feared the worst for her lack of devotion earlier. "Father McNulty would like to speak to you," Sister Bede said, her scowling face as frightening as ever.

As she walked down the steps to the Mother Superior's parlor, she stretched out her fingers, which were cramped up in a fixed position every afternoon, six days per week, and often on Sunday as well when she had to finish up a piece that was needed in the outside world. Facing Reverend Mother Laurentia was such a rare occurrence that Nuala was convinced she was in for it, and the leather strap on Friday night was beginning to seem lenient compared to a session with the Mother Superior. At least the pain of a flogging had a definite beginning and end, whereas Reverend Mother's punishment was unknown and potentially severe.

"I saw it in her eyes, Reverend Mother," Father McNulty said, speaking of Nuala as if she were nothing more than another piece of furniture in the gloomy room. "There is a passion for Christ that is expressed there, not unlike the missionaries I have met. That is their God-given gift, an irresistible attraction that draws converts to them. I liken it

139

to a beacon, God's light shining in the darkness, calling out to the heathen to seek shelter and salvation."

"Do you wish to become a missionary, Lilith?" the stern, wrinkled prune of a face intoned solemnly.

Quaking in the presence of the Mother Superior, Nuala could not make her tongue move. The Father must have recognized her terror, because he jumped in, almost rudely, to rescue the potential prodigy. "I will ask that in my interview, Reverend Mother, after we have had a chance to get to know one another. If we could be alone for a few minutes, I can assess the level of her dedication."

Up until that time, Nuala had never seen anyone deal with Reverend Mother as anything less than a higher being, one notch below the Holy Mother of God, but McNulty had a different rank. A priest, even one fresh from the seminary, was held up above the nuns because he was a man and women were naturally inferior. It was a known fact that a woman had led a man astray in the Garden of Eden, it became rote that men had to be better than women from the very beginning of time, and so the Mother Superior deferred to her chaplain. She obediently backed out of her parlor at once, meek and submissive in her attempt at a smile, while Nuala stood silently in awe of Father's power.

Two chairs stood on either side of the fireplace, and McNulty took Nuala's hand with the gentleness of a big brother. Sitting her down in one chair, he plopped casually

140

onto the other, radiating ease and friendly confidences. The fire that blazed in the grate accented the warm atmosphere that the priest created, in direct contrast to the unheated dormitory that Nuala was accustomed to.

"Can you name one of the seven deadly sins?" he asked with a voice so kind that Nuala was shocked dumb. "Pick the one that you think is your greatest enemy, the one that you have battled as valiantly as Brian Boru once fought."

Calling upon lessons that had been drilled into her head for almost two full years, Nuala recited from memory. "Pride, Father," she said, her face crinkling into a serious frown. "Pride that goes hand in hand with vanity, leading down the road to lust."

Leaning forward, he smiled with indulgence, a charming twinkle in his eye. "You recognize your enemy, and that is remarkable for a woman as young as you. You know him, but do you fight against him, or do you allow him to govern you meekly?"

"No, Father, I fight against my sins."

"Do you realize how amazing this is?" he asked, taking her hands as if he were touching a saint. "Most women do not know what lies inside them, working to bring about their downfall. How old are you?"

"I am nine, Father," Nuala replied.

"What I have seen, and what Sister Ursula has seen, does truly exist. You have a vocation, a call to serve God. Do you wish to serve Him?"

"Oh, yes, Father, yes," she gushed, enraptured.

He left his chair and retrieved his valise where he kept his vestments. With a smile and a fatherly wink at the special orphan, he extricated a doll, dressed in the habit of a Poor Clare.

"I know that the dolls that appear in the playroom are removed after the inspector leaves," he confided. Nuala could hardly believe her ears as she heard the truth tumble from the mouth of an adult. "Too many girls, and not enough dolls to go around. They would be torn to shreds and fought over, and the sin of greed would stain every soul. My doll is a Poor Clare, like my aunt."

The rag doll with the celluloid head and hands was placed in Nuala's lap, while she gaped wide-eyed at Father McNulty. He pretended to fuss a bit over the toy's skirt, smoothing it as a little girl would do, while encouraging Nuala to play. She hugged the cloth nun with delight, joy and pleasure filling her heart until she was afraid she might cry.

"Your sister Jenny touched the old apple tree that belongs to the Little People," Nuala whispered to the toy. "You must pray for her release, Sister Mary, and I will become a nun too and we will both pray together."

"Tell me about Sister Mary," McNulty said, putting Nuala on his lap. "Is she an orphan girl?"

"Yes, Father, she was taken from her mother because her mother was sinful after her father died, and she became a Poor Clare to atone for her mother's sins. She lives in the cloister and prays all day long, and she never gets tired of talking to God."

"Would you like to be a holy Sister? But not like our little Mary, not to be locked away in the cloister."

"Yes, Father."

"You must be obedient to your Mother Superior, and most of all, you must be obedient to the priests, even if they ask you to travel to the most dangerous corners of darkest Africa, where the black people have not met Jesus. You must obey the priests."

"I would, Father, I promise."

"You would not be afraid?"

"No, Father. God will protect me."

"Can we share a secret?" he said, looking around the room as if searching for spies. "When I was baptized, my father named me Terence in honor of his grandfather. What name did your father give you when you were baptized?"

"Nuala, Father. It's an Irish name."

"It's a beautiful name, Nuala, as beautiful as Lir's daughter Fionnuala. Can I tell you another secret? I have a head full of ideas, and you are part of them. The cleverest of *the orphan girls should be given an opportunity to become missionary sisters, and bring the word of God to those who hunger for it. It's easier for an orphan to travel, because they don't have a father telling them to stay close to home. Your father can be with you wherever you go because he's in heaven, don't you think?"*

"Would he know that I was far away?"

"Of course, and you would be closer to him because you would be closer to God, and since God lives in heaven, you would be nearer to paradise." The priest paused, studying her reaction. "I think of all the souls that could be saved if only one girl entered into God's service every year from St. Anne's Orphanage. You are the one that I have chosen, Nuala, because you have a strong vocation and you have shown me that your heart is ready for God's love."

"But who will give me a dowry, Father?"

"My goodness, you think clearly. I cannot believe that you are only nine years old. I have thought of this as well, and my solution helps you, and it helps others. There are many people who have been blessed by God, not only in Ireland, but in America as well, and they want to repay Him for His generosity. They want to put their money to the best use, and I cannot think of anything that would be better than providing dowries for those who are poor but strong in their desire for missionary work."

"How can I be the one, Father? I am a very naughty girl, and I am always disobedient and I sin and sin every day."

"You are the one, Nuala, because you see your faults and you do not try to cover them up, you try to destroy them. Don't ever tell the Sisters that I told you this, but they confess their sins to me. Yes, the nuns, they sin, they are not without sin. Only our Holy Mother is without sin."

"They sin?"

"Of course, they are human like you. And like you, they recognize their faults. A woman who is immoral, who confesses her sins again and again without a true desire to repent, is truly wicked. A woman who sins, one who is proud but comes to confess with true and sincere regret, that is a woman who serves God. Do you know the story of St. Mary Magdalene?"

"That she was a great sinner," Nuala said, struggling to recall the life of yet another saint.

"Slothful, full of lust, and so very wicked that her own sister was ashamed of her," McNulty added. "Yet Jesus forgave her, did he not? And she became one of his disciples, did you know that? Most importantly of all, Mary Magdalene was the first person to know that Jesus had risen from the dead, and she delivered the glorious news to the Apostles. Jesus loved her very much, because she stopped being sinful and asked to be forgiven."

His fingers brushed a few stray tendrils away from her forehead. With paternal affection, he touched his lips to her cool skin, and Nuala responded to the pleasure of human contact by hugging Father McNulty with all her might. It was the first act of tender affection that she had experienced since she arrived at the orphanage, and one that she yearned to prolong.

"Did you have a favorite uncle who bounced you on his knee?" he asked, but he did not seem to be interested in receiving any reply.

It was odd to see Mother Superior still waiting in the foyer twenty minutes later, looking like a guest in her own convent. She perused Nuala with a blank expression, but the girl held on to her very workable, very glum demeanor, the expression that Father had ordered her to put on her face, to guard their secret. McNulty followed closely behind his experiment, using a firm hand to hold her in place before he pushed her back to her everyday existence.

"Have her in the chapel at half-past five, Reverend Mother. I am taking charge of her religious studies personally," he commanded, not at all like the kind man who had interviewed a frightened child only minutes ago. "I appreciate Sister Monica's efforts, but she has earned a rest. A novice should become well versed in the care of vestments. This girl is to be looked on as an oblate, Reverend Mother, and accorded the same discipline."

146

The slightest suggestion of a smile was flitting timorously on the Mother Superior's lips. She began to crow about her convent, her orphanage, the source of dedicated Sisters that would be funded by donations from America. The saving of heathen souls by the relatively worthless inmates of St. Anne's was such a brilliant scheme that Reverend Mother Laurentia was surprised that she had not thought of it sooner, but then, it took a man of Father McNulty's wisdom to put things into motion. The nun seemed to be thrilled that she could generate useful employment for girls with little future, but she was much more excited about the money that could be raised to help fund the religious orders.

Told to return to the crochet room, Nuala moved slowly, eavesdropping as long as she could. Father McNulty was not a very large man, not much taller than Reverend Mother, but he used his voice and his posture to tower over the nuns. Whatever he said, the Sisters murmured their assent, exuding a stream of agreements with uncommon humility. It was obedience personified, a demonstration of power that reinforced Nuala's understanding of her situation, and of her life. She never wanted to be bounced on his knee again. She had no choice in the matter.

9

Mr. Treacy was up to his ears in old records when he was interrupted. The office he worked out of at the Dun Laoghaire Institute of Art was tremendously cluttered, with files piled on top of crates of more files and not a seat free to sit on. If the visitor were not someone who could possibly help him with his research, he probably would have asked her to come some other day.

"Yes, back then this was an industrial school," the graduate student said. "By and large, the system began to contract as the Church began to change after Vatican II. Many, many such facilities are serving other uses these days."

"I don't know that I can tell you very much," Molly said. "My father had little to say about his life in Ireland. It's almost as if he was born when he got on a ship to Norfolk and signed on at the first recruiting office he came to."

"That's understandable," Treacy said. "The emotional and physical abuse were psychologically damaging in their own right, but many of the former students were traumatized again when they entered the outside world."

"Unloved and unwanted all around," Eoin suggested.

"To an extent, I suppose that's true," Treacy said. "Many of my father's patients were loved by their parents, but due to extreme poverty those same parents had to give up their children, if only to ensure that they would be fed."

"Does he specialize in treating people from industrial schools?" Molly asked.

"Not a specialty per se, but his practice has seen an influx in the past several years, particularly since the last laundry closed. You may be familiar with it, Dr. MacNeill," Treacy said. "Our country is opening up quite a bit these days."

They veered off on a tangent, discussing the changes that the booming economy brought. There were new faces on the streets, immigrants from other lands, and while their fresh ideas helped, Eoin was convinced it was the expansion of financial resources that sparked the revolution.

For some reason, Molly felt as if she had dropped back into Gross Anatomy, where the students dissected and probed, looking at things that were a part of them, but at a safe distance from reality. Pick apart and tease apart, examine each tendon and nerve and artery, but never see the parts as the whole that was once a human being. It was as impersonal as walking down Michigan Avenue and looking in the windows of Water Tower Place. It allowed Mr. Treacy to speak of corporal punishment, but never feel the sting of the cane.

"The legend of the Apple Lady," Treacy said as he displayed a photo from the archives. "The only act of kindness these lads ever knew, in our great Catholic nation."

149

"We had fruit trees in our back yard," Molly said, enveloped in a shroud of melancholy. "God bless the Apple Lady, my father used to way when we picked the apples. He always loved apples."

According to Treacy's theory, the Emergency was a boon to men like Frank Devoy, who found jobs far away from the land that reviled them, even if it meant risking their lives as soldiers. He offered up anecdotes he'd collected, about men so wholly unprepared for the outside world that they had no idea what an erection was for, and didn't that prove the human will to assimilate or there'd have been no second generation. If anything, the rebound was so complete that he could count the number of industrial school inmates who had joined the priesthood on one hand.

The nuance and detail of life was lost to Frank, a fact that only made matters worse for Molly. He never learned how to be a father, how to be a husband, not with a few nuns beating dogma into his head. From such an artificial world, it was little wonder that Frank was so unlike everyone else's father. A shudder rattled Molly's knees.

"Many of the inmates never learned to form emotional bonds," Treacy said. "I've found in my research that their children share the same difficulty."

How many times had the surgeons made some comment, and not kindly, about her detachment from the suffering of the patients? She went about her duties with a cool head, counting sponges without ever once losing track, handing instruments with smart precision, but she was a machine and not a human being. Like a mechanical woman, she felt nothing for her husband and her main concern for her children was their survival, as if all she had were the most basic human instincts and she was unable to really connect on a different level.

The thing that her father saw in her, the thing that had to be cut out like a tumor, was deep inside her. It was why she felt lonely and isolated; it was the cause of her solitude. Her father had sent her all this way to find out what it was, but she had no idea how to get rid of it. What of her children, were they tainted by the industrial schools as well? Would it go on forever, down the generations, without end?

More horrors filled her every thought. Molly guessed that she had not been a loving mother, that she had been cold and distant and her father saw it but couldn't get past his own shame to call her out. Or was it merely a figment of Frank's distorted imagination, where he had some outlandish ideal of the perfect mother and Molly hadn't met expectations so he assumed she was marked by his legacy? The more she puzzled out the bits and pieces, the more she realized that there was something wrong in her head, something that could be fixed if she was brave enough to seek out a cure and expose her father's shameful past, the past he had worked tirelessly to keep hidden.

"At any rate, I suspect that the victims want to talk," Treacy said, "but they were indoctrinated into silence. It's a self-monitoring system, you see. The boys were taught to be afraid to talk, and so the abuse went on. The truth will die out and so all will be forgotten."

"I can't let it go," Molly said. It was obvious that her father didn't want it to end that way, with a silent whimper.

From a collection of old photographs, Mr. Treacy was able to show Molly the black and white images of her father's era, and she was thrilled to find her father smiling back at her in the snapshot of a theatre group. She admired his handsome young face in the photograph of the school band, pride in his posture as he held his clarinet with military precision, a pupil at the Carriglea Industrial School for Boys who did not yet know how reviled he would be when he was sent home.

Eoin exhaled a huge breath of relief when he walked out of the entrance. He looked back briefly at what had once been a fine Georgian mansion, straining to hear the yammering echoes of three hundred teenaged boys at the brink of manhood. "I'm glad you came here today," he confided. "To tell you the truth, I was worried about what might be lurking in the files. You had a bad time of it in Kilkenny."

"Not such a great time today, actually," Molly said. "Granted, I truly believe that my father was happier here, but he was scarred for life just the same. Even if the records show that his mother and his stepfather came often to visit, it wasn't normal."

"Not so very different from any other boarding school," Eoin said. "He was at the age where he was growing up and ready to leave Mammy and baby things behind. All boys go through that phase, to prepare their grand entrance into the big world and support a family. I have the feeling that girls don't mature in that way, because they never actually leave their mothers."

"You're right, girls don't truly separate from their mothers in the way that boys do. It's the opposite; we get closer to them and become more like best friends when we have babies and our lives become very similar." Molly stopped to let her thoughts catch up to her words. " I don't think that happened with my aunt and my grandmother, and I want to know why."

Eoin smiled, to boost Molly's glum spirits. "I'll do what I can to help you."

They drove for a while in silence, with Molly staring blankly out of the car window. "Would you take me home, please," she said, her eyes fixed on the oncoming traffic.

"Come back to my flat," he offered.

"Not tonight," she said. "I have to make phone calls."

"Call from my place, I don't mind," he said.

"Not this time, Eoin," she said.

Molly did not care if Mrs. Devlin listened in on the conversation because her respect for Irish people was slightly diminished. Without a doubt, Molly was certain that her hostess knew all about the industrial schools, and most likely considered the wretched inmates a pile of manure, as articulated so clearly by Con MacNeill. An entire generation had been raised with that prejudice, and Molly could not fault her father for taking off and never coming back. It was the rare man who could endure the life her father had lived, and then stick around for more abuse.

"I figured out why I married Stan," she said to her mother. "To make you happy. Why did you bug me until I broke up with Tom Kelly?"

"Molly, what's come over you?" Barbara asked.

"I need to know, that's why."

"Don't be snappy at me," Barbara scolded. "You're like a female version of your father sometimes."

"What was so wonderful about Stan?"

"He has drive, Molly, he's an entrepreneur. He has his own business now, and you're driving a Mercedes, my dear." Barbara tallied the benefits. "A big house, everything for the kids he pays for without complaint, what more could you ask of a man?"

"Is that why you picked my father, because he wore a sign that said 'Good Provider'?"

"A woman has to consider those things, Molly. What are you going to raise your children on, air? Is this about money? Is Stan's business going under?"

"Was Dad ever mean to you?"

"He was moody, and he wouldn't open up when he got in one of his states. Honey, Stan doesn't hit you, does he?"

"What do you mean by moody?"

"Down in the dumps for no reason. He'd tune us all out and go sit in his den, or he'd go sit outside under the apple trees. The last four or five years were the worst, don't you remember?

Some days all he had to do was look at you and he'd go mope for hours."

"Was he ever treated for depression?"

"No, he was fine, Molly, he was just a moody and quiet man. He was Irish," Barbara said. "Full of his own thoughts and shut up tight as a clam. You're the same way, you know. Molly, are you depressed? Have you been seeing a psychiatrist?"

"You know what I really think?" Molly said, almost laughing. "It's genetics. A genetic mutation."

"I wish you would confide in me." Barbara said. "Why are your children so unhappy at home? I can understand that Colette is at that age, but even Billy and Renee are saying they're never going back home."

"Mom, would you be ashamed of me if I did something wrong?" Molly asked.

"Like what, murdering your husband and covering up the whole thing?" Barbara made light of the question. "Honey, I can't get the kids to give me a straight answer about why they're avoiding their father. Stan hasn't called, not once, since you've been gone. No one wants to talk, and about all that Colette said was that he didn't knock them around or anything like that. Now, what could you have done that is wrong?"

"What if the neighbors were talking about me, what if there was gossip that went on behind your back? Would you be embarrassed?"

"Molly, are you drinking? Where are these questions coming from?"

"It's about Dad, and me, how we're alike. I can't explain it." Molly gave up, not ready to start on the final phase. "There's more to the story. I'll call you back later, when I have the pieces and I can put it together."

"Did your father kill his sister or something? What is shameful that the neighbors would talk about?"

"It's nothing, Mom, it's an Irish thing," Molly said, returning a cheerful note to her voice.

Ever since Rose had experienced her epiphany, she tended to cling to Molly as if the nurse were a life raft. After talking to her mother, Molly wanted very much to lie down and close her eyes, to block out the images she had been forced to see that day. Her mind played tricks, making her imagine the heartbreak if her son had been wrenched from the family at the age of five, and her stomach twisted with the pain. The last thing that Molly wanted was Rose and her pressing needs, when Molly did not have enough left to deal with her own miseries.

Her three children could squabble and argue like the bitterest of enemies, but in the end Colette would be protective of Renee. Billy admired his older sisters, followed them around when he was a baby, but would such bonds have formed if they had been separated at the ages of five or seven?

Molly could not conceive of a scandal so revolting that it would cause a brother to turn his back on his sister, any more than she could think of a reason for her father to reject Aunt Nuala. Viewing her world through American eyes, Molly presumed that the Irish people were not so very different, but then her ponderings came back to Eoin and his experiences. His former wife's father had been ready to disown his daughter for something that Americans had learned to grudgingly accept, and it must have been a credible threat because Eoin and Sheila got married. The Martyr of Kilrossanty had more courage than she had given him credit for, and perhaps her father had been the recipient of more respect than he was due.

"A messenger delivered a package for you while you were out today," Mary said, putting a comforting hand on Molly's arm.

Joining Rose in the sitting room, Molly sat down passively and accepted the parcel that Mary had placed on the table. "It says Booterstown on the label," Rose warned, implying something unpleasant.

"Quite a history, the convent in Booterstown," Mary said. "The Sisters of Mercy opened up one of their first homes there, well before the Great Hunger, to help poor women. A Catholic girl back then had no one to turn to, especially in Dublin, where so many girls came from the country to go into service."

"The road to hell is paved with their good intentions," Rose said.

Rose had tried to appear calm and be her normal self, but Molly could tell at once that the woman's ire was a new and very unwelcome phenomenon. Sitting back, Molly took in the show, to determine if Rose's mental instability was taking a different course. It was not done to butt in, but Molly did believe that she had a duty to Mary, to say something if Rose was becoming a danger.

"It's not right to paint all the holy Sisters with one big brush," Mary advised.

"You don't know," Rose said and then covered her face with her hands. "You can never know."

"Why don't you tell her, Rose," Molly said.

"Things best left unspoken," Rose burst out before fleeing back to the safety of her room.

"The Sisters always lived away from the outside world," Mary said, picking up her knitting as if nothing was wrong. "The big, high walls of the convents, you could look up at them and think that the nuns were separate from the rest of us, like queens in their castle."

Molly did not make a sound at first, but she did manage to babble out some noises to indicate her attention. It was unnerving to hear an oft-repeated phrase come from a stranger's mouth, especially because Rose used the sentence as Frank had, to be a warning and an end to further discussion. Some things were best not to know, and some things were best left unspoken, but there were times when it was better to bring the evil and the wicked out into the open for all to see. Molly had only to recall her father's past to find the truth in that philosophy.

"Things have changed so much that I can't imagine anyone with a vocation choosing to hide behind a fortress," Molly said. "I don't know about Ireland, but back home it's rare to find a nun living in a convent. They live among the people they serve."

"And all to the better, but people nowadays don't give them much respect, not like the old days," Mary said. "There was a time that a Sister never had to stand on a crowded bus. Everyone was ready to give up their seat."

"At least now that they've been released from their prison, they can really help people because they see what is needed. How could a nun judge my grandmother? Some shriveled up old spinster with three meals a day and a roof over her head, and she has the nerve to criticize a poor woman who's trying to raise two children."

"But they thought that they were doing good deeds, Molly," Mary said with some conviction. "Like a horse wearing blinders, they couldn't see anywhere but straight ahead, so they never turned right or left. I can't curse them for their blindness."

"Who was to blame, then, for my father's lost life?"

"Laying blame, now that's a race that never ends, always going around in the same circle. It was hard times and no one had money, and our country was just born with so many things to do at once. There was fighting for a long time, amongst ourselves, long after the British left."

"My father was taken away from his mother."

"Oh, I knew that before," Mary said. "I remember Carriglea's band, you see. I might have seen your father playing, back when I was a little girl."

"Did you think that they were a bunch of criminals?"

159

"Of course not. My father didn't always have work, and my mother took in washing and mending to make ends meet. They didn't always meet. We knew of boys, boys from the neighborhood, who were put away and then came back like frightened old hermits, and people would shun them. There but for the grace of God go my sons, my father used to say."

"He sounds like a very rare man who felt compassion."

"My father was a Christian man, Molly, pious and faithful to God's teachings. He was uncommon, yes, but that's human nature. Easy to preach, you see, and we were soaked in religion, but most of us don't like getting too wet."

"What makes no sense to me is that, if the State had the money to house all the children, why not give the money to the parents instead of giving to the religious orders?"

"Because the parents were unfit, or so they would say. There were real orphans, Molly, children with no parents living and no relatives to take them in. Listen to me, making excuses that I don't believe. I used to hold to them, when I was young, and they like to steal in every now and again."

"What made you change your mind?"

"Mr. Devlin," Mary said, her eyes twinkling merrily. "He was put away in Artane Industrial School, close to his home and that was truly a small blessing for his mother. Poor Rose, they sent her all the way to Cork."

"My father was hauled off to Kilkenny. I don't know how his mother could afford the train fare to visit him."

160

"When there's a will. Most of the industrial schools had at least one Visiting Day on a holiday in August, when the trains offered a special rate for the day. Half of Ireland must have been traveling, the trains were so crowded."

"How horrible," Molly said. "If your kids were spread out all over, how could you possibly see them in one day?"

"They didn't really want visitors, I don't think. You know, since the parents were bad, it wouldn't be wise to have them snooping about. The nuns knew best."

"Did you really think that they knew best?"

"They certainly did," Mary laughed. "And we never questioned."

"That's why all this happened, because no one asked questions."

"They do such wonderful things now," Mary said. "Out of the convent, they live among the poor like Jesus. It's better these days, to imitate Christ in every way you can. It's not good to raise anyone up on a pedestal, make them a god. The Bible warns us of false gods."

"That's it," Molly said. "Now that their altars are being pulled down, they don't like it. The worshippers are turning away."

"No one likes change, don't you think? Like Rose, she was kept in for ten years, and you'd think that the first thing a person would do is go outside. She couldn't change, though, she never felt right out of doors."

"She was fine when we went to the park and the cemetery," Molly noted.

"That's because of you. She's comfortable with you, that you'd be kind to her if she did something embarrassing. You're not ashamed to be seen with her."

"Has she ever considered therapy?"

"We tried it once, a few years ago, but she couldn't make herself talk."

"What could be that bad after half a century?" Molly asked.

"Didn't you read my memory book when we were clipping the articles?" Mary put down her knitting and reached for the folio covered by a gay floral print, a cheer that belied the contents of the pages.

10

Sister Monica was grateful to be relieved of her duties to Father McNulty. The man had a mercurial temper and precious little patience for a very old woman who could not move fast enough to please him. He did not hesitate to snap at her, which only left the half-blind nun flustered and quite likely to knock over the chalice and paten, sending the unconsecrated host to the floor. If the handle on the wine ewer was facing in the wrong direction, he tore into her after Mass, and piled on extra penance in confession. As much as Sister Monica wished to be useful in her retirement, she was not sorry to give up the morning duties.

On the other hand, Mary Josephine had to rise a half hour earlier to get Nuala out of bed, and she took it out on the girl by rousing her with a swat on the bottom or a cuff of the skull. None of that mattered to Nuala, who looked forward to Father McNulty's company and Sister Mary's companionship.

To get to the chapel, Nuala had to travel through dark corridors that echoed with gloomy silence. She had paintings and statues of saints for company, all reminding her daily that life was nothing but pain and suffering, with the only relief to be found in a heaven that was not depicted anywhere in St. Anne's. Walking as quietly as she could in her heavy hobnailed boots, she stole into the chapel when Father McNulty was lighting the candles on the altar.

"Good morning, Father," she whispered, respecting God's house through a pious tone.

"Come a little earlier tomorrow," he said. "You're old enough to light the candles."

She smiled from ear to ear, lapping up a compliment. Only a junior girl, she never felt so grown-up as she did at that moment. "I can come at five, Father, or any time you like."

"Good girl, good girl," he said. "Let's start in right off before the first Mass. Did you know that the Sisters go to Mass first? They come into the chapel through that door. Every morning, I want you to unpack my vestments and lay them out for me while I meditate. I must have complete silence while I pray, is that clear? And I must have everything done precisely as I tell you, or you will have failed in your duty to me."

"Yes, Father." She stood solemnly, growing nervous. A mistake could mean banishment, and that was too heavy a penalty to suffer.

Piece by piece, McNulty removed the many components of his uniform, explaining the significance and naming each part so that Nuala could respond quickly if he asked for

164

something. He quizzed her, telling her to pick up the amice, point to the cincture, lift up the maniple. In the case, only Sister Mary remained, waiting for a little girl to play with. Nuala could hardly contain her legs that wanted to leap for joy, her hands that wanted to clap with anticipation. Her entire body shivered with the effort and Father McNulty laughed in such a way that she knew he was just as happy as she was at that moment.

"Like the lilies in the field and the birds in the air, Nuala," he said. "You accept what is given and never ask for more. How blessed am I, to be allowed to minister to you and the other girls. Such sweet innocence."

Hugging the doll with delight, Nuala relished the few minutes that she had to be a girl like she used to be. She had earned the privilege, had worked very hard without crying or complaining, and Father McNulty followed through on his promise. A man who never lied was one to be trusted, and the good Father never lied.

"While I say Mass for the Sisters, you may visit with Sister Mary," he said. He turned his head and put his tongue in his cheek, pointing to the bulge and tapping, asking for a kiss. Along with a wet peck, Nuala threw in a hug for good measure. "You won't tell the Sisters, you must promise."

"I won't tell anyone, Father."

"Only God," he added. "You can tell God everything, because he does not get jealous. What we are doing here is

165

very special, and not everyone is fortunate enough to be chosen."

By now, Nuala had learned to take whatever good came her way, ignoring the bad because there was so much of it. If she had to sit on the priest's lap while she cuddled and chatted with Sister Mary, it was worth it because she had a chance to play with a doll. Besides, Father had to be close to her so that he could whisper in her ear, sharing confidences that Mother Superior did not need to hear. Nuala was aware of the punishments that would befall her if the nuns knew that Father McNulty complimented her lovely hair or told her that she was the prettiest girl he had ever seen. He wanted to make her feel better, to make her smile, and that was not allowed at St. Anne's.

"Your skin is so pale," he often told her. "You are a beacon, shining in the darkness of my soul."

In a routine that became a ritual, she named each component of his vestments as he put them on, usually drawing some murmur or even a word of praise. As soon as they heard the sound of thick rubber soles rubbing the stone floor of the chapel, McNulty kissed Sister Mary and then kissed Nuala. "Until this Mass is finished, you and Sister Mary may play, but very, very quietly," he cautioned. "Quietly."

She both adored and feared Terry McNulty, a man who explained his role as that of a father to a flock of children. Slight of build, it was the weight of his Roman collar that gave him his authority and garnered respect from all who spoke to him. Nuala thought of him often, dreading the next meeting but anticipating his kindness at the same time. With his fist ready to strike, she trembled when his tone grew angry, but that same hand could be cloaked in a velvet glove as he blessed her tenderly, the paternal guardian meting out both discipline and love. It was a tightrope walk every day, balancing on a high wire of ever changing demands from a priest whose mood shifted as readily as the wind.

McNulty's style of teaching incorporated dramatic swings from anger to love, which kept all the girls on their toes. From time to time, he would test their knowledge of the faith by lining up a few children at the altar rail, facing their colleagues in a rigid row of tension. Questions from the catechism would be intoned, with a correct answer receiving heaping praise, while an error drew a sharp slap. Every girl vied to be chosen for the test, so elated to gain the blessings of a kind word that they gladly risked a possible blow to the head. Nuala was selected often, to show the others how it was done, and she never once got it wrong. She prayed for a slap, hoping for a tough question that she could not answer, just so that she could be like the other girls, but McNulty tossed roses instead of rocks.

"Who is the third person of the Blessed Trinity?" he asked Nuala, but to the next girl he inquired, "How do you know there is such a place in the other life as Purgatory?"

"The Holy Ghost," was Nuala's swift reply, while 'Faith' stammered through a long, rambling paragraph that was impossible to memorize.

"There would be no use praying for them," the prize pupil tried to coach her friend, speaking like a ventriloquist at the Gaiety Theatre.

Sister Ursula kept a mental log of winners and losers, along with her roster of the week's miscreants. Like clockwork, she wielded her leather strap every Friday, taking advantage of bath night and wet skin. There was no better medium to raise stinging welts, to create a very visible message to all. Obey was the command, yield to authority and obey, and as an aside, the Sisters began to add a new dictate: never have anything to do with boys.

Nuala watched each day go by from behind the tall stone fortress that was the convent's borders. She never saw anyone except for the other orphans and the Sisters of Mercy, but she never forgot what it was like in the outside world. Mother and brother were kept fresh and vivid in her mind, where she held onto a recollection of her last Christmas at home. When she was frightened by terrifying nightmares, which was often, she lulled herself to sleep by pretending that she was back on Northbrook Terrace, waiting for Santa to come. An old, old habit returned, and every night, Nuala ducked under her blanket and sucked her thumb for solace.

Illness swept through the dormitory, often sparked by a new arrival and her new set of germs. There was one sickness that was epidemic, and one that was apparently incurable. No matter how often a person was made to carry her damp mattress through a gauntlet of jeering girls, no matter how many times a girl had a urine-soaked sheet wrapped around her head, there was no way to stop the bedwetting. The Sisters' heavy-handed treatments were ineffective, but they kept applying the same humiliation every day whether it worked or not. Nuala tried to keep her distance from people like 'Hazel' who were afflicted with the dreadful, and potentially contagious, malady.

There was another reason to avoid 'Hazel', and that was simply that she had no father. Illegitimate, she was an untouchable outcast in Irish society, and within the walls of the orphanage she was treated as such. As for the rest of the girls, they were lumped together into a congealed mass of sin and iniquity, but Nuala noticed that she was handled a little differently, as if she was elevated above the rabble. More was expected of her, and she was punished more severely if she slipped. In a way, she began to feel that the Sisters of Mercy were hovering around her, grooming her into their image with every slap, every biff and every dark scowl. The way that Sister Ursula looked at her at breakfast, the way that she whispered to Mother Superior while Nuala sipped her tea, reinforced an attitude that began to sprout and grow strong.

169

Nuala was of loftier status, somehow a little better than the rest, and by the time that she became a senior girl, her once terror-filled face had become a sullen mask.

No punishment existed that could erase her memory of Frank's birthday. She composed an invisible letter to her brother while 'Trudy' stuttered through a recitation. The pen moved through the air, hovering over a sheet of paper, while Nuala pretended to inscribe her real thoughts about her existence, pausing to wish Frank a happy birthday if such a thing were possible where he was held captive. Sister Assumpta asked her a question that she didn't hear, and Nuala burst into tears as she stood mutely at her desk.

Anyone crying had to be given a reason to cry, and Sister Assumpta had no patience whatsoever with emotional outbursts. Well-trained to the routine, Nuala walked to the front of the classroom and held out her hands, palms up, to be whacked with the cane that Sister kept hooked on the back of her chair. From fingertip to knuckle, Nuala's hands were already striped with bruises.

The nun could not suppress a gasp of shock, any more than she could hide the sweat on her fuzzy upper lip. Sister coughed uncomfortably and stated the obvious: Nuala had been disobedient already that day, and this was the first class, so she must have been bad at morning Mass. Putting on a grand show of penitence, Nuala solemnly agreed, rather than risk trouble from another source. Bad enough that she had dropped the paten before Mass even started, earning herself a severe biffing from Father McNulty. Should word get back to Mother Superior, it was possible that Nuala would lose her position and never see the precious doll again.

For the first time that Nuala could recall, the nun changed her mind about a caning and sent Nuala back to her seat. She told all the girls to put aside their books, fold their hands, and offer up a prayer to God. All eyes turned to the crucifix that hung on the wall, while Nuala examined Sister Assumpta to see if she had gone mad. A sparkle formed at the corner of the nun's eye, a drop that was hastily wiped away.

Nuala's mouth moved through a Hail Mary while her mind replayed the dreadful morning. It was all her fault that Father McNulty had to inflict such punishment. All her fault that she couldn't bend her fingers to fold his vestments after Mass. She had summoned his bad temper, his devil, by being careless, and she hurt him far more than he hurt her.

The fear of exile from his beneficence made her fall to her knees, begging to be forgiven, and he had come around after his anger cooled. She had to swear that she would never do it again, although she blubbered so that he couldn't possibly have understood a word she said. In a show of absolution, Father McNulty pulled a peppermint stick out of his pocket and shared it with her. Although she had come to despise the taste of peppermint, she would never dare to tell him so.

The group of girls that Nuala lived with was largely unchanging. On rare occasions, a new person might suddenly appear, along with a new cot added to one of the many rows that filled the room with cold precision. These fresh inmates were different because they had been raised outside for a longer time, and being older, they tended to struggle against the lifestyle that they were forced into. The Sisters would become so involved in training the recent arrivals that the long-term residents experienced a brief lull in the beatings.

"The virgin's aim is to appear less comely; she will wrong herself so as to hide her natural attractions," Sister Ursula read from St. Augustine's letters as the senior girls made tablecloths, doilies, runners and trims. Nuala had long since stopped listening, using the time to pray to her dead father in heaven.

"Please, Daddy," she begged in her thoughts, "send Mammy to take me home. Please help me, Daddy."

"Tell me, pray, where amid all this is there room for the thought of God?" the nun boomed dramatically, turning every word into a physical part of each girl's changing body, molding each budding woman into a Medieval penitent.

The isolation, the formidable walls and the harsh regime were the foundations of most religious orders. The nuns merely took what they knew and used the same techniques on the orphan girls, to bring them into line morally *and spiritually. Breaking down a sense of individualism was meant to bring about a communion with God, as the nuns had often told their charges, and it was something that every holy Sister had struggled with in her years of training. Keeping separate from the secular world was part of their mission, to serve God without distractions. That had to be the best way to live, and they knew what was best for the poor children because they were members of the clergy, a direct link to God. Nuala was being prepared for a world that had ceased to exist one thousand years ago.*

The phone was ringing but Mrs. Devlin didn't appear, so Molly answered herself with a cheery "Derry House" before stating her own name to avoid confusion with the person on the other end of the line. Her brother John burst out laughing. Her lodgings were obviously not of the standard hotel variety, and even for a bed and breakfast it was a bit more casual.

Word by word, John's tone took on an edge that signaled a serious discussion was on tap. All he had to say was that he had talked to their mother and Molly could guess where they were headed, straight into places she preferred to keep hidden from public inspection.

"Listen, Molly, we both know that you're more like Dad then the rest of us, but I'm just as buttoned up so I'm not blowing smoke," John said. "I know this is against type, but you can tell me if there's a problem at home. You know that."

"After seventeen years, it's not going to be champagne and roses," Molly said, hoping to blow him off but afraid that he was not so easy to sidetrack.

"How long has this been going on? I don't much like my brother-in-law telling me that my sister is a bitch who isn't welcome in her own home."

"John, it's, if Colette," she babbled. Realizing that her family's dirty laundry was hanging out for all to see, she could not think or speak clearly.

"Okay, let's go there. How long has Colette wanted to live someplace else?"

"I don't know."

"Don't know or won't tell?"

"He's my husband. I married him. It's not like I had to get married," she said.

"So Saint Molly made her bed and she'll lie in it, no matter what, even if it's a bed of nails," John said. "You can't cure everyone. For once, why don't you think of yourself?"

"John, Dad was locked up when he was five," Molly said. She wanted to talk about that part of her experiences, the part that didn't deal with her troubles at home and the fact that she had decided not to go back, but had no place else to go.

"What did he do?" John asked.

"I've felt sick all day," she said. "I saw all the records, the court transcript, everything. He didn't do anything. The government rounded up poor kids and locked them away in homes run by runs."

174

"So we've been touched by injustice," John said. "Poor old man. What was it, some kind of bizarre social engineering?"

"There's a shrink who makes a living out of putting the victims back together. A lot of the things that Dad did, it's because of that."

"But he still had a good life, Molly, and he was happy. What is past is past, it's gone, and you can't make it better. Dad was never bitter, he never complained about anything. Follow his lead on this one, will you?"

"I tried to drive by his old house but the neighborhood is so bad that the cops stopped me."

"You know what's getting at you? You're too sensitive to people's suffering," John said. "So our father came out of the slums, falsely accused of some crime he never committed, and how did he end up? Think about it, Nurse Molly, think about his cure."

"Living well is the best revenge." Molly repeated an old adage.

"Dad was going to work up a family crest once, remember when he was on that kick? That was supposed to be our motto."

When the oldest Devoy son graduated from Notre Dame University, with honors, no parent was more thrilled than Frank. At the time, Molly thought he was being weird, as usual, but the clouds were parting and her vision of her father was clearing. That was part of his drive, to live well, to excel, to produce children who excelled, and to all those who thought the

industrial school inmates were worthless, Frank's life was a
gesture that said "Fuck you."

Multiple copies of the photograph of Frank with Matt,
standing before the Grotto on the South Bend campus, had been
ordered and Molly realized that her father must have sent one to
every single person he knew in Ireland, to his friends and
colleagues and any nun or priest he could track down. Frank
Devoy was no treasured monument destroyed by barbarians. He
was a phoenix who rose from the ashes of his childhood and
managed to poke a few jaundiced eyes with the sharp stick of
achievement, beyond anything that his enemies could reach. All
that remained was the mental damage, the inability to connect to
others. How did that get cleaned up, Molly wondered. No
amount of money or fame would correct such damage.

"Did you get a funeral all lined up?" John switched
topics.

"Huh? Oh, yeah."

"And?" he probed.

"Mrs. Devlin, my hostess, her sister-in-law is going
through some kind of crisis," Molly said.

"Naturally, you've wrapped yourself up in it. Can't you
ever stop being a nurse and taking care of people?"

"Dad wants me to find his sister. I really believe it, and I
won't blow it off just because it's another trip through an
emotional meat grinder."

"Damn, if we'd known," John said. "Remember,
Christmas or family parties, when he'd get that faraway look in

his eye? We could have been supportive or something. Any details from your research?"

"He was put in an orphanage, beaten silly on a regular basis, broken down emotionally, you know, an all-around spectacular childhood," Molly said. "And now tomorrow, I'm taking my court order to some other place where Aunt Nuala was locked up. Same stupid no good reason, the crime of being poor."

"What a fucked up country," John snorted. "No wonder Dad left and never went back. Matt was telling me the other day that when Dad was there to bury Grandma, he stayed a week or so and came right back home. It's funny, now that I think about it. He never made a really serious attempt to visit Dublin until four or five years ago, and then he wanted to go back so badly that I thought he was getting a little obsessed."

"What I can't figure out is why he suddenly had to find her," Molly said. "I wonder if he felt guilty for mistreating her over some scandal, and he wanted to make it up to her at the end."

"If he did, I would imagine that there should be something in all that paperwork the lawyer gave to you. Did you look at it yet?"

Molly let out a little laugh. "Of course not, that would make sense. I've been a little distracted lately."

"We'll talk on Thursday," John said. "Let me know what you find, okay? And Molly, when you get back this weekend, drive up to Michigan, do you hear? Will you do that for yourself and for your kids?"

"Stan doesn't mean half of what he says, John," Molly said.

So ingrained was the dictum of keeping things bottled inside that Molly had not revealed the truth to her own heart. Her marriage was a disaster from the start, when she was not particularly comfortable around Stan or his boisterous family. To Molly, a husband was a man like her father, someone restrained and prudish, while Stan practically celebrated his bodily functions to Molly's disgust. Before they married she thought he was a boorish lout, but she had agreed to marry him anyway. For that reason alone, Molly felt that she was stuck with him.

Now that she had some idea of his past, Molly could appreciate how her father had raised her. He had given her all the freedom that was taken from him, the freedom to make her own decisions rather than being told what to do. She had been free to make her mother happy and brush off her father's warnings, but now she wished that he had, just once, come right out and said something. The poison that polluted Frank's past had filtered down to her, and Molly was tainted, trapped in a bad marriage and too ashamed to end it. There had been too much independence and not enough honesty; the sins of the past were not completely reversed, only reshaped. Somewhere in all this, the trip, the memoirs, the meetings, was the cure that her father prescribed.

When she returned to the parlor, her mind a jumble, she found Rose sitting in an armchair with her hands twined around a handkerchief. The television was flickering in the room, but the ladies did not seem to be paying much heed to the voices and the canned laughter.

"I'm going to Booterstown, to the convent," Molly announced, breaking a tense silence.

"Go on, Rose," Mary goaded. "Go on."

"You'll be wanting me with you, Molly," Rose murmured softly, her hands wringing in a manic contortion.

"Let's wait and see how you feel in the morning," Molly said.

"I'll feel the same," Rose replied, a newfound strength in her voice.

Not sure what to say or do, Molly looked over at Mary, but the woman was averting her gaze. Following the woman's gaze, Molly spotted the porcelain serenity of Our Lady of Knock, beatific on top of the television set. Below the statue, a program seemed to hold Mary transfixed.

"The bad news is, there's only two parachutes," the television priest told the clergymen who filled the cabin of the doomed airplane. The laugh track rose to the intensity of loud snickers as the character paused for comic effect. He continued with his lines, explaining the contest that would award the parachutes to the two priests who were judged to be the greatest and most deserving.

One by one, the other stereotypical Irish clerics rose to speak, drawing laughs from the mechanical audience as they touched on implications of homosexuality, snobbishness and dull wits. "I got my housekeeper pregnant and forced her to leave the country," was one proposal for a lifetime's achievement. "Should I put that down?"

The lead actor puzzled, the audience laughed, and he spoke with sarcastic sincerity. "Uh, no, I don't think so, Father." The crowd roared with glee over the standard joke of the fornicating priest, the holy hypocrite who had become the object of mockery.

"Did I ask you before, Rose, about Mass on Sunday?" Molly said. While the canned television audience sniggered and laughed, the two elderly ladies in the parlor were neither smiling nor amused by the fictional antics.

"I haven't set foot in their church since I was rescued," she said, the bitterness fully alive after fifty years. The scrapbook was lingering on the table, and Rose picked it up with authority. "Read it. Out loud."

To appease a mentally unstable woman, Molly did as she was asked. "Last Days of a Laundry," she began with the headline from *The Irish Times*. The first paragraph meant nothing to an American woman who had no idea what a Magdalene laundry was. "'Approximately forty percent of the women who came here in the past were single women who became pregnant and were rejected by their families.' So this was a home for unwed mothers?"

"You see how our own people paint roses on nettles?" Rose grumbled. "You hear charity in it, don't you? Well, read on, and tell me if you find God's love there."

Continuing to skim the long article, Molly learned that the laundry building was being sold, that it was as austere as any Dickensian horror, and that the last few residents were still there, unwanted by their families. When she got to the phrase, 'Being in moral danger,' Rose interrupted again.

"What does our fine Irish journalist say about moral danger?" Rose seethed. "Being with child and unwanted, or so the nuns would say. Being a pretty girl, that was enough for them, but they'll not admit to it now."

After finishing the article, Molly did not know what to make of it. She was quite certain that her aunt had been living at home after her father finished school, because he had mentioned how they lived together in tight quarters. Molly was interested in orphanages, not homes for the unwed. Apparently, though, this must have been Rose's personal demon, and Molly had foolishly helped to release it. Having started something, she could not, in good conscience, drop the whole affair. Rose was too delicate to be cast adrift without another buoy to cling to.

"I'll take you with me, Rose, but only if you've made an appointment with a psychiatrist to deal with these issues," Molly said.

"It's too late for me," Rose said.

"That's my deal," Molly said, her arms folded across her chest.

Defeated, Rose got up from her chair and left the room in silence. Mary watched her go, a sense of great pity tugging down the corners of her mouth. "This was the closest she's come. I thought we might finally discover what broke her and get her pieced back together."

"Don't give up on her, Mary, not yet," Molly said. "It's two steps forward and one back, but if you stay with it she'll get into therapy and make rapid progress."

"I should have been more firm the first time she thought of it," Mary said. "Does she have enough time for the back steps, that's what worries me."

"My father ran out of time," Molly said, thinking out loud. "And I didn't help him when he asked."

11

In a display of juvenile petulance, Rose stayed in her room while Mary and Molly ate breakfast. Her temper tantrum did little more than reinforce Molly's impression of a woman who was mentally unhinged, traumatized by some past experiences and now refusing treatment to alleviate the condition. Molly was a surgical nurse, not a psychiatrist, and there was nothing that she could do for Rose, as much as she sincerely wanted to help.

The best solution was also the most painful. Someone, and that would be Mary, had to force Rose into therapy. Helping the woman to remain shut in was more cruel, in the long run, but it was the easier course for anyone who wanted peace and quiet, no conflict. If Rose were to be treated properly, there could be no peace.

Mary seemed to be wavering, happy that Molly's confidence had been a beacon to her sister-in-law. Like some kind of pied piper, Molly had played the right tune to catch Rose's ear and get her to follow, out of the house and into the mouth of her personal hell. A gap opened in the conversation and Molly reiterated her belief that psychiatric therapy would work wonders. She had seen a little of it in Frank, who took up gardening on his doctor's advice, to lift his gloomy moods with physical labor. Not that pulling weeds was a cure-all, but it helped a little. What would have helped the most was if Frank had opened his mouth, but Molly knew that silence was a fortress not easily breached.

Before making the short drive to the Sisters of Mercy convent, Molly sat down in her room, where the vigil candle continued to glow next to Frank's crypt. She had some preparations to make, since she was supposed to read her father's outline before seeing the location to be visited. After the fact, she studied his recollections of Carriglea Industrial School, where she found the same story of the apple lady that Mr. Treacy had related. There were very brief sentences that referred to stories that Pat Grady had shared, but other than that, all that remained was a list of names and addresses. Several of the men tallied had passed away since Frank began his roster, and there were several entries that had been lined through, with a date of death scribed in the left margin. Of those that remained, all had been invited to the Thursday wake and burial.

Turning to the Booterstown chapter, she saw her father's handwriting, large block letters that were alarming and intense. "Find Nuala's story," she read, Frank's last request of his daughter. What little information he had acquired was all written down, and Molly was disheartened when she found that very little was there. Apparently, her father had begun his search without ever telling anyone in his family, and he had died before he could find out where Nuala had gone. The clues that he left behind were aggravatingly vague.

Frank knew all along that his sister had been put away in St. Anne's Orphanage, which was located near University College Dublin, to do time until she, too, turned sixteen. She came home not quite right in the head, as the hazy image had always been displayed, and somehow along the way she disappeared. Molly was heartbroken to discover that her father had contacted a Dublin solicitor five years earlier, when he had begged her to go abroad. It must have been a last chance to see Nuala or meet her children, and Molly had let her father down so that she could preserve the façade of her strong marriage. He was trying to take her away back then, to give her a way out, but at the time, she was not ready to surrender to defeat.

Sitting on the train with Mr. Clancy, feeling ecstatic in a new suit of clothes and awash in freedom, Frank watched County Kilkenny fly by. The wretched life at St. Patrick's was fading into the distance, to be replaced with the joy of Carriglea Industrial School for Boys, a life that held much promise.

"Are you off on holiday, young man?" a gentle matron asked Frank.

Going on holiday meant going away, as far as Frank had experienced. He was going away, and he answered honestly. "Yes, ma'am. I'm going to a new school."

His fellow passenger in the compartment laughed as if she were charmed by his fair features or the dark color of his wool jacket. "Would you like a damson?" she offered, reaching into the paper sack that she held on her lap.

"Go on, take one," Clancy grumbled from behind his newspaper. "It's something to eat. It's fruit."

Having never before seen a plum, Frank bit into it carefully, dazzled by the sweetness and the river of juice that flowed into his mouth. Here was a delectable tidbit that must have been reserved for the rich boys, the outside boys who had parents and a home and a dog named Toby. Devouring one, he greedily accepted another, and then a third.

"You're fond of them, then," the old lady marveled. "My grandson could eat a bushel full."

Satisfied, his belly full, Frank sat back and looked out of the window. It was grand to be ten years old, to be going off to secondary school for a fine education. Best of all, he was going to be much closer to home, and closer to Nuala, even closer than his mother and Uncle Joe. Thinking of his sister, he felt sorry for her, because she had to stay at the same convent and miss out on the thrill of a train ride, and the absolute glory of leaving one place to go to someplace better.

After a very long walk in the hot September sun, his feet blistered in his new sandals, Frank arrived at Carriglea's imposing Georgian façade. Much to his surprise, Mr. Clancy did not take him into the parlor, but went around the back to the schoolyard. There, Frank was ushered into a paradise of boys at play. Hurling and general horseplay filled the space, along with the cacophony of voices mixed with the sound of balls being hit against the wall. The yard at St. Patrick's had always been eerily quiet. A man who said he was Brother Comerford strode over and shook Frank's hand, welcoming him as one adult to another. Frank felt his spirits soar; he was truly going to be happy here.

At St. Anne's, the scores of girls that filled two dormitory rooms bathed in distinct age groups, so that the younger ones were never exposed to the wonders of puberty until they reached that milestone. At the age of ten, the first changes began, much to the humiliation of the first young lady to develop tiny breasts. By the time a girl became a senior, she did not necessarily understand what was happening to her body, but she could determine that it happened to everyone else, and such safety in numbers was consoling.

Backed up against one wall of the senior dormitory was the linen press, an enormous cabinet that held the clean bed linen for seventy-five cots. On a special shelf, accessed only by the older girls and the infirmary nurse, lay the bundles of rags that were used for mysterious purposes that all were too embarrassed to define. It was the object of hushed whispers that the nuns and the senior monitor Julia were constantly trying to stop, adding to the intense curiosity that enveloped the girls who were approaching that certain age.

"It's the curse," was as much as anyone would say. "You'll get it, too, just wait, and you'll wish you didn't."

There was something unusual involved, because a girl experiencing the curse was not allowed to bathe, having to make do with a washing up. Nuala had heard rumors of bleeding in relation to this peculiar curse, but she had bled plenty when the dental students came in and ripped out everyone's baby teeth when she was eight. Father McNulty had hemmed and hawed, but he did tell Nuala that the woman's curse was part of Eve's punishment that had been passed on to her daughters, like the pain of childbirth, but beyond that he did not elaborate. He slapped her for even asking, so she knew that it was quite an evil thing, and not a subject for discussion.

Like all new arrivals, the one christened 'Sarah' by the Mother Superior was swamped by the other girls when she first appeared in the recreation yard. She possessed news that all craved, a glimpse of the life that had been left behind. Talking of the outside world was forbidden, but the tens and elevens had found that a game of tag, or anything that involved running from one person to another, provided an

188

opportunity to pass on brief snatches of gossip. Sometimes, if things fell into place, they could slip in a word or two in the course of their normal play-acting, and 'Sarah' was an eager participant.

"The outside girls go to the convent school, but we don't see them," Nuala explained the ropes on a warm September afternoon. "We're not good enough to be with them, not us."

"But Lilith is more special than the rest of us," 'Faith' continued. "We're nothing, but Lilith is Father McNulty's helper. She's going to be a missionary nun."

Under the strict regimen of both McNulty and Reverend Mother Laurentia, Nuala began to buckle and break down in tears over nothing. She was expected to be smarter in every subject, from catechism to mathematics. The most pious girl, the most self-sacrificing girl, the most devout girl in Booterstown, she cried herself to sleep almost every night, even if Julia tore off the sheets and caned her bare bottom to make her stop. The only minutes of the day that were happy were those spent at play, and they were cherished to a degree that was out of proportion. The rest of the day, her face was pinched into a frown, glowering and brooding.

Over the course of a few days, it was learned that 'Sarah' was given up to the nuns by parents who were too poor to keep her. Floundering in abject poverty, her mother had done all that she could to appear neglectful, to get the attention of the parish priest so that the children could be placed in what was thought to be paradise. Her father described a cozy home, with breakfast, dinner and tea served every day without fail, and a school that would provide a real education. 'Sarah' was incarcerated on the day that the inspectors came, an event that the nuns were regularly warned about, and the lovely china plates and piles of toys that greeted her were straight out of heaven. The minute that the inspectors left, the toys were stored away and the china plates disappeared. Confused, unhappy, she begged to be sent home, but the nuns only increased their efforts to rein in her free spirit. It became a tug of wills, with 'Sarah' chafing under the restrictions, but she was determined to stand up for herself no matter how often Nuala warned her about the consequences.

"I renounce forever Satan, his pomps and works," the steely-eyed Sister Ursula led her charges in evening prayers. Walking up and down the aisle between the center rows of cots, the thud of her heavy shoes on the wooden floor had an ominous quality that vibrated through every girl, sending ripples of fear into seventy-five hearts. The quivering of trembling children mingled with the quake of floorboards until Nuala imagined that she was on a ship, tossed by enormous waves. If she stretched out her foot, she would have been able to touch 'Sarah', who was laying face down at the head of the line, her arms outstretched in penance for cursing the holy

name of Jesus. The nun's skirt brushed the victim's arms as Sister paced, stepping on a hand if 'Sarah' dared to let her weary arms touch the floor.

For forty-five minutes, Sister Ursula intoned one prayer after another, stalking along the columns, while 'Sarah' struggled to maintain her pose of penance. "I deliver and consecrate to thee, as thy slave, my body and my soul," the girls prayed along, with one girl's sobs providing a horrifying backdrop, "for the greater glory of God."

Constant prayer and endless repetition was meant to drill the orphans into shape, to erase forever the wicked attributes that came their way because they were female. 'Sarah' cracked quickly, begging for forgiveness thirty minutes into her punishment, and hysterically apologetic at the end of the session. "Through my fault, through my fault, through my most grievous fault," she wailed repeatedly, admitting to every sin if it would only make the nun stop.

A loud handclap announced the moment to climb into bed, and the children obeyed. For a long minute, Sister Ursula stood at 'Sarah's' head, the toes of her black shoes in line with the girl's eyes. "You are forgiven," was spoken at last, and 'Sarah' flew to her bed and bawled into the pillow. Nuala burrowed under the covers, her thumb jammed tightly into her mouth. It was strictly forbidden to get out of bed, a violation of the rules to talk at night.

McNulty applied his leather belt to Nuala if she went to the infirmary instead of the chapel, so that she quickly learned to ignore the scratch of bronchitis that plagued her during the winter, and she shook off the fevers that accompanied a summer cold, measles, and mumps. When an attack of bronchitis began to torment her after Christmas, she focused on his radiant face, the way that his hair curled up on the back of his neck, as he kissed the stole while dressing for Mass. Watching his dull brown eyes as he mindlessly picked up the chalice took her mind off her endless rasping and her upset stomach.

Friday was always a fast day, and that helped to control the vomiting that typically followed an intense coughing spell. Unfortunately, the constant hacking had kept her awake most of the night, and she was so sleepy that she dozed off during the noon rosary. Waking with a start as the last Glory Be was intoned, she knew that there would be a price to pay that night, on top of the price she had already paid before morning Mass.

All the girls lined up for their session with the leather strap, leaning over the filthy tub to watch the dirty water slowly drain away. Sister Ursula walked the circuit, doling out one hard lash without bothering to name an infraction. When she reached Nuala, she paused, sighed sadly and bemoaned the fact that another group of children had left childhood behind, *and now she found herself in a room filled with God's most reviled creatures, a group of women.*

"Enticing men with the curves of your women's bodies," she carried on, her tone as fiery as hell's fury. "The day is coming when you shall be released from the safety of this convent, outside of the protection of our walls. Beware of cosmetics, and avoid clothing that is meant to attract and beguile. Stay away from boys. Don't ever let a boy touch you. The good Sisters cannot protect you forever from sin. Soon, you will be responsible for the salvation of your soul, and when that time comes, remember my words."

The leather strap landed across the back of Nuala's thighs as Sister Ursula warned the other girls about the importance of obedience, unquestioning and blind faith, and the glories of passive submission to a higher being. Nuala felt the words come into her ears, but they were only sounds that clogged her head, like a foreign language that had no meaning. "I do this because I love you, my child," the nun said.

The result of two beatings in one day left Nuala with welts from her shoulders to her knees, too painful to lie on her back in bed. The first flogging had been severe, given by Father McNulty as a form of penance following her heartfelt confession. She did not want to be a missionary any more; she did not want to go with him to Africa, just the two of them, to minister to the black people. He called it a rejection of God's love, a personal affront to a priest, and an act so selfish that he was disgusted with her. If she had not pleaded with him for mercy, begging for a chance to pray and ask God for guidance, she truly believed that McNulty would have beaten her to death.

"I've been sick, Father," she had sobbed, cowering at his feet. "Please, please forgive me."

"After all I have done for you," he had said, his face purple with rage, "and now you do not want to share a life of devotion? Either you join me, or I will cast you aside, plucked out because you have offended Our Lord."

While he intoned the Latin service for the nuns, Nuala was made to ponder his terrifying threats. Only as an oblate could she attend to him before Mass, and only as an oblate could she play with Sister Mary. Forced to meditate through the Sisters' early Mass, she had contemplated her future while Sister Mary sat in a chair and watched the wavering novice. When McNulty returned to the sacristy after Mass, Nuala had crawled to him on her knees.

When Nuala was called down to the Mother Superior's parlor, she thought nothing of it. At least once a year she was invited to tea, one time with Sister Ursula's sister, the missionary from South Africa, and she had met with a Benedictine nun from the Congo only a few months before. That had been a fascinating conversation, and Nuala was hoping that today's session was going to be more of the same.

This time, however, it was Matron who was waiting for Nuala, and the twelve-year-old girl feared that her visit to the parlor meant trouble.

Despite the case of bronchitis that had hit her two days ago, Nuala had continued to follow routine, terrified of upsetting Father McNulty. She had refused Matron's order to go to the infirmary, thinking that the chaplain took precedence over the school's nurse. Taking note of Reverend Mother Laurentia's stern visage and Matron's cold stare, Nuala was afraid that her comprehension of the hierarchy was inaccurate.

Arriving in the parlor, she was immediately escorted to the infirmary, where a bed had been curtained off in the farthest corner. Matron was not at all angry, much to Nuala's relief, and she was her usual reserved self as she helped Nuala into a nightdress and instructed the girl to lie down and wait.

"We have had several girls coming down with appendicitis recently," Matron said. "Doctor O'Connor has come to examine everyone."

Because it was work done for the holy Sisters, Dr. O'Connor charged a reduced fee, and Sister Ursula claimed that he reduced the quality of his services in equal measure. He was obviously in a great hurry when he appeared behind the curtain with Matron, and his manner was rough and brusque as he jammed his fingers into Nuala's insides, from the bottom, and pressed down hard on her abdomen.

195

"Perforated?" Matron tentatively quizzed, while the physician mumbled a curse under his breath.

"Holy Mother of God," he growled, pushing his fingers through Nuala's stomach again, his face compressed into an angry frown. "How old is this one?"

"Twelve, Doctor," Matron responded promptly. "Thirteen in September."

"When was your last period?" he barked at Nuala.

"I'm sorry, sir," Nuala began to blubber, scared into incoherency. "I don't understand."

The nurse recognized a bad case of fright, and she moved closer to Nuala, to stand at her side and take her hand. "She hasn't begun to menstruate yet," Matron said, casting a tender smile at Nuala to relieve a little anxiety.

"No?" Nuala asked, trying to control sobs of pain from Doctor O'Connor's internal examination.

"I'd like to know what kind of children's home these nuns are running," the doctor said, but he stormed off before Nuala could discover the answer. Matron took off right behind him, fleeing from the sad truth and leaving Nuala alone behind the screen.

With nothing else to do, she looked up at the high ceiling, her eyes sliding down the long cord of the light fixtures from top to bottom. No one came for a long time, and when she simply had to go to the toilet, Nuala took a chance and got up. When she returned from the yard, there was still no one there, and she crawled under the bed to poke her fingers through the bed slats, stabbing at the mattress and pretending that she was someplace else.

Over the course of the past four years, the orphan girls heard rumors about the occasional convent student being quietly transferred to another school, and it was always the girl's father who made the excuses. "Mary would be happier at St. Helen's," or "Maeve promises to be a better pupil if I send her to the Sisters of Charity" were said to be the excuses, in the hope that the Mother Superior would understand without the need for specifics.

The outside girls were often heard whispering about the chaplain at St. Anne's, warning new pupils to steer clear. Siblings passed stories between them, and the schoolgirls often snickered at Father McNulty behind his back. No one would ever think to speak openly, not when it involved disparaging a priest. Instead, all those who were able to avoid the clergyman walked around the problem. The orphan girls were dependent on Mother Superior's vigilance, but she was blinded by unquestioning faith.

The chatter went on for months, until Monsignor Fitzgerald started showing up at the convent to have private meetings with Mother Superior. Nuala detected a slight change in Father McNulty, a new droop to his shoulders and an absent look in his eye, but she never understood what he meant when he said he had confessed everything and his soul remained

197

troubled. *Of course he confessed; everyone went to confession every Saturday without fail and she did not expect a priest to be any different from any other Catholic in Ireland.*

Nuala did not know the Bible well enough to follow along when the priest spoke of Deuteronomy and the laws of Moses, of trials by fire and enduring penance. He told Nuala she would have to wash away her sins, scrub her soul until it was white as snow. Maybe Father McNulty had been tippling the communion wine. He had babbled on so, making no sense whatsoever.

12

"Do I pass the course, Professor?" Molly's throaty whisper tickled Eoin's ear.

He stared up at the acoustic tiles, his body relaxed in rapturous fatigue. "You've taken all A-levels," he said, the bliss of lust satisfied playing on his lips. "I can't believe you did this. My secret fantasy made real."

"You were never seduced by a student who needed a good grade?" she teased him. "Am I your first, Professor MacNeill?"

"First and best, Miss Devoy," he said, pulling her closer to him. "I hope you take all my courses and come to me for tutoring every day."

With the convent so close to University College, Molly had agreed to meet Eoin at his office. He wanted to show her where he worked, just as much as he wanted to show off his prize to whichever of his colleagues was around for the summer term. No one had ever judged him handsome, but he had a very attractive lady on his arm these days, and the boost to his ego was tremendous. Introducing Molly Devoy from Chicago was as gratifying as making love on the floor of his humdrum office.

"What are all these papers?" he asked, coming down to earth as he put his pants back on.

"Today's assignment, Professor," she said. "My dad put together these packets for each place that I go to. Like the day I met you, he had a few notes written out for my drive through the Liberties. I finally looked over the material from Kilkenny and Dun Laoghaire. Here, this is my father when he was an altar boy at St. Patrick's."

The envelope was spilled out onto the desk, and Eoin picked up the yellowed snapshots, recognizing a style of dress that matched his parents' era. The boys in the picture wore wool shorts that covered their knees, wool stockings that disappeared under the hem of the trousers, and wool jackets that defined the cut of the early Thirties, a time of great poverty in an impoverished nation.

"These are the actors in the school play, the same photo that Mr. Treacy had." Molly pointed to her father again. "Oh, gosh, I remember another story, it must have been this play that Dad talked about. See this boy with the crepe moustache? He was so nervous with stage fright that he had to run outside between acts to throw up, and his moustache fell off and landed in his dinner. The character showed up for the second act clean-shaven."

"Was everything that he told you a happy, a good memory?" Eoin asked, studying a picture of Frank with a schoolmate. Both boys were smiling.

Molly shrugged. "He wants me to listen to his old boys and decide for myself. What I've heard so far sounds like a typical experience in an all boys' school. My dad was like that, wanting me to think for myself and reach my own conclusions."

"Sounds like a bit of residue from his orphanage days. The adults would have done all the decision making for the children, and never have given them any choices. I'm amazed that your father was able to survive, let alone excel, in the real world. How can anyone go from one day to the next without being able to think and reason, to know how to choose A instead of B?"

"You join the army and your commanding officer does it for you," Molly said. "My father found that out when he signed on after Pearl Harbor. That's when he noticed how he was, and he changed himself."

"The resilience of the human spirit," Eoin said. "We are resilient, aren't we? Do you realize what an enormous leap your father made? Emigrating was a wise idea for a man with his drive and determination. He never could have gotten very far under our system, with the old prejudices intact."

"Because of the industrial school thing?"

"In part, but the fact that he lived on James Street would have crippled him. Think of the worst ghetto in Chicago, and imagine some desperately poor young man from that street turning up at the hospital, looking for a job. Where do you think of putting him? In the casualty ward treating patients, or mopping floors?"

"So my father was Irish white trash?"

"Is that what you call them?" Eoin asked. "Dermot's generation doesn't see it at all, not after the Celtic Tiger prowled our streets. My grandchildren are unlikely to ever hear of the sort of class system that we kept after the British left. Poor boys did not become barristers, and rich idiots rose to power. Well, some things don't change."

"It's sad that everyone has been so ashamed to speak of the orphanages. History should be preserved, oral history at least if no one writes this stuff down."

"Then tell your father's story. Write it all down, get it published, send it to your local newspaper as a human interest piece. He sent you here for a reason; maybe that's it."

"He wanted me to find all this out, but why didn't he just tell me? I heard all about his experiences in the war, and about going to college on the G.I. Bill. Why not just tell me about the trial and the orphanage and the industrial school?"

"Because he was Irish, Molly. You'll never find a television program featuring Irish families airing their family secrets for all the neighbors to hear. It's easier not to talk about it."

"I've never seen this before," Molly said. She had opened the Booterstown portfolio, and a photograph tumbled out.

"What a pretty little thing. Must be a First Communion portrait."

The image was one of angelic innocence, with Nuala's eyes gazing serenely at her folded hands encased in spotless white gloves. Her fair complexion was softened further by the pure white of her elaborate dress and the cloud of veil that floated around her strawberry blond hair. Someone had penciled in the name 'Nuala Devoy'.

He held the picture next to Molly's face and noted the resemblance, although Molly was more broad across the cheekbones in a reflection of some Slavic inheritance. Returning the picture to the envelope, he imagined Molly's grandmother scrounging for pennies to buy the dress and the veil, then bringing them to the orphanage and not being allowed to see her child in all her finery. All Maire would get was an image in black and white, lifeless. The very idea saddened him, and he could keep it to himself, but he had found out some information that he needed to share with Molly and that would be far more depressing than contemplating the origin of a photograph.

"I've been working on a project with a good friend of mine in the social sciences, examining the repercussions of the convent work programs," Eoin said. "My line is the economics of the slave labor that was employed, and she looks at the people involved."

"Do I need to hear this?"

"Molly, if someone asked to tour an old Southern plantation, would you tell them all about slavery if they had never heard of it?"

"Well, of course I would."

"Wait, that's too far in the past." He pondered carefully, mentally reviewing the worst of American history. "Let's say that

203

we were watching a documentary about school segregation in the American south, and newsreel footage came on, showing your mother screaming and spitting at the black children. Would you hop up and say, look, there's my mother, isn't she wonderful to curse them?"

The slight frown that settled around Molly's eyes told him that he had found the right place for a comparison. Church and State were kept apart in America, to a degree that Eoin found to border on fanatic hysteria. With that in mind, he understood that Molly could not appreciate the atmosphere that polluted Ireland when the nation was struggling to find its bearings. Racial intolerance and sexual repression seemed to spring from the same filthy stream, running with hatred and a greed for power and dominance over others.

"I think I see what you mean," she finally answered.

"Later today, if something similar should happen, I won't leap to my feet and shout, look, there's my father and all his contemporaries, aren't they grand when they spit on the women. When I was a little boy, Molly, that's the world I saw walking past the butcher shop every day. I accepted it because I didn't know anything else."

"How could you know any better when you were little?"

"Did you read the plaque at Glasnevin Cemetery?"

"The women from the laundry? Was there a fire or something?"

"When the word got out that the nuns had over one hundred laundry girls buried in unmarked graves, they were swamped by relatives who had sisters and aunts put away, women they never saw again. These were people, Molly, who had no idea what had happened to their girls. The nuns didn't even know the names of all the women who were buried on their property."

"Are you trying to tell me that my aunt is part of a big pile of ashes in a cemetery?" Molly asked. "What was going on, some kind of death camp, like a Catholic Auschwitz?"

"No, I mean, it is possible that your aunt ended her life as a laundry girl, sent to the laundry from the orphanage and disappearing into the gulag."

"She was home when my dad started working, I'm sure of it."

"Well then, the story won't be so grim as I was making it," he said. "I was afraid that we might hear the worst, and I wanted you to know what happened. You can probably expect more of the same as your father's situation at St. Patrick's."

She returned to the miscellaneous bits of paper that comprised her father's records, finding a bundle of letters and postcards that were tied together with bits of faded ribbon. Able to mentally travel to a better time, Molly read the messages on the backs of the postcards that provided a timeline to her parents and their annual vacations. Greeting from the Grand Canyon had been included her oldest brother Matt, while Niagara Falls had been seen by Matt and Mark. Lake Geneva, Wisconsin, and the Wisconsin Dells played host to Matt, Mark and Lucas, while Las Vegas, Nevada was for adults only.

"Romantic get-away?" Eoin asked, trying to make as many light-hearted remarks as possible to keep Molly's spirits up.

"My brother John had to come from somewhere, and I sure wasn't dropped by the stork," Molly said.

She thumbed through a pile of birth announcements, all names that meant nothing to her. Eoin noticed that there was nothing in the collection that included Molly, her birth coming after her grandmother's death. All the family stories that would have been passed down from one generation to the next were lost, along with traditions and holiday recipes and all the small details that connected families. Who could say if the stress of separation from her children had damaged Maire, shortened her life, or if it was only a simple case of poverty and deprivation taking its toll.

Several letters from son to mother were put aside unopened, the contents expected to be too personal for Molly or Eoin to read. She sorted through them, looking at the same return address from Illinois, making a quiet and wistful comment about her father taking care of his mother until the day she died.

"Who was Peter Benedetti from the American Embassy in Dublin?" Eoin asked nonchalantly, waving a yellowed envelope. "It's addressed to your father in care of the GPO."

The old paper was cracking in the creases, and Molly had to slow her frantic pace to flatten the sheet. "This is weird," she mumbled. "Dear Mr. Devoy, I have in hand, blah, blah, blah, commendable desire to serve in the United States Army. I am writing to you in regard to a woman who may be related to you, and I am taking the liberty of asking you some very personal questions. Are you possibly related to, or do you know where I might find an orphan named Nuala Devoy?"

"What's the date of the letter?" Eoin asked.

"1941," Molly looked up at Eoin, her jaw slack. Returning to the old letter, she read on. "Eoin, she had a sweetheart, listen to this. I love her with all my heart, and I cannot get her out of my mind. She is everything to me. Took her for granted, took advantage of her innocence, and he says that she disappeared three years ago. Can you tell her that Pete loves her, and that he wants to get married more than anything?"

"How very peculiar. She was being courted and she vanished into thin air," Eoin said.

"Here's another one," Molly said with glee. "Where is Rathmines?"

"South of the river. This one must have had some money."

"Irishmen are so much more poetic when they write of love," Molly said, paying a sincere compliment that was directed at Eoin. "You are my heart and I am your soul. We are one person, incomplete when we are apart, yearning to become one flesh, longing to share God's love in service to Our Lord."

"We are famous for our literary traditions," Eoin bragged.

His façade remained perfectly intact, without so much as a crack. Nuala Devoy had left the orphanage and messed about with boys, and all that Eoin could think of was an anecdote that Mairead O'Meara had shared with him when they were compiling their notes for the research paper. What she had told him was much more than he wanted Molly to know.

There had been so many girls put away, and all for the heinous crime of having a boyfriend, of looking at a boy, of being looked at by a boy. What an offense it had been, to be happy and carefree, to be young and pretty. It was so perverted that he could not bring himself to tell Molly that her young and pretty aunt might have been incarcerated for the crime of being sexually attractive, the way that God made her through no fault of her own.

"So, she was confined to the laundry, and she'd be there today if her brother hadn't gone chasing all over Dublin looking for her," Mairead had said. "The nuns gave him the runaround for three years, trying to hold on to the girl because they thought she needed to be saved from sin."

Matron came back at dinnertime, her cheeks streaked with tears. "I am so sorry, little one," she said repeatedly, feeding Nuala like a baby. The thick slice of bread, soaked in milk and sprinkled with sugar, was a disgusting concoction that Nuala hated, but she had to eat it because she was in the infirmary and that was all that there was. She choked down each spoonful, only to begin coughing again as her throat and lungs tickled into a rasping bark. "Doctor prescribed some medicine for you. It will take away the pain."

Nuala figured out what was happening then. She was going to die, judging by Matron's sad face, and no one wanted to tell her the truth. She had been praying for years, begging her father in heaven to rescue her, and surely he was making good on her pleas. Taking the bitter dose, Nuala lay back and prepared to meet God and her daddy again.

Throughout the night, Nuala's sleep was tormented by demons and monsters, frightening dreams that she could not wake from. The nurse hovered over the bed only to float away, and later Reverend Mother Laurentia fluttered around, but she looked like an angel in Nuala's fevered mind. Then Nuala began to fly, like a bird she rose towards the ceiling, her arms outstretched as her nightdress wings caught the warm breeze that blew off the shore. From the sky she fell, to find that small dogs were biting her legs while Doctor O'Connor put his fingers inside her, and she cried out in pain. She called for her mother, but her mother did not come, and when she tried to shout out for her father, her throat seemed to shut up tight and she could not speak.

Hacking and wheezing, Nuala woke from her narcotic slumber, disappointed to find that she was still in her bed in the infirmary. She looked up, but the cracks in the ceiling were missing, and the lights were arranged in a different pattern than the one she knew so well. Afraid that she had wandered during the night and gotten into the wrong bed, she tried to get up, but the bed sheets were tucked in so tightly that she could not budge. Agitated, her coughing started anew, a deep rasp that made her ribs ache.

From far across the room, she heard a woman screaming in pain while another woman spoke in a strange, almost singing way. Disoriented, Nuala began to wonder if she was dead after all, and transported to Purgatory because she was a naughty orphan girl and not a worthwhile outside girl. The noise that emanated from the distance was frightening, not like any sound she had ever heard before, and Nuala accepted the possibility that she was actually in hell.

No one came when she called for the nurse, but then, it would have been difficult for anyone to hear her small voice over the wailing that roiled the air. The screaming brought to mind the pain that Nuala had experienced when her teeth were pulled, and the possibility of that happening again filled her with dread. She battled against the bed sheets, squirming and wriggling in an attempt to escape, to run to the chapel and hide under a pew until the dentists were gone.

With a start, she remembered that she had her important duties with Father McNulty to see to, and that thought added to her agitation. Being late would mean punishment, floggings for a week, and Nuala began to cry, begging someone to help her. The only response to her entreaties was more caterwauling from the mysterious suffering woman, and Nuala wondered if she was even at the orphanage any more. Maybe she was supposed to lie back and wait for St. Peter to send for her, or maybe this was where she was to relax before standing at the Throne of Judgment. Reverend Mother's upholstery was comfortable, like the bed, and her parlor was warm, like the infirmary, and Nuala pictured God's sitting room, where heaven-bound souls had to wait for their turn to see Him. With her brain swirling in a fog, she fell back to sleep.

Before the sun rose, the Mother Superior turned to an old friend for advice. "What am I to do, Monica?" she moaned, sitting in the austere cell of Sister Monica. "Have I failed?"

"Have you prayed for guidance?"

"For hours, Monica, I have prayed for hours. I cannot see how she can be prepared for a life as a religious now. It is impossible."

"You are too hasty. We must ask God for a sign, if he still calls her to serve Him. The need is great in Africa and China, in India and Asia, far away from Ireland. Away from Ireland, taking this scandal with her, leaving behind an institution that is cleansed of its sin. If the Lord still calls Lilith, He will show us that her soul is pure though her body has been defiled."

The best solution was always the simplest, and transporting the shame to a foreign land was a brilliant strategy, and one that melded perfectly with earlier plans. It was unlikely that the girl would ever find out what had happened, particularly if she went from Booterstown to the Benedictine Mother House in Connemara. If she did figure things out, it would not matter once she was ministering to the wretches of the Congo. Keeping 'Lilith' in a state of ignorance was going to be close to impossible, but it had to be done.

"What would you do in my place, Monica?" she asked.

"My clouded eyes no longer see, and I must rely on Ursula's opinions, which I respect. She has praised the girl's lace making. Do you find her skilled?"

"She will be hard to replace, not only because of a talent but she works quickly. I could put her with Sister Perpetua, in the crochet room. Those girls have been with us for a long time, and they keep to their prayers and devotions."

"What is to be done for her education? Has she completed her first level?" Monica asked.

"You have an idea, Monica, I have never seen you so animated."

"My idea is a selfish one," the ancient woman said. "My greatest love was teaching, until it was lost to me in blindness. Send her to me, as you once came to me, and I will teach her from memory. I do not need to see, not when the knowledge is stored in my mind. I have my books with me; mathematics, science, literature, it is all here."

212

"Can this be the sign that I pray for?" the Mother Superior said with relief. "She has been looked on as an oblate, and only as an oblate can she enter our convent."

"Sister Perpetua can be relied on, and taken into your confidence about our unfortunate incident," Monica suggested. "If we can keep her away from the concerns of the flesh and fill her with spiritual sustenance, she can follow the path that you once walked."

"Hard work and prayer, Monica; she will be given to God. Do you see me in her?"

"I will not live to see it, Laurentia, but when you are my age, you will entertain a Mother Superior from a foreign land who will come back here to thank you for all that you did. She has the fire that burns in you yet, and she will do great things one day."

"When we give her to our colleagues at Kylemore Abbey, they will receive a woman who is whole."

"Then we shall set off on this course without wavering. We shall never speak of this again."

With subtle coercion, Sister Monica sought to absolve her sin. There had been a cry from the little girl and the retired nun had heard it when she listened in at the door of the sacristy, to be sure that her replacement was performing her duties properly. Though able to see little more than light and shadows, Sister Monica's hearing was acute, and she was aware that the odd sounds and hushed words were not being

213

sighed in preparation for offering the Mass. The cry was one of fear, one of pain, but a lifetime of indoctrination prevented the nun from questioning or speaking out against a priest.

Making entreaties to God had been Sister's solution, while her conscience warned her that her actions were needed. Recognizing her culpability in the girl's debasement, she prayed for a path to forgiveness, and the solution presented itself to her. The best, most perfect life that any girl could have was that of a holy nun, and by giving that life to 'Lilith', Sister Monica tendered her apology for failing the child. Through a career of prayer and service to God, 'Lilith' would be sure to enter into heaven, and that was going to be Sister Monica's gift. Together, they would sacrifice, fast and pray, work without tiring and suffer with joy, to save 'Lilith' and do penance for a very great sin.

13

Loud shouting woke Nuala again, with a racket so scary that she pulled the blankets over her head to hide. As the noise washed over her, she pondered and puzzled, coming to grips with the possibility that she was in the waiting room of hell. She had been told often that she was a sinner and a disappointment to God, so it was logical to conclude that God did not want her either. The nervous jittering that accompanied her dark thoughts brought on more hacking, but this time someone came. The white robed figure looked frightening, her face a mask of anger and exasperation. Grabbing Nuala by the nose, she yanked the girl's mouth open, tossed down a spoonful of medicine, and slipped out behind the curtain again.

Nuns in hell became the concept that Nuala started to consider, but her eyes were suddenly too heavy to remain open. She began to float above the bed, to hover near the dangling lights, where her chest did not hurt from coughing anymore. Filled with peace, serene and warm, her mind saw babies, her cousins' little newborns, and she felt their warm, soft bodies in her arms, mouths gaping as they cried for their mothers.

"It is time, Lilith," came an old woman's voice through a fog of warm mist. "The final test is at hand."

Opening her sleepy eyes, Nuala focused on the frightening cataracts that blinded Sister Monica, the iris of the left eye almost completely white and the right one a cloudy gray. "Have I missed Mass?" Nuala tried to rise. "Father McNulty will be angry."

"That is all past, Lilith," Sister Monica said, speaking softly. "Do you know who I am?"

Every single girl in the orphanage knew who Sister Monica was, because she liked to stumble through the corridors and poke her head into the classrooms. Her white eyes and her unseeing stare were the stuff of many a girl's nightmares. "You are Sister Monica," Nuala replied, shrinking away from the bony hand that reached towards her.

"Do you see the tray at the foot of your bed? I have brought you your dinner. Go on, move it to your lap and eat while I talk to you."

She always did as she was told, and Nuala consumed the sticky mass of stir-about and the dry bread. The menu helped to restore Nuala's sense of place, because it was the same food, served on the same tin plates that she knew from the orphanage.

216

"You are here to wash away all traces of your sins," the nun said. "You are here to pray, to seek God's forgiveness through penance and prayer, to break your will. At the end of your trial, you will be ready to join the Benedictine Sisters, to become a Bride of Christ, one of my sisters, a sister to all of the religious all over the world."

A smattering of coughing was given in reply as Nuala choked on her tea. She did not want to be a nun at all; she wanted to go home. Sister's pronouncement brought the tears tumbling down Nuala's cheeks.

"Father McNulty has been sent on another mission by his bishop," Sister Monica said. "You are on a new mission as well. Put away all childish things, Lilith, and together we will walk into God's holy light."

Torn from her mother and now from her priest, Nuala began to sob uncontrollably with a crushing sorrow. Everything that she had asked for was given in its opposite form, as if God were half-deaf or entirely contrary. "I want my mammy," she bawled, as she had wailed on the last days of March all those years ago.

"Our Lady is your mother, and to have her, you must reach up to heaven," Sister preached. "Do you not wish to please our Lord by honoring His mother?"

"Yes, Sister," Nuala said.

"Women are lustful, they are the source of original sin that is washed away in baptism. Women are temptresses,

217

enticing men to sin, corrupting their souls. You are a woman, Lilith, you are sinful, and if you wish to enter into the Kingdom of Heaven, you must repent. Do you wish to repent of all your sins, to renounce Satan and all his works?"

"Yes, Sister."

Apparently satisfied, Sister Monica nodded her head and backed out, exiting behind the curtain. Like a magician's trick, another nun appeared instantly, a different person who was all suppressed rage in contrast to Monica's beneficence.

Pulled out of bed roughly, Nuala was stripped to her knickers by a stern faced woman who radiated age but was not very old at all. "You are One Hundred Twenty. Don't forget it," she stated coldly.

Taking a strip of calico, she wrapped it around Nuala's chest and tied it tightly under the girl's left arm, flattening Nuala's small breasts. The discomfort and pain made Nuala wince and fidget, drawing a sharp crack on the skull from Sister's heavy gold wedding band, the emblem of a Bride of Christ.

A shapeless dress of gray wool was dropped over Nuala's head, the voluminous fabric falling to her ankles. Handed a pair of thick, heavy stockings, she stood for a time, uncomprehending, and Sister hit her again. The black hose was swiftly tugged onto two spindly legs. The long plait of strawberry blond hair was tucked into a white cap, and Sister completed the outfit by attaching a cape over Nuala's shoulders, the hem reaching nearly to her wrists. Everything was too big, adult proportions, when Nuala was undersized for a twelve-year-old.

"Put on your shoes and follow me," Sister Perpetua said. "We observe silence at all times. When you speak, it is because you are praying or responding to a Sister. Is that clear, One Hundred Twenty?"

"Yes, Sister," Nuala answered, thoroughly confused by everything that was happening.

As they walked through the gloomy corridor, Nuala's head spun around in circles, taking in holy pictures that she had never seen before. Bewilderment returned, as Nuala once again lost her bearings in a place that appeared to be the Booterstown orphanage but was not quite as it had been before she fell asleep. A dim sound of machinery was growing ever louder as she walked along behind the nun, following meekly into the economic engine of the Sisters of Mercy, the industrial and moneymaking center of the enormous complex.

Sister opened a door and stood to one side, allowing Nuala to pass. The girl looked into the room and saw a long table, around which were sitting eighteen women, mindlessly working crochet hooks. Given a sharp push, Nuala stumbled in, turning her head and discovering a desk on a riser, as if this were a long and narrow classroom and the teacher presided from its head. A woman in an ugly black dress was sitting at the side of the desk, an open Bible on her lap. Nuala stared at her, and the lady stared back, but her eyes were empty, devoid of any human emotion.

Lining the walls were straight-backed chairs, each one placed near a window where the light was best. At each spot sat a very old woman, vision clearly impaired with age, and at each place the women were connecting crocheted emblems into tablecloths. Nuala observed their hands, which were gnarled and deformed, the result of years of hard, physical work and endless crocheting. She was so involved in studying the dreadful scene that she did not even notice when the woman in black guided her to a place at the table and put a crochet hook in her hand.

To her left was another dead-eyed being in black, her crochet hook bobbing steadily. Turning to her right, Nuala had the company of a washed out hag, her face without expression as her fingers twirled the thread into a lace rose. Eyes wide with fright, Nuala's gaze went from one laborer to the next, circling the table until her vision fell upon Sister Perpetua, seated now at the desk with the open Bible, and reading from St. Paul to the Ephesians.

"What is this place?" she asked the gray form. Getting no answer, she put the same question to the black shroud.

"No talking," the shroud, decorated with the emblem of a Child of Mary, said while her eyes remained fixed on the crochet work in her hand.

"What am I to do?" Nuala pleaded for guidance.

No words were used, only hand gestures, as the trusted lackey pointed rudely at the tools on the table and waved a sample lace cuff in Nuala's face as if the girl were an imbecile. Pointing with great impatience at the other women, working away like mechanical automatons, the apparent supervisor indicated that Nuala was to do the same. The steady drone of Sister Perpetua's voice rose in volume, to demonstrate the policy of this particular department. "For they have given themselves up in despair to sensuality, greedily practicing every kind of uncleanness," was spoken with a chill that Nuala felt on the back of her neck. "As regards your former manner of life, you are to put off the old man, which is being corrupted through its deceptive lusts."

Their eyes met as Sister Perpetua directed the lecture to the new arrival, scrutinizing and analyzing while Nuala tried to make her body shrink into nothingness. There was an accusation in the curl of Sister's lips, in the slight flare of her nostrils, as if the nun knew that Nuala had once wavered about her calling to serve God. In the background, the factory noises were mixing with the drone of Sister's voice, a steady undertone that was vibrating through the girl's fingers, making them tremble slightly. This was a trial, unlike the first trial that had sent her to the orphanage in the first place, and still she did not know exactly what she had done wrong, anymore than she knew what to do to show everyone that she was better. She would gladly repent, if she only knew what she was supposed to be atoning for.

Averting her gaze from the glare of the nun, Nuala twisted the fine thread around two matchsticks, as Aunt Orla had taught her long ago. The movements were familiar, done every day in the orphanage, but this new setting was unworldly, that of a tomb filled with the dead. The eyes of every woman at the table and lining the outside wall were hollow and blank, set into the heads of corpses that moved like machines, without seeing or feeling. Since the age of seven Nuala had prayed for a release from the orphanage prison, but God was punishing her even more for having the audacity to ask anything of Him. Answering her prayers, He had sent her to a hell on earth.

Great racking sobs poured out of her mouth, while torrents of tears cascaded down her face. Hell was eternal, hell offered no chance for salvation, and the rush of despair knocked Nuala to the floor. No matter how many prayers were offered on her behalf, no matter how many Masses were said to save her soul, she was one of the damned and would never see her father again.

A steam whistle blew loudly at six o'clock, but Nuala had no idea how long she had been under the table, using the seat of her chair to support her elbows as she knelt in supplication, begging for mercy and forgiveness of her grievous sins. The lace makers rose as a unit at the sound of the alarm, and they shuffled out of the room without so much as a glance at Nuala. For the first time in her young life, she felt utterly and completely alone, abandoned and non-existent, a ghost.

Another strange face appeared, surrounded by the wimple of the Mercy Sister's habit. Another cold visage locked eyes on the little girl, sending a fresh wave of terror through Nuala's beating heart. The little gasp was heard again, a sound of surprise as Sister Victor mumbled something about small size and youthful appearance. The hard mask cracked, revealing a rather pretty young woman who could not have been very long a nun.

"You are to come with me," Sister Victor spoke evenly, though a hint of a smile tickled the corner of her mouth. "Every evening at the close of the work day, you are to attend to Sister Monica for instruction."

"Instruction, Sister?" Nuala said, amazed that her mouth was able to form words after an afternoon of silence.

"You have done nothing but pray all day," the nun continued, speaking over her shoulder to her shadow. Her highly knowledgeable comment could only have come from information delivered by the woman who was in charge, the one addressed as Eighty-Nine. She had clung to Nuala's side all afternoon, even hovering at her shoulder when she went to the yard, but Eighty-Nine was not like the tired out wrecks in grey capes. The other women had parted as the pair approached, scurrying away like mice fleeing a prowling house

223

cat, nervously whispering about the Child of Mary. "If you truly wish to atone for your sins, you must work as well as pray. Pray while working, pray while walking, pray always, but work. Work hard, work tirelessly, and you'll be a Child of Mary quite soon."

"A Child of Mary?" she began, curious about what exactly it meant.

"In time, you will join the ranks of those who are sanctified, just as you will eventually take your final vows." Sister Victor slowed her pace, lowering her voice at the same time. "To think that you asked for this, to break your will as a penitent, is remarkable. Sister Bede thinks that you must be out of your mind, but most of us admire your desire to give thanks to God that your abdominal tumor is benign."

"Must repent," Nuala thought back to Sister Monica's speech.

"We are all sinners, but by sharing this life of prayer and work as a Magdalene, you will find God's mercy, as I did during my novitiate. We must walk the path that God has chosen for us, and not seek our own route."

Her empty stomach growling, Nuala was escorted into the inner sanctum of the convent, the most private of places where only the religious could enter. Sister Victor pointed out the water closet, aware that the penitents all rushed to the toilets in the yard at six o'clock, and Nuala followed their lead. Feeling better, she imitated the nun's manner of walking, with her arms across her middle and hands tucked into the opposite sleeve. Down the long corridor she processed, counting the doors until the parade stopped at the end of the hall, where an enormous statue of the Sacred Heart reminded all of Christ's suffering.

Like everything else in a convent, the door's hinges were quiet, not daring to squeak as they rotated. Nuala entered the compact space that had only enough room for a narrow cot, a very rough chair, and a tiny wardrobe. Society ladies and daughters of the well to do became nuns, and their cells were frequently a reflection of their upbringing. Sister Monica was the exception to type, having entered the religious life seventy years ago to turn her back on the avariciousness of the Victorian era. Her cell was bare, cold, and wretchedly uncomfortable. Every minute of Sister Monica's existence had been given over to atonement for the sins of the world. The lack of amenities was designed to add to her body's mortification, she dedicated her life to teaching under a veil of poverty, and so Sister Monica carved out a route that followed God's path on the way to paradise.

After six, the laundry girls had dinner and then an hour of recreation, during which they were permitted to talk. As the nun elaborated on the future, it was clear that Nuala was singled out, once again, and that her hour of recreation would be several hours of education. She would converse with Sister Monica after a day of silence, not to gossip but to learn useful

225

information from textbooks. For the next three and one-half years, until Nuala was old enough to join the Benedictines in the wild and craggy wastes of County Galway, she would be given private instruction, the sort of education that only the most wealthy and privileged girls could receive. Oddly enough, Sister Monica did not expect her pupil to be grateful. The nun made it seem as if she was the one who should thank Nuala, but for what, Nuala had no idea.

Surveying the room, she noticed that shelves overloaded with books lined the walls, affixed above the bed and the washstand, and on up the wall next to the door. Her gaze flew over the titles, with works of literature and philosophy intermixed with school textbooks and devotional tomes. To be brought to this private library was as unnerving as waking up in a strange bed and being forced into silence for hours. When Sister Victor closed the door, Nuala jumped out of her skin.

"This will be our classroom, child, and we shall be teacher and pupil," Sister Monica explained, elation brightening her chalky-grey face. "Now, above the bed you will find the history books. Let us begin with world history."

The private tutoring continued until seven-thirty, when a hump-backed troll of a woman arrived with a tray. Nuala made the acquaintance of Sister Bridget, who had come to Booterstown as an orphan sixty-eight years ago, and had never left. Because she was poor, she could only become a lay *sister, but she earned the position of housekeeper to the convent through dedicated service. Too old now for such a demanding job, she was put in with the other retired sisters where she continued to do the housework. Meek and passive, she stood like a dumb animal as Sister Monica related her history, unfazed as she plodded through a routine that looked as rigid and set as the movement of a wind-up train.*

"You eat the same food as the orphans, Sister?" Nuala said, shocked by the cup of tea and slice of bread streaked with greasy margarine.

"We are all here to seek God's salvation," the teacher continued with an ongoing lesson that had been ingrained in every girl who had ever passed through St. Anne's. "We must all do penance, and we must all deny our bodies the earthly pleasures that corrupt mankind. This will become a part of your life, child, if you wish to see God."

Another ninety minutes of study rounded out the day, concluding with the evening prayers that Nuala was missing in the laundry girls' dormitory. "Let it be done to me," the nun enunciated a passage in the prayer. "Deliver yourself to God, and follow the example of our Blessed Mother. Repent of your sins and become as Mary Magdalene, a disciple of Christ. You are not worthy of God's love, but if you follow Him, as she did, then you too will find salvation. Let us dedicate your life to St. Mary Magdalene, then, and pray that she intercede on your behalf for God's guidance and wisdom."

By the time that the Troll Lady came for the tray, Nuala was feeling quite relieved to know that she was not dead after all, but had a chance to redeem her soul. Thanks to her great good fortune, she was one who was chosen by God, one of the lucky few who had a strong vocation. Nuns being closer to God, she had a leg up on the average woman when it came to entry into Paradise, and Sister Monica made it very clear that she would not rest until One Hundred Twenty had achieved the highest of all professions open to women. Sister Monica would never give up on her, and did not seem to hold to the creed that the orphans were just so much human rubbish. Her gentle demeanor, her generosity and her love of learning had a profound effect on Nuala's outlook. The affection that had been held for Terry McNulty was transferred to a retired nun.

"Return now to the penitents, and become one of them," Sister Monica intoned gravely at nine o'clock. "Tomorrow, you will meditate upon the life of St. Mary Magdalene while you work. You will work diligently, to please God, just as you pray diligently to please Him."

"Yes, Sister," Nuala vowed. "When I take the veil, Sister, I would like to take her name so that she will always be my guide."

"Sister Mary Magdalene," she said, sorrowful as if she had lost something valuable. She reached out and took

Nuala's hand, the fingers icy cold in the chill of the small room. "Yes. Sister Mary Magdalene."

Sister Victor was waiting in the hallway, much to Nuala's surprise, and she silently escorted her charge back to the dormitory. "Don't expect any special treatment," Victor warned when they reached the door of the sleeping area.

"Yes, Sister," she said, an automatic response to every phrase, whether ignored or heard.

Without another word, she showed Nuala to the dressing room, effortlessly gliding to a cubbyhole and displaying a nightdress and a change of underclothes that had come from the orphanage so that the knickers fit. Drifting like a ghost to the front of the room, the dormitory nun pointed at an empty cot as she went past it, while one hundred twenty-nine pairs of eyes furtively watched Nuala take up her post for the evening rosary.

"Fresh sheep," she heard someone whisper.

"Spring lamb," came the witty retort, the rest of the sentence drowned out by the increased volume of the praying women who surrounded the newcomer.

Accustomed to doing what everyone else was doing, Nuala hurried to the foot of her bed and folded her hands, jumping into the prayers with serious devotion. Her eyes, however, were very busy moving from side to side as she analyzed her situation.

229

Nearby were older women, the youngest possibly the same age as Sister Laurentia, but in other parts of the room were women in their late teens or early twenties. It was a hodge-podge of age and figure, with some thin and some plump, some pretty and some homely, and some that were mentally handicapped. They shared one common characteristic, and that was the fact that they were all exhausted and completely lifeless. No spark or spirit flowed from a single penitent as they stood like a troop of the living dead, with all joy extinguished and all hope snuffed.

When the devotions were concluded, Sister Victor paused and looked over the group. "One Hundred Twenty, you made no effort today to redeem your soul," she shouted for all to hear.

"Yes, Sister," Nuala agreed, because it was true that she had done little more than touch the thread before giving in to the malaise that lingered still.

"Do you now understand why you are here, and what is expected of you?"

Shaking with fear over a possible punishment, Nuala struggled to speak above a nervous whisper. "Yes, Sister."

"Will you ever spend another day in idleness?"

"No, Sister," she replied strongly, hoping to ensure that Sister Victor would not make the same accusation in the future.

"You are forgiven," came the reply, with a tone that seemed to tell the others that here was their example to follow. "Thirty-Four, you refused to work today. Come forward to seek our forgiveness."

Nuala had seen the pose before, and she was overjoyed that it was not her laying on the floor, arms outstretched. There was no avoiding humiliation in this place, something that Nuala had learned from experience, so she swallowed hard and offered silent thanks to a merciful God for sparing her from the same torment, when the Sisters had no mercy.

For every infraction listed, Thirty-Four repeated the psalm of her disgrace, finally breaking into tears when the abuse grew too heavy. The accusations and intonations were spewed out against a backdrop of women's voices murmuring out entreaties to God, with one hundred thirty women canting in shame. As Nuala would come to learn, the nightmare scenario was a regular occurrence, and every woman in the dormitory would be put through the wringer until she became a hollow corpse, devoid of life.

Sister Perpetua's clanging bell announced the start of a new day, one that Nuala's neighbors did not greet with pleasure. "Good morning," she whispered to the woman in the next cot, but all she got back was a cold glare. When Seventy-Five bound Nuala's chest, to show her how it was done, she tugged a little harder and tied the calico a little too tight, eliciting a wince of pain. It was a message, a warning without words, an alert given through punishment, and Nuala never again tried to speak to Seventy-Five.

The penitents processed to Mass at seven, after they had washed and dressed. Nuala attempted to seek out the younger girls who were closer to her age, but the older women trailed her and blocked her access, keeping her hemmed in. No one spoke, and no one was to be given an opportunity to speak, not when the tamed residents of the Magdalene laundry acted as enforcers of the rules. The system was based on the vigilance of the nuns, then the alert ears of their trusted underlings, and finally, on the indoctrination of the laundry girls. Pitting women against women, the Sisters of Mercy wielded complete control.

Father Byrne was the oldest man that Nuala had ever seen, a priest in retirement who loudly proclaimed that he was filling in for Father McVeigh, as if Father McVeigh had been the chaplain all along and Father McNulty never existed. His Mass was slow and ponderous, evoking great adoration of God while promoting self-sacrifice. Nuala watched her fellows, to find the kind of humble adoration that she saw in the orphans, but the younger penitents were void of feeling for the word of God.

More prayers accompanied breakfast, where conversation was again banned. Surrounded by warm corpses, Nuala could whisper all she liked but it was a one-sided *dialogue because no one would break the rules. She looked around as she drank her tea, meeting the glances of others like her, relative newcomers who longed for friendship. At meals and prayer sessions, Nuala would say hello with her eyes and the lonely laundry girls would reply with winks.*

Cooped up in a single, freezing cold room from eight in the morning until half-past twelve, Nuala thought that she would go mad with restlessness. The only respite was a trip to the yard, which she lengthened as much as possible by walking slowly with her gaze searching the sky for passing birds. Even bathroom breaks did not provide a moment to sneak a few words, because the same gaggle of hags surrounded her wherever she went, just as another batch of biddies tailed the other young girls. Divided and parceled out among the more trustworthy inmates, the women were forced into silence because there was no way to get around the barriers.

While the weak and infirm worked on tablecloths for the export market, Sister Perpetua led prayers and sang hymns, which all were to join. Through an onslaught of sacred words, the women passed the day in asking God to forgive them, everyone begging for mercy. Given a half hour for lunch, they ate and prayed, and then they returned to work and prayed. Without tiring, Sister Perpetua spewed out the cant, grinding the listeners into submission. By the time that the whistle screeched at six, Nuala thought that she would go completely out of her mind.

"You have a gentle touch," Sister Monica complimented her pupil. Nuala had thoughtfully wiped a crumb from the nun's chin as they had their tea together in the comfortless room. "This is a talent that should be put to use. Nursing Sisters are always in short supply, as Sister Domenica observed recently. I have a book above the washstand, with the science texts, that deals with first aid."

Recalling the kindness of the school nurse when Dr. O'Connor was so rough, Nuala had to agree with her mentor that nursing was just the sort of profession in which she could excel. For the final hour, she read from the book, but Sister Monica encouraged her to continue reading while she offered enough prayers for both of them. "My time is running out, and we must race to secure your novitiate before God calls me home," Monica said. "The sooner that you join the Benedictines, the better for all of us. When you are wedded to the church, Mary Magdalene, you will have time enough for prayer. Then you must pray for me, that God forgives me my sins."

Turning off of Blackrock Road, Molly felt a chill run through her. A sense of foreboding hung in her head, a fear that she would be shown to a grassy field where her aunt's bones lay, hidden from view for many long years to hide the shame. In the back of her mind, she wondered if her father had not been mistaken, that perhaps his sister had not come home from the orphanage after all, and it was only wishing that had created a false memory of the family reunited.

"More left than stayed," Eoin said suddenly, catching sight of her trepidation. "And you don't know if she had a falling out with her stepfather and that's the reason she went off. Family squabbles are often covered up so that the other children don't know of them."

"I know," she agreed, without convincing him that she did.

The convent building was set well off the road, an island in the middle of a booming city. Molly could readily picture the place seventy years ago, when the city of Dublin was not anywhere near as big as it was in 2000. Her aunt would have been sent to an equivalent of Siberia, inaccessible to the rest of the world behind the dismal façade.

Walking through the portal elicited a gut reaction, as the same smell of polish and disinfectant hit Molly full in the face. She stood in the visitor's reception room, looking up at the high ceilings and the plaster rose in the center where a gas chandelier once hung. Sister Lucy knocked on the open door to announce her arrival.

"At the time, the term Magdalene meant a public sinner, female of course," the nun chatted over a pot of tea. "I can't use that word, frankly. It turns my stomach, to think of the connotations."

"How do you feel about the system?" Eoin asked, sounding like a man running an interview for his research project.

"In those days, we took in girls who were rejected by their families because of an unwanted pregnancy. It's not so long ago that it was a blow to the family honor," Sister reminded Eoin. "Even in America, there was a time when single mothers were reviled and shunned."

Molly looked up, trying to focus her thoughts when her mind was sailing from one place to another. She had been overwhelmed by the enormous size of the complex, feeling that she had come into a different city, a principality that operated under its own government. Cold chills ran across the back of her neck, until she adjusted her scarf to cover the bare skin. She sipped at the tea, hoping to settle her stomach.

Sister Lucy elaborated on her order's mission, to find families for the children taken in by the orphanage. They catered to troubled youth, to chronic runaways and provided shelter for children from abusive homes. The building that once housed the laundry facility was now classroom space, much needed for the development of the residents. When Eoin asked if parents brought their daughters there to be confined, Molly guessed that he was asking the sort of questions that she would have asked if she knew as much about the system as he apparently did.

"We made mistakes, Professor MacNeill, we admit to them, and if a mother turned up at my door with her daughter, I would tell her to get lost." Sister waved her hand to strengthen the point. "I'd never refuse to take the girl, of course, but we would counsel the mother to show her that we do not hide people away."

"What about the orphans, the children taken away from their mothers?" Molly asked.

"When our republic was first created, there was a strong desire to correct the abuses that had befallen the poor by molding our children, to eradicate the old and make everything new and Irish. And Catholic, yes. Everyone believed that the religious were better than the rest, that a nun or priest could do no wrong. If our religious community was more enlightened in the Twenties, this never could have happened. We can all thank God that it will never be seen again."

"I understand that the order issued an apology," Molly said.

"Yes, but we both know that a mouthful of words cannot change anything. By continuing our mission to help the disadvantaged, and by opening ourselves up to modern ideas and even outside inspection, we express our sincere regret better than any press release."

"Do you have any records of my aunt's time here?" Molly turned to business, to get what she came for and then get out quickly, before the ghosts of Booterstown's sprawling compound took possession of her soul.

"In defense of my predecessors, I would like to add one thing," the nun said as she rose from the armchair. "We are speaking of an age when women alone were in danger. Most of

237

the girls did not have a hope in hell of surviving on the streets. Girls have gone on the streets and been murdered. I've seen it happen."

After Sister Lucy left to collect the papers, Molly let loose with a hushed stream of vulgarities. She had seen women in the operating room bleed to death from knife wounds, stabbed by a husband in the safety of the family home. Who was this sheltered nun to proclaim the streets as a place of great danger, when worse things had happened inside the walls of the very institution she was running? An orphan was better off on the streets in the Twenties if the only other option was incarceration.

A few words from Eoin did nothing to relieve her distress. Of course she was more aware of the dark side of cities than the nun, but there was a different kind of darkness in the Booterstown facility that wasn't describable in words. In response, Molly raised her hands, fingers stretched as far as she could draw them out. She was filled with tension, a caged tiger type of stress that was reflected in her inability to sit still. Eoin began to tighten up as well, and then she knew. He had studied places like this, factories that sucked in innocent little girls and frightened young women, and the way that he drummed on the armrest and tugged at his chin was a clear warning. The dirtiest corners of a dark past were about to be revealed; a cloud of filth was about to be freed, but she would not let it settle back down. She would stir it up, sweep it out from under carpets, shake it out so that everyone choked on it.

A banker's box of documents was turned over, along with Sister's apology for the sorrow that had been caused. Molly did not listen, too engrossed in the contents of her aunt's childhood.

"This is the same as my father's record," Molly said out loud, perusing the typed card that reiterated Nuala's crime. "My grandmother dared to have a boyfriend, and my aunt was crucified for it."

"There was almost an insanity about sex outside of marriage," Sister Lucy stated calmly. "The most remote possibility of physical contact was a crime. Young girls who so much as walked out with a boy late at night were brought in and confined to save their purity."

"So this wasn't just about saving lives?" Molly brought the fact out to air.

"No, it was not," Sister said. "It was about controlling people, about the religious being the morality police and the sexual turnkeys. The Catholic Church was like a spring, wound tighter and tighter through years of British occupation. When they decamped, the spring exploded, and too many people were hurt by the recoil. Now we are paying the price, the religious community and our country. The second largest religion in Ireland is no religion. And we are running out of priests, to minister to our half-empty churches."

"Usual run of childhood illnesses," Molly noted as she continued to page through the folder. Her casual air was infected with a slight case of bitterness and sarcasm. "For things like this, I'd be on the phone to Family Services so fast it would make your head spin." She began to snicker, and then a full, throaty guffaw echoed in the parlor. "Better off in here than on the streets. A nine-year-old girl with recurrent bladder infections."

"I know that this will sound disgusting in our modern age of indoor plumbing, but the children shared a bath. Over twenty bodies in the same water. It should be no surprise that infections would be seen," Sister excused the report.

"No, it's not bath water or soap," Molly said. "The gynecologists call it honeymoon cystitis."

Eoin was watching Molly with increasing concern, aware of some news that had hurt her deeply. She was clearly angry, but in a subdued way that was far more dangerous, more coldly ominous in its chill foreboding. All Sister Lucy did was to wrinkle her brow, not quite seeing what a nurse could understand so easily and a lover hear so distinctly.

"The school matron even signed off on the chart. Vaginal trauma and laceration, Jesus Christ, my aunt was raped when she was nine and the matron put it down on paper like it was a goddamned sniffle."

A gasp escaped from Sister's throat, a sound that she stifled with her perfectly groomed fingers. The room grew silent, with no one knowing what to say. The only noise at all came from the file of papers as Molly thumbed through each sheet with crisp exactness. Eoin heard a warning, an admonition that the decades old cover-up at St. Anne's orphanage was about to be made public. With every page that crackled, he grew more and more certain that Molly was boiling over, ready to explode.

"Eoin, would you mind driving me to City Centre?" Molly finally spoke. "I have to see my father's lawyer immediately."

It was exactly the pronouncement that he was expecting. The closing of the Gloucester Street Laundry, coupled with the openness of modern Irish society, had unleashed a barrage of queries that sprouted from the last of the laundry girls and had not stopped blossoming yet. The press was not pacified by the descriptions of mentally challenged women finding refuge when there was no one else to care for them. A reporter had decided to probe further, and he found two women who were dying of cancer, exiles in England, who were willing to talk before it was too late to tell their stories.

All of Ireland soon heard of the brutality, and then the lawsuits began. It was such an American sort of reaction, to press for damages and bleed the guilty party. When the attorneys got involved, the government had not stepped in to aid the clergy, but then the fledgling Irish Free State had been a huge cog in the shameful machine. The courts, the judges, and even the Garda Soichana were all as wrapped up in the horror as the clergy. The Dail Eireann was doing its utmost to keep out of the way as the blame was levied.

"We were part of the penal system," Sister admitted. "If I had known what the Sisters of Mercy did in those days, Miss Devoy, I don't know that I would have joined the order."

"I hope everyone knows before I'm through," Molly said.

"By avoiding the truth, we are making a lie of our teachings," Sister Lucy said, picking at an invisible speck of lint

241

on her navy blue dress. "How can we tell the faithful to find solace in the confessional if our deeds do not reflect our words?"

Eoin took the file box, uncomfortable with Molly and her aunt's horrible experiences. He was as much a part of the dark past as the rest of the nation, as blameworthy as his father for ignoring what was known. The way that Molly's eyes clouded over looked like a sign that she was thinking the same things, that she did not want to be with him, as if the morning's lovemaking was years ago and they were meeting now as strangers.

"You'll join the law suit?" he asked, searching for an opening.

"What suit?"

"Some of the survivors have filed a grievance. The government pretty much brushed them aside, but they're still fighting. According to official policy, the women went in voluntarily. Don't say anything; let me finish. Irish politicians are among the most corrupt in Europe, and they would like all this to go away. It's a lot of things, Molly; it's fear of a backlash that would harm tourism, it's fear of a financial debacle if they have to pay compensation. You're in for a long fight, but I hope you don't ever back down."

"Thanks, Eoin," she said, gently touching his arm.

"Sean O'Rahilly is handling the case. I've gotten to know him through Mairead O'Meara, the leader of the research project I told you about."

"That's the same attorney that my father contacted before he died," Molly said.

"Then he knew, Molly. He must have known, or at least suspected."

"It's best not to know. I heard that so many times."

"I'd say he reached the point where he did want to know. When did he contact O'Rahilly, about four years ago?"

"How did you know?"

"That's when this broke open, hit the fan as they say. News reports, a couple of novels, documentaries, there was even a film. You would never have heard of it because it's an Irish phenomenon. I doubt that many people in the States know about the laundries, and if you were to tell someone, I don't think that they could believe it."

Through the short ride back to O'Rahilly's office, Molly held the box on her knees, going page by page, until she cried out. The sudden sound alarmed Eoin, who slammed on the brakes. "Oh, dear God," she said. "She was sent to the laundry when she was twelve."

14

Nuala had been sheltered in the convent, kept away from everyday life and the routines of human existence in the slums and streets of Dublin. All the same, she was not blind, nor was she stupid. Twelve of the laundry girls were in varying stages of pregnancy, a physical condition that Nuala easily recognized. As a child, she had gone everywhere with her mother and seen countless women who were on the way. The bulging belly was unmistakable, a marker that drew praise and attention from the shoppers on Thomas Street who delighted in babies and cooed over mothers-to-be.

Due dates and guesses about boys or girls had penetrated her ears, the phrases penetrating her ears as a little girl learned of motherhood. Her own future was part of it, and she saw that having a baby was a happy event and a joy to celebrate. The laundry girls were never happy or joyous.

Aware that she was here to prepare for the convent, she could accept the presence of the many old and middle-aged women, because widows and spinsters often tagged along with the nuns even though they never took the veil. What made no sense was the presence of expectant mothers. If not for Sister Monica, Nuala never would have learned that all the laundry girls had come to repent of their sins because they had been imitating the life of Mary Magdalene in the outside world, and like Jesus' beloved disciple, they chose to follow Christ through a new life of contemplation and penance.

Nuala trusted her keepers, and with no other source of information, she took Sister Monica at her word that old and young, even those who were with child, were here to seek God's mercy and forgiveness. Kept apart from the others, she went on with her studies, becoming ever closer to the nun in a sort of friendship that became a lifesaving outlet. Their conversations were not lighthearted or giddy, but for Nuala, it was a blessed chance to talk, with the added bounty of the opportunity to think and reason. It was not long before she was in the habit of kissing the old woman goodnight, as if Sister Monica was now her beloved grandmother.

Women came and went in the laundry, but there were many who had been essentially abandoned to the nuns, some great shame overwhelming family ties. Of those who slaved without complaint and shouldered the heaviest burden, the nuns did their utmost to keep them employed, forever telling them that they were not yet saved and needed to stay on. Nuala sometimes overheard one of the Sisters tell a penitent that the family wanted to take her home but the Mother Superior had talked them out of it, for the sake of the laundry girl's soul. It meant that there was no guarantee that Nuala herself would be sent to the Benedictines if Mother Superior didn't agree. She concentrated even harder on her studies, to prove herself and prove her worth to the missionaries.

Some girls saved their souls quite quickly, within weeks or months, and they were allowed to leave. Nuala had seen some of them on their way out the front door, but she never did understand why the girls who slacked off at work or stirred up trouble in the dormitory were usually the ones sent home after a short stay, when a longer period of prayer and introspection seemed more sensible. Keeping her ears open, she discovered that a girl could be put away by her father as punishment for some infraction that was so minor it didn't take a lot of work to wash away the sin.

In June, a flurry of absences disrupted the normally smooth operation of the laundry. Several girls went back home, and two of the pregnant women went into labor. Then another pair of girls escaped over the wall, leaving the factory short of skilled hands. Without new girls coming in, Sister Therese was in a tizzy, laundry trolleys backed up and the drying sheds half empty without workers to fill them with wet sheets. While the penitents ate breakfast, the nuns from the laundry engaged in a heated discussion, and Nuala was tapped to leave the crochet room and put her young, strong back to good use.

For the first time, Nuala entered the laundry, where the abominable heat and steam left her limp within minutes. The noise of pounding machinery was coupled with the whirr of steam-driven belts that drove the huge washing vats, but one other sound filtered through the racket. It was the voices of the nuns, leading the workers in prayer.

Presuming that no one could be more trustworthy than One Hundred Twenty, the potential novice, she was put with Forty-Nine, a recent penitent who was somewhat recalcitrant. Sister Therese looked to One Hundred Twenty to proselytize if Forty-Nine tried to break the rules, answering chatter with the words of the Lord's Prayer. Pushing canvas carts side by side, the two girls followed Sister Berenice to the door, where they had to take turns going out through a narrow passage. After one trip to the drying sheds, they were on their own, and on the next trip, pushing and groaning at the exit, Forty-Nine took advantage of a place where the ears of the nuns did not reach.

"How old are you?" she whispered, her lips barely moving.

"Twelve," Nuala muttered.

Under the watchful eye of Sister Berenice, who directed the hanging of wet laundry, and with their voices occupied in a loveless rendition of a hymn, the conversation had to stop. Nuala lifted the wet, heavy sheets out of the cart and pulled pillowcases from the bottom, straining under the weight. When both trolleys were emptied, the girls pushed them back, repeating the single file arrangement at the door.

"Who's the father?" Forty-Nine rasped.

"Father?" Nuala asked in response. She had no idea what her associate was talking about.

"Your baby," Forty-Nine quickly explained, pretending to help Nuala with her cart so that she could touch the girl's middle to be more specific.

Inside her body, Nuala had been feeling some peculiar sensations that Sister Monica claimed were due to the tumor that was congesting her intestines. Dr. O'Connor was going to remove it, the nun assured the girl, as soon as he decided the time was right. Based on her mentor's explanation, Nuala was picturing some kind of enormous boil that was going to be lanced when the infection was close enough to the skin. Suddenly, a girl who had been living on the outside until two months ago was claiming that Nuala was pregnant, and since Nuala tended to believe the newcomers, she was thrown into a dizzying confusion.

As an orphan, Nuala had discovered that girls just entering the facility had a great deal of knowledge, and things had been said that were later confirmed by the Sisters, which proved that recent arrivals possessed facts. Without a doubt, Forty-Nine knew the world that the cloistered nuns shunned, and she had no reason to make up tall tales when an opportunity to talk was too precious to be wasted on nonsense.

During the dinner break, a time of meditation, Nuala pondered the suggestion that she was with child. From her studies, she had learned that the Blessed Mother was very young when God chose her, and the Virgin Mary had been completely taken aback when the angel told her she was going to be the mother of the Messiah. She argued with the angel, in fact, stating that She didn't know man. As far as Nuala could determine during the half-hour break, she knew not man either, since she was not married and did not have a husband.

"The Savior," she gasped, her hand on her belly. "He is coming, as He promised, He is coming back to earth to redeem His people."

Sister Perpetua had been reading from the Gospel of St. Luke, and Nuala's sudden outburst struck her dumb in mid-sentence. Catching sight of Nuala, she observed some rapture or radiance. "Are you unwell, One Hundred Twenty?" she demanded. An eyebrow lifted ever so slightly, asking the fledgling nun if she was trying to communicate through a secret code of prayer between master and spy.

"My soul magnifies the Lord," Nuala said, tears of joy streaking her cheeks.

Sister Perpetua switched gears at once, joining Nuala in a recitation of the Magnificat, while the other women followed along out of habit. Over a plate of potatoes and cabbage, Nuala discovered that she was indeed very special, chosen to be a nun and perhaps chosen by God Himself. Her prayers were going to be answered, she was sure, and one day she too would be assumed into heaven, to sit at the right hand of God where her dear daddy was waiting. God works in strange ways, she had often heard, and if this was His way to get her out of St. Anne's, she would grab the opportunity with both hands and be grateful for it. The penitents passed their time at table with Marian devotions that day, concluding with a dull rendition of the Regina Coeli, while Nuala abandoned her food and fell to her knees in adoration of her Savior.

Word of Nuala's religious fervor quickly spread to Sister Monica. That evening, she reinforced the emotion by lecturing on the lives of the saints, explaining how the greatest often came from middle-class or wealthy families. "From comfort, they sought a life of poverty," the nun said. "You have come to poverty through no fault of your own, but I see God's hand at work here."

"Yes, Sister," Nuala said, half-listening while she read Ivanhoe.

"Such is my hope for you, that you become, not merely a religious, absent-minded in your devotions, but a leader of women. Our own blessed Mother McAuley was such a woman, and I will teach you to follow in her footsteps. Can you imagine founding an order, child?"

"Yes, Sister," Nuala agreed. Very slowly, she turned the page, careful not to make a sound.

"I have heard that a family in America, in Boston, has made a donation to our convent. Your dowry is very generous, but then, your vocation is exceptionally strong."

"I am blessed," Nuala said.

*"Perhaps God sent you to us to teach us humility,"
Monica said, her hands twisting about in her lap. She beat her breast, as they did every morning at Mass. "I thank thee, Lord, that I am not like that sinner. We forget His lessons so easily."*

Eager to learn more of her new friend, Nuala pitched in with a vengeance to push the wet laundry through the wringers, to race to the door with a full trolley and have three or four words with a girl. Forty-Nine took command of the conversation, however, being more skilled at social interaction than a child who had been locked up for almost six years.

"Mary Reilly," Forty-Nine introduced herself.

"Nuala De-scended into hell; the third day he arose again from the dead," Nuala masked speech with the Apostles' Creed.

"From County Wexford," Forty-Nine said on the return trip.

"The Liberties," Nuala shared her hometown. It was her last trip of the day to the sheds, and Nuala was promptly returned to the crochet table where Sister Perpetua welcomed her back with prayers to the Blessed Mother until six.

251

"Read from *The Lives of the Saints*," Sister Monica groaned wearily, the oppressive heat of July taxing her feeble body. "If you encounter any difficulty or wish to discuss a passage, speak freely. It would be wise to be an authority on St. Benedict before Reverend Mother comes to interview you."

"You look pale, Sister," Nuala observed, gently touching the woman's forehead. Using her first aid training, she took the bony wrist and felt the pulse. "No fever, and your heart is steady."

"It is only age," Sister Monica said. "Pull the chair close to the bed while I lie down. Do not feel that you are interrupting me with your questions, even if I appear to be sleeping. For a long time, I have fought against my body, and it is very difficult now that I am old. If you wake me when I doze off, you are actually helping me to overcome the pleasures of the flesh. Do you understand what I mean?"

"Yes, Sister. We must suffer to be closer to God."

Lately, the elderly woman was too tired at the end of the day to teach, but Nuala had long had the ability to pick up knowledge through reading and memorizing on her own, without the need of lectures or exercises. For weeks, she had studied mathematics and worked out problems unaided, leaving the papers behind for one of Sister Monica's retired colleagues to review during the day. Essays on history, catechism, or literature were treated the same way, with

Sister Monica dictating her notes and corrections for Nuala to analyze after work. Not quite thirteen, Nuala had become a serious scholar, diligent in her studies because she longed to please her mentor, her friend and companion, the matriarch of her make-believe family.

Taking advantage of the nun's failing eyesight, Nuala selected her books without fear that her teacher would be aware of what she was reading. With the chair pulled up even with Sister Monica's head, Nuala settled in and opened Alice in Wonderland, a secular work the nun had acquired when it was a new work of fiction, suitable for entertaining little children at bedtime.

Sister Monica had an extensive collection of novels because she was a firm believer in reading aloud to the little ones to instill a love of literature that made it easier to teach them later. Through the nun's personal library, Nuala was given access to the tales of Ivanhoe and Rowena, the sagas of Robinson Crusoe and Moby Dick, and the adventures of Tom Sawyer, the Three Musketeers and Robin Hood. In the pages of books, Nuala found impressions of the outside world that she wanted to join, with a desire that grew stronger every day. Like the heroes of novels, she wanted to do great deeds, to help others, and even though she did not really want to be a nun, she was ready to accept the position because it was a way out of Booterstown.

Sister Ursula's family had sent several nursing manuals to the convent when they were made aware of Nuala's interest in medicine, and Nuala had devoured every word, every picture and every diagram. Having completed the Lewis Carroll story, she went back to the medical texts, her curiosity peaking. In the quiet of the cell, she touched her belly where the movements rippled, closing her eyes and searching her oldest memories, going back to the time when her cousin Loretta was expecting her first baby. The tremors in her fingertips were unmistakable, for they were the same funny tickles that had emanated from Loretta's big belly when she let her little cousin feel the baby kick.

Absolutely positive now, Nuala was certain that she was not growing a tumor, but a child. Casting a glance at her teacher, confirming that she was asleep, Nuala returned to her nursing books and concentrated on the pages dealing with prenatal care. Forty-Nine had known that Nuala was pregnant, which indicated a level of wisdom that Sister Monica did not have. By the same token, she had asked after the identity of the father, which had to be significant. The way that the question had been posed, nonchalant and humdrum implied that there might not be some divine interference after all. Nuala had no idea how babies were made in the outside world, and it would have been pointless to ask a celibate nun. Seeking information from her books, the girl could find nothing in the chapters on maternal health to tell her how a woman came to be with child, no matter how many times she read the pages.

Somehow, she had to find out from Forty-Nine, a woman who might know, and if that failed, Nuala was determined to learn from one of the many other penitents who were carrying children. Before she announced that she had been chosen by God to bring forth a new Messiah, Nuala thought it best to eliminate all other possibilities. It was easy to envision the sort of humiliation that would befall a girl who blundered, and Nuala had learned to be cautious in her actions, to keep things inside rather than risk being laughed at or mocked. She had time, hours of time every day, to think things over very carefully before she was ready to confide in anyone.

After Mass that Friday, the girls had prayer for breakfast because every Friday was a day of fasting. While drinking her mug of water, Nuala made eye contact with Forty-Nine, manipulating her brows to indicate a desire to talk. She was anxious to get to the laundry that morning, to push the trolley to the door and say as many words as she could in the short span of time that was available.

"How can I tell?" she pattered rapidly on the way to the sheds, using the entire moment for her sentence. On the way back in, she finished the thought, "Who is the father?"

Sister Perpetua reclaimed her lace maker early in the morning after Clery's buyer had called and pleaded for his order, urgently needing to replenish his stock. Having to wait for her answer until Saturday, Nuala was about ready to jump out of her skin, and her nervous agitation was expressed by her steady rocking, back and forth, as she frantically crocheted. The crack on the head that Sister Perpetua administered to make her stop moving had no effect whatsoever. At lessons, Nuala could not seem to stop pacing to and fro as she verbally worked out the algebra problems, and Sister Monica indicated her displeasure by applying the leather strap to Nuala's bare back with stinging force during their weekly corporal mortification session, to articulate her annoyance.

The wheels of the carts creaked under the load, the trolley almost overflowing with men's shirts. Going through the door, Nuala pulled and her colleague pushed, their heads leaning closer together over the steaming clothes. "The one who puts," Forty-Nine said, finishing the sentence after the shirts had been hung in the shed to dry, "his thing in you."

"What thing?" was all that Nuala could get out without being seen talking.

Thoroughly enmeshed in the puzzle, Nuala did not realize that the laundry girls were saying a rosary as she helped Forty-Nine unload another machine. Sister Bertha gave her a sharp swat on the head with her big ring of keys to wake her up, a blow that dropped Nuala to the floor. "Forgive me,

Sister," Nuala said at once, surprised that she had been oblivious to her surroundings when she normally kept one ear and one eye open. Lately, she had been feeling so weary that it was almost impossible to think clearly, let alone remain vigilant.

"You are needed in the ironing room," Sister Bertha said. As they walked past the mangle where the pillowcases were pressed, the nun leaned close to Nuala. "I have spoken to Sister Perpetua about you."

"Yes, Sister?" Nuala's heart began to race. Things could be worse for her, much worse. First her mother was gone, then Father McNulty was gone, and they could take away the whole world if they wanted.

"I am pleased by the example that you set for the penitents."

"Thank you, Sister." Her knees began to buckle.

"Do you need to see Matron?"

"No, I'd like to keep working."

If Sister Bertha were capable of smiling, the miniscule crease at the corner of her mouth was the equivalent of a broad grin. At the brink of adolescence, Nuala was discovering the underlying weaknesses of humanity, and she was learning how to manipulate them. She thought about smiling, but decided against it. Instead, she apologized for seeming to make a decision on her own, and quickly asked Sister Bertha for an order, to iron or see Matron, as Sister thought best.

Besides Christmas, Sundays were the only days that were holidays from laundry work, but there was no rest for the penitents. They prayed instead of washing, kept occupied so that they could not talk to each other beyond the limited times permitted. Friendship was expressly forbidden, and given the climate that pervaded the facility, none of the women seemed to trust one another, as if each one was nothing more than an extension of the nuns. Nuala had been told that they were forbidden to talk of their past, of their families, or the world that they left behind, and she was under orders to report any infractions to Sister Bertha. Given such all-encompassing limits on chatter, along with the dangers of breaking a law, it was difficult to see what the girls could even talk about when they did have a chance to speak.

Sunday dragged on, while Nuala struggled with the answer to her query. During Mass, Nuala wondered what a man had put inside her. The only men she had seen for years were priests and the handyman who fixed broken door locks and changed the light bulbs. What thing did they have, she asked herself, and her thoughts turned at once to Dr. O'Connor.

She had been living in the orphanage, going to school and living with children her own age until Dr. O'Connor came along and touched her insides. For a large part of the day, Nuala had pondered the physician's actions, wondering if he had done something wrong. Matron had been apologetic and she had been watching the process, leading Nuala to conclude that it might have been Dr. O'Connor rather than God who had impregnated her. While eating dinner in silence she looked over at Forty-Nine, deciding at that moment that if Forty-Nine had meant fingers, she would have used the word. By calling the offending article a thing, she implied an item that was unique to men, and Nuala turned to her memories once again to help her solve a problem.

Out in the yard, walking in a circle surrounded by old women and black-garbed Children of Mary, Nuala looked up at the sky, the only part of the outside world that she was ever allowed to see. Someone, at some time, had shown her how to change a baby, a boy baby specifically, but the images in her mind swirled out of focus. Unable to recapture the picture, she tried instead to recall her brother Frank's body, and how it was different from hers. Aware of someone trying to get her attention from across the yard, she looked over and saw Forty-Nine making gestures with her hands, the movements small and compact, but the meaning very clear.

Hysterical screams filled the exercise yard as Nuala threw her body to the ground, rolling in the dirt with an agony that was immeasurable. Everything that ever happened in the sacristy was buried deep within her memory, impossible to dredge up and look at in the open air, but always gliding just below the surface. The hand gestures reached there, creating

259

ripples that distorted the pictures and images, making them more clear instead of more obscure. Subconsciously, she had her answer, and she fought with all her strength to submerge the smells, the sensations and the sights that rose up, calling to her, commanding her to look because the memories would never really leave her.

When Matron found One Hundred Twenty restrained in a bed, the nurse was not in the least surprised. She spoke of girls who cracked under the brutal regime, falling victim to overwhelming despair and depression that was expressed in temper tantrums, fights, and outlandish religious fervor. It was bad enough when a girl knew why she had been put away, she said, but it was much worse when a child was made to atone for sins that she could not possibly have committed, let alone comprehended. Blunt talk fell on deaf ears. All Nuala understood was the prescription to relieve her illness: a regimen of grinding, backbreaking physical labor to exhaust both body and mind and reinforce the message that it was futile to resist.

Only because it was deemed medically necessary did Sister Perpetua accept the loss of her most competent lace maker. For a period of one month, Nuala was moved into the laundry, to push the heaviest trolleys and carts piled high with dried sheets, to lift and tote until her shoulders were hunched over from the physical effort that such hard work required. She had to deal with heavier loads than her body could handle, *leaving her arms and back aching at the end of every miserable day.*

Profoundly exhausted by six o'clock, Nuala found the energy to continue her studies with Sister Monica through pure determination not to be broken. Limited by age and infirmity, the nun encouraged Nuala to teach herself through careful and thorough reading, and so, night after night, Nuala poured over one book after another, absorbing the knowledge that sprang out of the words. From her own studies and Sister Monica's lectures, Nuala discovered the truth of God's word in the Bible, while also uncovering the falsehoods and lies of the Sisters of Mercy, expressed daily in their actions. At a time when girls approached womanhood and started to spread their wings, taking a few tentative flights before they were not afraid to soar, Nuala grew increasingly cynical about life.

Sitting in Sean O'Rahilly's office on a cloudy Wednesday afternoon, Eoin had an uncomfortable sensation of being on the outside looking in. Molly had not changed her appearance or her demeanor, but she was not the same person. Somehow, Eoin detected a gap opening up between them, a chasm that expanded with every word that O'Rahilly uttered.

"It was classic techniques of torture," the barrister elaborated as he reviewed Molly's information. "As soon as your aunt was incarcerated, they took away her name and gave her a new identity. I've heard nuns attempt to rationalize it, but their excuses are bunk. It was step one in the dehumanizing process."

"Is that why she was a number in the laundry?" Molly asked.

"Definitely. By making a person an object, they stripped away their humanity. Brutal tactics, but highly effective. A few months of that, and self-esteem would be gone. The women that I am representing are all permanently damaged."

"What can you do with the rape?" Molly continued. Eoin shifted uncomfortably in his chair.

"The perpetrator is long dead, and his identity is not noted in these records," O'Rahilly said. "The matron, the nuns, all gone to their reward. All I can do is pursue the Sisters of Mercy for lack of vigilance, neglect, that sort of thing."

"I haven't read all of these documents," Molly said. "I don't know if I can, without getting sick."

"Is it worth her while to examine adoption records?" Eoin postulated. If it was a heartless suggestion or a brilliant idea, it did not matter. He only wanted Molly to have something, a living relative or a meager hope.

"The adoptions were separate from the laundry." O'Rahilly shot down the idea. "And we have found that inaccuracies as to the mother's identity were quite common. I have heard rumors that official birth certificates were often filed listing the adopting parents as the actual parents to completely hide a child's illegitimacy, effectively erasing a birth record. Back then, the nuns actually believed that bastards were barred from civil service and public sector occupations. So they rounded up the girls born out of wedlock, locked them up in the laundries, and congratulated themselves for giving them jobs and a roof over their heads."

"My father's burial is Thursday, and I leave Friday afternoon," Molly said. "Can I get photocopies of these records? If you could look through them and find something that would help me find my aunt, that's all I want."

"She might have been looked on as an object of shame by her mother and effectively removed from the family on purpose, as if she had never existed," Eoin warned. "You know, Molly, it's possible that she bought into her exile, and she's passed away without your father knowing it."

"Maybe so, but my father wanted me to find her just the same. I'm doing this for him, Eoin. I'd just as soon leave this God-forsaken country right now."

The discussion veered off into an analysis of Mairead O'Meara's project and how it dovetailed with O'Rahilly's efforts on behalf of the laundry girls. Molly took advantage of the new topic to retire to the lady's room, while Eoin watched her leave the office, eyes fixed on her retreating bottom.

"This is none of my business, Eoin, but, is there something going on between you two?" Sean inquired tactfully.

"Do you think a long-distance romance has much of a chance?" the economist mused, his head in the clouds.

"You do know that she's married, don't you?"

263

Eoin eased back into his chair, casually draping one leg over the other. "When it's being given away, Sean, I'd be mad not to take what I can get," he said.

The smiling countenance fooled even an experienced lawyer, despite the chipping around the edges as Eoin's heart crumbled to dust. In public, he held up his mask, letting it fall when he was well away from Sean's office. Feeling betrayed and used, he had to sit in a car with a cold-blooded adulteress, something he did not think he could do with grace.

As soon as they were in the middle of a traffic jam on Pearse Street, he let loose with his pain. "How could you do this to me, Molly? I'm not a prude, my girl, I'd have fucked your brains out for the enjoyment of it and I wouldn't complain. Why didn't you have the decency to tell me first?"

"It's not...you don't understand," she mumbled, her lower lip held painfully between her teeth.

"Do you do this often, go off on holiday and screw men who think you're the answer to their prayers? Do you enjoy tearing out guts; is that your game, disemboweling your lovers? I feel shit right now, congratulations. Are you happy?"

"No," she said.

"I really tried not to, but I fell in love with you. There, does that bring a smile to your face? I'm the gobshite, I'm the hypocrite, is that it?" He nearly rear-ended the garda patrol car that was stopped at the traffic light. "Christ, I could – can I have something besides silence? At least make up a feeble excuse."

"I can't."

"Have you avenged your family now? I've got friends, Molly, would you like to destroy them too? Have a go at every male in Ireland until your father and your aunt can rest in peace, their honor restored on an altar of broken hearts."

Traffic ground to a halt, and Molly jumped out of the car, quickly disappearing into the crowd of people on their way home from work. He had no intention of going after her, if that was what she expected. As if she did never been there, Eoin continued to drive, steering his car towards home. He pictured the letter that was sitting on his desk, ready to be posted, but he did not think that he could follow through after all. The honor of presenting a paper at the economics symposium at the University of Chicago had seemed like a glorious opportunity only a few hours ago. Now it appeared to be a pointless trip.

15

Watching her body change was a marvelous wonder, something that Nuala did secretly under the bedclothes after the lights were out. She stroked her belly, amazed at the creation of life inside her, while carefully listening for the dormitory nun's footsteps. Admiring her body was punishable as a display of vanity, and she did not want to be paraded naked through the gauntlet, as One Hundred Twelve had done last week. The laughter and derision of the laundry girls, the nuns and the monitors was more than Nuala could tolerate.

"The father?" Forty-Nine asked again when she and Nuala were pushing trolleys at the same time.

"McNulty," Nuala stated on the return pass.

"Bastard," Forty-Nine growled on the afternoon run.

"He loves me," Nuala explained.

"He used you," Forty-Nine told a naïve child on Wednesday.

"No," she stated with certainty.

"'Tis a crime."

"I'm guilty?"

"He is."

"I'm guilty," Nuala reiterated her fear.

"He abandoned," Forty-Nine hissed strongly.

"Did I sin?"

"He did."

By the end of the week, and from only a few words, Nuala came to see that something had gone wrong, but having to analyze on her own, she could not actually understand what her companion was driving at. Forty-Nine had been deserted by her boyfriend, and her bitterness filtered through in her explanations to Nuala, creating a web of absolute confusion over guilt and innocence, crime and punishment, and who paid the price of sin. There was no one to ask, no one to help her understand. The only person she had was Sister Monica, but the poor old woman could not even tell that her student was up the stick.

Sister Berenice must have been more vigilant than Nuala realized. Every time that the nun sniffed around, or had one of her spies poke a nose nearby, Nuala made sure that she was reciting prayers under her breath, intoning rosaries and murmuring entreaties to Saint Mary Magdalene and St. Benedict for good measure. Even so, Forty-Nine disappeared about one week before Nuala finished her laundry penance. Returning after an absence of three days, the penitent had bruises on her face and neck that showed all the marks of Sister Bertha's punishing keys. Nuala's last source of information was put at the sinks, where women scrubbed until

267

their knuckles were raw and bleeding. No one would ever again try to make friends with the youngest Magdalene. Her position in the laundry was clear.

Loneliness and oppressive silence dogged Nuala's weary steps. Her sessions with Sister Monica became the only light in the day, and Nuala started to take advantage of the nun's drowsing to capture an extra few minutes of reading, missing evening prayers and avoiding the Friday night beatings. When Sister Monica did administer the leather strap, she carried on half-heartedly, not disguising her boredom with the monotonous routine and demonstrating a tendency to spoil her pet.

"I set myself above the holy Sisters and conducted prayers without their guidance," Nuala took the cynical approach one Friday night. The belt fell across her shoulder blades, barely leaving a mark.

The flick of the strap was accompanied by a bored sigh. "Your sin is that of impatience. In the fullness of time, you will be called upon to teach and conduct prayers in a hospital where you will provide the only light in a very dark place."

"I confess my sin of impatience," Nuala responded, the drill well known. Two weak lashes were doled out for the crime, confirming for the penitent that she had not actually done anything wrong at all. It was some kind of silly game, done to amuse the nuns in their behind-the-looking-glass world, where kindness was cruelty and love was hate.

"You demonstrate your impatience by asking me when your tumor will be removed because it is causing you discomfort," Sister Monica said. "When God has determined that your illness should end, it will end. Accept the discomfort with patience, Mary Magdalene, accept all suffering with pleasure in God's will."

"I am guilty of impatience, Sister," Nuala spooned out another dollop of sweet insincerity. She expected another swat, but none came.

"I, too, am guilty of impatience. Do you hear my impatience, when I call you Mary Magdalene, well before you are consecrated? My time is short, child, and I am guilty of selfishly asking God to give me the years to see you married to our Church, when I can kiss Christ's newest bride. My confession is meant to show that we all are human, filled with all the faults of humanity. As long as you are a woman, for the rest of your days, you are a sinner, a daughter of Eve."

"Yes, Sister."

"You must forever guard against lust and temptation, and all pleasures of the flesh."

"Yes, Sister."

"Do not give in to base desires or depravity. The devil works in clever ways, to steal the souls of God's servants. He may wear many disguises."

"Yes, Sister. You have taught me that evil takes many forms. It may come to me as a priest or nun, is that possible?"

"Any form is possible, Mary Magdalene. Any form, both beautiful and hideous, can be used by Satan. Your only weapon is knowledge of God's word, to judge good from evil."

A knock on the door interrupted their religious studies, but the lecture had run on for so long that Sister Perpetua must have gone off in search of the prodigal penitent so that the dormitory could be locked up for the night. "When you pray before retiring, Sister, you might like to include Twenty-Seven in your prayers. One Hundred Twenty and I will offer up our prayers while we walk back to the dormitory."

"So she has passed away," Sister Monica said, sorrow in her voice. "I taught her when she was a student at the convent school."

"How remarkable, to remember someone after forty years," Perpetua said. To Nuala she added, "We would do well to also add Forty-Two to our prayers. She has just learned that she lost her mother."

Stunned into shocked silence, Nuala could not seem to make her legs move when Sister Perpetua motioned to her to leave. With a yank on the arm, the dormitory nun shook Nuala back to earth, catching her as the girl stumbled. "I am sorry, Sister," Nuala apologized, but her words were hollow noises.

Nuala had come to know Twenty-Seven from her month in the laundry, where the cancer stricken, middle-aged woman had a job folding pillowcases, the easiest task available. She also recognized Forty-Two, who worked the mangle that

270

pressed the pillowcases flat and smooth. Mother and daughter had labored side by side, and the work detail had been arranged to add to Twenty-Seven's penance for bearing a child out of wedlock. For eighteen years, the woman had stood next to her daughter and been banned from speaking, from making herself known. Nuala stared at Sister Perpetua, to look beyond the black habit, to gaze through the looking glass.

"You feel something strongly, One Hundred Twenty?" the nun asked.

"Yes, Sister," Nuala replied. "I see so clearly now. I understand."

"You are making great progress with Sister Monica. She is one of the finest teachers I have ever known, and you are blessed to have her as your tutor."

"Yes, Sister."

Lying in bed, listening to a storm rage outside, Nuala talked to her father in heaven. "I tested them, Daddy. They see lies as truth, and they worship evil. God doesn't live here, Daddy, please, help me get away."

In the dim light of dawn on Saturday morning, the delivery wagons came to the convent to pick up the clothes that had been dropped off earlier in the week, all cleaned, pressed and packaged neatly for the hospitals and private homes that paid the Sisters of Mercy to handle their laundry. Only the nuns were allowed to see the teamsters, while the girls were kept occupied in the chapel or at breakfast. The

271

men were under strict orders to be quiet when they came, so that the loud shouting in the yard was unexpected, an alarm that roused the laundry girls from bed, to flock around the windows.

"Forty-Two escaped," one young girl gasped, the excitement and hope of the desperate so evident in her voice.

Not every escape was successful, and the Garda could be counted on to bring in any girl they found wandering the streets of Dublin who was dressed in a shapeless gray dress, the style more in keeping with 1865 than 1934. Even so, not every runaway turned up again in the dormitory with her face covered in bruises, the result of Sister Bertha's clanging keys.

"Remain in your beds," Sister Perpetua barked, coming out of her cell to see what the noise was about. It was not long before Sister Marian and Sister Bertha turned up, striding rapidly to the wash room.

With the nuns out of the room, the code of silence fell away, and those with a view of the yard reported back what was happening. An ambulance was seen coming in, and several garda cars were reported, parked among the various delivery wagons. Men below were calling up to the wash room window, out of sight of the girls in the dormitory. So many men were barking orders that they began to contradict one another, but finally, one cry rose up and was repeated along a chain of command. Someone was to bring a ladder.

*Finally, one strong voice took charge, the sound deep
and confident. "Climb up and get hold of her, Maher, while
Quinn comes up behind to catch the body when it falls. Show
some respect, man; even a whore is entitled once she's dead.
Careful there, boys, we don't need to drop the poor girl on the
ground like a load of coal. Looks like a suicide, Mr.
McSweeney. Right you are, Reverend Mother, she's a suicide."*

*"They killed her," Nuala whispered to those around
her. "They killed her."*

*"Go on, Sister, cut the sheet off the drain pipe," the
man in charge shouted.*

*"That's one way to escape," Nine chortled, beginning
to laugh. "Garda can't bring her back, not her."*

*At morning Mass, Nuala prayed for Forty-Two's soul,
explaining to God that the young woman was not a suicide,
despite appearances. "I know that you aren't here," she said.
"But I believe that you hear me when we talk like this. Don't
abandon me, God, please, let me see my Daddy again. If you
help me get out, I'll do anything to save souls. I promise."*

*As the salver was passed from chin to chin at the
communion rail, Nuala skipped her turn with such swift ease
that the chaplain did not notice that he passed over one head.
Her mind was made up, to never again participate in their
rituals and sacraments. She was dealing with the devil's
handmaidens, and she recognized them for what they were
thanks to Sister Monica's teaching. Weekly confession would*

273

become a play, with the same lines delivered for every performance. The real prayers would be spoken directly to God, the God she had come to know in the New Testament. She was sure that He was out there, not in the chapel in Booterstown, but somewhere, and she was going to find Him.

When Molly slipped into the bed and breakfast, Mary was waiting for her in the parlor, full of cheer. "There's a lovely article in the *Times*, Molly, come and see," she sang out when the front door closed. "Holy Mother of God, you look like you've seen death."

"Mary, is Rose insane?" Molly asked.

"No, not insane," Mary said, her brow crinkling with incomprehension. "Damaged, I'd say."

"Broken? Broken down?" Molly probed.

"Was your aunt a laundry girl?" Mary asked.

Not pausing to answer, Molly ran back to the kitchen and returned quickly with Rose, knowing now that she had to change, longing to find the power to fix things, starting in a bed and breakfast in Dublin.

"Tell her, Rose," Mary pleaded, her eyes glistening. "It's best to hear from you, can't you see that? Look at her, Rose."

"I'm suing the Sisters of Mercy. Throw me out of your house if that bothers you, but I'm going after them. I want evidence, Rose; I want it all. I won't stop until I've wrung the life's blood out of them."

274

"You can make them pay?" Rose asked. "Could I get my wages? They made us work all day, every day except Sunday, and I never saw a penny. It wasn't fair, Mary, when I could have done the same job at a public laundry and helped my mother. I didn't mind working."

"If you go to a solicitor, Rose, you'll have to tell him what happened. And again, in the dock, you'll have to tell everyone," Mary warned.

"Or you can keep your mouth shut, and they'll win," Molly put in. "Lay down and die for them because they terrorized you into silence, and they've beaten you again."

The phone began to ring, breaking the wave of energy that had begun to surge through the room. Molly wanted to shake Rose's shoulders, to wake her up from her fifty year slumber. All Rose had done was to prove that her parish priest was right, that she was a bad girl, when she did not need any help in protecting her purity. For her entire life, she had never been touched by a man, never experienced the pleasures of love and children and family. It had all been for nothing, Molly wanted to tell her; it had been a complete waste of one woman's life, all for nothing. They locked her away and she stayed locked away, but it was not too late to break out of her self-imposed prison.

"We can expect quite a fine crowd tomorrow," Mary said, changing the subject. "The phone has been jangling all day, with that lovely notice that was in the newspaper. Every man calling says the same thing, Molly, that he looks forward to meeting Frank Devoy's little girl."

275

In the turmoil of the day, Molly had forgotten about the wake. If she could have started over, she would have dug a hole on the day she arrived, buried her father and then hopped the first plane back to Chicago. This trip had accomplished nothing, except to make her miserable. She was depressed by her father's stolen childhood, defeated by her aunt's destruction, and agonizingly sorry that she had been so cruel to Eoin. That above all caused her the greatest pain.

She was a hypocrite, in essence, for pushing Rose to fight back when she knew that something wasn't right about the way she avoided close relationships. Talk was too easy, and Molly recognized her ability to goad others while she hung back, not doing what she should have done before leaving a trail of unhappiness behind her. It was as if her father's fear of discovery, his ingrained sense of shame, had acted as a poison to alter his genetic code. The fear of embarrassment became a trait, along with blue eyes and fair skin, a gene that Molly feared she had passed on to her children. The key turned in the lock, the door was opened, but still she was afraid to walk out, to be free.

Thursday dawned behind clouds and mist, a gray day that suited Molly's mood. She had to face her father's old mates, all the orphans from Kilkenny and Dun Laoghaire who were as close-mouthed as her father had been. Entertaining strangers was going to be impossible, as impossible as going home. Molly did not want to stay in Dublin, but she did not want to go back to her old life either. Feeling disoriented and essentially homeless, she carried the box of ashes to Mary's parlor and waited for the onslaught.

The dining room table was set for a feast, with breads, ham and boiled bacon piled on platters. Bottles of whiskey and pots of tea were paired with cakes and biscuits to welcome the mourners and toast to Frank's memory. Molly stood near the door of the parlor, meeting, shaking hands and forcing her lips to smile.

"All these boys were stolen by the Church," Molly overheard Pat Grady say to his son. "Ned, go on, tell my boy about your life after you left the industrial school. It's time he heard it."

Molly slipped into the parlor to listen, hoping for a tale of triumph to alleviate her oppressive depression. "We had the opportunity to learn a trade, you see, and I chose tailoring," Ned began. Molly's mind wandered, knowing that Ned was the tailor who made her father's shirts many years ago.

"Less than a shilling a week?" Pat's son Robert looked at the tailor in disbelief. "That's all they paid you?"

"And I wasn't to speak to the farmer's family or he'd give me the sack," Ned continued his tale. "I had to take my meals apart from everyone, like a dirty animal they treated me. I'd get my bowl of stew at dinner and go out to the shed where I slept, trying to keep the snow out of my food on cold days. It must have been the coldest place in Ireland, that shed in Ballaghadereen."

"Excuse me, but aren't you Ned the tailor?" Molly broke in.

"How I became a tailor," Ned crowed, taking a sip of whiskey. "I was a tailor, Molly, but my employer had a farm and I had to work there as well. A cow kicked me, broke my leg, so I was sacked. I ended up in hospital, and lucky for me that James Dillon happened by. He saw to it that I was taken care of, and when I recovered, I went straight to Dublin with my back wages that he got for me. I opened my shop then, and it's still open today."

Yet another tale of cruel abuse was sickening, making Molly feel worse than she already did. She did not see the humor in the tale that made Ned and his cohorts chuckle as if they had pulled off a clever prank. Seeking refuge, she avoided Pat Grady fortifying his resolve in the dining room, and retreated to the kitchen to escape. Even there, she could not get away from Rose's voice, filtering through the gap around the door, boldly proclaiming that she had been put away in a laundry and rescued by a brother who never gave up looking for her. It brought to mind the unknown dead at Glasnevin Cemetery and the unknown fate of Nuala Devoy.

"Molly, Mr. O'Rahilly phoned," Mary poked her head in. "He's getting a summary typed up for you, about your aunt. Have a drop of the jar, it'll do you good."

The little cottage on St. Anne's Road was packed with old bodies, filling the rooms with the thick brogue of the country and the delicate wisp of Dublin. Frank Devoy was brought back to

Molly for a moment, resurrected in an inflection and a musical cadence that was flavored with a few words of Irish. A wave of nostalgia brought tears to her eyes, while a sip of whiskey burned down her throat.

"RAF," the acknowledgement popped up around the parlor and dining room, along with, "Irish Army. Leeds Rifles; Jesus, the likes of you drove a tank? Royal Fusiliers, Lancashire Fusiliers; go on with you, you were one of McAlpine's Fusiliers. You mean navvy, not Royal Navy."

"Of course we signed on during the Emergency," Mike O'Keefe said. Eoin was interviewing a group in the parlor, fascinated by their stories and their remarkable ability to laugh over past tragedy, revel in the present, and hope for the future.

"It was a golden opportunity, lad, to chuck the misery we found out there," Dan said. "After Carriglea, we thought we had it made, with a topnotch education under our belts. Then we get out and discover that all of Ireland thought we were no good, a bunch of jailbirds and delinquents if we weren't some whore's bastard child."

"Not only that, Danny, but the only life we knew was the regimented life," Mike put in. "They raised us up for the military, I'm telling you, and we fit right in like putting on a glove."

"There are many of us who stayed in England after the war," a balding old gentleman added. "No one knew our past and we were treated like normal people abroad. To this day, I haven't told my family about St. Patrick's, not even my wife."

"Well, my boys, I'm proud to announce that, in honor of our old friend Frank Devoy, I've told my son that I was put away in an industrial school," Pat declared. A stunned silence settled over the parlor. "Frank's told his little girl, indirectly I'll admit, but he's opened up his past. I won't be ashamed any more."

"Well, aren't you the little crusader?" Eoin sneered in Molly's ear when she drifted by.

"You didn't have to come," she said, squirming away.

"I want to know why you treated me like shit, that's all. Tell me and I'll be on my way."

"I'm sorry." Molly tried to back away but Eoin kept following her, shadowing every move.

"I'm not a handsome man, Molly, it can't be my looks. Is it my cock? Do you find me attractive from the waist down?"

"Stop it, Eoin."

"What'll it be, one last ride before you go back to your husband? I'm willing to give you a grand send-off. You're good in bed, my girl; I'd like to be fucked one last time. Except we'll both know what it's about, won't we?"

"You don't understand."

"No, I don't. Good on you." He folded his arms across his chest, daring her to speak. "Let's try the question again."

"It's best not to know," she uttered a pat phrase that sounded like an old custom.

"Will you at least kiss me goodbye?"

The look in her eyes startled him out of his tantrum. Somehow, he realized that things had gone wrong for Molly, that she had gotten hopelessly lost. He saw a deep hurt, a pool of depression and defeat that he had helped to fill. Reflected back at him was the day in Kilrossanty, as if Con MacNeill's insults about industrial school boys and the fallen women of the laundries were raining down, a torrent of cruelty and abuse. Reflected in Molly's eyes, Eoin saw that the prejudice was splashed onto an economics professor who once scorned Ireland's disgraced. It was not vengeance that Molly sought, but a route to take her away from those who injured her father, a man she loved and admired.

"I'll be in Chicago in August for a conference," he said, not sure if he was making a threat, a promise, or a plea for forgiveness.

"August." She paused, as if thinking deeply over his pronouncement. "I have to get back." she pointed toward the parlor, where the whiskey had done its job by raising the volume of the men's voices.

She lost herself in the swirl of mourners, making the acquaintance of Gerry O'Flaherty over a shot of liquor. "You all ran away, just like my father," she said.

"Not running, lass," Gerry chuckled. "A man wants a family and he wants a good job to keep them. Why be a fool and stay here, to be spit on and cheated? We weren't ready for the outside world, that's the worst of what they did to us. We were like aliens, landing on a strange planet and then trying to fit in. Where's the glory in being the whipping boy? We moved on, and those who mocked us after we'd made something of ourselves only hated us the more for our success and their failure. It's grand, Molly, to stand on top of the mountain and watch those who tried to hold you back struggling for a foothold at the bottom."

Wandering through the rooms, Molly listened to the St. Patrick's boys recall the electrocution machine, the beatings, and all the disappointments of an orphan's solitary, unloved, life.

"What I would have given for a tuck-in at night," Liam sighed sadly.

"Even a cuddle when you were frightened," another gentleman added. "A kind word, something of the like. I used to cry under the bedclothes at night so the older boys wouldn't hear me. They'd mock a little boy's tears, wouldn't they?"

"Once he got out, he ate himself to death," Liam recalled another boy from St. Patrick's. "To this day, I check the breadbox every morning, to be sure that there's a loaf of bread in the house. I'll never get over it, that fear of being hungry again."

"Did your dad ever told you how we used to strip the brambles clean when we found a patch of berries on our Sunday walks?" Tommy Nolan whispered. "And the blessed Sisters of Charity, dining on roasts and vegetables every day, and begrudging us an egg on Easter Sunday."

"The day they sold the band," Molly came upon Pat Grady in mid-story. "Now there was a sad occasion."

"I ran into the band director in London about five years ago," Mike said. "We were on holiday, me and the missus. He was a Carriglea boy as well; did you know that? He stayed on after he earned his leaving certificate."

"He had no family at all, you see," Pat mentioned to Molly.

"He left the school after they sold off the instruments, and he became a teacher," Mike continued. "Training the mentally handicapped in tailoring. One of the finest, most Christian men I've ever known."

"So he never married?" Molly asked.

"No, no, never did. He had his pupils, I suppose, and they made a fine enough family for him," Mike said. Drifting off on another tack, he went to another time. "I still recall the smell of the peat fire. You thought that when you were a senior boy you'd get the warmth of it, but that little grate didn't heat much more than the night watchman's chair."

"You lived in unheated dormitories?" Molly asked.

"We soon got used to it," three men said at once.

"The senior boys, I remember, used to sit around the fire with Brother George before lights out," Dan continued. "Do you recall that, lads, our intellectual discussion with Brother George? We were regular philosophers back then."

"It's the newspapers that I enjoyed, when he would paste them in the windows of the recreation yard so we could stay abreast of the world. Lindbergh's flight was big news in those days, and then when his baby was kidnapped, that was a sad, sad tale." Mike smiled wistfully.

"The wireless was grand, wasn't it?" came the next recollection, and Molly retired to the kitchen to find some solitude.

Rose was merrily puttering around, making more tea and refilling the trays of sandwiches. Only five wives had come with husbands, and Rose put great stock in impressing the few ladies.

"In the laundry, Rose, do you remember books and the radio?" Molly quizzed.

"Not in the laundry, lass," Rose laughed. "We had prayer. When I was older, I saw one or two films of a Sunday afternoon, but no, not the radio. At the end of the day, we were so worn out that all we wanted was to drop into bed and sleep."

"So the boys had the best of a bad lot?"

"It's a man's world, Molly, yesterday and today," Rose said.

"I've never seen you so happy."

"You've set me free, and I'm out of the cage, free to fly," Rose effused. "There's another lady here, Molly, put away like me. She's been through it, and had sorrows as I had. What a lovely chat we've had, about the nuns and the consecrated girls, and so much alike, our time in the laundry."

"Some man at the orphanage sexually abused my aunt," Molly stated, seeking relief by sharing her burden. "She was put away in the laundry because she was pregnant."

"I met a girl who was put in the family way by the parish priest, and then he put her away to hide his sin. There were girls who went astray with a boyfriend and found themselves alone.

Then there were the illegitimate girls, sent from the orphanage to the laundry. Mrs. Kiely told me of a girl who was put away even though the boy wanted to marry the girl he wronged, but the priest thought that the girl needed punishing. There were all sorts, Molly, as many excuses as there are stars in the sky."

"What excuse did they use on you?"

"I was considered a pretty girl. My father was dead, and Father Considine stepped in."

"So they went after the powerless? A bunch of bullies in Roman collars and starched wimples," Molly grumbled.

"They wanted to clean up the slums, to fix poverty by taking the children and remaking them. The intention was good, Molly, it was the way they did it that was wrong."

"Please, Rose, they had the good intentions of a Mussolini. Ask the Italians about Mussolini, and they'll tell you how he made the trains run on time, or they'll tell you about the free education he provided. There's some good intentions for you, and don't mind the war that got in the way."

"It's human nature to look for the good and keep that warm. You'll make yourself bitter if you feast only on cold sorrow."

"I wish that I had come with my father when he asked me before. Maybe he could have shown me what is so wonderful about Ireland. I don't ever want to come back here."

"*Muise*, you've spent your time here mucking a manure pile," Rose clucked. "Just go listen to your father's old boys a while, and you'll find the beauty he knew."

285

"No, I can't listen to them anymore. The abuse, the cruelty; it's nauseating."

Grabbing Molly's ear, Rose gave an affectionate tug. "I don't think you hear clearly."

Eoin had his hand on the door, ready to push it open, but he could not bring himself to interrupt. He wanted to ask her what she thought the twenty thousand dollar check was for, to see if she realized it was a twenty thousand dollar guffaw. It was clear to him that the money was a loud laugh in the face of all those who claimed that Frank was worthless, a sneer at those who kept their sons away from an industrial school graduate. She was too deaf to hear the cry of victory that her father had shouted from the grave, a bold announcement that he had won in the end. It was a shame that she did not make the journey with her father, because he could have explained things to her. As it was, she missed the point completely, and Eoin felt nothing but pity for her.

"We'll be sorry to see you leave," Rose went on.

"I don't have any place to go," Molly said. "I can't go back home, Rose."

"You're welcome to stay," Rose offered.

"I don't want to stay," Molly sighed. "I don't want to go home. Maybe I'll get lucky and the plane will crash."

"I wanted to die, when I was trapped in the laundry," Rose said. "I think we all did."

Pat came by, to poke his head into the kitchen to tell Molly it was time for the removal, to head out to Goldenbridge

Cemetery and bring the story of Frank Devoy full circle. Eoin heard her sniffling as the kitchen door closed. Not sure what he should do, or what his position was, he waited for a moment, hoping that she would make the next move, the one that he heard her beginning to make.

When a few of the penitents began to stir up trouble, Nuala was put back in the laundry to be the ears of Sister Bertha. She was sent all over, pushing trolleys overflowing with heavy wet laundry or stuffed with piles of ironing. Lifting, reaching, stretching and standing for five and one half hours each day, her feet and ankles were swollen by dinnertime. The heat in the laundry was unbearable, with clouds of steam adding to summer's warmth until Nuala thought that she would sweat out every drop of fluid in her body. The Sisters liked to remind the inmates of the fires of hell on the hottest days, to reinforce the imagery, and Nuala did look on the Magdalene laundry as a corner of a large, industrial hell.

The incessant pounding of the machines, coupled with the oppressive heat, triggered explosions of rage and frustration among the laundry girls. They were here against their will, treated worse than animals, and subjected to endless mental torment. Nuala heard the complaints and learned of the plans, whispered secretly out in the yard or mumbled from the corner of a mouth during work. She kept

287

her lips sealed, and when Eighty-eight went out on strike one hot August day, Nuala pretended that she had never heard a thing. If the plan worked, however, she had every intention of copying the girl, always hoping to find some way to be set free. Eighty-eight would turn up in the laundry two days later, the bruises on her face still livid and purple. She never repeated her protest, and Nuala grew despondent.

By October, she was tempted to trade a beating for a few days of rest. The work had always been hard, but now she felt so wretchedly weary that she could scarcely roll out of bed in the morning. She fell asleep during morning Mass, and her thigh was black and blue from the constant pinching that Seventeen used to rouse her. Even so, as soon as she set foot on the polished wood of the convent's quiet floors, she felt refreshed and full of energy, as if she had just woken up from a restful sleep.

"Very soon, this tumor will be ready for removal," Sister Monica informed her pupil. "After you have recovered, it will be a good time for Sister Domenica to come and see you, to have a serious discussion and perhaps began to chart the course for your final years with us."

"Thank you, Sister," Nuala replied mechanically.

"I have something for you. You received a tin of sweets for your birthday, and you have earned a reward this evening."

"Thank you, Sister, but I would enjoy it more if you ate it," Nuala said, a master of the game.

"Bless your consideration, Mary Magdalene. There are two bull's-eyes. We can share and allow this one indulgence."

"Thank you, Sister."

The birthday had come and gone a month earlier, without a word from Maire or Frank. It had always been that way, because Mother Superior reviewed the mail and decided if there was anything worth relating to the girls. Birthday greetings and such were unimportant, and death notices were often forgotten for months because Reverend Mother was so busy. The candies came at Christmas and again in September, but the sweets were stored away, to be doled out by Sister Monica in accordance with her lesson plan. The shillings from Aunt Maggie and Aunt Celie were forwarded at once to the Benedictine convent in Connemara, much as the gifts would be donated to the order when the oblate became a full-fledged novice.

"Do you wish to lighten your load?" Sister Monica asked with a maternal affection.

"No, Sister," Nuala lied.

"But you will do as I instruct?"

"Of course, Sister."

"When Sister Perpetua comes to you in the morning, to return to the crochet room for a full day of work, you will not protest over the ease of the job when I know that you long to exert yourself."

"I will go where I am needed, Sister, I will not complain."

The nun placed her hands on Nuala's middle, gently gliding her hands over the hump that was not particularly noticeable under the voluminous penitent's uniform. Where Sister touched, Nuala felt her baby touch back, an action that brought a tear to the old woman's eye. Just as she was about to tell her beloved mentor that it was not a tumor at all, Monica rapidly changed her face and changed the topic.

"Yes, soon, but not soon enough for my impatient student," she said, gently teasing her beloved pet. "You must not labor at difficult tasks until you are restored to health."

"I am not worthy of special treatment, Sister." She felt incredible pity for Sister, a woman of great wisdom but no knowledge of the world outside of a convent's sheltering walls. "But I will always be obedient to my superiors."

"It is not a question of worth, child, but a simple matter of health. What is the good of working yourself to death if you have not yet gained a seat at the Lord's table? If you apply yourself to a lighter task with equal diligence, you extend your life and the amount of time that you can give over to repentance and penance."

The advice was crushing, providing a reminder that Nuala had three long years left to her sentence. The isolation from other girls her own age was growing more intolerable every day, and the fact that she was denied an hour of idle *chatter after slaving for ten hours made the suffering that much worse. Kneeling at Sister's feet, her head fell into the nun's lap, to pretend that she was someplace else for a minute or two. With Monica's bony, cold hand on her shoulder, she found no relief from the loneliness, the solitude, or the misery.*

No one ever told the pregnant child what was going to happen, so when Nuala woke up at four o'clock one morning with her guts in a knot, she presumed that she was sick. With the chill of early November icing the windows and blowing in through the cracks, it was too cold in the frigid dormitory to get out from under a warm blanket. Having learned to tolerate illness, she stayed in bed until Sister Perpetua rang her bell, and she went through the routine of rising, swiftly making her bed to cover the bloody, wet spot on her sheets out of fear of being punished for soiling the bed linen. The breast binder was donned so loosely that it was falling down before she had her shoes on, and she marched off to Mass as she always did. For two days, she endured the pain, hoping that everyone had been wrong and that she was going to die. Finally, the throbbing was so great that she could stand it no longer, and Sister Perpetua rushed to her side in the crochet room when she screamed out in agony.

For a third day, the contractions rippled with force, while Nuala sobbed in the infirmary, so sick that she prayed for death. Only by chance did she get a clue that the baby was coming, when she overheard Matron tell someone to send for Dr. O'Connor at once. The patient had spiked a fever of over one hundred degrees, and labor was not progressing.

Nurse Hassett tied Nuala up to the delivery table so tightly that the girl could not even bend her legs. Her entire body was pulsating and vibrating, her mouth was wide open and her lips dry. The room was filled with screams, the noise of a woman in agony, but several hours passed before Nuala realized that she was the one who was wailing. She struggled against the restraints, thinking that she could find relief if she could get away. Her throat ached and the cries grew hoarse, but she continued to yell for her mother and shout for her father while Dr. O'Connor put his hands inside her.

"High forceps," he said to Nurse Hassett above the din.

"It's almost over," the matron soothed, an unexpected sympathy in her voice.

"Here we are, just as I told them. A large cranium and a small pelvis," O'Connor continued, very angry. "Bring her to my surgery, I said, she needs to be sectioned, but what does herself do but turn a blind eye?"

"We didn't know," the nurse said.

"The head was engaged when I arrived. Engaged, Matron, and stuck in place."

"Shall I send for Mother Superior?"

"I'll make the decision, thank you. Better to have a medical man act sensibly than bring in a woman with no training in reality. I could have solved the problem months ago, and kept my mouth shut. Well, I'll solve the problem now."

"For the health of the girl?"

There was no answer, only grunting that accompanied a strange new sensation, that of cold metal that felt like an opening trap, expanding inside until Nuala truly believed that the doctor was going to tear her in half, from her bottom up to her throat. The pain that had been overwhelming was only getting worse, and she struggled even harder to get away before she was drawn and quartered

Down low in her stomach, where the pain had first started, something wiggled in her, and it did not hurt quite as much. She could breathe again, great hiccupy gasps that filled her lungs again and again. Gently, Matron sponged Nuala's face with warm water, talking over the patient as she conferred with the doctor in medical jargon. Doctor O'Connor replied with grumbling, the only sound in an infirmary that had grown silent, eerily still. Looking down between her legs, Nuala watched his white haired head bob up and down as he worked behind a sheet. It was almost over, she overheard the doctor, but whatever else he said was a jumble of irritable mumbling and vulgarities.

Their eyes met when Dr. O'Connor rose, a wad of bloody sheets in his hands, and he averted his gaze at once, unable to face his patient. "Stillborn," he groused, short-tempered. "There's no need to record it, Matron. There's no point at all."

"The Mother Superior should be pleased," Miss Hassett said, pressing Nuala to her breast as if she did not want the girl to hear what the adults were saying. "It's the best outcome."

"For her," Dr. O'Connor said, canting his head at Nuala.

"There, now, it's all over," the nurse said, giving her undivided attention to a child who was shivering, weeping and gasping for breath, a tethered animal. "Let's get you into bed and you'll be right as rain in no time. You'll bleed from your privates every month now, like the other big girls."

"She never thought about what she'd do with it after it was born, did she?" O'Connor bellowed, while Matron tried to shush him. "Who was going to feed it, a thirteen-year-old girl who didn't know she was going to have it in the first place?"

Matron took the doctor's arm, to lead him away, but he would not be stopped, and Nuala began to wonder if he had been drinking. She could hear his voice echoing through the empty infirmary, bouncing down from the high ceiling. "Offer up a prayer of Thanksgiving, Reverend Mother, and thank God that he denied life to the abomination. It's all been erased; it never happened."

A few minutes later, after Nuala had been tucked into bed, the doctor came back, with a distinct smell of whiskey on his breath. He told her that he had prescribed injections for the pain, still without looking her in the eye. "Now stop carrying on," he advised. He cleared his throat, ran his beautifully clean hands through his thinning hair, and spoke to the wall. "The surgery was a complete success. No complications. You'll be on your feet in no time."

Nothing could stop the tears, as Nuala mourned the demise of her last hope. In her childish fantasies, she had looked on the baby as a replacement for her precious Jenny, the celluloid and cloth doll that she had prized as an outside girl. She had nothing anymore, no family, no home, no baby, and no one who loved her. When Matron delivered an injection of morphine, Nuala did not even feel the sting of the needle. Drifting on a cloud of hazy lethargy, she prayed to her daddy in heaven.

"Daddy, God can't find me here, and I'm so small, can you show him where I am? Please help me, Daddy, help me get away. Tell God how terrible it is here, so he can save me. Please, Daddy, don't forget me."

Numbed into oblivion, Nuala lost track of day and night. She would sleep and then wake without knowing how long she had dozed, half expecting to open her eyes in her bedroom on Northbrook Terrace. Always, she found her sights fixed on the same ceiling, her bottom sore and throbbing. Her chest hurt as well, and when she touched her breasts she felt two wet spots, perfectly round, as if her body was crying as well. She was filled up, unable to hold in anymore, with a powerful urge to release everything and feel the sweet sensation of emptiness.

Struggling to her feet, Nuala was surprised at how weak she was, as if her knees were made of aspic and her head was floating about on its own. Tottering at the edge of the cot, she noticed a roll of bandages and a scissors on the bedside table, next to a syringe and a small bottle of clear fluid. What little she knew of the human body had come from the first aid manuals she had memorized, miscellaneous facts that drifted through her brain like wispy, soft clouds. She had an inkling, as she took the scissors and embedded it into her wrist, that she could hit the spot in between the bundle of tendons if she pushed hard enough. The blood flowed in a steady stream, warm against her skin, and she slid to the floor to watch the red stain grow ever larger on the white of her nightdress. With difficulty, but with determination, she pulled out the scissors and attacked her left wrist.

"I'm coming home, Daddy," she whispered weakly. "I can't stay here anymore."

16

It was not St. Peter who greeted Nuala when she opened her eyes again. Dr. O'Connor was trussing her up like a turkey while he criticized Nurse Hassett's error. "I told you to watch for hallucinations. Prescribing narcotics to babies is risky, and I thought that I made that clear," the physician glowered, a touch of angry impatience in his voice. Mumbling under his breath, he spoke to the air. "If I had fixed her the first time I examined her, we wouldn't have to do this now. Tell me about sins and crime, will she, the old bat. Just as blind."

Realizing that she was still in the same nightmare, Nuala began to cry, going so far as to plead with the doctor to help her get away. For the first time, he looked her straight in the eye, and Nuala saw a man who was just as helpless as she was, knowing what was going on in the laundry but unable to question the sacrosanct Sisters of Mercy. The doctor was tied up, just as she was, bound so tightly that he could not move a muscle.

"Be a good girl," he counseled quietly. "If you make trouble, they'll have you locked up in the lunatic asylum and that's far worse than this. Do you understand?"

"I want to go home," Nuala wailed anew. "What did I do wrong? Why can't I go home?"

"Stay out of trouble and you'll go home in three years," the doctor said. The dejected girl only screamed and sobbed, struggling against the restraints that held her to the bed. "Do you hear me? Shut up, keep your head down and you'll go home in three years."

One of the living dead returned to work two months later, an old woman without life or spirit, shoulders hunched against the weight of living. Her mouth was too tired to move, to respond to the priest's incantations at Mass, to repeat the Stations of the Cross or to recite the rosary. Confession was the same every week, a made-up list of errors that was meant to fool the evil beings that ruled the Booterstown empire. Nuala survived by shutting out the hymns and prayers of the Sisters during the workday, focusing instead on her supplication to the true God, the God of the Bible.

"She is remarkably accomplished," Sister Domenica decided, impressed by their brief interview the following winter. "Her knowledge of Scripture is amazing for a grown woman, let alone a child of her years."

"We find that she has developed quickly," Mother Superior put in. "Within the past year, I would say, she has grown remarkably calm, serene in fact. I have the impression *that the girl has risen to a higher plane, where our simple prayers and devotions are inadequate, leading her to seek out more scholarly texts."*

"She has shown extraordinary insight into the teachings of St. Benedict," Sister Monica boasted.

"You have been her tutor for some time, Sister Monica," the Benedictine said. "What is your opinion?"

"My opinion is highly biased, Sister, because my heart overrides my reason," the elderly nun demurred. "We have become very close over the years. She is my caretaker, as much as my pupil, sharing my cell and being my legs, my eyes. I am old, old and frail, and my heart tells me to keep her by my side, for my own selfish reasons. My mind tells me that I must let her go, that she is ready to take the veil and it would be wrong of us to hold her back."

"I agree completely with Sister Monica," Reverend Mother jumped in, rather abruptly. "Until she is sixteen, she will be under our supervision, under the continued tutelage of Sister Monica. At that time, it would perhaps be best that she be sent at once to Kylemore Abbey, before she could fall under the influence of the outside world. Without doubt, Sister, she is prepared to enter the convent now, but with another two years of education, she will be more advanced than any novice I have ever met."

"I see no reason to postpone her entrance until she is eighteen," Sister Domenica agreed. "She is mature beyond her

years, and considering her mother's questionable morality, it would be our duty to keep them separated."

"She is rather an impatient person," Sister Monica warned. "Her strong urge to do penance for her mother has been the impetus to speed her through her studies. However, I can understand her haste, and if we can save a few precious years, I would not correct her eagerness in this matter."

Maggie Devoy Ryan was fiercely obstinate, a woman not to be trifled with, and she struck terror in the hearts of those who tried to cross her, including the Mother Superior of the Booterstown convent. As godmother to Nuala, the woman took her position seriously, and she sent countless letters to the convent over the years, asking after her niece and demanding answers. Her perseverance had as much to do with her duties to Nuala as it did with her particular attachment to her brother's firstborn. Maire had once feared that Nuala was going to end up like her aunt, so similar were their personalities, the sort of woman who wore the pants in the family.

Maggie liked to think that her niece was more like her than any of her three daughters had turned out to be. Due to her close connection with Nuala, she worked tirelessly to get a definite answer from the walled compound near the coast. Unlike Maire, she would not settle for empty words, and she hounded the nun as July came to a close, to make

arrangements to pick up Nuala on her sixteenth birthday.
Maire was counting the days when her children were returned
to her, and she trusted to the nuns to make good on the terms
of the court order. When Frank came home for his week's
holiday in August of 1937, they set about making preparations
for Nuala's homecoming, having no doubts that it was going to
happen, especially with Aunt Maggie at the helm.

September crawled by, without a word from the
convent, and Maire began to fear that her daughter was dead
or, worse, put away. It was not unheard of for girls to
disappear into the laundries, with concerned family members
left to chase from one institution to the next, running down
leads that went nowhere. October came in with warm breezes
and went out with bitter winds, but still Nuala did not come
home. Inquiries to the convent were met with silence until
Reverend Mother Laurentia informed Mrs. O'Brien that her
daughter Nuala Devoy had been accepted as a novice to the
Benedictine order.

The ecstatic response on James Street was echoed all
across Dublin, in the homes of innumerable aunts, cousins,
friends and acquaintances of the Devoy clan. As a nun, Nuala
would reflect glory onto her family, something that they
lacked in their hovel on James Street. Maire looked forward
to the respect that would come her way, but she was more
grateful that her daughter was the recipient of a miracle.
Having been reduced to penury, Maire appreciated the fact

that Nuala's job would provide her with meals, housing and clothing for life with care in her old age, freeing her from the common worries of the world, and some stranger had donated the dowry that made it all possible.

It was all well and good with Aunt Maggie, to lay claim to a Benedictine in the family. She prattled on endlessly as she described the day when Nuala would grace her home with her blessed presence, a day that Maggie would broadcast throughout the town so that she could show off to the neighbors. Before all that was to happen, however, Maggie wanted to see her godchild, and Maire was helpless in the face of Maggie's insistence. "When the good Sisters tell me to come," Maire said, afraid of rocking a boat that might not turn out to be seaworthy.

"I've been waiting nine years," Maggie replied. Her jaw was set, her hands on her hips, and no one, especially not Maire, could move the mountain.

Egged on by an assertive sister-in-law, Maire rode the tram through Dublin, walking for a good part of the way because she could not afford the fare for the interurban train. With two days remaining before Christmas, and with Maggie's convincing arguments as ammunition, Maire did not think that she was asking all that much of the nuns, to let her daughter come home for the holidays.

"At the present time, Mrs. O'Brien, your daughter is completely enmeshed in a period of introspection in *preparation for the next part of her journey," the Mother Superior prevaricated. She took a seat next to the fire, inviting Maire to join her for tea with all the respect that was due to the mother of a religious.*

"Surely she can be spared for three days, Reverend Mother," Maire fought back politely. "Before she enters the convent, at least to see her brother again. Her aunt, Mrs. Ryan, is keen to speak to her."

The subtle reminder of Aunt Maggie was entirely intentional. In her last letter, Maggie had been both restrained and blunt, suggesting that she was prepared to use her financial resources or go to the authorities if necessary to seek Nuala's release. It was far more bold than Maire cared for, and she was now very much afraid that Maggie's harsh tone had set Reverend Mother Laurentia's mind against the holiday.

"I am concerned, you see, that the temptations of the city, the trappings of immodesty, might tempt our novice. Her vocation is truly the strongest I have ever witnessed, Mrs. O'Brien, and I fear that she may be swayed," the nun warned with a stern arch in her brow.

"Time are hard, Reverend Mother, and I'll tell you honestly, I can't hope to give Nuala anything grand. All I can offer is a chance to see her relations and say goodbye to the family before she takes the veil and leaves us to serve God.

303

She'll be a missionary, Reverend Mother, and I know what that means. Please don't deny us this one visit."

"Then you will return her to me?"

"I'll bring her to Connemara when they call for her," Maire made a counter offer. "If I have to sell everything I own to pay the fare to Galway myself, I'll give Nuala the life that God has chosen for her."

"May I trust you to deliver your daughter as promised? You are quite certain that you have the means to get her to Kylemore Abbey?"

"Reverend Mother, how can I go against the will of God? I promise you, I would shamelessly beg for pennies on the street if I had to."

Satisfied, Reverend Mother smiled with sainted beneficence, patronizing yet sincerely warm. She rose from her chair, asking Maire to remain seated while Sister Agnes prepared One Hundred Twenty's suitcase. Nervously, Maire's hand wiped across her forehead, to see if her puzzled frown was as evident as it felt. Prisoners in Mountjoy and the Curragh had numbers, not schoolgirls or orphans in convents. Reverend Mother was back in no time, and she poured out another cup of tea as if nothing were amiss.

While they waited, the two women sat next to the peat fire and chatted, with the Mother Superior describing the beautiful setting of the Benedictine Mother House, perched on the edge of a lake and surrounded by mountains. She detailed the evidence that had appeared over the years, proving that the girl had a gift for nursing. The conversation quickly turned into a rehash of Sister Monica's last days, when her adoring pupil cared for her with love and tenderness, feeding and bathing the old woman, hauling bedpans without complaint, and spiraling into intense grief when the ancient nun succumbed to the inevitable.

"At the end, she encouraged Sister Monica to make a complete confession, to find inner peace and contentment. They were on very intimate terms, and I suspect that something was troubling the Sister in her final days. After she spoke to our confessor, she appeared so radiant," Reverend Mother emoted with rapture. "Her last words to your daughter were, 'You have saved my soul, Mary Magdalene.' Your daughter has dedicated her life to St. Mary Magdalene, by the way."

Maire wiped her tears, overcome with emotion at the inspiring tale, and struck speechless to think that it was her daughter who was the heroine of the saga. "It's all been to the best, Reverend Mother. My son is enrolled in one of the finest schools in Dublin, and to hear that my daughter has grown in God's love; I have been blessed."

"Sister Monica was my inspiration as well," the Mother Superior's smooth voice flowed on. "When she singled out your daughter as one worthy of advanced scholarship, I knew *that this convent had been chosen to enrich the life of another Bride of Christ."*

"And you say that Nuala will be trained in nursing?" Maire asked, unbelieving.

"There is a great need in India, where medical care is lacking and the Word of God is seldom heard. She demonstrated a remarkable gift when she looked after Sister Monica. Not only nursing, Mrs. O'Brien, but ministering to her spiritually; bringing her tea to soothe the body and reading Scripture to feed the soul."

After a long wait, the parlor door finally opened, and Maire rose from her seat, a smile as brilliant as one thousand suns glowing brightly on her face. Her scream of horror echoed in the warm room.

A scrawny, hollow eyed creature shuffled into the parlor, her legs too weak to lift the feet that were encased in heavy shoes. The girl stumbled, fell to her knees and clutched at Maire's hands. "Take me out of here or I'll kill myself," the grey-faced being rasped. "I won't miss this time."

Looking down at the bony features of a very old woman, Maire saw a stranger who vaguely resembled her late husband, but then she noticed the dead look in two haunted eyes. "What have you done to my daughter?" Maire screamed hysterically, her arms waving as she tried to envelope Nuala in a protective embrace.

"One Hundred Twenty," the Mother Superior began, "has been fasting and praying, actively seeking penance to atone for her many sins."

"She's half-dead," Maire raged, getting Nuala to her feet while grabbing the box of clothes that Sister Agnes was holding in her hands.

Turning to the nuns, leaning on her mother for support, Nuala straightened her spine and spoke with firm resolve. "My name is Nuala Devoy," she enunciated each syllable. "My name is Nuala Devoy."

Quickly, nearly overcome with nausea, Maire hustled her child out of the parlor and through the door, walking as fast as they could down the long path that wound through the convent grounds and led to Booterstown Road and the train station. Nuala was trying to run but her feet could not follow her legs as she tripped and then regained her balance. Seeing the entry gate at the road, the former penitent began to cry, great sobs of relief mixed with fear that the gate would be closed in her face.

"It's all right, Nuala, it's all right," Maire murmured, clasping her daughter to her side, to become her legs and half-carry her along the road.

"Why didn't you come for me?" Nuala wept freely. "I wrote and wrote and you never answered."

"I never heard from you, Nuala, I had to wait for the Mother Superior to write. She always told me you were doing well. Did you pray for your baby sister as I asked?"

Stopping short, Nuala tore away from her mother. "You've mistaken me for someone else. I don't have a sister. I have a brother."

"I had a baby, Nuala, didn't they tell you?" Maire put her arm around Nuala's waist again, to continue the trek. "I had a little girl and we named her Maude, for Uncle Joe's mother. She died, Nuala, she died six years ago."

"The baby was dead," Nuala mumbled. "Was it a girl?"

The words were garbled, the phrase of a madwoman, and Maire feared that her daughter had lost her mind. "Did they tell you that Uncle Joe and I were married?"

Exhausted, her daughter had to make an effort to think, as if the act of remembering was as difficult as lifting five hundred pounds. "Yes," she said at last, "they told me. Please don't let them take me back, please don't. If they think I've gone over the wall, they'll send the gardai after me."

"No one is going to send anyone after you. You're free, Nuala, and we're going home." Nuala's shivers pulsated in her mother's arm, slowing Maire's gait. "You left without your coat."

"We don't have coats," Nuala stated the blunt fact, her voice lifeless. "We don't need coats. I'm used to being cold."

Realizing that her daughter could not possibly walk to the tram stop, Maire dug through her pocketbook and gathered what little capital she had before heading for the train station near the coast. While they sat side by side in the depot, Maire studied her child, a person who was as much a stranger to her as the other people waiting for the train. As a girl of six, Nuala had been outgoing, a vivacious person with rosy, plump cheeks and twinkling blue eyes. Today, on a chilly December afternoon, Nuala Devoy was like a corpse, ashen and gaunt. Her eyes were empty, her hair limp, and her shoulders were as hunched as an old dowager. The plump and rosy cheeks were drawn, sunken, and of a sickly pallor that resembled a cadaver so thoroughly that Maire had to take the girl's hand, to see if it was warm. It was impossible to believe that this shriveled, tiny woman had once been a happy, effervescent child.

"I thought of you so much, and I prayed for you, for this day to come," Maire babbled with excitement, delirious with the pleasure of touching her little girl once again. "Frank's coming home for the Christmas holidays, just from Dun Laoghaire, did they tell you that he was sent there for secondary school? He's so thrilled, Nuala, and Aunt Maggie is throwing a hooley to welcome you home."

"Who?" Nuala spoke without looking at her mother.

"Aunt Maggie, your aunt, your dear daddy's sister. The one who lives near Jacob's Biscuit factory, married to Uncle Mike, do you remember her?"

The act of recalling another lifetime must have been too much for Nuala, who shook her head with great weariness. An answer came after a minute or two, but it was a voice that echoed out of a tomb. "Jacob's biscuits. In a tin. With circus animals."

"Yes, that's it, she gave you a tin of biscuits with animals painted on the sides when you were a little girl. She sent you a packet of biscuits this past Christmas."

"No, not to me, not to a sinner," Nuala muttered. "On Northbrook Terrace."

"I've saved all year for our Christmas dinner. We'll have a pig's cheek, and the plum pudding is hanging to age already, you'll see it when we get home and then it will come back to you."

"Will Santa come?" Nuala turned to look at her mother, and her face was transformed into that of a small child, covered by a veil of tormented misery.

"Hang up your stocking and you'll see," Maire said. Grasping at the tiniest sign, she believed that Nuala was coming back, slowly and cautiously, but returning nonetheless, to make the family whole and complete once again. "How did you spend Christmas at St. Anne's?"

"We prayed," Nuala said. "We prayed that God would forgive us our sins. Please, let's not talk about it. I don't know how to talk anymore."

Nuala turned her head away, to watch the people come and go in the noisy terminal. When her mother took her hand, she passively allowed it to happen, but there was no other sensation, no sense of family or feeling of affection. The rupture was thorough, and Nuala was isolated, a solitary figure surrounded by strangers, making her escape from the Sisters of Mercy. The sounds that floated around her meant nothing as she became deaf to the people who approached her mother. Novice, holidays, Benedictine missionary, empty words swirled around her head like pesky flies while gauzy images drifted through her vision as people stared at her, speaking to her when she could not hear. She waited for someone to ask her about the hunger strike, so that she could tell them how difficult it had been two weeks ago when she started. Terence MacSwiney and Thomas Ashe had shown her the way, she would tell anyone who wanted to know. She had been set free, but she was as ready to die as they had been, ready to give up her life in the cause of justice. She would talk about that, and nothing else.

"The train is here, Nuala," her mother's voice penetrated the mist of confusion.

"But I don't have money for the fare," she protested. Removing the silver cross that hung around her neck, the emblem of the Child of Mary, Nuala handed it to her mother. "Will you take this in exchange? I never want to touch it again."

Wisely, Molly had rented a car and driver to get her party to the cemetery. Too distraught to think clearly, she knew well enough that driving would have been a mistake. Her father's urn sat on her lap, held carefully and with an unwillingness to let go. For as hard as she tried, Molly could not understand why her father wanted to be buried in Irish soil, when the Irish people had abused him and torn apart his family. He did not know what had been done to his sister, that was obvious, or he could not possibly have asked that half of him be planted in the old sod, embedded in cruelty.

Looking backwards, Molly saw Eoin following right behind, although why he turned up was a mystery. By rights, he should have stalked off, to get drunk and ridicule her to his friends. She could not begin to explain things to him, because that would have involved an airing of her life, exposure that her father had avoided for his entire life. Probing her own psyche was too painful, and best saved for some other day when she could find the strength.

Some day, she might ask him what it felt like, to love someone so much that you stayed, even while the object of affection was focused on getting away. No longer sure what love was, how it was shown, Molly hugged the urn and analyzed the ache in her heart that was her loss. All her life, her father had held them all at arm's length and she had copied him, only to learn that her thinking was all wrong. Seeking her own company was taken as rejection by normal people; avoiding close attachments was abnormal behavior but she wanted to be normal, to be able to share space. Eoin had been hurt, Stan had been hurt, and God only knew what a mess she'd made of her children.

Put her in an operating room and she was confident, the headstrong nurse who brooked no nonsense from staff or patient. Out of her scrubs, she was cold and heartless, not greatly disturbed if someone didn't make it out of the recovery room because Molly never got close to anyone. All her talk about psychiatric care came back to her, the speeches to Rose and Mary that applied to her as well. Be strong, she had urged, while her own heart laughed because she herself was weak.

"Rose, this lawsuit is not something to jump into without thinking it over," Molly warned, turning to her strong points to get through the day. Running other people's lives seemed to be more in her line, telling someone what to do while she did the opposite.

"There's no other way," Rose said, accepting harsh reality. "And I doubt that I'll live long enough to see it finished. I'll go down fighting, like the great chiefs of old. Irish to the core, Molly, and I'll do battle against the worst odds for the sake of my pride."

"You see, Molly, during the Rising, most people were against it," Mary said. "My own father confessed to jeering the rebels when they surrendered, and he mocked Countess Markiewicz when she was marched off to prison. But after the

Brits started in to executing the leaders, one after another, and their blood ran out from under the door of Kilmainham, then my father took up a gun. Ireland loves a martyr, I suppose. We understand sacrifice, and giving up all you have to serve the greater good."

"I hate to see you suffer, Rose," Molly said. "And you will, you know. People will curse you for criticizing the Church."

"They did wrong, and if some want to turn a blind eye, well, maybe if I give my heart then they will see clearly." Rose was perfectly at ease, like a condemned woman putting the noose around her neck with bold courage.

"You've put your name out in public as well," Mary reminded Molly. "Rose won't want for company."

"But I'll be thousands of miles away," Molly said. "I don't expect to make any money, that's not why I'm doing this. I'm really hoping that someone might recognize my aunt's name and help me find out where she went."

"It's harder to find women," Rose said. "We change our names, and if a lady marries twice, it's easy to forget a name, and then the grandchildren don't remember, and just like that, your aunt could have disappeared into the city or gone to another county."

"Do you think she was married?" Molly asked.

"A lot of the laundry girls went into service in England," Mary said. "Not only to get away from their shame, but men here thought that a girl from the laundry was a tramp, to be honest. A lot of women wouldn't hire one to work in the house, especially if she had a boy old enough to mess around."

"Insults piled on insults," Molly griped. "And I'll bet that every one of those bitches was running to Mass every day."

"Sure, it's easy to talk of Christian charity, and it's another thing altogether to be a Christian," Rose said. "They took everything from me, but they couldn't take God. That army of hypocrites. I don't need their church to follow Jesus and be a Catholic."

"Do as I say, not as I do," Molly said. "There's the motto they could have used back then."

Father Cahill met the funeral cortege at the cemetery, where several other people had gathered for the graveside service. Even the sun peaked out from behind the clouds, to witness the internment of Frank Devoy. The party was beginning to walk to the grave when a distinguished looking grandfather touched Molly's arm.

"You're the very image of your aunt," he said. "Your father always said that he saw Nuala when he looked at you, and I see it for myself now."

"Did you know my aunt?" Molly asked.

"If only she'd have taken a look at me, but I was only Frank's friend from the GPO," he sighed in mock sorrow. "Tom Hennessey, Miss Devoy. We were great pals, your dad and I. The obituary, when I read it, what a surprise to learn that Frank was an industrial school graduate."

315

"Yes, he was," Molly said, ready to defend her father's honor.

"I suppose he wasn't proud of it," Tom said. "Back in those days, so. It made me think back, about how your father was. He was so innocent and naïve as a boy, and that must have been why. The older lads used to tease him terrible, letting the air out of his tires, pushing him around, laughing at him when he didn't get their bawdy jokes. It didn't let up until he got into a fistfight with the biggest of them. Your dad took a whooping, but the other boy broke his hand and was out for three weeks. Frank was a hero to the lads after that."

"Getting bullied is a recurring theme, Mr. Hennessey," Molly said.

"He got the best of us, in the end," Tom said with a sly wink. "Oh, I know all about you and your brothers. Successful in all that he did, that's how I'll remember him."

"He asked me to find my aunt," Molly said.

"All I know of Nuala is next to nothing. We used to go off on weekends for bicycle tours, me and your dad, out to the country for a picnic lunch and then back home, sometimes spending the night sleeping rough and going to Mass at a country church. Once, we saw Nuala with her sweetheart, but she didn't see us. I was jealous of that Yank, I have to admit. What a crush I had on her, pretty as a picture, tiny as a bird she was. Five feet tall if she wore high heels and a big hat." Tom chuckled at his impression. "She was like a porcelain doll."

"Who was the boy?"

316

"Frank found out that he was a guard at the American Embassy. A big man, tall and muscular, that's how the soldiers at the gate were back then. I think he was dark, swarthy, as I recall, like a Spaniard or a Greek."

"Peter Benedetti," Molly said.

"Could have been of Italian extraction, could have been." Tom paused, pondering for a moment. "That must be why Frank didn't know what marmalade was. We used to trade lunches, and once he asked me what was on my bread. You've never had marmalade before, says I, and he looked a little embarrassed. Sure, he never had it before."

"I don't suppose that he had much of anything in an orphanage," Molly added.

"Oh, he had pluck," Tom rejoined. "I always admired him, your dad. A humble man, but a man who accomplished much. I always looked up to him, but more so now, knowing what hardship he had to survive before he got where he did. That Nuala, what a fair colleen."

"Do you know where she went?"

"No, she just seemed to vanish and Frank never mentioned her again. There was talk of her becoming a missionary nun, but I'd hate to think that she took those pretty blue eyes to some jungle. Let the homely ones serve the Lord, I say," Tom said. "So that's all that's left of Frank?"

Molly cradled the casket in her arms, unwilling to part with her father for all time. "Half of him, at any rate."

"That's like Frank, close to his family and his roots. It was a pity that he never could talk your mother into coming here for a visit. He wanted to come back, he said to me many times, to visit his old friends. What a lazy sot I was, turning down his invitations to pay a call in the States. Laziness is all it was, always putting off for another day. So, here we are, with no more days and the opportunity lost."

"I'm sorry that you two let it slip away."

"Water under the bridge. You'll keep in touch, won't you? Let me know about your little ones, and your brothers' families?"

"Of course, Mr. Hennessey, of course. And my dad's invitation is still open, if you ever have a mind to see Chicago."

"Yes, the spitting image of Nuala," Tom sighed, a smile of youthful delight brightening his face.

"Frank's got the last laugh," Pat Grady nudged Molly. They looked up to see Father Padraic Cahill, prayer book and holy water in hand, take his place at the grave. With Mike's hand on her shoulder, she handed the casket to Pat.

"Forcing the heartless bastard to speak words of praise over his corpse," Mike snickered into her ear. "His Holiness there won't be calling Frank Devoy a derelict today, you can bet."

"You're a good girl, coming all this way to find our why your father had to prove he was better than the rest," Dan said. "It was himself there, getting under Frank's skin, preaching God's word and thinking he was pure as snow because he paraded around town in a clean cassock. And underneath, the heart was black as coal."

318

"He thought his family was so holy, with him in the seminary and his uncle a priest," Pat grumbled. "He wasn't so God Almighty righteous when his uncle's name popped up in connection with the scandal at Goldenbridge Orphanage. Nowhere to be found then, and wouldn't you know Frank would send him the clippings from the *Times* and pretend he was all concerned."

"This can't be the same McNulty as your uncle, now," Mike mocked. "It stuck in Cahill's craw and choked him half to death. Frank Devoy had a wicked sense of humor. Tush, tush, Your Eminence, who'd have guessed your uncle was so fond of babies."

"He liked a good laugh," Pat agreed. "We'd get on the phone and say two words, and spend the next half hour roaring like little boys. Used to drive my wife mad with the racket."

"We made a good life out of what we had," Dan remarked wisely. "The likes of Cahill couldn't break us in the end. You'll never beat the Irish, Molly."

A proper funeral required a drop of whiskey, and a flask was passed among the men who had once been confined to an industrial school because they were poor. Molly looked at their faces, a mixed assortment of features that reflected the hard times of the Depression and the horror of war. Teasing at the corners of the men's eyes was the sadness of a miserable childhood, but for the first time Molly saw the softening of the harsh edges, a result of life's blessings.

On the other side of the grave, she watched Eoin take a drop, to toast to a man he had never met but wanted to honor just the same. She could guess that she had broken his heart, but the fact that he was there, standing only a few feet away from her, must be some kind of sign, a message that he agreed with her. It was not a meaningless affair or a holiday tryst, not if he came all the way to the cemetery. Without realizing it, she was staring at him, and when his gaze met hers she could not hold in the tears any longer. Mike put an arm around her, strong and solid, while she looked at Eoin and tried to tell him, without words, what she was going to do next.

17

Frank was nearly running down the street, racing home to spend his fourteenth Christmas as he had longed to do, with his entire family. Barging through the door, he came to a halt, surprised that his mother had a guest. The old woman was dressed in a shapeless black dress that was more of a shroud, hanging well below her knees when the fashion was much shorter. Thick wool stockings, also black, were paired with heavy, hobnailed boots, completing a severe habit.

"Frank, don't you remember your sister?" Maire said. "It's Nuala. Don't you remember her?"

The gaunt creature with stooped shoulders and dead eyes was not Nuala, or at least she was not the playmate Frank recalled. She held out her hand, as much a stranger to him as he was to her.

"How do you do, Frank," she spoke quietly, almost afraid to utter a word.

For years, Frank had been imagining a happy reunion, with tears and hugs, laughter and strong embraces. He had been separated from his sister in a courtroom, but the length of their parting was not nine years. Looking at the woman before him, he realized that he had lost his sister. They had grown up apart, without common experiences to make them one family, and the bonds were shattered, irreparably broken.

"I'm glad you're home, Nuala," he stammered. "Mammy and I like to go to Midnight Mass on Christmas Eve. Will you come with us?"

"No," she stated bluntly, a corpse speaking.

"She's tired, Frank," Maire said. "Why don't we go in the morning, after Santa's been by to leave presents for my darlings?"

They were in their teens, but they still believed in St. Nicholas because no one had ever broken the spell by telling them otherwise. Eagerly anticipating a visit from St. Nick, Nuala retired early, finding great joy in climbing into her old bed, even though it was not on Northbrook Terrace anymore. She almost could not wait to go to bed, giddy as a child to take Jenny in her arms and cuddle her doll again. Frank saw his big sister in her, the person who had let him sleep with her on her last night at home, when they were both too frightened to be alone. The image gave him some hope for the future, to take back the past and jump over their lost years, to be a family again.

In the cramped space of a single room, Frank had to sleep in the same bed, head at the footboard. Maire had tied a string between the head and footboards and draped a sheet over it, to act as a wall between brother and sister and create a sense of propriety when there was no other solution. As a lark, Frank lifted the screen on Christmas Eve, to whisper Happy Christmas, but he dropped the sheet at once. Nuala was sixteen years old, but she was clutching her doll, with her thumb stuck in her mouth like an infant.

"Mammy, what's wrong with Nuala?" Frank said to his mother when she came over to kiss her children goodnight.

"She had a hard life at St. Anne's," Maire stifled a sob.

"She's not right in the head," Uncle Joe put in, still hurt by Nuala's accusation that everything that had befallen the Devoy family was all his fault.

"What happened?" Frank asked.

"It's best not to know," Maire ended the discussion. "Off to sleep, or St. Nick will pass us by."

No one said anything when Nuala made no attempt to go to church on Christmas morning, but then, Uncle Joe never went to church and Maire never criticized his lack of piety. Frank had to assume that his sister was not well, and when Uncle Joe offered to watch over the invalid, his guess seemed to be confirmed. He prayed for Nuala at Mass that morning, asking God to restore her health when she looked so frail.

Dinner was tense, as if four strangers had somehow ended up at the same table. There was little conversation, with Maire constantly looking over at Nuala to ask her if she liked the meat, if it was too tough or too soft, if it was salted enough or too much. She danced around topics, searching for something that would not spark an upwelling of tears in

Nuala's sad eyes. Even Uncle Joe had a difficult time of it, not sure what to say to the person at his right hand.

It took Nuala forever to eat, because she had not used anything but a fork since she was seven years old. She had forgotten how to cut the meat, and Frank was shocked by Uncle Joe's patience as he held Nuala's hand, teaching her a basic skill. Like one who had been marooned and then rescued after nine years, Nuala chewed slowly and tasted everything completely, searching for memories of a certain flavor as she tried to find her past. By the time they were enjoying the Dundee cake and plum pudding, Nuala appeared to be regaining her bearings, using her sense of taste to guide her until she figured out where she was. The entire experience was unnerving, to sit at the polished mahogany table, its grandeur a reminder of his father's comfortable home, with Jenny's painted eyes staring back at him while Nuala's hollow eyes looked at nothing.

"Did you have anything special to eat at Christmas?" Frank asked, hoping to make conversation and ease the oppressive tension.

"No," Nuala replied. "No work. We prayed instead of working. No rest."

"Did you have a gramophone? We have one, and we listen to the wireless at night," Frank continued, to learn of his sister's life.

"I listened to girls cry at night." Nuala burst into tears and fled to the corner, where she could hide behind the curtain.

"Hush, Frank, leave her be," Maire scolded. "She didn't have any such treats. Don't be a braggart over your good fortune."

"But I wasn't boasting," Frank protested, confused over Nuala's heart wrenching sobs and his mother's attitude. He looked at Uncle Joe, seeking some answer to the puzzle, but his stepfather only sat there, gumming the pudding.

"Heaven help us, we've got to live through a day with Maggie," he groaned, to break the silence that was filled by one girl's muffled grief. "That targer will be the death of me."

Aunt Maggie's St. Stephen's Day hooley was a tradition, and one that Frank looked forward to now that he was permitted to leave Carriglea at Christmas. Even though Nuala claimed that she remembered Aunt Maggie's parties and admitted that they were grand, she said that she did not want to go. It took Uncle Joe's stern command to get her out of the house, and Maire backed her husband in the matter, even though Nuala cried and pleaded to be allowed to stay inside. If she could have come up with some reason, Frank was certain that his mother would have backed down, but all Nuala offered was a simple, "I can't", and that was not good enough.

Normally, they would have walked all the way to South Summer Street, a long trek that took them across the Liffey. As a concession to Nuala's weakness, they boarded the omnibus while Uncle Joe grumbled about the expense. Frank sat next to his sister, watching her shrink into nothing as she shivered in Uncle Joe's old jumper and Maire's borrowed cardigan. He sat a little closer, offering his physical presence as a shield to protect her from the mysterious unknown force that terrorized her. She pulled away.

A hooley at Maggie and Mike's involved food and music, washed down with a couple of kegs of Guinness and a bottle of port for the ladies. Frank took charge of his sister, to show her what wonders could be seen on the sideboard in the dining room, where the floor itself seemed to groan under the weight of the bounty. All the things that he had dreamed of in St. Patrick's were presented here, with pies of every kind, plum pudding and tarts, and elaborate cakes that were a feast for the eye as well as the belly. The children were given bread and butter to fill up on before they had a taste of the sweets that were given first to the adults, and Frank goaded Nuala to eat until she thought that she would burst. Aunt Maggie indulged her favorite relation by piling on an extra slice of jam cake, determined to put some meat on Nuala's bones before she went off to India and certain starvation.

"Won't you favor us with a song, Maire," Uncle Mike would typically begin the festivities after his guests had eaten their fill.

"Oh, no, I'm not a singer at all," Maire demurred always, to be polite. "Well, if there's no one else, I could give it a go."

Aunt Bridget perched on the piano stool, while Mike called for quiet, relaying the word through front and back parlors that Maire was going to sing. Taking her place next to the piano, Maire launched into an old tune, a song that Frank quickly recognized as his sister's favorite, something that was sure to alleviate her funk.

"After the ball is over," the lovely voice soared through the house, "after the break of morn, after the dancer's leaving..."

Seeing a chink, a faint gleam of joy beginning to steal into Nuala's dull eyes, Frank offered her a goodie. "I saved the peppermint stick for you, Nuala," he said. Pushing the candy towards her face, he urged her to take it. "Go on, I know that peppermints were always your favorite."

Her pale face blanched whiter still, and Nuala's hands flew up to her mouth. She jumped out of the chair and raced to the water closet at the back of the house. Alarmed by her daughter's abrupt exit, Maire ended her tune as quickly as possible and tore off after the girl. Mr. Dooley filled in at Aunt Bridget's side, regaling the partygoers with a few selections that had been popular in the music halls during his youth, which was forty years past.

The revelers did not notice that Maire and Nuala were gone for at least thirty minutes until Maire's screams resounded through the house, penetrating the merrymaking of the hooley. Aunt Maggie, frightened into a tizzy, dashed down the hall to see what unpleasantness had taken place in her water closet, fearing a mouse in her spotless home. When she came back to the party ten minutes later, she asked her husband for a glass of whiskey, something that she had never touched before.

"Jesus, Mary, and Joseph, are you taking a drop of the jar, Maggie?" Mike bellowed, laughing loudly.

"Maybe she's drinking to forget," Tom Cassidy babbled, his lips grown numb from porter. Snickering, he gave Maggie a nudge and a wink. "Forget him and remember me, eh, Maggie?"

Drunken male voices rang in her ears while her head began to spin. Waves of riotous laughter pounded against her ears, the sound of merrymaking and hijinks that was suddenly out of place. She wanted the whiskey to erase Nuala's words, to wash them away because they could not possibly be true. Not that the girl was lying, it was only a dream, a bad dream that she had when she was put away in the orphanage. Surrounded by nuns and priests, it would be no wonder if she dreamed of a priest, a childish fantasy that seemed real.

Another mouthful of liquor burned down Maggie's throat, and when she went to take more, she discovered that the glass was empty.

"Here, darlin', enjoy the evening," Mike staggered over, pouring a generous serving. "Tonight's my lucky night, boys."

The whiskey released the voice from the back of her head, the voice that spoke with logic and reason. How could a girl know the details of the things that married people did, in the dark, in secret? How could a girl describe a man's smell, or have the faintest notion of the way a man's face twisted up at the end of doing it? How could a girl know about certain practices that were against the law they were so indecent? How in God's name could a child know of the pain of giving birth?

"I'll not have the Sisters of Mercy in this house again, Michael Ryan," she hissed, gulping down the last few drops in her glass. "Never again, and may God forgive them."

"Not in the condition you're in," he joked. "Let 'em come on Sunday, and we'll have our fun on a Saturday night. How's the girl?"

"She's gone and eaten too much, and don't be making a fuss over her when she comes back," Maggie said. "Pass the word, Michael, let's not embarrass the poor child."

The alcohol spun in her brain as she roamed through her house, pretending that everything was fine. Force of will was all that kept her from going out to the garden to be sick. Not listening to the music, Maggie kept asking God why he did not clamp her mouth shut when she demanded that Nuala explain why she was so agitated by a peppermint stick. The girl's words were not erased by two shots of whiskey, and the look on Nuala's face was forever etched into Maggie's mind. Her feet took her back, past the guests who were walking back and forth to the keg of Guinness in the garden, back to the door of the water closet. She lifted her arm, to knock, but her fist only wobbled. Feeling woozy, she leaned forward and banged her head against the door. "I believe you," she said quietly. "I believe you."

When Frank went back to Carriglea on Monday, wiping away the sad tears of another depressing departure, Nuala asked to walk part of the way with him. Their mother treated the pronouncement as if it were the best possible news, to hear that her daughter was willing to go beyond the yard of the tenement for the first time in days.

Gifts of money had been given to the children, sixpence and shillings, and they had accumulated a pound each. As they walked down the street, Nuala explained to her brother that the money represented one hundred twenty tram fares, a means of escape from the dismal back room on James Street, and freedom from their mother's disappointment. Uncle Joe had turned out to be mean, nasty and thoroughly unreliable, marrying Maire for her money and then dragging the Devoy family into penury as he threw everything away on the horses. Sadly, Maire was stuck with Joe for the rest of his days, but Nuala would not be tied down to her mother's mistake.

"Where will you go today?" Frank asked, glad of Nuala's company all the way to O'Connell Street.

"Just to look at Dublin," she said. "I might call on friends."

"You'll come on Visiting Day, won't you?" Frank pleaded nervously.

"Unless I have a job and can't get away," she prevaricated. "Off you go, then."

Having lost the sense of security that was Frank, Nuala had to navigate streets that she did not know. As a little girl, she had gone shopping on Thomas Street with her mother, but she had never been to O'Connell Street before, and the din and clatter of so many people, cars, wagons and horses was terrifying. Wandering slowly, she found herself at Clery's Department Store, a familiar name from Booterstown. Overcome by curiosity, she entered the store and just as quickly wished that she had not. The setting was too unfamiliar, too intimidating, but when she turned to go, she realized that she had forgotten where she had come in.

"Can I help you, miss?" the floorwalker inquired politely.

With her heart beating wildly and sweat beginning to pour from her temples, Nuala could do little more than stammer like an imbecile. "The yarns, please," she mumbled. "I make lace."

"Of course, convent lace," the gentleman smiled warmly.

"Yes sir, the Benedictines have accepted me," she said, as if she were being grilled by Sister Perpetua.

"My wife has been ill, troubled by rheumatism. Would you be so kind as to remember her in your prayers?"

Shocked and surprised by a gentle demeanor, Nuala looked up to meet the gaze of a very pleasant man who was smiling at her. At that instant, she concluded that he could not possibly have guessed what she really was, a being so far beneath him that she was not deserving of the slightest kindness. "I would be honored to pray for her return to health, sir," Nuala said, her expression calmly serene in its blankness.

"If you have a moment, I could introduce you to our lace and trim buyer in the dressmaking department," the floorwalker continued, returning a spiritual favor with a secular reward. "He purchases convent lace for wedding and christening gowns, and it must be the finest quality. Make an appointment to bring in some samples, and I am sure that he would be pleased to do business with you."

Floating on a beautiful cloud of anonymity, Nuala carefully visited the outside world that she had been dropped in. No one pointed at her, or cast suspicious glances her way, and it made her head swim, to think that she could pretend to be like everyone else and not be noticed. Summoning up every bit of courage she had, she asked the first person she saw on the street to give her directions to the library, where she could make an escape that she had made every day for years. Literature and scholarship had been her salvation in the laundry, and she turned to her old friends once again when the world pressed in too closely. For a small reading fee, something that meant walking home to save money, Nuala found a safe haven in Dublin that would last her until her Christmas money gave out.

Walking everywhere to save money, Nuala escaped to another part of Dublin where she could disappear into a sea of strangers. As she wandered through the Phoenix Park, her mind explored the few options that were open to a woman in the city who was marred by a shady past, but there were few alternatives available for any woman during the close of the Thirties. Out of nowhere on a cold January day, she had an idea, something that she childishly acted on as the impulse struck her.

"Excuse me, sir, but I would like to emigrate," she informed the uniformed guard at the entrance, interrupting two men sharing a dirty joke.

333

A pair of United States Marines looked over the Irish girl. "Where do y'all want to go exactly?" the leering one asked in a most bizarre accent.

"I want to go to America, sir," Nuala explained further.

"Now what would a pretty little thing like you do in America?" he teased.

"I'd work, sir. I can make lace, I can read and write, and I'm not afraid of housework."

"Think you could make some lace for my mama?"

"Yes, sir," she bubbled with excitement. Removing the well-worn sweater, she extended one arm to show the artistry of the cuff she had fastened to her postulant's severe black dress.

"You made that?" the other guard whistled. "I'd like to get a hold of some of that for my girl back home."

"Tell you what, sugar, y'all come see me Saturday and we'll talk about getting you to America, how's that sound?" the swarthy man offered. "We'll buy some of your lace if you bring it round, too."

When Saturday dawned, Nuala was already out of the door and striding purposefully to her destination, to make a sale and make arrangements to get out of Ireland. As far as she was concerned, she was an embarrassment to her family because she had been put away in the Magdalene laundry, and it would be better for all if she could support her mother and brother without having to be seen with them. She was

334

particularly concerned with Frank's future, afraid that her reputation would hold him back or spoil his prospects. America was the best place to go, because the nuns made the greatest fuss over American parents coming to adopt Irish babies born to the penitents. It was far enough away to disappear, but close enough to get money to her mother without much delay. The United States became a distant beacon of deliverance.

The gentleman on duty found her story amusing, though incredible. Since Nuala had not asked for names, she had no idea who she was supposed to see, and the idea of two burly Marines buying lace was too farfetched to be acceptable.

"Don't you have a coat?" the guard said. "Here, come inside while I send word to the chuckleheads in the barracks."

The waiting room of the United States Legation was as grand as the chapel at St. Anne's convent, though much lighter and definitely more cheerful. Electric lamps glowed brightly, and Nuala noticed at once that the room was warm, so warm that she had to take off her sweaters and wool scarf to keep from perspiring.

"Lookie there, my girl's come early for our date," the Marine boasted to his colleague as they strolled into the empty foyer.

"Your sweetie doesn't know your name, jarhead," the other man scoffed.

"That's okay, I don't know hers neither," he said, laughing with a booming resonance that echoed. "Come on, little girl, I'll tell you about moving to the States and see what I can do to help you out."

"I've brought all the lace that I've finished, sir," Nuala said. "I'm hoping to get four shilling for the cuffs, and the lace edgings I can make to order for eight pence per yard."

"Honey, I don't know shillings from shinola," he snorted. Leading her down a long corridor, he opened a door and escorted her into a room that contained a desk and two chairs, the furniture arranged for consultations and conducting business with a consular official. "Have a seat, little lady, and we'll talk about the whys and what fors. First off, you have a sponsor over there?"

"I don't know anyone at all in America, sir," Nuala admitted.

"First up, you need a sponsor, say, an uncle or a cousin to take you in. Once you get that, then you go to the embassy office down on Merrion Square and fill out a form, wait for the government to give you the okay, and that's it."

"I'm an orphan, sir. I don't have anyone to sponsor me."

"You got money to pay for the boat ride over?" he asked.

"Not yet, sir. I hope to save up."

"That's too bad," he sighed with sympathy. "You got a sweetheart over here?"

"No, sir." She blushed crimson, dropping her eyes to her lap.

"You want one?"

Her response was to shuffle her feet, fidget nervously and move her mouth without being able to think of a thing to say.

"You sure are the prettiest thing I ever did see," he continued, pitching woo while Nuala wished that she had never come in the first place. "I mean that, I'm not just saying it."

"Please, sir, can you buy my lace?" she stammered nervously.

"Sure, I'll buy it from you." He reached into his pocket and pulled out a roll of Irish money, peeling off the top bill. "How much can I get for this?"

"I don't have as much as all that, sir, not for a pound. I can make more, though, and you can trust me, sir, I'll get two more collars done by next week, or a long piece of trim if that's what's needed, and I'll bring it right away."

"Hold on." His snickers rumbled in his throat. "Don't sell yourself short, sister. These things are worth a buck a piece at least."

"I'm not a Sister, sir, I'm not a nun," she corrected him. "I crocheted in the convent, but I'm not a nun."

He started to laugh at her, but then he looked at her
again, a glint of sympathy in his eye. "That's the best news
I've had all week," he said. He extended his hand in greeting.
"Name's Pete Benedetti. Come out of Florida, Orange County,
and I've been freezing my tail off in this country."

"My name is Nuala Devoy," she said, her evening
prayer. "From Dublin, sir."

"My, oh my, if that isn't the prettiest name to go with
the prettiest face," he said. Leaning over the desk with a
charming smile plastered on his face, he kept up his courtship.
"You like the picture shows, Nuala Devoy?"

"The what, sir?"

"Picture show, you know, the movies. Clark Gable, you
like him?"

"I don't know him, sir."

"Call me Pete, sugar, I like to hear the way you say
things. You ever seen a moving picture, Nuala Devoy?" Her
face fell, too ashamed to tell him that she did not have the
money for such an extravagance. "Would you do me the
honor, Miss Devoy, of accompanying me to the picture show?"

"I don't know if I should," Nuala fidgeted even more.

Leaving his spot behind the imposing desk, Pete knelt
at Nuala's side. Looking into her eyes, he took her hand and
put the pound note gently in her palm. "Of course you should
go," he said. "Fellas take their girls to the picture show all the
time back home. You're my girl, ain't you, Nuala Devoy?"

"Do you want me to be your girl, Mr. Benedetti?" she asked, her eyes wide with wonder.

"And how," he said with a smile, his teeth like white pearls set into the cool shade of his olive skin. "I want you to be my girl, mine alone."

Her breathing began to grow more rapid while her chest seemed to tighten. He touched her cheek, complimenting the porcelain tone of her complexion and marveling at the contrast between her pale skin and his darker color. Her skin was as white as orange blossoms, and he told of the petals that fell from the trees in his father's grove, soft and sweet, as soft and sweet as she was. His hand pressed into hers, where she felt the money growing damp with her sweat. Thick, strong fingers twined in her hair and he pulled her head towards his, so close that she could smell the lingering odor of cigarettes and American soap. She could feel the slight coarseness on his cheek where he had missed a spot with the razor, a brush that sent an electric current through her entire body. His lips were much softer than she expected, warm yet firm, as his kiss enveloped her in sensations that she greedily accepted.

"You ever sold it before?" he asked with great kindness.

Unable to open her eyes, let alone speak, she shook her head slightly. This was the first time that she had approached anyone to help her, but she was not begging, she was merely *trying to make a living by doing what she did best. This was going to be her job, engaging in the same craft that had saved many a family during the Great Hunger. Somehow, the words would not come out, and he kissed her again while his hand reached under her dress, sliding gently along her thigh.*

"You're my girl," he whispered, his breath hot on her neck. "I won't hurt you, sugar, don't you be scared, now. I love you, Nuala."

She knew what love felt like, and Nuala yielded because she was starving for love, the very thing that she wanted more than anything in her life. His touch was tender and his voice was soothing and low, offering compliments and endearments rather than the harsh threats that had filled her head for nine long years. On the floor of the empty office in the United States Legation, Nuala let Peter make love to her because she craved affection and could not resist, needing love to sustain her as much as she needed food to stay alive. It was not a sex act that satisfied her, but a caress, flattery, and the look in his eyes when he finished.

Side by side, they lay on the floor, looking up at the ceiling. Without a word, Pete got up and took her crocheted bag, stuffing three pound notes into it before tugging the strings tight. His smile was infectious, and she smiled back at him as he coyly dangled the purse. "I don't know if this is the same as three bucks," he said, giving her a hand to help her to her feet. "I don't want to shortchange you. Hell, you're worth more than that. Come on, now, let's get you something to eat."

"Can we see a film?" she asked, hungry to learn of moving pictures and Clark Gable.

"I promised, didn't I? Listen here, you get yourself something pretty for next time," he said, watching her tie up the ugly hobnailed boots. "Get rid of those stockings, and buy some lady's things."

"Mr. Benedetti, I can't make enough lace in a week to earn three pounds," she protested, admiring the sight of the bills in her handbag.

"You're my girl, ain't you? You call me Pete, sugar," he began to puff up proudly. "That ain't for the lace, Nuala, that's to help out my girl make herself pretty for me. I want you all decked out when we go out on the town."

He chuckled at the expression on her face as she attempted to interpret his gibberish. Out of nowhere, he lunged and gave her an enormous hug, taking her in his arms while laughing with joy, lifting her off her feet as if she was a wisp of a cloud. "You're my girl, Nuala."

"Yes, sir," she agreed, startled by his sudden movements, his overwhelming mass and his strength. "Yes, Pete."

"Don't you go kissing any other boys," he warned with imitation severity. "Save all those kisses for me. Give me some sugar, Nuala."

Watching My Man Godfrey *was an incredible experience for a girl who had not seen a talking picture before. Nuala clutched Pete's arm, awestruck by the characters on the screen, by the sounds that came out of their mouths, and the beautiful clothes and hair of the actresses. She had seen one film in 1927, though she could not remember much about it anymore, and to be transported from a convent to a cinematic American home was more than she could fathom.*

"What comes next, Pete?" she whispered with excitement as each scene ended.

"Just you wait and see," he said happily, holding her hand.

Day after day, Nuala wandered off early in the morning and drifted back to James Street at teatime, not volunteering any information and giving out precious little when she was questioned. Until bedtime she would sit and crochet with deft speed, rocking back and forth until Joe snapped at her to sit still. She took to sitting out in the yard so that she did not have to listen to Joe's dull ramblings, coming in when she could no longer see the fine thread that she turned into beautiful strips of lace. By the light of a paraffin oil lamp, she continued to work, ignoring Uncle Joe when he asked her where she got the money for the new dress and shoes, for the lipstick, for the loaf of bread or the pack of tea.

On the day before he turned fifteen, Frank dressed in a new suit of clothes and said goodbye to all his old mates at Carriglea. Having completed his studies a year early, he had already passed the National Examination and obtained a position at the G.P.O. He had accomplished all that the Christian Brothers expected of him, and they were sending him home, setting him free. As a final send-off, Brother Conrad rode the bus with him to the city, chatting comfortably and offering all kinds of wise advice before bringing the boy to the General Post Office.

"Apply yourself, and keep to your books," the cleric urged over a treat of tea and cakes. "You'll go far, Frank. We have provided you with a foundation that you can build on. Persevere, and you will find yourself driving your own car one day, dining in restaurants and wearing a fine suit of clothes."

Brother Conrad left him at the Post Office, while Frank felt the pangs of homesickness tearing at him once again, but this time, he longed to return to Carriglea. It was all that was familiar to him, and having to face the strange city of Dublin was frightening, nearly overwhelming in its noise and bustle.

Along with eleven other boys who had earned employment at the lowest entry level, Frank was fitted for a uniform and then the Inspector of Messengers affixed his official badge to his wool jacket. From that time on, he would be Messenger T51, with a secure job and a pension waiting for him at the other end. Frank had never been more nervous in his life.

He was exhausted when he came home to James Street after his first day on the job, tired out from stress and strange places. Walking into the dingy room, he did not recognize Nuala, who was transformed into a modern woman with her hair fashionably cropped and curled, powder on her face and lipstick coloring her mouth. All at once it struck him; the family was back together, he was working to support his mother and sister, and life was going to be grand. The horrors of the industrial schools were behind them all, with only their innermost memories to act as cruel reminders of a stolen childhood.

18

There was one glaring omission in Frank's dreams, and that was brought back to him every time he walked in the door. His mother saw nothing but glory on the horizon, with her son working and her daughter on the verge of a lifetime's commitment to God. Only one thing would add to her happiness, and Frank took the initiative to give his mother what she had lost because of Joe O'Brien.

"The inspector's here, Nuala," Frank called out on the all-important day. Mrs. Thomas Ashe had followed through on her promise to help the family obtain corporation housing, and only the inspector's negative report was needed. "Try to get in his way as much as you can to make this place look more crowded."

"There's no effort in that," she snorted, tossing her permed curls saucily. "One look at our bed, Frank, and we'll be out of here in two minutes time. You'll be thanking me for pulling down the curtain, just you wait and see."

Discovering that teenagers of the opposite sex had to share such close quarters, let alone a single bed, horrified the inspector beyond measure. Within a week, the family was moving the collection of old furniture, gilt mirrors and broken clocks to a brand new, government-built housing development in Drimnaugh. At the time, slum clearance was achieved by moving people out to the suburbs, rending the social fabric of the neighborhood and removing people to areas far distant from their accustomed church and shops. None of that bothered Maire, not when she had a house of her own, a garden and plenty of room to throw a hooley.

"Where do you go every day?" Frank asked his sister, walking his bicycle as far as the tram stop to keep her company.

"I meet friends. I check in with the dressmakers for orders," she replied, somewhat vaguely.

"What happened in Booterstown? Why can't you tell me?"

"The Sisters of Mercy, that's a joke. They have no mercy, those stealers of souls. A gang of liars leading a pack of gobshites and idiots. Don't ever have anything to do with them, Frank, I'm warning you. They'll tell you it's black and I promise you, it's white. If a Sister of Mercy tells you it's raining, I guarantee it's a sunny day."

"Is that why you're joining the Benedictines? Before you go to Connemara, can we take in a show at the Gaiety? I'll treat."

Nuala laughed, a nasty and sarcastic sort of snort. "They'll not take me, the blessed Sisters. I slaved for them, they took every drop of sweat and blood out of me and they kept all the money for themselves, while Mammy did without. Where's the sense in that, Frank?"

"But Nuala, to become a nun," Frank gushed.

"Why? So that people on James Street won't call me a tramp anymore? Did you like being called a bastard to your face, Frank, because that's what the holy nuns did for us."

"That's all in the past," Frank said. "We don't have to tell anyone where we went to school, and now that we're out of the Strand there's no one here who knows us. We're just an ordinary family again. I have a respectable position, and you'll become a nun, and that's all that anyone around here needs to know. I've made an end of it."

"Exactly, I'm making an end of it," she said in agreement. "Here's the tram, off I go. I'll bring home a bit of cheddar for tonight, and jam if there's a penny left over."

Venerations on Holy Thursday and Good Friday were observed at a different church that year. Maire's only disappointment was the fact that Nuala did not join her now that they were in Drimnaugh and well away from their past. On Holy Saturday, the girl disappeared as she usually did on a Saturday, and she was off again at dawn on Easter Sunday, wearing a brand new hat and a very smart coat. She did not come home for dinner, and when she was still gone at teatime, Maire was beginning to think that it was time to call the guards to report her daughter missing.

347

The sound of a car pulling up outside was followed by Nuala walking in the door at eight that night, and Frank could not recall ever seeing her happier. Rushing to the window, he had a glimpse of a private automobile going down the road, the headlamps glowing in the darkness. Even Maire ran to get a look, so rare was a sighting of a fine car in the corporation estate.

"Mrs. Adams wouldn't let me walk so late at night," Nuala explained. "She made her husband drive me home. She's been very kind to me."

"They were very thoughtful to bring you home in their car, so grand," Maire said. Her heart ached at that moment, with a sad realization that her daughter did not seem to be returned to her at all. There were secrets hidden just below the surface, private thoughts and actions that a daughter would never keep from her mother, but Nuala was holding back.

Gradually, the gap grew more narrow as Nuala started to occasionally confide in her mother or Frank. She became more open about her daily jaunts, sometimes telling Maire that she was going to help Mrs. Adams at a church rumble, or mentioning how she was learning the art of flower arranging in exchange for teaching friends of Mrs. Adams how to make lace. The impression that Maire formed of her daughter's activities was rather dazzling, because Nuala was moving in a circle of well-heeled Dubliners, finding all sorts of odd jobs from Mrs.

Adams and her high toned friends that earned the girl a few extra shillings.

Certainly, Maire was pleased that Nuala was doing well for herself, and contributing all that she could to the family's resources. Uncle Joe, on the other hand, found that he was being shuttled off to the sidelines, like so much excess baggage or cast-off belongings. Legally, he might be the head of the household, but Frank had essentially taken over the post by finding them a better place to live and becoming the family breadwinner. Joe's resentment was expressed in his bullying, tormenting Maire a little more each day. His petulance added to the strain of keeping a family on a minimum budget, and the gray hairs began to sprout more noticeably on Maire's head. "Humor him, for peace's sake," became her mantra as she struggled to get through each day, while the children found ways to stay away from the house in Drimnaugh.

In July of that year, Sister Domenica and Sister Theresa came to call on a warm Saturday, but Nuala was nowhere to be found, as usual. Fully aware of the general public's opinion of industrial school girls, the Sisters were not concerned that their potential novice ran away from those who knew her past, to seek the company of strangers. They took it as a sign of Nuala's cleverness and her ability to cope with life's difficulties. Learning that Nuala had found a way to attend Mass where she could worship anonymously, Sister Theresa turned to her colleague and nodded, impressed with an apparent case of deep piety that could not be quenched by rude comments or catcalls. The interview proceeded, with the two nuns very pleased to learn of Nuala's selfless generosity to her mother and her ceaseless hard work in support of the family. The Benedictines were sure that they had found a worthy soul.

Since Frank was meeting a friend for a cycling trip, he was excused from the ordeal of being further examined by two steely-eyed martinets. Pedaling along a country lane, enjoying the fresh air and the sense of freedom he relished as he rode wherever he wanted to go, he discovered where his sister wandered off to every Saturday, thanks to Tom Hennessey's sharp vision. While two Benedictine nuns sat in his mother's parlor, talking about Nuala's holiness, the subject of the discussion was not looking particularly holy.

"Isn't that your sister?" Tom whispered, peering over the stone fence that separated the messenger boys from an open field. On the other side of the wall, a picnic was underway. "That's her, Frank, as sure as I'm standing here."

"Jesus, those are two of the biggest men I've ever seen," Frank whistled. "Soldiers, do you think?"

"Yank soldiers," Tom said. "The other lady, that one with the baby, she's different looking. Must be a Yank too."

For the first time, Frank saw his sister as something other than a sibling or a novice. She was sitting on a blanket, smoking a cigarette with the panache of an American film star. Not only that, but she was actually attractive like a film star, smiling and laughing, brushing her curls out of her eyes with a languid hand. On the other hand, the burly Yank with black hair cut short and muscles rippling under his shirt was so incredibly homely and intimidating that Frank could not understand why his sister was attracted to him.

"I'd sell my soul to be him right now," Tom mumbled, observing the couple kissing when the other pair ran off to chase their toddler.

"Go on, it's just my sister," Frank scoffed, transfixed. Only recently had he learned that men and women kissed and embraced when they were in love, his knowledge acquired from films and the other messenger boys' crude remarks. He was swept with admiration for his big sister, who knew so much more than he did about the world of courting and romance.

"She's just five months older than me," Tom continued. "Can't you put in a good word?"

"What does she want with a messenger boy and his twelve shillings a week?" Frank cuffed his pal, and then turned to go. "And a bicycle instead of a car?"

The letter from the Benedictine Provincial House arrived in late August, asking Miss Devoy to kindly report to Kylemore Abbey on or about her seventeenth birthday. Maire was so ecstatic that she scraped together every coin she could gather, and threw a grand hooley for the family and any neighbor who wished to share in the joy. Not only was Nuala slated for the convent, but it had also been suggested that she was destined to move up the ranks, with the position of Mother Superior mentioned as a very realizable achievement. From the ashes of Family Court ten years past, a golden future was arising, an answer to countless prayers and petitions coming forth in a shower of glory.

"Where's the guest of honor?" Uncle John Devereux blubbered, half drunk by seven o'clock.

"She'll be along," Joe said. "Such a good girl, she collects her payments and gets more work for herself every Saturday without fail, and comes home to us with her contributions. If not for my bad back, I'd be out myself, but it's the cross I bear for my military service."

Sticking to her schedule, Nuala returned to Drimnaugh after eight, eyes bright and smile radiant. Requested to sing with the party in full gear, she politely declined "I'd rather hear Mammy sing from The Bohemian Girl," she said.

"Mammy said I could ask for a leave of absence to go to Galway," Frank informed his sister as the party careened into the wee hours.

"Don't go worrying about that, my boy," she said. "They can't have me."

"Why is that?" Frank teased, ready to ask about a certain big, plug-ugly ape.

"I'm not going to Galway," she stated simply. "I can't go anymore; I fixed it."

"Getting married, are you?"

"Maybe I am," she said. Sipping on a glass of port, she winked at her brother.

"Who is he, Nuala? Go on, you can tell me, I'm your brother."

"Come for a walk with me," she said. Once outside, she pulled a green packet of Lucky Strike cigarettes from the pocket of her dress. "You tell them in there that I'm smoking and it'll be the end of you."

Strolling around the cul-de-sac, Frank and Nuala shared confidences, the start of a return to their former life. His sister was not the same girl who had played with him as a child, but Frank also admitted that he was not the same little boy who was fascinated by road tar on a hot day. From their tête-à-tête he discovered that Nuala was far more embittered, more filled with hate, than he could ever be. She managed to transfer a great deal of her pain to him, and as she smoked one Lucky Strike after another, he incorporated her revulsion of the Sisters of Mercy into his very being.

Her words had a lifelong effect, embedded permanently into Frank's psyche because it was the last time that they would have a serious, grown-up chat, with an *intimacy that reflected a family tie struggling to reunite. On the fourteenth of September, Aunt Maggie threw a hooley to bid a fond farewell to her favorite niece. Nuala was expected at six, but she never showed up. By eight o'clock, Maire was so concerned that she sent Frank home on his bicycle, but the house in Drimnaugh was dark and empty. The telegram was waiting on the floor of the foyer where it had landed after the messenger boy shot it through the mail slot. Sent from the telegraph office in Dun Laoghaire, it was a simple thank you to Mrs. O'Brien for her kind consideration, a message that said goodbye.*

"Mom, I don't care if he gives me the Hope Diamond," Molly said, tightly gripping the telephone receiver. "I've had it with him and his games. I'm not a whore, to be bought when he wants something."

"What am I supposed to tell your aunts?" Barbara said. "He doesn't beat you, he doesn't get drunk, he's a good provider, and you want to move out?"

"I'm not going back."

"Listen, this is all because your father passed away and you're upset. You were very close, Molly, and now you've lost him, that's all that's wrong with you. It's a disruption in your life. Go home; adjust to a different way of doing things, without your father. You'll be closer to Stan in the long run."

"Is that what you want?" Molly said.

354

"You can work things out, honey. Don't be so hasty to dump everything overboard."

"I have to call the boys, to tell them about the funeral. Dad's old boys are the best, Mom, really great people. They're sad, too, the same way Dad was."

"Irishmen are too moody," Barbara said.

"They've got good reason for it," Molly added, but she did not elaborate.

For over an hour, Eoin attempted to reach Derry House, but the line was engaged. He had an urge to ask Molly if she could see inside his thoughts, if she had watched the newsreel footage that he replayed behind his eyes, scenes of a summer evening in Kilrossanty. If not behind his eyes, he wanted to know if she had the angle from the street, outside of the butcher shop looking in, to observe the MacNeill family as they watched the road. Molly would have seen Anne Crilly in the back seat of Father Duggan's car, being driven to the Magdalene Laundry in Waterford City on a cold day in 1962.

Everyone in town tried to avoid staring at the girl, sobbing and pleading in the back seat with her father, who sat rigidly next to her with his head held high despite the shame. Imagining that Molly could view his memories, Eoin feared that she saw a ten-year-old boy standing in his father's butcher shop, face pressed up against the window in the door as the dark sedan slowly went past.

"She's a filthy whore," Con mumbled under his breath, his cleaver hacking angrily at a rack of lamb.

"She did nothing wrong," Eoin's mother countered, the same heated argument that had raged all week. "It was her cousin, the filthy pig, and no mother in this town has ever let a girl near him because we all know what he is."

"She dressed like a tramp and egged him on," Eoin put in, echoing a phrase that was meant to please his impossible to satisfy father. "She brought it on herself."

"Mind you own business, Eoin," his mother barked.

Eight years later, she moved to England with his sisters, but by then, he understood why she left. If he could paint a complete picture for Molly, show her what was happening behind the scenes, he was sure that she would forgive him and they could work things out. Eoin had abandoned that era, given up ideas that he never really held close to his heart, but he had to make that clear to Molly. By ten o'clock, he figured that she had left the phone off the hook on purpose. She was not willing to listen to him anymore, or give him another chance.

"They were called bastards or jailbirds to their face because everyone assumed that they were juvenile delinquents," Molly said to her brothers. "The old boys I saw today, they haven't even told their own families to this day. It's so sick it's pathetic."

"And Aunt Nuala vanished?" Mark asked.

"Off the face of the earth. If she had killed herself, I wouldn't be at all surprised." Molly paused, to push aside the recollection of the conversation with her mother.

Talking about it made her sick, and having Rose not twenty feet away reinforced the nausea. Psychological torture on a phenomenal scale, and their father had held it in for the rest of his life. Matt tried to ease the tension by suggesting that his wife would be relieved to learn that there was a good reason her husband didn't open up and share his feelings. Then John picked up on it, describing a new disease called Devoy-itis with 'don't ask, don't tell' as its key symptom. Listening to their banter, Molly thought back to their childhood, to their public relationships with their spouses and children, and decided that she was the one who had inherited the birth defect while her brothers might be looked on as carriers who didn't exhibit the full-blown illness.

"Well, I'll be glad to see this place behind me," Molly said. "Two-faced people, smile at you and then spit on you when you turn around."

"I thought that you liked the people you're staying with," John said.

"They are the sweetest old ladies I have ever met, but one of them has been living in exile for most of her life because she was put away for no good reason. She's not right in the head after the experience, and it's her own people who did it to her." Molly sighed, checking her anger. "Irish hospitality applies to the guests. The family has to eat the garbage, and make sure that no one sees them."

"Jesus Christ, are you ever in a bitchy mood," Matt complained. "Don't forget, Miss Molly, that Dad loved Ireland."

"Heaven help Dad if he called you Nuala by mistake," Lucas said. "How can you forget her name, Frank, Mom always ragged him about it. Of course, she'd look me in the eye and say, Matt, Mark, John before she got to the right one."

"Oh, Lord, when you took medals in set dancing and couldn't keep off Mom's feet when she taught you how to polka," Mark said. "You turned into a full-blooded colleen, Molly, no matter how much kielbasa Mom tried to stuff into you."

"So, making a fresh start when you land at O'Hare?" Matt asked.

"Oh, please," Molly said. The last thing that she wanted to do was discuss her private concerns. One word of consent would lead to an hour of questions that she couldn't answer, not when she honestly didn't know what she was going to do once the plane landed in Chicago.

"Why do you think Dad bought that house, the one you liked so much," Matt reminded her. "For you to have someplace to go so you could get divorced."

"Don't make up stories," Molly said. "It was an investment. Wasn't it?"

"Did you listen to the lawyer?" Matt asked. "Dad left it to you, and it's so tied up that Mr. Asshole can't touch it."

"I'm running up the phone bill. I've got to get my bags packed," Molly said.

"Sure, run away," Matt said. "Dad didn't run from anything. Do it for him, if you can't do it for your kids or for yourself."

She didn't expect her brothers to read her mind, to know what she was planning. They didn't care for Stan, and Molly saw that as the foundation on which they acted. What they did understand was the relationship, with Stan the absolute ruler and Molly the humble servant. Her brothers had seen it from the start, while she was too preoccupied with her mother's advice to settle down and raise a family. Granted, it was true that Stan gave her so much, as her mother constantly reminded her, but everything that he gave was nothing that she wanted.

Seventeen years ago, Stan had made Molly quit smoking, and until Eoin came along, she had not touched a cigarette. Grabbing her jacket, she took the pack out of her purse and shoved it into a pocket, along with a book of matches. Her head pounding, Molly walked out the door and walked across the street, to watch the Grand Canal flow by and find peace with a cigarette and solitude. After the last cigarette had been tossed into the water, she watched the butt sink from sight.

"It's lovely out here, isn't it?" Rose crept up, startling Molly and setting her heart to pounding. "Does it help, to watch the water?"

"Sure, when you need to think," Molly said, an answer without thought behind it.

"Are you thinking about Mr. O'Rahilly? I've been thinking. Maybe I've made a mistake."

"No, it's not a mistake," Molly said. "You've taken on a heavy burden and the weight is surprising you, so you want to put it down. Keep carrying it, Rose, and you'll find out how strong you really are."

"Mrs. Kiely won't talk to the solicitor," Rose confided. "She's happy to let things lie."

"Most people are," Molly said, feeling bombarded by the truth as it hit its target.

"Would you think less of me if I backed out?"

"No, I'd never do that, Rose. Would you think less of me if I told you that I run away from my problems?"

"Go on with you," she said. "About your aunt, you won't back out, will you?"

"Never, not even if they threaten to excommunicate me. It's the hierarchy that we're up against, not God or Jesus. The religion doesn't change; the message hasn't changed because my aunt was abused. What happened to you and my aunt has nothing to do with our faith, does it? That's what the bishops don't get, Rose. It's not them that we respect, it's the word of God, and they're only the messengers, the office boys and middle management. Every one of them could dive off a cliff and we'd be no worse without them. I won't let them drive me out; I'll run them off first."

"The chapel in Cork was so beautiful, Molly," Rose said. "The Good Shepherd Sisters had it remodeled, and at what cost?

If they had used that money to help the poor, instead of gilding their chapel, I might have been able to forgive them."

"They just didn't get it, Rose," Molly said. "Jesus was born in a stable, and they want to erect palaces to make it up to Him. Sorry for the lack of accommodations, sir, but we've upgraded you to first class and thank you for coming down to Earth. Okay, so your kingdom is not of this earth, but we're building castles anyway, and we might as well call ourselves Princes of the Church."

Rose began to chuckle, a tiny snicker that blossomed into a hearty laugh, the silly kind of giggling that was typical of giddy young girls just approaching womanhood. Hearing the sincere merriment, Molly began to laugh as well. Living well was the best revenge, but for Rose, the very act of living was going to serve as her reprisal. Molly had given her a boost over the barricade, but now the nurse felt that she was left behind to find her own way over.

19

Before the mourners came to pay their last respects to Mrs. Smythe, Martin stole down to the church hall, only to find his son Keith already there with little Hilary balanced on his hip. "Now, let's kiss Gran goodbye," Keith said, a tear dropping from the end of his nose.

He was the stoic while she had been the source of affection, the one to kiss the children goodnight while he stood at her side like a clerical Beefeater. It was not a surprise to see Keith weeping over his mother's death, not when that same woman had been prone to weeping over the slightest emotion. When Keith earned a fellowship to study vascular surgery, she shed copious tears, while Martin gave their son a hearty handshake and congratulations for a job well done. They were well suited, Martin and Ginger, with differences that drove them closer together and created children that were firmly grounded and very well balanced. If anyone doubted that opposites could attract and flourish as one, they had only to look at Martin and Ginger and the Smythe family.

"You have her warm compassion," Martin said, looking again at the lifeless body that had once been his wife.

Struggling to maintain a stiff upper lip, Martin turned his face away, embarrassed that he might reveal the deepest intimacy between man and wife. He was a renowned theologian and lecturer, but his existence had been nurtured on one woman's love and support, just as the family had thrived under her care. He was no more a tower of strength than a pile of sand, but only Ginger knew that.

"And your cool reasoning," Keith countered. He put Hilary down so that he could retrieve a handkerchief from his back pocket.

"Our wedding picture," the Anglican priest indicated the framed eight by ten that was set in a group of photos on a side table. "She went to Clery's that morning and bought the best suit that she could find."

"The corsage is as big as her head," Keith chuckled.

"That was quite au courant," Martin said. With his finger, he gently touched the black and white image. "Only yesterday."

The day was still quite vivid in his memories, even though thirty-one years had passed since he left Ireland with his beloved Ginger at his side. There had barely been enough time to pose for the photographer at the pier before they ran to catch the three o'clock mail boat to Holyhead, his departure already delayed for two weeks while he worked up the courage to ask for her hand. He could never forget the hearty cheers and best wishes of the other passengers on the boat, who recognized a honeymoon couple by their Sunday best clothes and the stars in their eyes. Through the heaving Irish Sea, they held hands and appeared to be lost in the clouds, smiling broadly as each traveler came up in turn and offered congratulations to the bride with the oversized corsage.

"I always thought that if I looked up 'minister's wife' in the dictionary, I would find a picture of Mummy," Keith said. "She was your doormat, you know."

"She was a good, dutiful woman, Keith, and she loved me so deeply," Martin confided. "Women always make the greater sacrifice in marriage. She never minded, you see, but I knew she did everything she could to make me comfortable and happy. I appreciated it, and I never missed an opportunity to tell her so."

"We'll be inundated by her flock, I suppose," Maureen warned, joining her father at the display of photos. "Mrs. Dee will be a limp rag in no time without Mummy to prop her up."

"She always used to tease me about the size of my congregation," Martin's eyes grew damp. "Her life's work was to bring in new members to my parish. She was completely dedicated to God's call when it came to converting the agnostics. It's a difficult life, to be the wife of a minister, but she sincerely enjoyed it."

"Reverend Smythe, the florist shop from the West End has sent a lovely arrangement." Mrs. Dee popped in, a deliveryman trailing behind her. "Mrs. Maghera did it herself, she said, to be sure it was to Mrs. Smythe's liking. Over there, young man, next to the spray of yellow roses."

From the day she arrived in London as a new bride, Ginger had launched her mission, to help women down on their luck or cast adrift. The flower arranging classes had been the first foray into occupational training for the many Irish girls who turned up in the city, their reasons for emigrating as varied as the girls themselves. Despite her shy, retiring nature, the minister's wife had doggedly pursued every florist in England, Scotland and Wales to secure positions for her pupils, offering a fresh start with no questions asked about their past.

Martin suspected that many of the young ladies had been released from industrial schools or Magdalene laundries, women with little hope for any kind of decent life in Ireland. Every now and then, an unwed mother would arrive at the kitchen door, but no stern lectures about morality were ever issued at St. Andrew's vicarage. His home was more of a dispensary, where advice, charity and a helping hand were prescribed with selfless generosity to anyone who came in search of aid, guidance and a reference.

The night before, as the children reminisced about their mother, Maureen and Louise described a woman who never seemed to be still, always in motion and always working on her causes. When they were little, they actually believed the suggestion that every maid, laundress, seamstress and florist in London had obtained her position through their mother's persistence, leaving Dublin's upper crust without hired help. Never once did the Smythe girls think that their mother's endless activity was at all unusual or rare, because she had made it seem so commonplace and ordinary. If anything, she had taught her children how to be charitable without being patronizing, and they had learned that it cost nothing to give to others.

Even so, the charity was not entirely free, because Mummy proselytized her charges, and every convert to the Church of England meant a great deal to a woman who worked tirelessly to bring God to those who had given up on Him. She had gotten Mrs. Dee to the baptismal font after only a month, and Martin had laughed to recall that Ginger had begun to work on the woman from the time they met on the mail boat as it left Dun Laoghaire on the way to Holyhead on a sunny September day. Over the years, there were dozens more who joined St. Andrew's, all people who were drawn to Mrs. Smythe and her indefinable charisma, and almost all were Irish women who had left the Catholic Church.

Gradually, the church hall began to fill with parishioners, the ladies in furs and the gentlemen in cashmere coats. Their old friends stood out, dressed in a more subdued mode that took note of the current trends of short skirts and bold colors but refused to be shackled by Carnaby Street and eternal youth. Friends of his children and colleagues from the Humanities Division at Oxford strolled in, a shaggy headed group that stood in sharp contrast to the conservative core of the parish. Looking over the throng, Martin took in the full gamut of London society, from old age to infancy, from Peers of the Realm to simple scrubwomen who betrayed a sense of inferiority by the look in their eyes. They had all come to pay honor to his wife.

"Mrs. MacNaughton would like a word, Dad." Keith had to interrupt when Mrs. Hardwick would not take a cue to stop chattering.

"I can't believe she's gone, sir," the stoop-shouldered woman mourned. "We were talking just the other day about seeing in the new decade and putting these unsettled times behind us. The poor dear left us too soon."

"Yes, thank you, she had been taken from us too soon," Martin said, fishing around for a topic to mull over. "Are you from Dublin originally, Mrs. MacNaughton?"

"From the Strand, Reverend, and happy to be here, saved from eternal damnation in baptism," the grandmother said. The former Catholic had become an Anglican twenty years ago, and her religious zeal had not waned. "The good die young, they say, and here's the truth in it."

"Heavy smokers die young, Mrs. MacNaughton," the minister added gently, making an attempt at lighthearted humor.

367

Many nights, he had come upon his wife in the lounge, an ashtray nearly overflowing with cigarette butts as she puffed away, engrossed in her Book of Common Prayer or another reading of the Bible. She called it wrestling with her demons, but she never told him what could be troubling her in the middle of the night. He chalked it up to her addiction to nicotine, a craving that she had never been able to master. She would light one cigarette with the butt of the other, chain-smoking until her heart finally had enough.

"How I shall miss her delightful drinks parties," Mr. Peacock said, barging in as if Mrs. MacNaughton were invisible, but then, she essentially was. "As a hostess, Martin, she was unsurpassed."

"When we married, she only just knew how to boil water," Martin said. "She worked so hard to learn how to do everything perfectly. I've been so proud of her, of all that she's done."

"I didn't realize she was so young," Mrs. Peacock interjected.

"I never told anyone this before," the minister spoke in hushed tones. "We married a week before she reached the age of consent. She was afraid that I would leave her behind if I knew, the poor dear. She didn't tell me that she had lied about her age for weeks."

"She was mad about you, absolutely mad." Mrs. Peacock gently touched Martin's arm. "Who could blame her?"

"To find such a specimen as this to be irresistible," Mr. Peacock made a stab at something cheerful, "she must have been blind as well."

"Excuse me, Father," a middle-aged lady touched Martin's shoulder. "I'm sorry to interrupt, but I'm minding my grandson and I don't like to leave him too long with my neighbor. I only wanted to let you know that your wife saved me, truly rescued me from a nightmare. If she hadn't been there at the train station, looking for girls just come from Ireland, I don't know what would have happened to me. My husband and I own a haberdashery. He's a tailor, and a fine one."

"That's a marvelous testimony to my late wife," Martin said, shaking her hand with gratitude.

The woman's hair was streaked with gray, but her blue eyes were still bright as Mrs. Foy smiled at the cleric. "I converted, to Church of England," she bragged. "It was grand, Father, to walk into a church and feel God's presence. I thought He was gone from this world, but I found Him through Mrs. Smythe."

"Her sentiments exactly," Martin said, his thoughts returning to Dublin again.

Every Sunday, he had seen her in the back of Christ Church, looking a little lost. Coming upon her in the library at Trinity College was nearly a miracle, as if God answered his prayer that he find the courage to approach her, to sail off on *a sea of witty repartee and somehow be allowed to touch her lovely hands. He wanted to gaze into her blue eyes, to study the arrangement of her facial features and determine if she were a very young child or an older woman because she looked both young and old at the same time.*

"I'm divine," he stammered, meaning to say that he was a Doctor of Divinity before adding that he was on sabbatical.

She started, a little frightened, but then she giggled ever so slightly, finding his remark amusing but not wishing to hurt his feelings by pointing out how foolish he seemed. "I don't understand," she said, gentle and kind, giving him a chance to rephrase the remark. The words just poured out of him then, not witty because he was not a joker, but she was mesmerized by every syllable.

"Although I may, indeed, be divine," he went on. "May I offer you every opportunity to assess my qualities?" They spent the next four hours over a pot of tea and a plate of biscuits at the Country Shop, and he did not want the day to ever end.

Her interest in religion was sincere and heartfelt, and when he began to spend Sunday afternoons with her, studying catechism or debating the theses of Martin Luther, he knew that he had found the perfect wife. Having been raised by a Catholic grandmother after she lost her parents, Ginger wanted to renew her ties to the Church, and Martin became her religious instructor. Reverend Adams baptized her on Holy Saturday, along with the other converts, but Martin only noticed one beautiful smile of perfect joy that day. She took communion for the first time on their wedding day, an event that left her glowing for weeks afterward, although Martin liked to think it was his lovemaking that put the sparkles in her eyes.

Her faith was remarkably strong, powerful enough to see her through the many miscarriages that broke her heart repeatedly. She wanted children, as many as Martin could afford, but in the end, only four survived, although Ginger never complained or blamed God for cheating her. Instead, she would insist that she had been blessed, always finding the silver lining in the darkest cloud.

"Christ, here's Mummy and Daddy in Majorca," Frank said, not pleased by a photo of his parents looking moony and love struck.

"That's where you came from, isn't it?" Keith ragged his baby brother. "A romantic getaway to sunny Spain, and here is their souvenir."

"Shut up," Frank hissed. "You're not at all funny."

"They must have taken off their clothes at some point, Frank, or none of us would be here."

Martin could not suppress a smile, catching Keith's eye with a knowing wink between married men. "Oh, and don't think I never saw the way you looked at Mum," Frank warned his father. "You could have set the tea table on fire."

"I always thought it was sweet," Louise said. "So romantic, Frank, and Mummy and Daddy rather old and stodgy. You have no sense of romance at all."

"Dear me, Louise, if your mother should see you now," Martin said, exasperated by his youngest daughter's penchant for micro mini-skirts and overabundant eye make-up.

"I wore this because she bought it for me," the girl replied, storming off to greet her friends from art school.

"It's been years since I've seen this." Martin took the framed photo, the tears beginning to trickle from the corner of his eye. "Such a beautiful woman, yet so modest. She always dressed elegantly, but she never put on a display of any kind. Only a touch of cosmetics. Gilding the lily, I liked to tell her. We were so perfect together. She was everything to me."

Surrounded by his four children, Martin found the strength to bring his sorrow under control. Frank gave his father a warm embrace, a strong hug to lend support when the fifteen-year-old was just as heartbroken. Blowing his nose quietly, Martin returned the picture to the table and set his shoulders, to carry on through the reception with bravery.

"We were just recalling the blitz, Martin," Lloyd Jones welcomed a new voice to the conference. "I was telling them how strongly your wife protested the relocation of the children to the country."

"Yes, she was rather vocal about that," Martin agreed. "Passionate, in fact, and quite unlike her. Well, she was orphaned, and I came to find that the lives of children and the well being of families were of great importance to her. I must admit that she was quite right, about the reaction of the children to being separated from their mothers. Quite traumatic, exactly as she predicted."

"Did she really threaten you with a frying pan?" Sylvia Jones inquired, seeking the truth behind an old rumor.

"Keith was not quite a year old, and if anyone tried to take him away from her, I think she would have flailed away with her skillet," Martin chuckled, bringing to mind a memory of his wife, but the skillet was not there. She was standing in the kitchen, a firm grip on Keith and a firm grip on the carving knife. Madness filled her eyes, her threat to kill him if he tried to take Keith very real. He backed down after that and let them stay home through the blitz, never once bringing up the episode. He accepted her unwavering, almost suffocating love for her children, and he brushed aside one incident that was brought on by intense stress. She suffered a stillbirth and a miscarriage during the war, and in the end he was glad that she had Keith in her arms to help her keep her sanity when so many people were cracking under the strain.

"The organist wants to play a special song for Mummy."
Louise scurried over, giggling behind her hands.

"Good heavens, you didn't tell him that he could wring
show tunes out of that instrument, did you?" Martin huffed.

"But Mummy liked My Fair Lady very much," Maureen
said in defense of the iconoclastic musician. It was like her, to
stand up for others. She frequently stood up for her mother,
claiming that Mummy took her vow of wifely obedience much
too seriously. He had bickered with Maureen about it,
insisting that Ginger was perfectly happy, but Maureen only
countered his arguments by pointing out that no one could
possibly know whether Mummy was happy or not. Ginger did
have a great imagination, and had reveled in games of make-
believe with the children, but it was also true that she was an
extremely reserved and private person. Even in bed, in their
most private moments, he never truly felt that she was giving
herself completely to him, but she was that sort of person and
he accepted her reticence.

There were some things that he could never tell his
children, the intimacies that were shared by a married couple.
Some day, he hoped that his daughter would come to know a
man as her mother had loved him, to worship the very ground
that he walked on, to sublimate her being because she adored
him. It would not do, to confess Ginger's weaknesses to their
children. Maureen would not understand how much her
mother needed her father, or how much he needed Ginger,

until she was married for several years and had been through life's ups and downs. He never had to know precisely what his wife was thinking or feeling because she told him many times that he was everything to her. That was all that was needed, a simple understanding, and Maureen would have her opinions until the right man set her straight. Her current boyfriend, a long-haired architect, was definitely not the right man for the task.

"Your mother would be humiliated by such a display," he said. "This is a funeral, girls, not a stage show."

"It's supposed to be a celebration of Mummy's life," Louise complained, the seventeen-year-old who lived in a state of mutiny against her father's authority.

"We shall have a celebration tonight, just the family. I'd say we could all use a bit of cheering up, to think about Mummy and how much she loved us." Martin cleared his throat, to remove the sobs that would not quite retreat into the distance. "I apologize for snapping at you, girls. My nerves are on edge, as you can understand."

A warm hug and a peck on the cheek told the minister that Louise forgave his bout of temper. He could not say anything more to his daughters because the press of mourners intruded, offering their condolences and providing a blessed screen of distraction for a sorrowing husband. His wife's converts, the humble Irish women, were of the greatest comfort as they alleviated a modicum of pain with the glow of hope for the future. They came in all shapes and sizes, but they came, repaying his late wife's kindness and filling his aching heart, taking the love that had been given so generously and returning it tenfold.

"Excuse me for a minute, Dad," Keith said. "I'd better pop into the other room and look in on Mrs. Dee."

The family's housekeeper had taken the death very hard, keening in the manner of an Irish peasant when she was told that Mrs. Smythe had passed away. Having joined the Smythe clan from its inception, she was as much a part of the family as any of them, and her sorrow caused a great deal of concern. Keith in particular was attached to her, even though he knew absolutely nothing about her background or even what part of Ireland she came from originally. His mother had thoughtfully refrained from speaking of the past, and her silence had become as much a part of Mrs. Dee's history as the woman's penchant for an occasional whiskey to warm her bones.

Some time after Keith entered university, he was told that the timid lady was on the ferry to Holyhead because she was pregnant and unmarried, having been abandoned by her lover. She was running in fright from the Catholics, who imprisoned unwed mothers and innocent young girls, forcing them into slave labor and a lifetime of servitude. The Smythe children often wondered if Dee was really her name, but their mother, citing respect for the unfortunate woman, abruptly

376

terminated the discussion. In the same vein, no one was allowed to ask about Mr. Dee, and Keith presumed that such a spouse did not exist.

There were shadowy memories of Mrs. Dee's little girl, who died of whooping cough near the end of the war. Keith had played with her, as if she were his big sister, but he remembered very little about the child except that she was rather a homely creature with dark hair and an olive complexion. Like so many other unpleasant topics, Mrs. Dee's dead daughter was something else that was not discussed.

"I knew that I could find you awash in biscuits," he teased the housekeeper, to bring a twinkle to her pretty eyes. "How very thoughtful, Mrs. Dee. You've put out Mummy's collection of biscuit tins."

They were a collection of junk, purchased from second hand shops, with bits of rust and flaking paint, but highly treasured by his mother. She kept her secrets in them, she used to tell the children, but when they opened up the tin with the circus animals painted all around, they found only their baby teeth, scraps of thread, bits of lace and crochet hooks, locks of baby hair and photographs of the family. It was Mummy's pretendings that were in there, he discovered, and the biscuit tin could hold whatever she wanted to put in it. He had put things in there as well, like a piece of agate from Scotland and a smooth stone from the beach in Brighton, pretending that he had the entire country and the whole resort locked up in Mummy's treasure box, bundled in with a family and a corner of Dublin.

"Most of London will be here," she said, wiping a linen handkerchief under her nose.

"Except for any representatives of our neighbors at St. Mary's Church," Keith sarcastically noted.

"She snatched girls right out from under the priest's nose, didn't she?" Mrs. Dee brightened. "Your mother preached the words of salvation to us, Mr. Keith, and those black-robed vultures wanted to eat us alive."

"Yes, well, she never attempted to make friends with them," Keith said, sorry that he had brought on another long-winded tirade against the Catholic Church. Mrs. Dee could wax prolific on the topic.

The relationship between St. Andrew's and St. Mary's was icy for as long as Keith could remember. Things had become downright hostile ten years ago, when Monsignor Leverick accused his mother of being the ringleader in a scheme to adopt Irish babies into Anglican homes. There had been infants brought from the Mother and Baby Home at High Park in Drumcondra that turned up at the baptismal font in St. Andrew's, but his father pointedly ignored all of Leverick's protests. At the time, members of the Church of Ireland were being castigated by Irish Catholics, and Keith saw his parents as crusaders against religious intolerance, doing their part to help the pitiful Irish immigrants who fled from their oppressive homeland.

"You remembered the Jacob's Biscuits," Keith said. He had grown up with those same treats, served daily at teatime. "Hilary loves the Jaffa cakes, but too much chocolate is not good. Let's keep her little hands out of the tin, shall we?"

"Oh, Mrs. Dee's favorite," Louise said, poking her head into the classroom that was to serve as a refreshment area following the internment. "I'll save some for you, Mrs. Dee."

"Those biscuits are for the guests, Miss Louise, and not for the help," Mrs. Dee informed her sternly. "Nor for family either if the supply runs low."

"Mrs. Dee, you're crying," Keith said, hurrying over to console a woman who had come to rely completely on her patroness. "We shall all miss her terribly, but Mummy would want us to carry on her work. No matter what, you must stay and look after Daddy. He's bad off, and he will need you to be his rock."

"Those horrible nuns, they lived forever, and a good woman like your mother is taken too soon." Mrs. Dee fumbled with her handkerchief. "My faith is shaken, Mr. Keith, and now your mother is gone and who will restore my spirit?"

"God still watches over us," Louise said. "And maybe Mummy is watching, too. Still telling you to give up cigarettes while she lights up in heaven."

"At any rate, she's no doubt hounding God right now to touch your heart," Keith said, easily picturing his mother on the phone to the Lord, badgering until He gave in to her demands.

With a refreshed smile, Mrs. Dee wiped her nose and cleared her throat. "Go on, the both of you, and see to the visitors. Although there's not a drop of whiskey in the place, and that's not much of a proper wake for an Irishman."

"Do you think God's throwing a hooley in heaven, Mrs. Dee?" Louise suggested in jest, bringing the sparkle back to the woman's eyes.

Charging in on her little legs, Hilary made a dash for the table, with her mother close behind. "Not more chocolate," Diane ordered, giving a warning to her husband.

"The lure of the Jaffa cake and the custard crème," Keith said. He swung his daughter into his arms and nuzzled her tummy.

"Your dad is," Diane began.

"Bad off, yes," Keith agreed. He handed Hilary off to Louise.

"Did I ever tell you about my first impression of your mother? I was terrified of meeting her, you know," Diane said. "Everyone told me she was more of a missionary than a minister's wife, and I was picturing some sort of bulldog spouting hellfire and damnation. But when I actually saw her, all four feet and ten inches of her, I was speechless."

"My mother?" he laughed. "She was afraid of her own shadow. I'm sure that she was far more frightened to meet you."

"Yes, she was, I think. She was rather shy at first. In fact, she was the most unique woman I ever met. She was a shadow, Keith, she was your father's shadow, and she was perfectly happy with it. I can't understand how she did it, badgering everyone she knew to get positions for her Irish girls, unstoppable until they gave in, but as soon as your father asked for his tea, she just dropped what she was doing and ran to the kitchen."

"It's that generation," he shrugged. "She could lecture the ladies' guild about the need for women's rights, but she was still an old-fashioned wife and mother. Ahead of her time, do you think?"

"Straddling the line between old and new," Diane said. "I shall miss her terribly."

The curate of St. Andrew's had volunteered to conduct the funeral and deliver a eulogy, but as the time approached, he found that he was cracking with emotion. Looking over his notes, he reviewed the words that he would speak, to pay homage to a woman who had worked tirelessly during the war to help those who lost everything in the bombing raids. Her domestic economy had been an inspiration, her salvage drives still talked about among the older parishioners, and all the while, she rescued Irish girls who came to her for help.

381

Glancing up, to get a feel for the atmosphere he might find inside the church, Reverend Stevenson discovered some of the recent arrivals gathering near the door. He had met several of them, all naïve young girls who gave in to a boyfriend, only to learn that men could make themselves scarce if they wanted to duck the responsibility. There was quite a medley taking seats in the pews, from scrubbed-face nannies to hard-edged women who were more than likely making a living on their back. Saint or sinner, all they ever had to do was turn up at the vicarage and say, "I've come from the Good Shepherds" or "They'll send me to the laundry if I go back", and they found aid and comfort from Mrs. Smythe. Their haunted faces looked back at Reverend Stevenson, and that was when he felt the lump form in his throat. With a loud harrumph he focused his mind on his duties, a sound that sent the undertaker scurrying back to the community room.

The mortician appeared, discretely catching Dr. Smythe's eye to let him know that it was time. "I believe in God's mercy, Keith, and I believe in His love," Martin said, struggling to accept his loss.

"And Mummy believed, Daddy, without doubts or even a question. Her faith was unshakeable, and that's been my example to follow. She'd be disappointed in you if you dared to question the Almighty."

The pallbearers were ready to shoulder the heavy casket, a large coffin for such a small woman. Only they remained in the room, standing inconspicuously near the door while the Smythe family had their last moments alone with their beloved matriarch. Diane touched her fingers to Hilary's lips to pass the wet baby kiss on to the lid of Gran's coffin, and each child in turn touched their lips to the brass plate engraved with their mother's name. Keith put an arm across his father's stooped shoulders, surprised that the once lively man looked more than his sixty-two years, and waited for Martin to finally accept the death of his precious little Ginger.

"I've changed my mind, Mr. Spaulding," Martin said to the funeral director. "If you would, please open the coffin."

"Dad, you have to say goodbye," Keith said. "We can't keep her, and you know that."

"One more time, that is all, and then I will accept what God was willed," Martin assured his family.

Only when Keith nodded to Spaulding would he work on the bolts that sealed the coffin. With the sextant's help, he removed the top and stepped aside, while Keith prayed that his father would not have to be forced to relinquish his wife's dead body.

Although flecked with gray, her hair was still the color of ginger, the color that gave rise to Mummy's pet name. She was as tiny as a songbird, as Daddy often said, one that feasted on love and affection, thriving on kind words and a bite of flattery. For thirty-one years they had nurtured each other, offered support and endless patience that seemed

383

limitless, and yet it had suddenly come to an end. He did not want to cry any more, but Keith could not hold in one last sob, one last whisper, "Mummy."

"Her lovely, lovely hands," Martin said. The fingers of the left hand were stained yellow from cigarettes, a permanent scar of her only bad habit.

"Daddy, please," Keith said, more forceful, more insistent

Hesitating, Martin carefully laid his hand on hers before he smoothed the worn fabric of the once white dress, felt the celluloid nose and smiled with contentment at the blond eyebrows, the paint worn off until only a suggestion of a line remained.

"No, no, I was right the first time," he backed off, gesturing to Mr. Spaulding that the casket was to be closed. "I have no right to keep her. She shared our bed every night, but she belongs to Ginger. She never went anywhere without her Jenny. Never went anywhere without her."

Fr. Stevenson donned his surplice, the one that Mrs. Smythe had given him to welcome him to St. Andrew's. With love, he touched the lace band along the bottom, the lace that Mrs. Smythe had made because she was that sort of person, generous and kind, always giving to others. A tear escaped and rolled down his nose, to be hastily wiped away with a laugh. Mrs. Smythe had crocheted shamrocks as part of the

theme of the piece, to make Stevenson an 'honorary Irishman'
as she had so charmingly teased him.

Standing at the altar, the curate looked over the crowd
and silently asked God for the strength to continue without
breaking down. "We have come here today," his voice rose
powerfully, "to remember before God our sister." He paused
in mid-sentence, momentarily forgetting her real name.
Everyone had always called her Ginger.

Dublin Airport was bustling on a Friday, with a crowd of
American tourists sharing Molly's flight to Chicago. They were
boisterous and noisy, a group tour that must have made one last
stop at the Guinness Brewery for a liquid breakfast, while Molly
yearned for solitude and quiet so that she could think. They were
crowing about Belleek and the Waterford Crystal that they had
picked up, "a bargain, Estelle," came the brag above the chatter.
The mention of Waterford brought Kilrossanty to mind, not
glistening crystal artifacts. Kilrossanty did not call up glass
blowers demonstrating a trade; it only reminded Molly of her
aunt and all the women like Rose Devlin.

She had sat up with Rose most of the night, as the long
submerged memories bubbled up and broke on the surface. The
despair appeared again, coupled with sounds and smells that
Rose related through tears, the images striking out in her
nightmares when she closed her eyes. Listening all night to
Rose, the feeling of hopelessness had rubbed off on Molly, who

sat in the waiting room of Dublin Airport, staring blankly at the holiday revelers.

"Say, are you traveling alone?" A jovial grandmother approached Molly. "Come sit with us, we've got plenty of room."

"Thank you, but I'm fine, really," Molly said, politely declining.

"Are you sure? You're welcome to join us. We took the Horizon tour; are you in a group?"

"No, I came for a funeral."

"Oh, I'm sorry, honey. Anyone close?"

"My father."

"That's too bad. So he was Irish? My great grandparents came from Cork. I don't know where exactly, but the tour bus took us out to the country to see the farms. Beautiful country, Ireland."

"Like blighted potatoes," Molly said. "That's how I heard a man describe it. Lush and green on top, black and stinking underground."

The older woman shrugged and laughed. "I guess. I never saw a blighted potato, so what would I know?"

"Rosemary, will you leave the girl alone?" a man said. "Always making a new friend wherever we go, she's got to talk to people."

"Her father just died, Sid," Rosemary said. "Do you have family here still?"

"No, my grandfather died when my dad was a baby, and my grandmother died the year before I was born," Molly explained, finding comfort in confiding in a stranger. "My aunt disappeared right before the war, so I don't know where she is."

"Wow, that's quite a mystery," Rosemary said, clearly intrigued.

The copy of the *Irish Times* that Molly had been reading was folded to the article about the ongoing suit against the Sisters of Mercy. Turning to the newsprint on her lap, she picked up the section and glanced at the name of the newest members of the class, Miss Rose Devlin and Ms. Molly Devoy on behalf of Nuala Devoy, whereabouts unknown.

"We're digging up some clues to find her," Molly said, bouncing the newspaper on her knee.

"Isn't it terrible, how those people are suing the nuns," Rosemary said, pointing at the headline.

"For what those nuns did, they should be drawn and quartered." Molly's grin was menacing. "I hope they bankrupt them and drive them out of business completely."

"Oh, well, I don't know all that much about it," Rosemary spluttered.

Leveling a penetrating stare at the tourist, Molly offered her advice. "It's best not to know."

That was enough to send Rosemary scurrying back to the safety of the pack, to immerse her thoughts in souvenirs and sights seen. Molly contemplated the brief article again, focusing on her father's name. Without clear instructions, she did not know with certainty that this was what Frank wanted, but Molly decided to do what she thought was the right thing. Instead of running away, she was going to stand and fight, although she was cowering behind Mr. O'Rahilly and his tower of legalese.

Alone again, the flight delayed due to a storm, Molly stared out of the window and saw her life, a life of running to please others while running away from relationships. As much as she tried to be fair and give equal weight, she could reach no other conclusion but one. When she made her father happy, she was happy too. She became a nurse at his urging, and she loved her profession. Irish dancing and volleyball had been her passions as a child, and Frank had savored every minute of it. With her father, she shared interests and tastes, but if it was genetics or training she could not determine. It simply was how things were, and she accepted the inevitable.

Two week ago, Molly thought that her father had run away, but she saw now that she had been mistaken. He had stormed off, to show all those who spit on him that he was better than they were, and he proved his point. Even the washed out old priest at Goldenbridge Cemetery had admitted to past conduct that was inexcusable while lauding Frank Devoy's ability to overcome the obstacles that the Irish people placed in his path. Many of the old boys had done the same, by turning to England for a fair shake and then making the best of what they had. They recognized the barriers, vaulting them with effort but getting over. Frank wanted Molly to see how it was done, so that she could do the same. It was possible to recover from the legacy of the industrial schools and the Magdalene laundries.

"Miss Rose Devlin has been a virtual prisoner in her late brother's home." Molly scanned the article again. "But with the help of Mr. Sean O'Rahilly, she is fighting back. Like many other former laundry girls, Miss Devlin will need psychiatric care to aid in her recovery."

Clearly, it was never too late to put up a struggle, even if years had to pass before the boxer could get up off the canvas. Rose had been knocked around, as Molly had learned the night before, but she had a little left in her, a scrap of pluck still remaining. Like the martyrs of 1916, the laundry girls waged an unpopular uprising but they would draw support over time, as people saw the justice of their cause. Rose Devlin believed in her country, admired its history, and she stopped running away so that she could turn and stand her ground. If it meant certain slaughter, so be it, but Rose meant to go down fighting.

"You have to think like the Irish, Molly," Rose had advised the night before. "It's not fleeing, it's the need to recuperate. Gather your forces and make ready for battle. We're allies now, you and I, and I'm coming out of exile because you're with me. Do you know our legends and our myths, our brave warriors? That's the stuff we're made of, your father and I, and you as well."

By this time tomorrow, all of Ireland could read that Nuala Devoy had been sexually molested while a ward of the Irish Free State. It was not the sort of publicity that Molly would willingly seek, but her father had asked her to speak for him, and those were the words that came to mind. Told in Frank's unusual way, Molly had uncovered a story that was a testament to the resilience of one man to bounce back from a horrible childhood, to reach for the heights and achieve his dreams. It seemed fitting that Nuala's saga should be revealed, to lay bare the secrets and put an end to the decades of silence that were supported by the thinnest frame, the victim's fear of shame and the culprit's fear of the truth. It was left up to her to fight her battle, the second generation's war to eradicate the last remaining fragments of stolen childhoods.

"We may open a back door," O'Rahilly had postulated when they discussed the course of action he was taking. "Those whom you seek may come out in search of you. If your aunt joined a religious order, they may swoop down on me to put a stop to our resurrection of the past. If she married and had children, they may come forward to either proceed or stay, but whatever the situation, we can acquire some information that we do not have now."

"Or maybe everyone will keep quiet because it's best not to know," Molly said.

"Possibly. Just as it is possible that you passed her on a Dublin street, yet another elderly woman in a flowered dress and sensible shoes." O'Rahilly thought for a moment, and then smiled. "From now on, I suspect that you will be staring down every grandmother you encounter."

Molly realized that she was doing exactly that, watching the people in the airport in search of a familiar face or a family trait. Rubbing at her eyes, she calculated that her aunt would be almost eighty if she were even still alive. Frank's obituary had not shaken any Devoy relatives out of the rafters of Dublin, except for a few distant cousins who had sent cables of condolence out of a sense of propriety. Slapping the newspaper against her thigh, she cursed under her breath at the religious congregations who had dug up and then cremated the unnamed remains in Drumcondra. The DNA was destroyed, and with it, any hope of identifying Magdalene St. Therese of the Little Flower or Magdalene St. Rita of Cassia.

Rummaging through her carry-on bag, now sadly empty, Molly discovered the guidebook she had brought along and never opened. No travel writer would recommend her itinerary, deep into the black rot of the past, and she flipped the paperback into a nearby trash bin. Fingering her Irish passport, Molly stopped her cleaning task abruptly. With a sense of purpose, Molly shuffled through the miscellaneous scraps of paper and notes that she had tossed in the bag that morning, almost laughing when she found the phone card.

A bank of telephones lined the wall across from her seat, patiently waiting for the traveler to lift the receiver and punch in the chain of coded numbers that would connect two people. Living well was the Devoy motto, and Molly declared that the time had come for her to live well, to display the best revenge. Her father never told her, he showed her, a man of few words using pictures that were worth one thousand words. She had the strength, the strength of Frank Devoy that was in her genes, forces gathered and ready for battle. One by one, the numbered

391

buttons were depressed, as Molly's head tabulated a list of wrongs to be righted. The phone began to ring on the other end of the line.

THE END